The White Seahorse

ELEANOR FAIRBURN was born in the west of Ireland, her childhood horizon dominated by the outline of Clare Island. She was educated at a St. Louis Convent and studied art in Dublin and Liverpool. She now lives in Yorkshire.

Her other historical novels include *The Green Popinjays*, *The Golden Hive*, *Crowned Ermine*, and *The Rose in Spring*, among many others. She has also written several mystery and crime novels under the pseudonym 'Catherine Carfax'.

The White Seahorse

ELEANOR FAIRBURN

WOLFHOUND PRESS

The White Seahorse was originally published by Heinemann (London
1964), and reissued in paperback by Allen Figgis (Dublin 1970).

This edition published 1995 by
WOLFHOUND PRESS
68 Mountjoy Square,
Dublin 1.

British Library Cataloguing in Publication Data

A catalogue record for this book is available from
the British Library.

ISBN 0-86327-456-0

Cover illustration by Katharine White
Cover design: Joe Gervin
Printed by Guernsey Press Co. Ltd., Guernsey, Channel Isles.

Graunuaile was one of the most extraordinary women ever born in Connacht, the western province of Ireland; yet, not once is her name mentioned by the Irish annalists of her time. It is only from the State Papers of Elizabeth I's reign that she emerges as a real person – 'a most famous feminine sea-captain' (Sir Henry Sidney), 'a nurse of all rebellions in Connacht' (Sir Richard Bingham) and 'a woman who has overstepped the part of womanhood' (Lord Justice Drury) – to quote only a fraction of the correspondence to which her turbulent career gave rise, directly or indirectly.

Author's note: Many Irish words have been rendered phonetically.

Maps showing the Province of Connacht and the whole of Ireland appear on pages 3 and 17.

Chapter 1

THE September tides were running silver with herring. From every hump-backed island in Clew Bay the black curraghs were launched, and their high prows pointed westward towards the open Atlantic. They dipped their nets and gathered the shining, gasping harvest while sea-birds screamed and circled overhead.

Across the wide mouth of the bay stretched Clare Island, one thousand five hundred and twenty feet high, a fortress battered by the ocean. The air was so clear today that the curraghmen could see the sunlit strand, and the huddled dwellings, and the summer residence of O Malley on Clare although it was thirteen miles distant from Murrisk.

Owen O Malley of the Black Oak, lord of Upper Umall, was watching his catch being landed. He saw the herring not as fish but as currency: topped, tailed and salted, packed in barrels and shipped to Spain and Portugal, the 'chicken of the sea' would bring back, by exchange, wines and spices, nails, iron and copper, alum, fruit and Grains of Paradise. Owen O Malley was a rich man in this year of fifteen hundred and thirty-seven, as well as being chief of wide territories on the mainland and among the other islands southward from Clare to Inishbofin.

His steward came striding up, bare-chested, from the beach, sand caking his feet and legs like boots. He bellowed in Irish, "O Maulya, they're all in now. A fine harvest, praise be to God. Will there be another run, do you think?"

The chief fingered his long brown beard and stroked the whiskers on his upper lip. He looked out to sea with mild grey eyes from which the Viking fires of his remote ancestors had died, leaving only a wealth of knowledge.

"No," he said, "no, the shoals will turn north before evening. We have enough without chasing them and, maybe, running into trouble with O Donnell of the Fish. Get the salting started."

"At once, O Maulya."

"I'd like to leave for Spain three days from now if the weather is right. You attend to the catch, O Toole. I'll prepare the fleet myself."

"You'll head straight for Biscay?"

"Aye: La Coruña. Then, if there's no swell, south to Vigo . . ."

The man plunged off down to the strand again, where the entire island population was noisily gathered. Girls and women in saffron-dyed petticoats were hauling the dripping creels of fish up out of the sea's reach to where a circle of old men worked with knives, gutting and cleaning. Farther up, on the short, cropped grass that was vivid green from dampness, salters and packers were busy. There was speed and rhythm here, a fusion of light-hearted noise and crude colour against the heaving grey backdrop of the ocean.

O Malley considered the scene for a moment longer, then began to climb towards Knockmore. He wanted to study the empty Atlantic, from whence came the prevailing winds, the sou'westerlies; and he wanted to read the sky as far in advance as he could before taking his trading fleet out under the Blue Ensign. Weather was almost a religion here, and the signs and omens were interpreted by the chieftain as if by a high priest.

The mountain towered on his right side, seeming loftier and more sheer because of the smallness of the marshy island which it dominated. Rare birds nested in its upper crannies and strange plants grew on the south and east faces – there was always colour here, brilliant or delicate, flashing in movement or caught in utter stillness against the blue slate and the grey limestone – but, to the west, was only complete barrenness, a sheer cliff wall of rock frowning down on an ocean which seethed and boiled and pounded even on the calmest day.

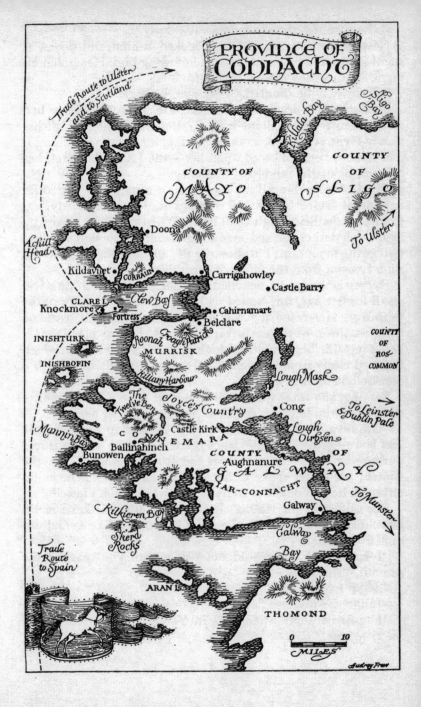

PROVINCE OF CONNACHT

Trade Route to Ulster
and to Scotland

COUNTY OF
MAYO

COUNTY
OF
SLIGO

Killala Bay

Sligo
Bay

• Doona

To Ulster

Achill
Head

Kildavnet •

CORRAUN

Carrigahowley

• Castle Barry

CLARE I.

Clew Bay

Knockmore •

Fortress

• Cahirnamart

INISHTURK

Roonah

Croagh Patrick

• Belclare

MURRISK

INISHBOFIN

Killary Harbour

Lough Mask

The
Twelve Bens

Joyce's Country

• Cong

COUNTY
OF
ROS-
COMMON

Munnin Bay

Castle Kirk

CONNEMARA

Lough
Oirpsen

To Leinster
& Dublin Pale

Ballinahinch

Bunowen

Aughnanure

COUNTY OF
GALWAY

IAR-CONNACHT

To Munster

Kilkieren Bay

Galway

Sherd
Rocks

Galway
Bay

Trade
Route
to Spain

ARAN IS.

THOMOND

0   10
MILES

Audrey Fray

As he climbed, the sky spun away dizzily. . . .

Now he paused, winded, and looked behind and down. A small figure in a white smock was following him. He circled his mouth with strong square hands.

"Graunya!" he shouted. "Graunya, go back."

She looked up briefly and continued to climb. Obedience had never been a strong point with Graunya O Malley in all her nearly-eight years and, as the only daughter of the chieftain, it had seldom been enforced upon her – the Lady Margaret, her mother, being the mildest of women.

The O Malley braced his back against a rock and waited for her, arms folded across his goatskin tunic, short sturdy legs tensed inside their rough wool braes. When the child looked up again, her father seemed menacingly solid as though he were part of the mountain; but she struggled towards him, her mouth slightly open from the effort of breathing.

Expressionlessly, he watched her dogged progress. She was small for her age, fine-boned with the enduring fragility of the thorntree. Her colouring was much darker than his, with no trace whatever of the early Viking blood: hair so black that it had a metallic blueness in the highlights of the curls; skin which bronzed easily from sun and wind; eyes intensely dark with a black circle around the iris.

Panting, she came abreast of him, and gave a little grunt of triumph. In spite of her disobedience, he caressed her.

"Graunya, I told you to go back," he said in Spanish. She was learning the language from the Grey Sisters on the island during the summer, and from the friars at Murrisk in the winter; her father spoke to her in Spanish whenever he could although he had only a merchant's knowledge of it himself.

She sniffed at the leather sheath of the hunting-knife in his kriss, then touched it with the tip of her tongue like a small inquisitive animal.

"I knew that you would not begin until you reached the summit," she said.

"Begin to do what?"

"Judge the weather."

"I must be alone when I do it. You have been told not to interrupt me."

4

"I will be quiet." She knew that the gift of weather prophecy was lodged by God Himself with the O Malley chieftains. . . .

"So let us go on." The father held out his hand to the child. "Why did you come after me?"

"I heard O Toole telling them on the strand that you were sailing in three days."

"Well?"

"I want you to take me with you."

"*No.*"

"Why?"

"You're too young. Not yet turned eight years —"

"I can handle an oar as well as my brothers can."

"That may be. But you're going to stay with your mother nevertheless. There's more to running a trading fleet than pulling an oar in her galleys. The high seas can be dangerous in more ways than one, and this is always a hurried trip in the autumn to beat storms and early darkness. Anyhow, you'd be in the men's way: that mane of hair would blow across their eyes!"

He gave it a playful tug and glanced sidelong at her face as he did so; instantly the underlip stuck out above the long chin, and the brows frowned.

"I'll cut it off," she said, a growl in the back of her throat.

"Fine sight you'd look then. The women would lock you up until it grew. Now, have sense, Graunya. When you're older, I'll take you to France or Spain with me and you can choose cloth and lace for your clothes; you'd like that?"

But she wasn't listening. A huge moth had alighted on her forearm and she was absorbed in its splendid markings. Then she stumbled, and the moth fluttered away on a northward slant, higher and higher against the dazzling silver sky. She watched it out of sight, standing motionless with her head raised. Without warning, she said, "I can see thunder. . . ."

The O Malley looked at her sharply with narrowed eyes. More than once, of late, he had suspected that the gift of weather prophecy had fallen to his daughter and not to his sons. If this were indeed so, it would be a terrible thing, for no woman could be elected to the chieftainship and no chief could survive without the gift.

"There will be no thunder," he said harshly.

The intense eyes searched his face, then slid away unblinking to the distant mountains that ringed the bay, from Mweelrea to Nephin Beg and around to the summit of Croaghaun in Achill. . . .

She turned around and began to scramble down the steep slope, running and jumping like a goat.

He sighed, and walked over to the White Rock – the sacred stone where O Malley chieftains were inaugurated – which faced the Achill peninsula to the north. The entire northern skyline shimmered in a haze of moist heat. Behind Croaghaun, other mountains marched, paler and paler blue, fading to infinity. It was a scene of utter peace until, suddenly, above the farthest rampart, he saw the beginnings of a pillared cloud formation which was the cradle of an infant storm. . . . Half an hour previously it had not been visible; now he felt its pressure.

He lowered his hand to his kriss, an instinctive movement when he was disturbed, to feel the solidity of his hunting-knife. The sheath was empty.

"Oh, damn that child!" he roared in the language of his fathers, and began to crash down in the path she had beaten.

There was no sign of Graunya on the strand when he reached it and, presently, he forgot about her in the urgency of other matters: the fish packing would have to be got under cover in case heavy rain fell and ruined the salt: stores already going aboard the ships would have to be protected too; several hours' work. . . .

It was thunder-dark when he reached the low stone-built summer-house. Before he crossed the threshold he became aware of the commotion within. The rare sound of his wife's voice raised in anger halted him.

"Margaret —"

She looked up at him distractedly, and dismissed her serving women. Her fair skin was blotched with frenzied weeping and her corn-gold hair stuck out in wisps under the folded white linen kerchief. He put his arms around her shoulders and she began to weep again.

"Margaret, in God's name, what has happened?"

6

"We'll have to spend the entire winter here," she wailed. "We can't go back to Belclare or Cahirnamart. Graunya —"

"*Graunya?*" Remembering the knife, he went rigid with fear. "What has she done? Speak to me, speak . . .'

The Lady Margaret stopped crying, and said with deathly calm,

"She has cut off all her hair."

He choked a bellow of laughter and turned it into a cough; evidently this matter was very serious to the womenfolk although he could not see the full tragedy of it himself.

"*All* of it?" he asked then in a funereal tone; and Margaret blinked away fresh tears.

"Have you ever known Graunya to do anything by halves?" she demanded, her voice rising, defying him to argue. He shook his head. "Well," his wife continued, "she's shaved it to the skull. *With a knife!* God knows how she didn't cut her head off. . . . At any rate, we can't take her back to the mainland looking like that; people would think she was a leper."

"Then there's only one cure for the situation," he said.

"What is that?" – hopefully.

"I'll take her to Spain with me in the trading fleet. Donald can stay at home to make space for her – he shames us all with his sea-sickness anyway! We'll be away nearly two months. By the end of that time, she will be presentable enough. Now, go and fetch her for me, Margaret; I want to see how bad it is . . ."

The sky outside had grown blue-black and huge drops of rain were beginning to fall. There was a scampering of feet on the shingle path; the door burst open and the two O Malley sons, Cormac and Donald, tumbled into the apartment. At the same moment, the Lady Margaret appeared at the opposite entrance, grasping her scowling daughter by the hand.

The boys' wrestling match froze into paralysis. They stared speechlessly at their sister. Then Cormac, the elder, laughed shakily and cried, "Graunya! Graunya *mhaol* . . ."

The word meant anything from 'bare' to 'tonsured' and he pronounced it *way-ull* in the fullness of the island dialect. The instant after he had spoken, a flash of green light illuminated the strand with unearthly brilliance; then thunder shook the house.

7

The boys began to caper about, shouting, "Graunya mhaol! Graunya-mhaol —" until they were made aware of their father's presence.

"Get out," he said to them quietly, and they slipped like river rats into the rear kitchens. "Graunya, come here to me."

She was too horrified by the results of her handiwork, and by the jeers of her brothers, to be able to cry. She felt naked, plague-stricken and quite unaccountably cold. She stared at her father with eyes so big and black that he thought of rock pools fringed with shining seaweed, but she expected him to recoil from the sight of her. Instead he reached out a hand and patted the spiked tufts which the knife had missed. She never loved him more than in that moment. . . .

"Graunya," he said, "there are people in this world who will have what they want, whatever the price. You are one of them. Fair enough! I'll take you to Spain with me in order to save your lady mother from embarrassment —"

"You'll *take* me? The day after tomorrow?" She could hardly believe it. She vibrated with anticipation like a plucked string.

"I have said so, and I will do it although it is against my will. It seems the only means of getting you out of the way. But remember this, Graunya, before we set out: the men of the fleet are likely to hit on the same nickname for you as your brothers have done. It may hurt: you deserve that. And it may stick for the rest of your life. . . . I advise you to become accustomed to the sound of it."

"Yes, my father," she said, very meekly. "Graunya mhaol! Graunya-mhaol. Graunuaile —" Like all words repeated, they ran together and lost their meaning. . . .

Outside, across the bay, stretched a really spectacular rainbow.

On the night before undertaking a long sea journey, the O Malley always ate a meal with his men. Because the summer house on Clare Island was small, this could never be a feast in the mainland tradition – where two hundred people might crowd under one roof at Belclare or Cahirnamart – but the islanders liked to sit under the sky anyway, whatever the weather. They grouped themselves around the chieftain's

8

residence, while he and his captains and his family dined within.

The newly caught herrings were sampled, slow-baked in earthenware ovens; then more substantial fare was brought – spit-roasted venison, beef and mutton followed by dripping honey-cakes washed down with ale and wine.

O Dugan the Bard sang, recounting deeds of dead heroes. . . .

Owen O Malley was well aware of his own failings as a chief. He knew that the young men outside regarded his trading as a shamefully mild occupation, and that they blamed him for keeping them so engaged, wasting the years of their youth and vigour when they should be fighting. A man had to fight to prove his masculinity, and some of the island youths were having to quarrel among themselves for want of another enemy; they were too young to remember the great – and futile – battles of Owen O Malley's own succession to the chieftainship, since when he had lived a life of determined amiability. Indeed, there was no prospect of any further bloodshed until the next *tanist*, or successor to the title, was elected.

O Malley felt their resentment as surely as he had felt the pressure of the coming thunderstorm. He knew that he had to act, now, before leaving for Spain; otherwise, there was liable to be trouble in his absence.

"Let my eldest son come and sit by me," he commanded, and the captains shuffled on their bench – where they crouched, facing the entrance, their shields hung behind them in time-honoured manner – to make room for him.

Cormac moved up from his low seat at the end of the board, where he had been sitting between his younger brother and Graunya, the latter wearing a felted wool cap pulled down over her ears. . . . He was a lad of about twelve years, fair like his mother, open-faced and honest. The brehon law of his country recognized no birthright for him to succeed his father in the chieftainship. The chief was elected by the people from any member of the ruling family. Thus, they could pass over a weakling elder son to elect his more robust brother or cousin or even uncle; this freedom of choice was fiercely defended by the clans.

But Owen O Malley was fairly certain that his son, Cormac, would be chosen as his own tanist.

"I wish to put this youth before you," he said now, "as my heir. If there are other candidates, let ye bring them forward in due time."

The captains leapt up and shouted the news to the crowd outside. Instantly, there was uproar. O Malley listened carefully to the tone of it. After a while he leaned back against the wall, relaxed: it was a friendly commotion. He exchanged a glance with the Lady Margaret, who smiled and nodded her veiled head, content that all was going well. Cormac would be elected tanist. He would choose his personal army from among the restless young men and would spend several years training with them. That would keep them all out of mischief until the day of the traditional raid on some unfortunate neighbour's cattle. . . .

Now everyone was shouting for the poet-harper.

"Let O Dugan sing! Let him sing. . . ."

"And what would you have me to sing?" asked the bard.

"The *Thaw-in*!" they yelled. "The Cattle Drive of Cooley."

It was a fully predictable choice, that of the greatest epic in the Irish language; a story that began in comedy, continued in majesty, ended in stark tragedy.

Graunya had heard it many times before; it was already part of the fabric of her consciousness, a thing familiar although not fully understood in its deeper implications, an emotional experience shared. Her response to it was an echo of her clan's response: when they cheered, she did likewise; when they wept, tears ran down her cheeks.

She clasped her small hands together in her lap as the first notes of the little eight-stringed harp rippled like water running over smooth stones. O Dugan's voice sang:

"Maeve, the Queen of Connacht, was very beautiful;
But she was arrogant and jealous also.
By her side lay Aillil, the weakling King . . ."

Now the bard recounted the famous argument between Maeve and Aillil about whose possessions were the greater. Finally, the only way to settle it was for them to gather everything they each owned on a great plain for comparison. When the count was made, it was found that a bull of Maeve's had gone over to Aillil's herd because —

"He thought it unbecoming in a bull to be managed by a woman!"

This line never failed to produce a roar of laughter. Graunya was too young to appreciate the satire, but she laughed with everyone else. In the same moment, she caught her father's eye and he was looking at her in a curiously speculative manner which made her feel uneasy, as though she had done wrong to laugh. She saw him place his hand over Cormac's on the table, as though to say,

'This is my son and heir, who will manage all our common possessions without argument. *His* bulls will not stray – because he is a man in the making.'

And, for the first time in her life, Graunya was aware of womanhood as a thing separating her from certain desirable pastures, like a prickly hedge. . . . She brooded on it, unaware of the song slipping away through heroic feats of arms, crashing in battle, sobbing to final defeat.

"*Then the Brown Bull of Cooley lay over against the Hill,*" sang O Dugan,

> "*And his great heart broke there.*
> *Thus, when all this war and Thain had ended,*
> *In his own land, 'midst his own hills, he died.*"

There was a mighty roar of approval from the crowd but Graunya frowned at her finger-nails. She was faintly dissatisfied with the epic this time. It was not that it had moved her any the less – her throat was still tight with tears – but that, suddenly, she was aware of a great inconsistency in it. *Why* did the noble bull have to die? He had chosen his own kind of freedom. Life seemed a high price to pay for it.

O Dugan leaned over her, his white robe brushing her shoulder.

"Have I displeased you, Graunya?" he asked. "You did not applaud me."

Her words came at him with a rush, spilling her thoughts: why, why, *why*? He drew her away from the noisy table where everyone else had already forgotten the story.

"Because," he said, "the Cattle Drive happened – not once, but many times. And it will happen again. When we recount facts, Graunya, we cannot expect logic; only fairy-tales have tidy endings. Can you understand me?"

"Yes," she said slowly. Then, "*When* will it happen again?"

"On a small scale, when your brother, Cormac, comes of age. He will steal a neighbour's cattle to bring on a fight."

"And is there something bigger than that?"

He pressed his lips together and smiled tightly.

"There is," he replied, "when one whole country invades another and drives its cattle off and shouts, 'I am the new chief!'"

"Like the King of England does to Ireland?"

"Like so, exactly," said the bard. "Remember, last springtime, how Henry Tudor wiped out the Geraldines by treachery, and took their lands, titles and herds?"

She remembered Silken Thomas and his five uncles. The entire country remembered in its shocked consciousness: six members of a semi-royal house gone to the block, the great Kildare estates broken. Now it was the duty of the bards to see that no one ever forgot: it was their vocation to keep the flame of resentment burning, just as it was the chanting of O Keenan that had fanned the spark of rebellion in Silken Thomas's soul. . . .

Instinct told the O Malley poet that Graunya was more responsive than either of her brothers, and that her influence, in the end, would be wider than theirs: she would marry the leader of another tribe; she would rear his children; and she would dominate everyone with whom she came into contact. Even now, with the absurd woollen cap on her cropped head, the vitality of her presence was disturbing.

O Dugan smiled again, thinking of the nickname which her brothers had given her and which the whole island was repeating with a grin. When he shut his mind to the meaning of the tacked-on word, the name had a curiously melodic quality for him.

Graunuaile. . . .

Her mother aroused her before dawn and helped her to dress in linen chemise, worsted petticoat and long leather jacket slit at the sides – fussing over whether she would be warm enough on the high seas, losing no opportunity to kiss and fondle her. Graunya bore all this with rigid patience, her ears picking up every sound of preparation from the harbour.

It was a cool, damp morning. The storm wind had dropped

to a steady north-westerly, rare enough here and providential for a voyage to Spain.

"I believe you're not going to miss me at all," the Lady Margaret said plaintively, fastening her daughter's frieze cloak with a heavy gold brooch under the chin.

The last thing Graunya wanted was a tearful scene with her mother; she, herself, was acutely aware of the pain of parting – it had been with her all night and the previous day – but not by a single sob would she admit to feeling it, in case the adventure were snatched from her.

"I will think of you often, my mother," she replied, "and Cormac and I will kneel and pray for you every morning and night. Good-bye. God stay with you!"

She ran out into the morning air and down to the dark strand. Clouds were sifting the first grey light of dawn. Ships and shadows and reflections were a misty jumble in the harbour. The water had a heavy smoothness like oil, and sea-birds flew low or stood motionless on distant rocks.

Men were wading out to the long galleys, carrying oars and bundles of personal belongings, while curraghs served the bigger ships anchored farther offshore. Women were kissing husbands and sweethearts. Yet, in spite of all the activity, there was a kind of muted quiet. Even the convent bell, when it rang, had an unusual softness.

The chaplain came out and blessed the fleet.

"Come, Graunya," her father said then, "Cormac is aboard this half-hour." He lifted her into a curragh, saying to the oarsman, "Take her out to the flagship."

The light craft moved quickly over the water. She looked back once, saw her father and mother embracing at the sea's edge, the woman's head haloed with the first flush of light from the east. A feeling of panic hammered in her throat: she had to go back — But her father's words came to her, 'Some people . . . will have what they want . . . whatever the price. *You are one of them.*'

She paid with a gulp and a snuffle.

Cormac was up on the poop-deck of the flagship, shouting and waving.

"Graunya! Hey, Graunya *mhaol . . .*"

She turned and shook her clenched fist at him as the curragh hove to. Then her attention was captured by the Blue Ensign at the masthead. It was streaming so straight that the emblem of the White Seahorse was undistorted by folds: no legless creature of the deep this, but a rearing animal, maned, deep-chested and hooved, such as the old gods rode across the Atlantic.

And she could almost read the O Malley motto underneath:
Terra Marique Potens – Powerful by Land and Sea

Chapter 2

O MALLEY's trading fleet was an odd collection of craft, assembled over many years.

The flagship was a Portuguese caravel, three-masted, square sterned – the kind of vessel in which Columbus had sailed from Palos nearly fifty years previously. She carried a big square sail and a topsail at her mainmast; her foremast bore a smaller canvas, with another above, and her mizen supported the triangular lateen which the Portuguese had adapted from the Arabian design. She had a forecastle and an aftercastle – each with dark, noisome spaces underneath – and a fair width of open deck although she was a small ship. In a heavy sea, she was apt to pitch. . . . Still, the O Malley loved her, crowded her with cargo and thirty men besides, and refused to alter the name which her original owners had given her, the *Santa Cruz*. Nor would he exchange his cramped quarters below decks on this ship for more comfortable ones on the two newer carracks of the fleet.

The carracks were unarmed but had formidable ramming beaks under the sinister painted eye which they had brought with them from the Mediterranean.

The rest of the fleet was made up mainly of barques, small open galleys and longboats, some carrying a single square sail but relying on oarsmen for propulsion with any but a following wind.

The galleys and longboats had little roofed-in spaces fore and aft, with leather curtains across the openings, and here the oar-crew slept in relays, two or four at a time. The galleys were very old. Their storage space was so limited that the men lashed their weapons to the gunwales, sat on their spare clothing and strung their food on thongs about their necks. Water vessels and cargo were stowed in the centre between the rowing benches, or were tied to cables – which ran from stem to stern, encircling the mainmast amidships – overhead.

The galleys' main contribution to the fleet was their speed and manœuvrability; if the bigger ships were attacked by pirates, the oared vessels would help defend them. And, sometimes, a becalmed ship could be towed by strongly-oared craft.

O Malley never voyaged without his ancient galleys although the Spaniards (who were building bigger and bigger vessels these days) were apt to jeer at them, calling them 'Leif Ericsson's grandchildren, five hundred years old!'

O Malley knew his coastline and his weather. He was rich enough to buy a tall galleass if he had wanted to do so: he was also intelligent enough to know that she would not survive one winter on the fanged seaboard of Connacht.

Before the sky was fully light, Clare Island was a distant rock on the northern horizon. As he led his fleet east of Inishturk, O Malley dipped his sail three times to honour the Island of Saints near by. Then the Twelve Bens of Beola reared up out of Connemara, their quartzite peaks aflame like torches from the rising sun. He nodded towards the mainland and said to Graunya, "There's O Flaherty country."

She gave it her entire attention, for O Flaherty history was closely bound up with that of her own ancestors; there had been marriages and murders between the two clans, alliances and dissensions. . . .

A barren and forbidding place their country looked to her, now, in the early morning, its peaks so high that the valleys were thick with mist and purple-blue shadow; but she knew that it could be beautiful, for she had heard much about its lakes and troutstreams, woods and heatherlands and sudden silver beaches by inland waters. The O Flahertys had been hereditary princes here since time out of mind.

Cormac came and stood by his father and sister at the swaying port rail.

IRELAND

SCOTLAND

ATLANTIC OCEAN

To Scotland
RATHLIN I. Mull of Kintyre
North Channel

TYRONE
PROVINCE OF
ULSTER
Tullaghoge
Dungannon
L. Neagh
ANTRIM

Donegal Bay

Sligo Bay

ACHILL
CLARE I.
INISHTURK
INISHBOFIN
ManninBay
Ballinahin
Sherd Rocks
ARAN IS.

PROVINCE OF
CONNACHT
Belclare
L. Mask
L. Oirbsen
Galway
Galway Bay

R. Shannon

Dublin
(The Pale)
Wicklow Mtns.
To Wales

PROVINCE OF
LEINSTER

Askeaton
LIMERICK

PROVINCE OF
MUNSTER

Smerwick

Dingle Bay

Kinsale

Waterford

St George's Channel

ATLANTIC OCEAN

Route to Northern Spain

0 10 20 30 40 50
MILES

Audrey Frew

"If I am elected tanist," he said, "I think I will raid O Flaherty."

For a moment, Owen O Malley did not move; then he raised his heavy hand, brought it down on Cormac's shoulder and spun the lad around.

"If that is your intention," he growled in his beard, "I will make it my life's work to prevent your being chosen. . . ."

"I – I was only joking." The boy was startled by his father's vehemence. "I wouldn't rattle a spear in front of an O Flaherty."

"Then don't speak about it," O Malley shouted, and strode away.

Cormac was embarrassed because his sister had heard this exchange, and tried to justify his position by youthful bluster.

"When my men are trained, we *could* do it! I'd be ashamed to raid a clan weaker than ourselves, and only the O Flahertys are our equals —"

Graunya forgot about the tragic Cattle Drive of Cooley, and the illogicality of raiding one's own countrymen when a real enemy was already within the gates.

"That's right, Cormac," she said fervently. "Of course you could!"

But, up on the poop-deck, O Malley was pursuing another line of thought. He knew that Cormac had not spoken out of his own mind: he was too young. The idea of raiding O Flaherty had been put into his head by others, the restless youths of the tribe with their thirst for blood and glory. Well, they would have to find someone else to goad into a fight. O Malley had no intention of putting a hostile coastline between himself and Spain.

There had been talk between him and Dhonal Crone O Flaherty – now chief, then tanist – once, about arranging a family marriage. That conversation could be resumed. . . .

The fleet passed well to westward of the Aran Islands and saluted two Spanish merchantmen making their way into Galway's busy harbour. The Spaniards had a great spread of red and yellow sail, decorated with crosses; their masts were equipped with fighting tops, and their hulls, although beautifully carved and gilded, were reinforced to bear the weight of cannon hiding behind shuttered ports.

The close view of these ships in movement – their every detail picked out by the brilliant morning light – made a lasting impression on Graunya's mind. For a long while after they had passed majestically into Galway Bay, she harassed her father with questions about them. In the end, he only gained peace by promising that she would see dozens more like them between Ireland and Biscay.

'And,' he added to himself, 'I pray God they're all peaceful merchantmen!'

The menace of pirates was ever present, some of them were extremely well equipped in the most modern manner. It was ironic that O Malley should pray to be saved from piracy, because, until his own chieftainship, it had been the main livelihood of his clan: the Blue Ensign bearing the device of the White Seahorse was still remembered with a shudder by old sailors, many of them maimed or blinded by O Malley hatchets and firebrands.

The chief did not wish to dwell on these things, nor did he allow his bard to glorify them in verse. Above all, he wanted to keep his children in ignorance of their violent heritage.

Thomond slipped by to port, then the mouth of Shannon and the toothed skyline of Kerry beyond the Great Blasket Islands. There was nothing now but open sea, with musical water bubbling under the ships' bows and fanning out in their wake.

Fifteen days later, Galicia was sighted, the north-eastern province of Spain.

Graunya had enjoyed every hour of the voyage but arrival disappointed her. She had expected everything to be different in this foreign country; instead, it resembled Ireland closely, even down to the fine drizzle of silver rain which blended sea and mountainous coastline. There were small stony fields with sheep and cattle grazing in them; stunted trees all growing at an acute angle away from Atlantic gales; deep, narrow sea-inlets. . . . And, over both land and people lay an intense awareness of threatened freedom – Torquemada had been dead for forty years but his Inquisitors lived on, to accuse after secret arrest, to torture and to murder in the name of religious unity; just as, in Ireland, spies of Henry the Eighth were reporting on the great monasteries prior to their fearful dissolution.

Graunya's father was too busy – disposing of his cargo, bargaining for a new one and reprovisioning his ships – to give her much of his time, and he sternly forbade her and Cormac to wander off alone into the town. Cormac was happy enough to trail around the warehouses with his father, but the order exasperated Graunya; she sulked and stamped until her harassed parent relaxed part of it.

"All right, all right – as long as you keep to the harbour walls. No farther. . . ."

So it was that her acquaintance with Spain was confined almost exclusively to shipping. She heard church bells pealing but saw no churches; she heard street vendors crying in the Gallego dialect but handled only the wares of those who came down to the quays. Thus her vision remained filled with ships: pilgrim transports from Santiago de Compostela; rich men's pleasure boats from Vigo and Pontevedra; iron and coal barges from Bilbao; busy merchants from all over the world – this wealth of craft was displayed before her every day in the harbour of La Coruña.

Her hair was beginning to grow again so that she could leave off her woollen cap. She deposited her frieze mantle aboard the *Santa Cruz* – for the weather was very warm – and bought a big rush hat from an Algerian sailor. Then she established a claim to a pile of empty barrels near the warehouses by sitting on top of them to eat her meals; thick fish soup, boiled lobster, fresh fruit, all washed down with the local wine, *ribiero*. Nobody attempted to move either her or the barrels although her presence on top of them excited some interest; it was obvious that she was not a beggar child, therefore people spoke to her without fear of being pestered for alms; what was not nearly so obvious was whether she were a boy or a girl. Apart from her cropped hair, she *looked* like a girl, but her attitude was entirely male. When a new ship arrived, she would go down solemnly to inspect it from every angle. When the captains began to invite her aboard, her blue-black eyes missed no single detail of steering gear or instrument, ordnance or tackle; and she would climb the mainmast shrouds, and slide down the halyard as casually as walk the deck, after tucking the back hem of her skirt into the front of her kriss to form a pair of peasant braes. . . .

By the time her father was ready to sail she had acquired the status of a visiting admiral. And, to the many who inquired what her name was, she replied clearly,

"Graunuaile," believing that it was more pronounceable for foreigners than Graunya Ui Maulya.

There were men at La Coruña that autumn who were to remember the name many years later. . . .

The weather had turned grey and stormy so that O Malley decided not to proceed south, where the coast was dangerous. His trading had gone well and he was ready for the homeward voyage. But he would not head straight for Clare Island.

Graunya had never seen the royal Irish city of Galway. She knew that it had been built by the Norman de Burgos on the site of an O Flaherty fishing village – those same de Burgos who now called themselves Bourke or MacWilliam, dressed themselves in Irish fashion and let their hair grow long, all to appease the furious O Flahertys who still contested the territory!

But the quarrel of the old Irish no longer lay with the Normans who had been in their country now for four hundred years. Instead, it had transferred itself to later English settlers, the Athys and the Kirwans, the Lynches, Blakes and Bodkins, the Brownes, Deans, ffrenches and Fonts, the Martins, Joyces, Skerrets and Morrisses; and, last of all, the d'Arcys. Before the bustling onslaught of these fourteen merchant families, the de Burgos made a dignified withdrawal, for the settlers had the might of England behind them and the Normans had severed all connexions with the Crown; they had no allies unless they made friends with the native Irish. And this they did, in a bond of surprising strength.

Now, it was Normans and Irish outside the walls, English within, the latter building warehouses for their wine and wool trade, and proclaiming – by numerous by-laws – their unwise intention of living isolated here in this walled city. . . .

'Neither the lord MacWilliam nor his heirs shall settle anything in the town without permission. . . . No man of the town shall oste nor receive any of the Burkes, MacWilliams, Kellies nor no cepte elles. . . . Neither O nor Mac shall strutte ne swaggere through the streets of Galway.'

The fact that nobody except themselves understood the English language troubled the Fourteen Families not at all. A more imaginative people might have had nightmares, feeling the pressure of hostile forces upon those walls which, alone, separated the citizens from tracts of enemy country. Unheeding, the English settlers continued to live their busy lives and failed to notice that their children and grandchildren were beginning to speak with Irish accents and to call a horse, a *coppell*.

The early October darkness was closing in as the fleet approached Galway Bay. O Malley looked to the north-east, puzzled: there was a red glow in the sky as though the city were on fire, and meteors of blue-white light shot upward at intervals from the dark land mass. He wondered if the O Flahertys had attacked again. . . .

He shouted to the nearest galley to row into the bay and find out what was going on. The galley was away for over an hour. Total darkness fell and a line of bonfires along the harbour was fiercely reflected in the black water, while, behind that, cannon belched and the bells of St Nicholas's seemed to dance in frenzy.

O Malley kept his fleet as far out to sea as he could until the galley returned. His mind was filled with a sense of foreboding.

The leading oarsman climbed on board the *Santa Cruz*.

"They are celebrating —" he said breathlessly. "News reached the city today that Henry the Eighth has a legitimate son at last!"

"I see," O Malley said quietly, and turned away.

This was the royal birth which all Catholics who adhered to Rome had dreaded. A male heir for thrice-married Henry meant the continuance of the new orders: to renounce the Pope and dissolve the monasteries. Mary, daughter of Catherine of Aragon, would never be Queen now, to reinstate the old form of religious worship. It was a bitter blow for those who had imagined that Henry's death would be the end of their suppression: he would live on in his son by Jane Seymour. . . .

There was no comfort, now, in remembering the report of two years back, when Anne Boleyn was Queen, of how Henry had stormed out of her bedchamber, shouting, "You will have no more boys by me!" – referring to the dead male child she had just miscarried. The live daughter, Elizabeth, caused Henry nothing but annoyance; he had winced at her birth.

'So now he has a son at last,' O Malley thought, 'after making do with the bastard Duke of Richmond for eighteen years. And this infant's mother was betrothed on the same day as Anne Boleyn went to her beheading. Queer times, when such a man says that he is Supreme Head of a Church!'

In the darkness, Graunya sensed her father's disquiet and her childishly selfish hope was that this would not prevent his docking at Galway. She didn't want to watch the celebrations from a distance: she wanted to be part of them – to feel the fire's heat and the thud of exploding powder, to dance and sing and shout with the people, whatever their tongue or religious persuasion. An infant was born in a royal palace; why pull a long face over that? Adults had such a great capacity for being miserable.

"Are we going in, Father?" She tugged at his mantle.

"Umm, we'll try. But it'll be too late tonight to have the cargo examined. We might have to stay on board."

A ship had to submit to inspection by the Mayor of Galway and his two portriffs whether she was selling her cargo in one of the city's seven market places or not. Tonight, His Worship would be too busy in any case; and tomorrow he might have a very sore head and not be inclined to admit any of the 'outlandish Irish' to his Mercantile City. Admission of the Irish into Galway was strictly controlled by licence; they might come on certain days only, between fixed hours, and make entry according to the wares which they brought for sale – hides and skins by the east and west gates, freshwater fish through the Little Gate, wool by Shoemakers' Tower. . . . The rules and regulations were interminable, a source of utter bafflement to the Irish, who could not read them, and who were always liable to arrest and imprisonment for their infringement.

The Seahorse fleet approached the harbour to find it choked with other vessels of various nationalities, and not a member of their crews present on any of them; everyone had gone into the city. With difficulty, O Malley moored his ships, and waited. No one came forward to collect harbour dues or licence money.

23

No one challenged him or asked his business, and the two strand gates were wide open. . . . He didn't really want to go into the city but sleep would be impossible in any case because of the uproar, and Graunya was pestering him to take her.

"Very well. We'll have to leave our mantles on board though. . . ."

It was cold and raining but no Irishman was allowed to walk the streets of Galway wearing a frieze cloak; the settlers had the most terrible suspicions of these garments, believing that – under cover of their hairy folds – any crime could be committed and any criminal hidden. The Spaniards, on the other hand, would buy as many *falanga* of Irish manufacture as they were offered!

O Malley took Cormac and Graunya and a few of the men with him; the rest remained behind to guard the cargo, none of which was to be sold because it represented winter provisions for the islands.

The great spaces of the fish markets were jammed with people, some sitting on empty hogsheads while they ate and drank and kissed one another; others lurching around in a wild dance, bawling out choruses from the broadsheets which had been printed weeks before in anticipation of a boy being born to Jane Seymour:

> *"God save King Henry with all his power,*
> *And Prince Edward, that goodly flower!"*

Up Kirwan's Lane and Kea Street, pickpockets and vagrants were busy. Along Cross Street and Lombard Street, the crowds were so dense that a man could hardly get his hand into his *own* pocket. Farther into the town, past the Market Cross and the Exchange, the great houses of the merchants were blazing with light; doors and balconies glowed with beribboned garlands, gates streamed with banners showing the armorial devices of the families. The smell of cooking food from the rear kitchens pervaded courtyard and street.

Still the bells of St Nicholas's clashed and pealed as though the Lord Deputy's visit of three months back had never happened, when he removed all the Church ornaments and sacred vessels, and heard Mayor and Aldermen renounce the Pope.

The thirteen cannon boomed from the Lion's Tower.

Along Great Gate Street and down High Middle Street surged the Mayor's processsion, reinforced by reformed clergy at Crooked Lane. Prosperous merchants of the town came out, with their wives, to see it pass, to cheer it on – torches, banners and music, all the trappings of a confident English settlement brought out for a royal event. Graunya's mouth opened in disbelief as she stared at the proud merchants, because she thought that their bodies must be the same shape as their clothing: monstrous in shoulder and hip, thin in the nether-stock, flat in the head. Cautiously, she stretched out a finger to touch a blue velvet cape, silver lined, but her father stopped her.

"I wasn't going to do any harm —" she said reproachfully in Irish, and then he put his entire hand over her mouth, shouting in her ear – for a whisper would have been drowned in the clamour all about – "You must not speak your own language. Spanish or Latin – otherwise keep silent; that is the law for those who do not know English."

She pondered this as the end of the mighty procession passed, and wondered why it mattered how one spoke as long as meaning was conveyed. She could hear the English tongue on all sides but understood no word of it; very forceful it sounded, full of hardnesses formed by the front of the mouth; and the people spoke more loudly, and on a higher note, than she was accustomed to hearing.

Midnight came and the city was still brilliantly awake. Several days late the celebrations might be – for news could not reach this outpost quickly – but they were doubly boisterous for that, rejoicing in a birth *and* in a christening. . . .

Five hundred crow-miles away in London, the royal infant was being carried back to the state apartments after his baptism by Archbishop Cranmer. Through all the vast building rang the words of Garter-King-at-Arms, reaching even the farthest away of the twenty score dignitaries who had attended the ceremony.

"God of His Almighty and Infinite Grace, give good and long life to the right high, right excellent and noble Prince Edward, Duke of Cornwall and Earl of Chester, most dear and entirely beloved son to our dread and gracious Lord, King Henry the Eighth. . . ."

The christening procession reformed; gentlemen of the household carrying torches, followed by bishops, abbots, chaplains and their choirs; the Lord Treasurer and foreign ambassadors; the Dukes of Norfolk and Suffolk, godfathers to Prince Edward; the Archbishop of Canterbury. . . .

Then came the twenty-two-year-old Princess Mary, who might have dreamed of wearing her father's crown one day had this infant never been born. Following her, the tiny red-headed Lady Elizabeth, declared illegitimate after the execution of her mother, and deprived of the title 'Princess'.

Henry Tudor lifted his son out of the arms of the Duchess of Suffolk. The infant could be no burden to so large a man and yet he stumbled as he received it. He was in his forty-sixth year and was already losing the magnificent physique which had once been renowned throughout Europe: he was growing fat and heavy and old. His physicians could find no remedy for the ulcer on his leg which had tormented him of recent years.

He approached the embroidered pallet where the young uncrowned Queen had sat upright for five hours. He kissed her forehead and found the fair skin damp and burning.

"Are you well, dearest?" he murmured, grasping her hand.

"Quite well, Your Grace." Her composure had helped make her a queen when Henry was wearied by Anne Boleyn's hysteria. She would hold fast to it now while the room dipped and swayed about her and even the taper-light seemed blurred. It was natural to be weak after so long and painful a labour as she had had – three days and two nights, terminated only by the King's order to remove the child from her womb, whatever the cost – but she would regain her strength, bear Henry another male infant to bolster the succession against the daughters whom he despised. . . .

Ten days later, Jane Seymour, Queen of England, was dead of puerperal fever.

O Malley sent his fleet home to the islands under the command of one of his captains. Then, with the children and a small escort, he set out by land for Connemara. Although he had bought six mountain ponies in Galway, only Graunya and Cormac rode – without saddles or bridles, as was the Irish custom – leaving the other four as pack animals. The men preferred walking to riding any day, and O Malley walked with them; their speed and endurance was unbelievable to a stranger.

Their route lay north-west out of Galway, following the banks of Lough Oirbsen to Oughterard, then westward into Connemara.

The Twelve Bens of Beola rose up on their horizon; they were making for the foot of one of these giants, Ben Lettery. There, there were three lakes; in one of them, an island; on the island, a fortress-dwelling of the new O Flaherty chieftain, Dhonal Crone of Ballinahinch.

Neither Graunya nor Cormac knew the reason for their father's journey, nor why he had chosen the land route instead of the sea: he could have sailed to Mannin Bay and covered the short inland distance from there. . . .

The farther they penetrated into Connemara, the wilder the scene became: bog and forest and mountain under a ragged sky that called out all the deep blues and purples of the autumn land. Oirbsen itself, a thirty-mile-long lake, had all the restless turbulance of the sea, now green, now slate-grey with toothed waves. Sometimes, from the dense woods, came the eerie cry of wolves, and the sound had more menace here than in the pleasant country of Upper Umall. Torrents leapt off the mountain faces for a brief shaking of white manes before diving into dark caverns that echoed under the travellers' feet; the entire territory was honeycombed with souterrains. Red deer grazed with black cattle on distant slopes, the eyes of the deer ever watchful for the eagles that could harry them to death.

Cormac had become more and more silent as they progressed, and now Graunya spoke his thoughts for him.

"This would be a difficult country to raid without the knowledge of generations behind you."

"Yes," he said.

"Even if you were to take the O Flaherty's cattle, you'd never drive them overland home to the Umalls."

He looked at the desolate miles ahead, one mountain range

peering over the shoulders of the other, with dark sinister passes in between and eerie upland lakes; and he knew that the country would beat him even if the ferocious O Flahertys did not.

"Maybe we'll sail on O Donnell of the Fish instead, when the time comes," he said. "We are not made for land fighting."

"That is so," Graunya nodded. "We were born for the sea."

They had this much understanding between them, the brother and sister, that each knew how an inland place oppressed the other. And the father, who knew them both, had travelled wisely and to good purpose; but he had one more stake to hammer home yet in the cause of peace and safety.

Chapter 3

THE O Flahertys were a mighty tribe of many branches and a thousand kinsmen. Their elected chieftain kept great state inside his many fortresses where he was served by members of other families, all having their hereditary duties: the O Lees and the O Canavans were his physicians; the chiefs of Hy-Bruin-Seola his Masters of the Horse; the O Colgans his standard bearers; the O Maelampaills his brehons or judges; the O Duanes his attendants at the common house; the Mac-Kilkellys, his ollavs in history and poetry. . . .

The O Flaherty was not a man, he was a tribe, older than the Hag of Bearra. He had only one superior after God, and that was O Conor Sligo of the Royal House of Connacht, now bereft of crown and title. Vikings and Normans and Englishmen might come and go, the centuries-old O Flaherty figurehead ignored them all unless they annoyed him; then he fought like a wild animal that has a million eyes and eight million claws and twice that number of teeth, for all the O Flahertys were represented in the body of one chieftain, elected by, and maintained by, themselves, so that they – and the lesser families – were an extension of him. He was a corporate monster, against whom the Galway Council spent a great deal of time legislating.

Graunya was shaking from head to foot by the time she was ready to meet him.

Granted, his boatmen had been good-humoured and civil when they rowed the O Malley party over to the island; granted, the Lady Eilish O Flaherty had given them gracious welcome, saying that the chief was out hunting but would be home for the evening meal; granted, too, that O Flaherty's daughters had given Graunya a gift of scarlet satin and gold ornaments to wear at table, and had sent five of their own women to bathe and dress her. But the sense of unreality engendered by the costly new robes only increased her apprehension.

The serving women held up mirrors and twittered, "There, there" delighted at the way her short dark hair curled around their brushes, "proud we are to feast the O Malley *thiarna*."

Thiarna: lord, chief, almost king. . . . Yes, that was her father's title and she drew strength and dignity from it, and from the remembered words of her brother, '. . . Only the O Flahertys are *our equals*.'

This fortress was no greater than the Hall of Belclare; and the Umalls of O Malley boasted as many attendant families. Only Belclare was familiar: Ballinahinch was not. The voice of the sea did not penetrate O Flaherty's walls.

The trestle tables were laid ready for the evening meal. Torches flared against grey stone, illuminating rows of shields. Ancient banners hung, like sleeping bats, from black oak beams, their Golden Lizard emblem tarnished by time and dampness. Behind the dais table stretched a huge tapestry into which the armorial bearings of O Flaherty had been woven: two lions counter-rampant supporting a red hand couped at the wrist; beneath this, a black galley, its oars in vigorous action; below that, the motto, *Fortuna Favet Fortibus*.

Men were stamping about the hall while ladies sat in little groups, talking and laughing. Massive wolfhounds were chained to rings in the walls beneath the shields and weapons. . . . Nothing had altered here during countless ages.

The windows, filled in with translucent horn, glowed like dark wine from the sunset sky outside as the family and their guests began to enter. O Malley led in Eilish, O Flaherty's large and placid lady; Cormac partnered his eldest unmarried daughter, and Graunya found herself holding the arm of the chieftain himself while he looked down at her, and winked, and told her about a litter of newly-weaned pups from which she might choose the one she liked best. . . .

Nothing had ever astonished her like this meeting with Dhonal Crone O Flaherty. He was the direct opposite of everything she had imagined; a small man, not old, but having the appearance of supple leather. His face crinkled all over when he smiled, and he had the intense blue eyes of sea-going generations. There was a spare, economical quality about him – even his hair and beard were trimmed shorter than the Irish usually considered necessary – and this brevity was echoed in his speech. Graunya sensed that Dhonal Crone's decisions would be as quick as his observation was acute.

When, later, she knelt beside him in the warm straw of the stables, and he said to her, "You choose *that* pup? Why?" she felt that he was questioning her choice for some deeper reason than was apparent. And she answered carefully, cuddling the blue-grey animal whose coat was still soft as brushed wool,

"Because he is independent and courageous – he was farthest from his mother!"

Dhonal Crone laughed and said: "Well, that settles the question of whom you must marry."

"I don't want to marry anyone."

"You'd rather take a nun's veil?"

"No. I want to continue sailing with my father."

"Hmm. Then he didn't tell you what brought him here? No; a man of his own counsel. That is why I have always called him friend. . . ." Dhonal Crone might have been talking to himself, sitting hunched up in the straw, his wiry hands clasped around his knees. The pups were climbing all over his head and the huge wolfhound bitch was licking his ear ecstatically. To Graunya, he looked like a benevolent *pooka*.

"What brought my father here?" she asked.

"A conversation we had, just after you were born. We discussed a marriage between you and an O Flaherty. Owen wanted it settled there and then, but I preferred to wait until I could see what kind of woman you'd make before binding you to one of our family."

He looked at her keenly with his bright blue eyes sparkling in the lantern light – saw the richness of the red satin and the gold ornaments against the blackness of her hair and the sun-bronzed skin. Her mouth was firm and strongly defined, as

31

though childhood were already behind her. He regretted the length and forward thrust of her chin : that must come from an ancestress who was a Norman Bourke. . . .

"Well, I am satisfied now," he said, "that only a grand-nephew of mine will do for you. Another Dhonal, who has all the makings of a chieftain."

"When will I see him?" she asked, not greatly interested.

"Your father wants a six-year betrothal. We'll come for you then."

Nobody except Dhonal Crone O Flaherty could have arranged so complicated a matter during the course of one evening. His mental eye had ranged over his entire family in search of a fit mate for this quick O Malley child and, keeping in mind the custom which rejected the weak and stupid, he had chosen young Dhonal, the apple of his eye, for her.

As they walked back from the stables together in the darkness, she asked no questions about her future husband. She was entirely occupied in wrapping the wolfhound pup inside the folds of her mantle.

Two days later, the O Malleys left Ballinahinch and set their faces northward for their own territory.

There, the seasons followed each other in gentle rhythm for Graunya; lessons at friary and convent during winter and summer; hunting, fishing, sailing with the fleet to trade autumn herrings and spring wool. News of the wider world barely concerned the inhabitants of the Umalls in their isolation; they heard that King Henry had married a fourth wife called Anne of Cleves and had divorced her the same year, but they were not even curious about the circumstances; to them, there had ever been only one real Queen – little Spanish Catalina, long since dishonoured and dead. . . .

When Graunya was in her thirteenth year, she went to Galway with her father one morning to help him dispose of a last of hides. They travelled in a longboat, surrounded by a cluster of black curraghs. Their business done, they took to the sea again without delay for there was nothing to detain them in the unfriendly city.

Galway Bay was clear and lovely on this evening in early

June – a great expanse of translucent green water bounded by low hills to the south. The small fleet headed into the setting sun, keeping close to the coast of Iar-Connacht; on their horizon lay the three Islands of Aran.

The sun went down in a fervour of fire-colours, leaving a few long clouds moored beyond Inishmore, their undersides red-gold. The green twilight of the West came, then the purple afterlight on a flat calm sea. In an hour, the moon would be up and she would be nearly at her full; meanwhile, the light was blue-grey and misty, so that O Malley looked twice before being sure of what he saw: a caravel with sails furled but oars poised, lying outside the mouth of Kilkieran Bay. At first, it crossed his mind that she was an O Flaherty ship but, as his longboat drew near to her, he thought, rather, that she was English. It was unusual to see any English vessel north of Galway except the small fishing trawlers which paid fees to O Malley and O Flaherty.

He hailed her but she did not answer. Instead, she dipped her bank of oars and bore straight down upon him. . . . O Malley flung himself across the tiller, yelled one word of command on which the men acted instantly, and saw the caravel's beak pass within a yard of him.

This unprovoked attack inside his native waters aroused a rare anger in him.

"By God and the Virgin," Graunya heard him vow, "I'll teach that ship better manners!" Then, shouting at the full power of his lungs, he summoned the scattered curraghs of his escort, and directed the longboat at the same time, making a dramatic turn before the larger enemy could control her course. He knew that his men were unarmed except for their short knives and a few tools, and that the boat was not equipped for ramming, so he decided on great speed.

The caravel towered over them as they shot across her bows.

"Break her oars!" the chief bawled. He saw his men raise their knives above their heads, then bring them down with slashing force, again and again, on the oarblades. He could hear the crew of the caravel shouting, hear her guns being dragged into new positions for the closer range. His own curraghs were swarming around now. A hooked rope snaked upward, formed a taut line from the mainmast of the longboat; then another and

33

another, enmeshing the caravel. The men began to climb upward like spiders. . . .

It was a brief battle, an easy victory. O Malley's impression was that the enemy was inexperienced and unco-ordinated; he found the whole business difficult to understand; no self-respecting pirate would trouble to attack a single open boat.

Then he boarded the caravel and came face to face with a group of dismayed young men who looked as though they couldn't grow a beard between them. By the cut of their clothes, they were English and Italian; by their chins, their average age was seventeen. O Malley had little sympathy with pirates but, when he ran across a bunch as inept as this, he felt it his duty to protect them from the sea. First, though, it might be best to save those below decks from his own men, who were swarming all over the ship, elated by the unexpected prize.

He bellowed them back under his eye.

"Is anyone dead," he demanded, "either side?"

There was a good deal of blood apparent, eyes were closing fast and there must be broken bones; but the only reply came from one of the O Dowds, who was staggering towards him with a body in his arms.

"A youth here, barely alive, I think."

"Put him down softly. He'll be cared for."

The O Malley walked up close to the group of beardless young men and scrutinized each one to know how badly hurt he might be; he decided that they were all capable of walking into Galway city when he put them ashore. The caravel was his by right of a fair fight, according to the ancient Maritime Law of Olneacht. By such means had the O Malley fleet been built. Now, for the first time, it was to acquire ordnance: two light culverins and a falconet. . . .

The crew was bundled ashore in the moonlight and the direction of the city pointed out to them. It would be a long walk through rough country but Irish wood-kerne and churls would help them.

Only the wounded youth sailed northward with O Malley, and he, being unconscious, knew nothing of his fate until once, during the night, when the moon was small and high above the mainmast, he opened his eyes. A huge man with long brown hair and a wild beard was bending over him; he could feel the roughness of frieze brushing his face.

"God's Blood," he muttered, "Irish savages . . ." and fainted again.

O Malley sat back on his heels looking at him.

"He'll survive," he said to Graunya. "This wasn't to be the plank of his death. Maybe God wants him for other matters."

She knelt down and cradled the young man's head in her arms. He was handsome in a delicate, girlish way, and she regretted the terror that had leapt to his eyes when he looked at her father. Inside the torn neck of his shirt, she could see a gold medallion on a chain and, when she examined it, found that it was a 'Saint Nicholas of Myra', reputed to bring all travellers and seafarers home safely.

As soon as the curraghs were drawn up on the island strand, and the caravel was anchored in deeper water, O Malley carried his charge up to the summer residence. There, the Lady Margaret and her women took command, with bowls and bandages and honey warmed before the fire. The liquid honey was spread on cleaned wounds and covered over with boiled linen; it would soothe at once and, eventually, it would heal, because honey was pure of itself and had a little magic in it from the sacred bees. . . . Confident of this, the women bustled away, to their cooking, their prayers and their needlework. Only Graunya remained behind in the cell-like room. After a while, the wounded man awoke from a kind of stupor, and his light-lashed eyes locked with hers.

"What is your name?" she asked at once, in Spanish and then in Latin.

Dazed, he whispered, "Francis Derham."

She repeated the words carefully. He got the impression that this was for the benefit of a monstrous hound which crouched beside her. Then she smiled — a flash of white teeth in a sun-dark face — and pointed to herself.

"Graunya Ui Maulya — Graunuaile!"

Francis Derham nodded imperceptibly and raised a feeble eyebrow in the direction of the glowering animal. The girl laughed aloud.

"Bran!" she cried. "Bran of Ballinahinch."

As soon as his name was spoken, the dog sprang to his feet. He was as tall as a calf but very slender under a long shaggy coat of bluish-grey hair. His nose was pointed, his eyes honey-coloured; he had the appearance of a creature which thought and reasoned.

Derham looked from the dog to the girl; she seemed to be about twelve years old or so, small-made, quick and full of aware-ness. When she laughed, the curve of her cheek was beautiful and her eyes had the sparkle of deep-coloured jewels; but hers was a face that needed laughter – in solemnity or boredom, it might be dull like a Spanish face; in rage or concentration, it might be too intense. . . .

"I will call my father," she said, and went out, barefoot, the animal padding close to her heels.

"His name is Francis Derham," she told her waiting parent, "and he understands Spanish and Latin."

O Malley went in to question him, Graunya following again.

"Do not be afraid," the chieftain said in his merchant's Spanish. "I am Owen O Malley of the Black Oak, lord of all these territories known as the Umalls. We will care for you here and then let you go. All we want from you is some history of the ship which we have taken, and for you to teach us how to use the guns. Do you understand?"

Derham nodded, relieved that the wild-looking man of his nightmare was not going to kill him.

"Good. What port did you sail from?"

"Out of Bristol."

"Your purpose?"

"Some trade, some preying if we got the chance —"

"We?"

"My friends, all partners in the enterprise."

"You and they have lost everything. How will you pay your debts?"

"I – I could approach the Queen for aid. We were friends once —" He seemed to regret the statement immediately and bit a pale underlip. O Malley misinterpreted the movement.

"We never ask ransom," he said quietly, "and you are not our prisoner. As soon as you are strong, you will be helped on your way. Only one thing more: why did you choose the sea? You are not of it. . . ." To O Malley, sea-people and land-people were as separate as north and south.

"I — I had to leave England . . . for a while."

"You are a criminal?" It was unlikely.

"*No. . . .*"

"When is it safe for you to return?"

"It might be safe now."

"Very well. I will pay you in gold for your share of the caravel in case your creditors pursue you. God stay with you and send you health!"

At the curtain, O Malley turned hesitantly.

"I am somewhat confused," he mumbled, "by the King of England's many marriages. Please tell me who is the present Queen?"

A flicker of panic showed in the young man's eyes: then he smiled easily.

"Her Grace, the Lady Katheryn Howard."

Every morning before lessons began, and every evening when they were finished, Graunya visited Francis Derham. They managed to converse at some length in snatches of Spanish and Latin and a little French. He was curious about the ways of the native Irish, whom he had believed, until a short time ago, to be barbarians, and she thirsted for knowledge of the enemy country, England. With intense concentration, she listened to his stories about the Court, about the city of London, about the lives of people, ordinary and extraordinary, both there and in the provinces. They did not seem to differ much from the Irish: they rose up in arms from time to time; they feared invasion, and resented laws which curbed their freedom or broke with old traditions.

"The monasteries are all gone now," Francis told her one day. "Fountains – Jervaulx – Bridlington – Woburn and Glastonbury – Waltham, all gone! Some of the abbots and priors have been executed; others pardoned and pensioned – those who gave in quietly and acknowledged the King as Supreme Head in place of the Pope. Perhaps the Irish will learn from this: I hear that a few of them are being somewhat obstinate."

She thought of the little sea-lapped friary at Murrisk whose only wealth was its manuscripts and medicines and its O Malley tombs; and she thought of the public burning of Saint Patrick's crozier by order of the new Archbishop Browne in Dublin.

"What harm do the monasteries do?" she cried. "They feed the poor, instruct the ignorant, care for the sick!"

Derham's face darkened.

"You are two centuries behind the times," he said. "Religious houses grow fat on wealth, grab land, treat their tenants as slaves; eat, drink, idle and lust. . . . They destroy themselves from within —"

"That is untrue."

"Perhaps so, in Ireland, although I heard recently of a Galway by-law, nearly thirty years old, forbidding priests from staying with prostitutes in the town; by-laws are only made to prevent crimes already known."

"Galway is an English town."

"We will not argue that. The rot may not have begun in your native houses yet. But, one way or another, the good will suffer for the bad."

"And where will the monks and nuns go if their buildings are taken from them, their lands given to nobles, all their possessions snatched by the Crown?"

"The sensible ones will adjust themselves to a new life. The others" – he shrugged – "some beg in the streets, some go out of their wits or die."

"And the ordinary people," she asked, "who cares for them when they are sick or become lepers?"

"That is a problem yet unsolved, even in England. There are no new hospitals —"

"It sounds like the chaos of hell!" She was so angry that her teeth chattered. Francis Derham laughed heartily.

"You're like a pet monkey I had once, when I was about fifteen!"

She ignored the insult to inquire, "Where were you then? What were you doing?" – because everything about him was of interest to her.

"Living at the old Duchess of Norfolk's place. Learning to squeeze through the barred windows of the gentlewomen's bedchamber. My companions were the young Arundels and the Bayntons and the Howards —"

"Howard, is that not the Queen's name? Was *she* there? Is that how you know her?"

"Yes, Katheryn was there," he said briefly, and relapsed into silence. Because he and Graunya lacked a fluent common language, there were many gaps in their conversations. Subjects became too complex, too subtle, required too fine a shade of meaning for any other tongue except their native one.

Suddenly, Graunya leaned over him on the pillow, her eyes bright with curiosity, her restless fingers playing with the chain about his neck.

"Tell me of the Queen —" and, for an instant, he had a double vision. He was lying on another bed, wearing only doublet and hose, and a girl was bending over him, laughing and teasing. Her hair was the colour of autumn leaves. Her chaperone, in the background, was looking the other way. . . . He took hold of the girl by the shoulders and kissed her on the mouth. 'Tonight, Katheryn?' – and she had nodded vigorously, her eyes tip-tilting at the corners – as Graunya's did – with suppressed merriment. . . .

"I said, *tell me of the Queen!*"

"Eh? Oh, she's brightly coloured and warm and gay, full of movement. She's reckless – generous – passionate."

Graunya was watching him unblinkingly.

"Did you love her?" she asked with the first stab of jealousy she was ever to know.

Without moving, he withdrew from her.

"You're too young to understand."

"I'm not too young," she shouted, blinking back tears. "I know everything. . . ."

"You cannot know until you have experienced," he said gently, and closed his eyes. . . . His own experience with Katheryn Howard had lasted over three years; the old Duchess of Norfolk, slumbering overhead, had remained unaware, during all these nights, of the gaiety and the feasting of her charges down below. Unaware, too, of what went on afterwards until dawn lightened the sky. . . .

Graunya's voice dropped to a pleading whisper.

"Please tell me, Francis, what it is like to love. I swear by all the saints that I will never repeat one word of what you say."

He was bored lying there in the tiny room. The explosive secret which he had carried for so long was pressing on his brain. He wanted to talk about it, even if the child did not understand. For the first time since he had been bundled out of England for knowing too much, he felt safe and relaxed; and he had an audience, a girl and a wolfhound.

"Swear, then, to be silent for ever?"

"I swear! I swear!"

Wide-eyed, she listened. And, listening, learned and grew a little older. . . .

"But, Francis, your rival – this man called Manox – what did he do when the Lady Katheryn spurned him?"

"He spied upon us all, then wrote a secret letter to the old Duchess, telling her when to surprise us. She stormed in upon us one night."

"W-what action did she take?"

"Belaboured with blows anyone within range, cursed us all and shouted for the Duke!"

"What did *he* do?"

"Nothing. He was more angry with Manox for telling tales than with us for kissing."

"And what happened afterwards?"

"Afterwards?" The light died out of Derham's eyes and his mouth set bitterly. "A gross and ageing King walked in a springtime garden. He saw my love and offered her a crown in exchange for her youth and beauty."

"Were her kinsfolk glad?"

He laughed sharply. "Yes, very glad. They assured Henry that Katheryn's heart belonged to no other man, then packed me off to Bristol with all speed."

"Would the King be angry if he knew about you, and Manox and . . . and everything?"

Derham did not hear Graunya's voice. Instead, it was the gruff whisper of the old Duchess which came to his ears, '*She cannot die for what was done before*. . . .'

"No," he said aloud, "she cannot. All this is in the past. It was for present misconduct that Henry cut off the head of Anne Boleyn."

After a few weeks, he was able to walk about and go down to the ship. He instructed the chieftain and his captains in the use of the culverins and falconet 'in case we should be set upon by pirates' as O Malley said, roaring with laughter.

Cormac and Graunya were never absent from these lessons and even the sea-hating young brother, Donald, crept aboard occasionally to watch. Donald was turned thirteen now, fair like Cormac, small-boned like Graunya, but more easy-going in his ways than either of them. Donald made no demands upon himself. He was a younger brother who would continue to evade the responsibilities of growing up for as long as possible. Mentally and emotionally, Graunya was ten years his senior. Sometimes, she protected and defended him; other times, bullied him unmercifully.

The youngsters were not allowed to handle the guns but they watched their loading and priming, and heard all the advice that Derham had to give concerning their care and maintenance. They were also permitted to be present when the caravel was sailed over towards Achill: the chief and his captains wanted to practise marksmanship on the spiked rocks which pierced the ocean there.

The noise was fierce and glorious among the sea-caves but, when Graunya turned to look at Donald, she saw that he had put his fingers in his ears and that his face was screwed up as though with pain.

On the morning of his departure, Francis Derham dressed himself most carefully.

He had chosen a fine outfit from the packs of his friends left aboard the caravel; a white lawn shirt, frilled and banded, to be worn under a doublet of dark blue velvet, this cut low at the neck to reveal the pearls of the sleeved waistcoat; a pair of grey stocks, puffed and slashed above the knees; a broadcloth jerkin lined with seal skin (to the horror of the entire O Malley clan, who never slaughtered seals, believing that they were bewitched humans).

41

Thus attired, Derham felt more confident than he had done for some time. He turned down the brim of his black velvet hat – no young man of fashion would be seen with an upturned brim these days! – and fluffed the plume. He was ready to step into the curragh that would take him to Murrisk. From there, he would ride the dangerous track to Dublin, and obtain passage back to England. His purse was heavy with O Malley's gold. He would buy his way into a good position at Court, backed by the influence of the Queen: Katheryn would not refuse this small favour to an old lover!

The islanders gathered to wave him farewell and to shower gifts upon him. His new clothing astonished them but they still considered him a most pleasant and handsome young man. Everyone had grown fond of him. The chief had even invited him to stay and settle in the Umalls. . . . But Derham was city bred; he missed the crowded streets, the familiar tongue. However harsh a welcome awaited him in London, he was hell-bent to return there.

"Good-bye, Francis," Graunya said in a muffled voice. Her throat felt tight and painful. She would miss him more than anyone else would. He had told her what it was like to love and she had understood.

"Good-bye, Graunuaile!" From about his neck he took the fine chain that had the little medallion of Saint Nicholas swinging from it. She had long coveted it. Now he pressed it into her hand. "For friendship. Silent for ever!"

It was only when the bobbing plume and the black curragh had disappeared into the morning mist that she knew she should not have accepted the medallion.

He had given her his guarantee of safety.

Chapter 4

Since time out of mind, O Malley chieftains had owned the fishing rights of the best waters in Ireland, and they had the power to lease these rights to foreigners. Now, in order to keep Frenchmen and Spaniards away, Henry the Eighth paid a fat annual fee to the Lord of the Umalls for English boats to fish exclusively. Payment of the fee hurt Henry, but he could find no legal means, as yet, of taking O Malley's traditional rights away.

It was not unusual for fifty English craft to be off the west coast at any one time during a good season. O Malley never encouraged them to land except to obtain fresh drinking water but there were occasions when the towering rage of the Atlantic drove the little boats eastward into Clew Bay. If they were in poor case then, the chieftain invited their crews ashore and entertained them at his castle of Belclare or his ancient fortress of Cahirnamart. So it was that, on a March evening in the year fifteen forty-two, half a dozen Englishmen sat down to dine with him, while, outside, great trees were bending away from the wind and even the normally placid river showed white fangs where it met the sea.

The Lady Margaret was confined to her bed with a fever so that Graunya sat by her father's side at the upper table. She had been taught to take her mother's place whenever necessary: in less than two years' time, she would be married, mistress of an O Flaherty household. . . .

The English captain's name was George Plessington. He

spoke some Irish, having once been a wool-buyer in Munster, and he and Graunya struck up a lively conversation; she was avid for news of the outside world, from which she had been cut off since October because rain had reduced the tracks to muddy impassability and no travelling man had visited the Umalls since long before Christmas. She questioned Plessington about this and that, and he smiled at her and remarked:

"You are surprisingly well informed."

"Thank you. I learned much from a guest we had in the summertime."

"Englishman?"

"Yes. We had hoped for news of him. . . ."

"Maybe I know him if he has a ship?"

"Er . . . no; I think not." She bit her lip; the caravel had been overhauled and renamed *Naove* after the Island of Saints, but O Malley did not wish to advertise her presence in his fleet and had warned Graunya accordingly: Englishmen might have different ideas about ownership. . . .

Plessington noted the awkward pause and it aroused his curiosity.

"What was his name?" he asked directly.

She fingered the Saint Nicholas medallion around her neck; there was no way out of the question.

"Francis Derham," she said.

All six fishermen stopped eating at the same moment, one with his knife still poised in mid-air. Plessington was the first to move or speak.

"Francis . . . Derham," he said carefully, "who was engaged in piracy around these coasts?"

Panic hammered in Graunya's throat. Something was wrong; she sensed it as surely as a nervous horse senses a wild animal about to spring. . . .

"Yes," she said, gulping wine.

"Then I have good news for you," Plessington beamed. "He will trouble you no more."

"What's that?" O Malley asked, leaning across the table. Everyone had become suddenly quiet.

"Francis Derham," Plessington said loudly. "He was arrested

at Court in the autumn. It was a most exciting trial. The entire country followed it. You had not heard?"

Graunya did not want to hear. But now her father and brothers and all the people at the other tables were looking towards the English captain, demanding to know what had happened. In his halting Irish, he was trying to tell them. The scenes came jaggedly, in strong crude lineaments – black shadows of the Tower, solid fabric of judicial pronouncement, orange glow of the torture fire. . . .

And Graunya's knowledge of how Derham would think and move and speak helped to join them in a nightmare sequence for her.

Francis Derham had reached England without mishap. The Court was already at York by then, where kneeling men made atonement to King Henry for the outrage of the Pilgrimage of Grace. Old skeletons rattled their chains above the battlements.

Derham had private audience of the Queen. Her gown was so stiff with jewels that he found it difficult to remember the softness of the body underneath. But the eighteen-year-old Katheryn read growing recollection in his eyes and quickly offered him the price of silence: the position of Usher to her Chamber.

"And take heed what words you speak!" she said lightly as she dismissed him. She was laughing. . . .

He bowed very low and withdrew, to join the ever-swelling ranks of those who must be kept quiet concerning the past. He knew that his love affair with Katheryn was over and he had no wish to compromise her position. She seemed happy enough without him now, although there was no sign of a Duke of York in the making. . . . It crossed his mind that she had taken another lover. No, that was impossible! Even her recklessness would not dare put horns upon the King who doted on her, called her his 'rose without a thorn' and thanked God publicly for his marriage to her.

Derham went about his duties and enjoyed the life of the Court. Everywhere were familiar faces from the old Norfolk establishment: there was Joan Bulmer, who had been present on the night of discovery; there was the maid, Tilney, who used to guard the door; there were the young Howards and Bayntons and Arundels, once partners at the love-feasts, all now rising steadily in position about the young Queen. Between them, they would help her to bury the past because their continuing success dovetailed with hers. A more discreet band of courtiers it would be difficult to find anywhere, and Derham's discretion was the most tightlipped of all; he even disciplined his eyes when the royal pair passed by – Katheryn, slender, radiant and vital; Henry, so obese that he had to be lifted up and down stairs, and short-tempered from the pain of his ulcer which was now closing to a frightening pipe-shape.

'How does she endure him?' Derham wondered, remembering the way she had rejoiced in his own slim body. And, again, the answer came to him: 'She has a new lover. . . . Look at her gleaming hair, the tenderness of her eyes and mouth; could Henry stimulate her to this beauty of gladness?'

To Derham, who had shared Katheryn's bed for three years, all was clear as spring water. And he began to be afraid.

Riding south with the Court in October, he passed under high bare trees that looked like gallows, where a solitary raven croaked; and, in the croaking, he imagined the voice of the old Duchess,

'She cannot die for what was done before.'

Before. Before. But this was *now*. . . .

Thomas Cranmer, Archbishop of Canterbury, passed a folded note to the King. ". . . Because, Your Grace, I cannot speak the contents!"

Henry read it and put out a hand to steady himself.

"Call a secret inquiry of all the persons named. . . ."

Throughout the night, there was a coming and a going of horsemen. The Queen was confined to her apartments and her musicians withdrawn from her, the order ending with the heavy words:

'It is no longer time to dance.'

Francis Derham was arrested on a charge of piracy. With others, he was interrogated in the Tower but, so far, the questions related only to the past – why had he been sent to

Ireland just before the royal wedding? – who financed the expedition? – who lost by it and remained silent?

The questions indicated the store of information behind them: a serving-wench had joked with her own brother about the Queen being 'light'; the brother demanded explanation of the term; his sister, still laughing, told him what she meant. Appalled, he took his outraged conscience to the Archbishop of Canterbury. And Cranmer acted with the speed of a snake. . . .

Derham confessed to having had carnal knowledge of the Queen before her marriage; Manox, to knowing a secret mark upon her body.

Now the floodgates were opened and the past swept the present before it. Servants talked: yes, the Queen had a lover called Thomas Culpeper, a Gentlemen of the Royal Bedchamber. She had met him on the backstairs of every resting-house from London to York and home again. She had written him a letter. She had tainted the blood royal and must die for it.

They all must die to purge the House of Tudor.

Francis Derham stood in the dock at Guildhall and heard the terrible sentence passed upon him and young Thomas Culpeper: they were both to be hanged at Tyburn, cut down alive, disembowelled and beheaded.

On the tenth day of December, Derham died thus. Culpeper's sentence was reduced to beheading only because he protested, to the last, the innocence of his association with the Queen.

On the twelfth of February following, in the evening, Katheryn asked that the block might be brought to her cell in the Tower, ". . . So that I can judge how to lay myself upon it."

Next morning, very early, while the river fog was still thick and icy, they led her out. She was nineteen years old. Her weeks of hysteria were past and she was calm. She said that she deserved to die.

They brushed the tendrils of hair from the back of her neck so that the stroke of the axe might not be impeded.

Except for the roaring of the wind, there was no sound in the hall of O Malley's fortress. Plessington looked about him, puzzled: he had done his best to entertain, but the faces in the torchlight were tight-lipped, flat-eyed as stone images.

O Malley stood up.

"You will go now," was all he said.

"*Go?*" The six Englishmen had dreamed of warm straw on the floor, a sleeping place among the servants and the dogs at least. Now they saw the chieftain's hand upon his hunting knife as a signal to his guards; felt the breaths of the chained wolf-hounds on the backs of their necks.

"Very well, we will leave," Plessington said heavily. "I suspect we go to our deaths on such a night." The fortress was shaking from the force of the storm and hail lashed the ancient stonework.

"That is as may be," O Malley replied. "You come of a race to whom life is cheap, and public execution an entertainment."

Plessington looked him deep in the eyes.

"And you," he asked quietly, "do you not fight and kill your own brethren for the sheer joy of it? Do widows and orphans not starve to death here, now that some of the monasteries are gone? Do you not plough by tying your horses' tails to the iron, and bury cats in sand or hang live goats from the masthead to call up a good sailing wind? Are we so wrong then to execute our criminals?"

"It is no crime to take a woman," O Malley said; he could not deny that the other things happened in his country and the tribes had no strong feelings about marital infidelity; most chieftains had bastards. . . .

Then Plessington went out into the rain-lashed dark with his men; and all of them cursed the name of O Malley.

"The Irish are savages!" It was their unshakeable conviction.

"The English are barbarians," O Malley was muttering, trying to resume his meal; but his hunger was gone. He turned suddenly to Graunya.

"See that no word of what we have heard reaches your mother. I would not want her to know that she saved a man's body for Tyburn."

Graunya nodded dumbly. Nobody would ever measure the full depth of her horror. It formed a well of darkness in her mind, silent and terrible, this first full awareness of deliberate human cruelty. Grizzly tales of the Spanish Inquisitors she could listen to impersonally; no one of her acquaintance was involved and Spain was a long way off, friendly towards Ireland. But England was moving in upon her country with new laws, and new methods of enforcing those laws. The ancient brehon code by which the Irish had lived for centuries – whereby a man made restitution to the victim of his crimes, but was not otherwise punished – was to be abolished. . . .

Derham had told her of the passion for which he was to die so horribly. She was never to rid her mind of this association – love and death. If one had to make a choice between living and loving, then she wanted to live.

Spring came suddenly in a burst of feathery green. The Lady Margaret's fever left her and she threw herself into the twice-yearly business of moving house. Graunya rejoiced always in going to the islands and worked willingly to speed the day of departure (it was a different story with her in the autumn: *then* she would look towards the mainland in despair and refuse to lift a helping finger!).

"I don't know what you'll do when you're married," her mother smiled, busily sorting linen. "Young Dhonal O Flaherty might like to live in the same place all year round."

"Then he'll have to do it without a wife," Graunya said shortly.

"You wait, my daughter! If you love him, you'll want to be with him always. If not – well, his children will tie you to the hearth in any case."

Either way, it sounded like the end of freedom. She was not looking forward to her marriage. The children she could accept but not the mystical bond that would make her one in spirit and desire with any man. . . .

"Is that your father I hear down below?" the Lady Margaret asked.

Small boats were scraping on the fortress steps, ready to carry the household supplies down river and out into the bay. Men were splashing about, loading them, and children played on the sun-dappled shingle.

"Yes. He has a foreigner with him."

"A *foreigner*?" Her mother came to stand beside her at the narrow window.

"A Spaniard," Graunya said, after further inspection. She had been to Spain four times now since her eighth year, and recognized a man of that country easily enough by his clothing. This one was dressed from head to foot in unadorned black; an Irishman would not wear black while there was any other dye left in the world, and an Englishman would use it only as a setting for jewels.

She followed her mother down the stone steps from the fortress wall to the river. O Malley came towards them, leading the stranger. He was a youngish man, thin, with shiny skin which looked as if it had been stretched too tightly. There was a suppressed intensity about him which at once attracted and repelled: one felt that a promise made to him would be binding unto death and that it was better to withdraw now before becoming involved.

"This is Don Pedro de Ricalde," O Malley said. "He is on his way to the north and wants to visit the MacWilliam first. He saw our fleet in the bay."

"But the fleet is heading west, not north," Graunya objected discourteously; she was afraid of anything which might delay the move to Clare Island.

"I know, my lady," the Spaniard said, bowing; his mantle opened to reveal a heavy crucifix thrust under his girdle. "Nevertheless, the matter is of sufficient importance for me to risk asking an awkward favour."

"Oh, it is easily enough arranged," O Malley told him, and began shouting for one of his boatmen. Then he had another idea. "We will *all* visit the MacWilliam! The weather is splendid and settled. I would have to do it next month in any case – eh, Margaret?"

His wife nodded and smiled, trying to erase Graunya's impoliteness.

The MacWilliam was O Malley's superior lord, and his territories lay across the bay, extending east and southward from there in a great arc to Castle Barry, where they met the lands of Upper Umall. The O Malley owed no rent to the Mac-William but only a rising out of men in time of trouble; twice

50

a year, he rendered an account of his fighting men so that the MacWilliam might calculate his own composite strength from among the tribes of Connacht.

Graunya could have wept with vexation. A visit to Carrigahowley Castle now would waste nearly a week. Other years, it might not have mattered; but *this* year . . . it was the last she would ever spend on the island with her family and she begrudged every day stolen from it.

Next summer, the O Flahertys would come for her.

The man who now held the MacWilliam title was David Bourke of Carrigahowley. He was standing on the jetty below his fortress to welcome the O Malley longboat. Two hundred years of Irish mothers had not altered the Norman mould of this family who came to conquer and remained to become absorbed: David Bourke was tall, longheaded, nose and chin hooking towards one another. . . .

He had buried one wife, who had left him three sons. One of these, Walter the Tall, was by his father's side now, gravely helping the Lady Margaret ashore. Walter was the MacWilliam's tanist, and resembled him closely both in manner and appearance. They looked more like brothers than father and son.

O Malley presented the Spaniard to David Bourke. The colourless Norman eyes betrayed nothing, but it was evident that David did not know Don Pedro de Ricalde, and had little interest in his coming. . . .

Graunya was curious to see the MacWilliam's second wife because she was an O Flaherty of Connemara, and half-sister to young Dhonal, Graunya's betrothed. Finola O Flaherty had a reputation for extraordinary beauty.

The visitors entered Carrigahowley Castle and ascended to the private apartments. Spring sunshine slanted through the windows, softening harsh grey stone but failing to remove the dank chill which winter had left behind in this most desolate place.

David Bourke opened a heavy door and ushered them inside. At first, all Graunya saw was a brocade curtain, rich and gleaming; then the MacWilliam drew it aside to reveal a room of astonishing splendour: rugs and tapestries, banners and armour covered the walls; the floor was creamy with deep piled sheepskins; velvet cushions in brilliant colours were tied to the heavy oak benches and, over all, lay the perfume of a woman's presence.

Finola, the second wife, was coming forward to meet her husband's guests.

Her progress was unhurried, consciously sinuous. She was a ripe, luxurious woman, red haired, green eyed, white skinned. Her breasts were high, as though pushed up by English corsets, but the movement of her hips was too free to be so confined, and the sand-coloured satin of her gown fell against her body without evidence of underclothing.

She greeted the visitors and bade them be seated, but herself remained standing, leaning against a high black oak chest. Around and around her finger she twirled the tasselled ends of her waist cord, first in one direction, then the other, forming a hypnotic circle.

Graunya sat on the edge of a bench. The apartment was very warm, the perfume heavy. All sounds from outside were eerily cut off. She felt breathless and imprisoned here after the windy freedom of the sea. All her life she had been vaguely uneasy in the presence of women, and this one alarmed her – made her fully conscious of her own rough, careless attire, her unformed body, her animal tenseness when confined within four walls by comparison with Finola's royally superb relaxation and exquisite appearance. Yet she could not take her eyes off David Bourke's wife nor cease listening to the lazy, confident voice which betokened a knowledge of all things. Oh, to be like this woman whose effect upon men must be dynamic! – even Owen O Malley was leaning towards her, oblivious of everyone else, and his smitten gaze hurt Graunya like a knife-thrust.

But Finola was not interested in the O Malley chieftain; it was towards Don Pedro de Ricalde that she was turning the full force of her personality, willing him to look at her instead of at a square of bare wall above her head.

Around and around her finger the cord twirled in ever-varying circles. . . . And, watching it, Graunya knew, with sudden blinding maturity, what was its purpose.

'If the Spaniard lowers his eyes to her face', she thought, 'to her breasts and her hips, that blurred circle will draw him towards her.'

But the black-clad man refused to let his gaze lock with Finola's. He had estimated her power and her intentions in the first instant. Her blue-green eyes were cast inward slightly towards the bridge of her nose, so that they focused at a point only a dagger's length from the human heart, transfixing it with their stare.

Don Pedro needed his freedom and the full plain of his senses. He came of an intensely moral race – which, nevertheless, begat bastards by the hundred thousand – and he knew when he was threatened. As now . . .

The tension was broken by a man-servant bringing wine and sweetmeats.

Finola said to him, "Find my son and ask him to come here." Then, deliberately, she walked towards Don Pedro and sat beside him, from which position she regarded him slantingly. "You seem like a man anxious to finish his business and be gone. I want you to meet my Richard before you do so."

The Spaniard answered formally.

"Madam, that would be a great pleasure. My mission concerns all members of every ruling house in the country."

David Bourke's eyebrows lifted slightly.

"Then we had better hear of it," he said.

The Spaniard took a letter from inside his black clothing and handed it to the MacWilliam. Graunya could see that it bore a heavy embossed design at the head and a flourishing signature. Bourke read slowly, frowningly, then passed the letter to O Malley, who merely stared at it because he could not read Latin.

"So," David Bourke said to Don Pedro, "you are a priest?" – and, without turning his head, managed to throw the information at his wife. Finola merely smiled. . . .

"Yes," the Spaniard said, "of the new Society of Jesus, founded by a soldier, my kinsman."

"You will need military tactics to conduct this" – Bourke glanced at the letter in O Malley's hands – "this Counter-Reformation."

53

"We are trained for it. And more besides."

"What more?"

"Logic. Argument. Knowledge of people and conditions."

"You are guilty of a miscalculation in coming to Ireland, then. Our own priests are flying abroad or roaming the country-side as beggars."

"We have come to organize them for resistance. I have one companion with me. Others will follow."

David Bourke stood up and began to walk in a tight circle.

"I am not entirely certain," he said then, "that we want you. How think you, O Malley?"

"I would prefer to hear more before forming an opinion." Not having read the letter, there were gaps in O Malley's grasp of the affair.

"Very well," Bourke said, "hear me first. The Spanish record of infiltration is a sorry one – ships heading for the New World with missionaries on their decks and racks and thumbscrews in their holds. Anyway, we have enough foreign elements here already; there is no need for Spaniards to come to Ireland; their presence can cause nothing but trouble. . . ."

"That is strictly a layman's view," the priest said swiftly. "Rome has decided that Ireland must be saved from Protestantism, whatever the price. I may die for it. You may die. It makes no matter. The work must go on —"

Bourke stopped pacing and leaned over him menacingly.

"Rome has decided, has she? All right: we agreed, once, to obey her and our obedience is constant. But, tell me, learned friend, are we not capable of defending our own Faith without foreign aid?"

"It would appear not. Many of your bishops have sworn to the spiritual supremacy of Henry Tudor; that is heresy. Dozens of your nobles have accepted abbey lands. My business with you is to ask you to refuse them if they are offered to you."

O Malley ran his fingers through his long brown beard.

"Don Pedro," he said, "there are five religious houses on my lands: Murrisk, Aughavale, Inishbofin, Kilgeever and Clare. If these should be dissolved, would you expect me to welcome strangers into my territories?"

"Yes. Inside a generation, you would have converted them

to your own way of living and thinking. It is a risk and a hardship, I know; but, if you accept the Church lands yourself, you will be required to swear an oath on the title deeds, renouncing the Pope. It is you the Catholic against you the chieftain. You know what your choice must be."

Graunya saw her father's eyes meet those of David Bourke over the priest's head, and she knew that, for these two, the division of duty was not so clear-cut. The Spaniard did not understand the sacredness of chieftainship, nor could he realize how suicidal it would be to allow Englishmen to settle on Church lands which lay deep inside each territory. There was greater conflict here than Don Pedro de Ricalde could learn about from the outside, however astute his teachers.

O Malley was troubled and disturbed. It was against his every instinct to allow foreigners to set foot in the Umalls. Better to take the abbey lands back into his own possession, as other chieftains had done lately, swearing the Supremacy Oath with tongue in cheek. . . .

"Well, my lords," the priest's voice cut across his thoughts, "can the Holy Father count upon your complete loyalty?" – and, before he could answer, David Bourke was laughing and saying:

"Certainly, certainly! So long as he sends us Vatican troops to bolster us against prolonged attack by Henry Tudor."

"I have no authority to promise military aid. But I think it might come. And from my own country also. However, it may never be necessary, you understand?"

"What do you mean?" O Malley asked. The priest spread his hands.

"We have – ambassadors and . . . er . . . others, at Court. They write long informative letters. It seems that Henry is a sick man. He has only one son and no prospect of another; this Prince is not yet six years old." He looked around him carefully but avoided Finola's gaze. "The English king will die soon. Can a child survive the burden of the crown? And, if it were to crush him, who could follow?"

"Mary," O Malley said, with a sigh of profound relief, "who would restore the old form of religion. . . ." This would be the solution of all problems.

The door opened and a young man came in, flushed and dishevelled from hunting.

"Ah, Richard!" Finola cried. She was instantly changed, no longer aware of herself or of her beauty or its effect upon others; her whole being surged towards her son, fiercely enveloping him.

He was a big, muscular youth, about twenty years of age, dark-haired, dark-skinned, with bold blue-green eyes like his mother's; these rested on Graunya for a long moment. . . . Finola caressed her son's arm and, when he became aware of the touch, his face expressed resentment of her pride in him. He mumbled an offhand greeting, bowed to the company in general and immediately excused himself.

His mother called after him in exasperation but he did not return. Then she leaned back against the wall, her maternal moment over, and fixed her strange eyes on Walter the Tall, her stepson, who had been silent all the while.

Graunya was never to forget the altered expression on Finola's face when she turned from Richard to Walter; pride became jealousy; desire to protect became determination to destroy. . . .

Chapter 5

F^OR a few days in early June of the following year, Clew Bay was a floating city. Carracks and coracles, curraghs, canoes and caravels all jostled on the sparkling water: red sails of O Flaherty; blue ensign of O Malley; pennants of O Donnell and O Sullivan Bearra; banners of O Dowd, O Hara, Costello and O Kelly; wine-red hand of the MacWilliam and O Conor badges.

Motionless background to the kaleidoscope was the blue-grey cone of Croagh Patrick – a beaked head thrusting skywards into the summer clouds, its foothills on either side like the spread wings of a nesting bird in the treetops of Murrisk.

Between mountain and water lay the Austin 'Friary of the Marshland' – guardian of the Black Bell, repository of priceless manuscripts; its austerity lightened now by garlands and glowing tapers and cloths of silver lace.

The wedding procession formed outside on the sandy grass. Past the O Malley tombs it filed with candle and crucifix, bell, canopy and chant; white linen; frosty lace; scarlet velvet and black watered silk. . . .

Young Dhonal O Flaherty stood before the high altar, awaiting his bride. He was a broad-shouldered youth with light-brown hair that curled on the nape of his muscular neck. He could feel the press of humanity behind him, crowding the single aisle; hear the voices of friars and nuns singing in Latin from the vaulted chapel on his left side. Sunshine picked out every detail of the carved and decorated interior – he could even see the wicker-work markings of the moulds which the friars had used to sustain the beautiful arches whilst the mortar which bound them was still wet. But his instructions were to stare straight ahead through the five-lighted east window and not to turn around. . . .

He sensed the rustle of excitement that began at the west door and spread up the nave – an entirely feminine sibilance, part whisper, part swish of fabrics.

Graunya was coming, hand resting on her father's arm, her maidens holding up her blue mantle that had the White Seahorse embroidered on it in pearls. Dhonal could keep his neck stiff no longer. Impulsively, he turned around, saw her slenderness against the expanse of sea beyond the open door, and the sparkle of the water was in her eyes and in her hair, and its flow in the fall of her ivory gown. Mesmerized, he kept his eyes upon her until she stood by his side. Then they knelt together, their mantles fanning out like the wakes of ships, blending the emblems of White Seahorse and Golden Lizard.

Graunya came out into the sunshine with her hand firmly locked in Dhonal's. She was hardly aware of the kisses and embraces of her kinsfolk, of the cheering and shouting which marked the union of two great families.

There was a stampede for the boats which would carry hundreds of people to Belclare and Cahirnamart for the wedding feast.

Peace and silence returned to Murrisk with their going; seabirds called; bees hummed among the woodbine flowers; dragonflies darted over the little golden stream that tumbled down from Croagh Patrick through the woods.

From the boat, Graunya looked back once at the friary where the bones of her ancestors and their family records lay, and a sudden desolation washed over her; hers might be the last great wedding this remote building would ever witness, for dissolution was creeping upwards from Iar-Connacht. Her last memory was of the friars grouped in the doorway, work-roughened hands hidden in their sleeves, their patient faces smiling. . . .

Dhonal's arm was around her waist, the heartbeat of his

masculinity close to her. Nothing and nobody should matter except Dhonal. It was scarcely two hours since she had first laid eyes upon him but he had been a part of her consciousness for six years and she was entirely satisfied with the sight of him: he was handsome and strong; he had a great gaiety. And, when he looked at her, she knew that he found her beautiful.

The feasting was still in noisy progress when they went to their own apartment. She had wanted to be alone with her husband, if only to disentangle him from predatory kinswomen below; but now, as the door shut behind them, she wished that she were still in the dining-hall, laughing with this splendid young man, giving him the surface of her emotions only.

The sudden silence frightened her, and the walls seemed to be closing in. At that moment, she would have given her right arm to be standing up in a curragh, exulting in the dangerous knowledge that only a cow's hide separated her from the depths of the ocean. The idea of submitting to the love-making of this boy seemed suddenly ludicrous. She felt timelessly old, as though every O Malley girl-bride since the making of the world were present, in spirit, within her; Graunuaile, to whom the elements spoke. . . .

Dhonal was not aware of Graunuaile, only of Graunya with her midnight hair and her little waist. He held out his arms to her and said, "Come here!"

She stiffened, backed against the door and regarded him down the straight length of her nose.

"*I will not be commanded.*"

He took a bewildered step towards her.

"Nobody is commanding you, Graunya —" Then he laughed, grabbed her by the wrists and kissed her. "There, I have come to you. Is that what you want?"

It was. And she was determined that it should always be so. . . .

Later, he lay with his arm under her neck, looking at her face in the moonlight – the dark smudges of her lashes, the opalescent skin; and he was entirely happy, undisturbed by her moment of rebellion when some strange animal had looked out of her eyes. . . . Perhaps she had been afraid of him. Yes, that was it. All was well now.

He was drifting towards sleep when, deep in his ear, the bitter angry voice of his dead father came to him from a moment in childhood. . . .

He remembered only that his step-sister, Finola, had been present, but not the context of the words – some quarrel or other . . . contention always surrounded the red-headed Finola.

The father was shouting,

'Woman wants from man only this: sons and the means of rearing them; sons, *sons*. . . .'

Now, on his wedding night, Dhonal O Flaherty tossed and murmured, "God rest my father's soul!" But the words still echoed in his brain – *woman wants from man only this: sons and the means of rearing them* – and, all at once, he was afraid that it might be true; that Graunya would never love him. There was a reserve of withdrawal in her, a determination not to be dominated. . . .

By the end of the month, the O Flaherty ships were back in their own waters and the young husband and wife settled, temporarily, at Ballinahinch Castle with the chieftain, Dhonal Crone, and his family.

Graunya had her moments of homesickness; at such times, she would slide her hand inside Bran's spiked collar and draw comfort from the rough warmth of his coat. But, on the whole, she was happy. Her responsibilities were few: the household ran itself as it had always done, radiating out from the bunch of keys carried by the portly Lady Eilish, who asked nothing more of her than that she should take the men and dogs out from under her busy feet as often as possible. This was entirely in line with Graunya's inclinations: every morning she rode out to hunt with her husband and the chieftain and the bands of men – there were few women at Ballinahinch Castle, apart from retainers – or she sailed with the fleet, to fish or trade, sometimes for weeks on end. The O Flahertys were a harder and more ruthless crew than she had been accustomed to at home; they lacked O Malley's sensitivity to weather and current, and forced the gap of danger with their men and ships more often. Still, nobody complained, least of all Graunya, who was learning new waters; and what she knew about the weather, she kept to herself for fear of offending Dhonal Crone and his captains.

The floodtide of summer passed and autumn dyed trees and heather. Now the nights were big with stars, frost-sharpened. The last evening of October came, when the *Shee*, the nameless Other Ones, would make their midnight ride from rath to rath, and mortals must remain indoors, playing games with nuts and apples.

There was a fearful din proceeding from the hall where most of the household was gathered for the Hallowe'en festivities. Lady Eilish sought the peace of her solar. There, Dhonal Crone was kneeling on the rush-strewn floor, grooming his favourite bitch.

"Have the youngsters returned yet?" he inquired.

"No," Eilish said, sitting down heavily. From the lake shore a wolf howled and she crossed herself. "Do you know where they are, Dhonal?"

He shrugged his thin shoulders.

"Night hunting with torches, maybe. They're often away until dawn." He half-envied young Dhonal and Graunya – their strength, their freedom, their utter disregard for comfort. Once, by accident, he had come upon them at daybreak, sleeping in a sandy hollow of the beach, the dog Bran at their feet; and he had stood looking down at them, his heart full of nameless regrets. "Oh, cease worrying, Eilish," he said now, irritably. "They're better able to take care of themselves than the Fianna!"

"The Fianna were all men," his wife pointed out literally.

"Nonsense. They must have had women. What about Diarmuid and the other Graunya? *She* bore him twelve children in the forest!"

"I wouldn't like to think," Eilish retorted, "that an O Flaherty would be born the same way. . . ."

"There's plenty of time yet."

"Less than five months. And the winter is coming on fast. I must talk to both of them. What do you suppose the Lady Margaret O Malley would say if she knew how her daughter was running wild?"

"She reared the child the way she is —"

"No. No, I doubt if she did. I heard it said at the wedding that Graunya and her father were inseparable always, that he

61

had had the training of her. Maybe that's why the men here accept her so readily among them. It's as though she were one of themselves. Sometimes it seems to me that she thinks like a man – small remarks . . . little things, you know – and I wonder how her husband —"

"You imagine a great deal, Eilish. Graunya is a young girl with a healthy body and a mind full of curiosity. Maybe she'd grow fat and dull if she were married to a stolid middle-aged husband: but I saved her from that. Young Dhonal knows how to amuse her."

"Dhonal isn't the only one!"

"Ho-ho! Jealous of the time I spend with her?" he teased.

"I'm too old for jealousy. But some of the captains' wives are not. There's a deal of talk —"

"Indeed?"

"– about her wearing a man's tunic and braes."

"And what should she wear at sea? Petticoats?"

"Dhonal Crone, you're deliberately blind and deaf: a married woman shouldn't want to *go* to sea! It's unnatural. . . ."

"That's for her husband to decide."

"Her husband does whatever he knows will please her; I think he is a trifle fearful of her! He never stops to think how his own chances of election for tanist might be affected, if he could be accused of needing a woman on his ships."

"I never heard that reason put forward by the ollavs for rejecting a man!"

"You might before very long. Do you think he's the right one for your tanist, anyway?"

"Yes, I do. He'll have my vote behind him. He'll be elected, you'll see."

"Umm, please God. When he has a son he might be a bit more responsible. *If* he has a son —"

The chief kicked a blazing log. "Why should he *not* have, in the name of Crum?"

Eilish turned on him swiftly.

"Because his pregnant wife is acting like a fourteen-year-old boy! Riding without a saddle, drawing a six-foot bow, rowing all over the three lakes. . . ."

Dhonal Crone began to chuckle.

"It's well she does it," he said fondly, "and a great joy to me to watch her. Ah, here they are now!"

Dhonal and Graunya came in, laughing, their cheeks and eyes bright with cold. They were full of talk about a wolf they had tracked half-way up Ben Lettery. Graunya put her freezing hands against Dhonal Crone's face but he went on grooming the bitch, and said, without looking up, "Child, you ought to be taking things a bit easier now."

Eilish nodded and Graunya went and knelt by her.

"Only a few more weeks," she pleaded, "then the snow will come and shut us all in."

"Snow?" Dhonal Crone said sharply. "We hardly ever have it."

"We will this year."

He drew the brush carefully over the bitch's ears.

"What makes you think that?"

Graunya did not answer for a moment and the silence stretched.

"Oh – the berries," she said, then, hurriedly, "There is always an abundance of them before a hard winter." She was looking at the burning log as she spoke and her dark eyes had points of fire.

Two weeks later, snow began to fall, piling in silent layers until the whole countryside was blanketed between the still black lakes.

Graunya knew that a mighty title like that of the O Flaherty was not passed on lightly. Even to have his name put forward for election, Dhonal had had to undergo rigorous tests and scrutiny. Now, in fierce competition with others, he would have to satisfy the learned ollavs that, eventually, he would make the best chieftain. The entire business would take many weeks; there was seldom any urgency about the election of a tanist because he was chosen while the reigning chieftain was still in his prime (as Cormac had now been chosen tanist to the O Malley).

Up to the moment of his acceptance, anyone might challenge, insult or libel him; afterwards, his name and person was sacred as the heir apparent, the crown prince. . . .

On a bleak February morning, when months-old snow lay

frozen on the desolate mountains, Graunya watched her husband and Dhonal Crone row away with their escorts. If the younger man returned as Prince of Connemara, the child now heavy within her would have his name inscribed in the family records as first-born of a tanist.

The ambition sustained her through the final weeks of waiting, when panic and impatience alternated in her mind.

"This has gone on far too long! I have been a prisoner for months. . . ." She was in a frenzy to be free of the child. Her feet and hands were blue with cold from lack of exercise, and her face alarmingly blotched. She was half glad that Dhonal was away, although his absence left an icy void in their bed at nights. At last she begged the Lady Eilish to come and lie with her, and kept that busy woman awake until cockcrow, asking, "What is it like?" and "How does it begin?" until —

"Oh, *sleep!*" Eilish yawned. "I have never met the like of you for restlessness."

In a little room near by were three women of the family O Lee whose menfolk were physicians to the O Flahertys. They had everything ready, bowls and towels and water. An empty oak cradle stood by the ever-tended fire, while linen sheets and brushed blankets hung from a petch above. They slept light, waiting for the call. It came, at last, on a March midnight. . . .

Graunya did not give birth easily. She was too small, too impatient and undisciplined. She fought the gigantic force which had taken hold of her, resenting it as a personal outrage. Storms which she had experienced at sea – and regarded as nature's violence in its most elemental form – were nothing by comparison with this towering dominance.

After twenty-four hours, awed and exhausted, she crept into the harbour of sleep where even the cries of her newly-born son could not awaken her.

Very early in the morning, the men came home. She heard the splash of oars, the stamping and the shouting. She recognized Bran's excited bark and heard him pounding towards her apartment; then Dhonal's footsteps, strangely hesitant and slow.

Her husband came and stood beside her, his face shadowed.

"Dhonal!" She forgot the reason for his absence, forgot everything except that she was the mother of a son, and that his

64

father's arms were around her. It was the happiest moment of her life, caught up in a kind of ecstasy, oblivious of everything except Dhonals' lips and hands, the solid support of his body. But she was fully conscious of her happiness and knew that intrusion must follow. She felt the beginnings of it in Dhonal's voice.

"Graunya, I am not the O Flaherty tanist."

It was a moment before his meaning penetrated her awareness: then she struggled free of him.

"You have failed!" It was an accusation devoid of all sympathy.

His quick temper blazed out.

"It was not I who failed, but you, Graunya. The new tanist's wife is a Moycullen O Flaherty, a strengthening link in the family chain. Mine is an O Malley, a competitive outsider. . . ."

They stared at one another like angry strangers; such words had never passed between them before. His rage was a simmering, fighting thing against what he felt to be an injustice: his name had been leading the other's on every count until the question of their respective wives had come up; then the circle of ollavs had deliberated, pored over the genealogies, called witnesses of character. . . .

'We consider that the strength of a wife is the weakness of a husband.'

It was the captains' women who had damned Graunya and delivered the deathblow to all Dhonal's hopes. Now she was blaming him as though for some personal weakness and, for a moment, he hated her. She saw it in his eyes and made a desperate attempt to save a situation which frightened her.

"Dhonal – forgive me —"

"For what?"

"For being what I am: unwomanly —"

"You are too much a woman." Suddenly, he took her in his arms, shutting out his anger with the curtain of her hair. She stroked and fondled him, and asked gently, "Do you not want to see your son, Dhonal?"

"Yes. Yes, of course. . . ."

She held him to her for a moment longer, then called for one of the O Lee women to bring the infant, and watched Dhonal's face as he took the child, awkwardly, out of the nurse's hands.

"What are we going to call him?" he asked; many names had been discussed.

"I thought Owen, for my father . . . unless you have some other choice?"

"No. Owen is a good name." They were treading warily now, determined not to offend each other. "As soon as we have eaten, I will row down the lake and bring the hermit-priest back with me for the baptism." It was a sad thing to have to say because, for centuries, O Flaherty children had been carried to the Royal Abbey of Cong, there to be christened by the Lord Abbott; but two years ago the Augustinians had been driven out by order of the King's Escheator-General. The Abbey was desolate now and, remembering, Dhonal was silent. Then he forced a smile and said, "Time enough yet to choose a tutor and a riding-master for you, young Owen!" – and stroked the infant's scant hair with one finger.

In the manor house of Ashridge, another tutor had been busy for several years. His pupils were Edward, son and heir of Henry the Eighth, and Elizabeth, unloved orphan of Anne Boleyn.

Both the Tudor children had red-gold hair, blue-veined white skins and the pale slanted eyes of their father. But Elizabeth would never inherit his corpulence: she was thin to the point of brittleness; even her bulky clothing could not disguise this. She was a sharp, suspicious child with a harsh voice. Her only claim to beauty, apart from her colouring and fine skin, lay in her long slender hands, the nails pink-flushed. . . .

Dr Richard Cox now directed his next question at her.

"My Lady Elizabeth, what is your royal father's policy in regard to his domain of Ireland?"

Without hesitation, she rapped out, "'Sober ways, politic drifts and amiable persuasions.'"

A smile twitched the tutor's lips.

"Yes – yes – but not in that tone of voice, surely?"

"I cannot help my voice."

"I was referring to the tone. . . . Let us continue. How is this policy being put into operation?"

"By appeals to the greed of the Irish nobility: Church lands in exchange for submission – they would rather lose their Pope than their territories! – English homes for the free education of their children, and newly-created titles to be passed on by primogeniture instead of by the ancient elective system of tanistry."

Dr Cox never failed to be astonished by Elizabeth's immediate grasp of any situation. If only her brain could be transplanted into the head of her brother Edward! The lad was neither slow nor stupid, he was merely average, but, for a future King, average was not enough. The educational programme mapped out for him would have taxed a much more acute intelligence, and occupied it for another decade at least. But had Edward that much time to spare before the Crown descended upon him? Rumour said no: the King was slowing down, his illness and pain increasing, his temper becoming more violent and unpredictable than it had ever been. This rot had begun with the execution of Thomas Cromwell, his most trusted minister, and then that of Katheryn Howard, the consort on whom he had doted. Now he was alone amid the great throng of the Court. His eldest daughter, Mary, who might have been the consolation of his old age, was so hounded and harried for her Popish obstinacy that, in her late twenties, she was a pathetic spinster living in real or imaginary fear of her life.

Richard Cox sighed and turned his attention to Prince Edward. The boy's education might have to be crammed into a very short space of time. . . .

Even so, King Henry had no intention of going to his grave without a final attempt at successful marriage.

As far as it was politic to do so, the young ladies of the Court kept out of his way because it was now an act of high treason for 'an unchaste woman to wed the King'. But there was a thirty-year-old widow present who would suit his old years better: this was the Lady Latimer, Catherine Parr.

When the April trees were dusted with green, Henry opened his heart to the lady of his choice.

Unable to conceal her dismay (for she was in love with the gay piratical Tom Seymour!) Catherine cried, "'Twere better to be your mistress than your wife!" – by better, she meant safer. But a wife-companion was what Henry needed, and a mother for his ill-used children. Catherine was a gentle and a kind woman. . . .

In July she went to her wedding at Hampton Court, trying not to look back down the tunnel of the years to where four former Queens of Henry – two of them headless – were entombed, and one still lived, divorced. She spoke no word of protest: to have done so might have endangered the man she loved, Thomas Seymour, uncle to the young Prince Edward. Instead, she took up her heavy burden and, miraculously, made light of it: humoured the irascible King, soothed Mary's shattered nerves, penetrated the glassy wall of Elizabeth's reserve. It was only Edward who presented no problem; he was too young not to recognize human goodness immediately with the clear eyes of a child.

For a while, all went well, in spite of wars and intrigues in Europe from which Henry could not disassociate himself. He had to watch the Church of Rome at the same time, for she was preparing the massive Council of Trent as counter-offensive to his Reformation. But Henry was confident that his enemies would cancel each other out, and he was good-humoured again by reason of his new marriage.

He was always merry in the early days. . . .

Graunya was playing in the sunshine with her six-month-old son, Owen. He occupied a great part of her time and attention, and she would not be separated from him, however good his nurses. Hers was the wary watchfulness of the she-cat when the kitten is handled.

Dhonal had hoped that, after a few weeks, she would tire of the infant sufficiently to need his own company more, but high summer had come and gone, and last year's idyll, when they had slept together under the sky, seemed a lifetime away.

'Woman wants from man only sons.' Slowly, he was coming to recognize the bitter truth of his father's words.

At first, pretending not to care, he had gathered his young men around him and gone hunting; then, he had led a small raiding party into the territory of O Kelly; a larger one into the

Joyce Country; a pirate fleet against Thomond. All the legendary ferocity of his forebears was rising to the surface of his thwarted nature while his wife kept him at arm's length.

Dhonal Crone, the chieftain, spoke sharply to him about these incursions. ". . . Reprisals will follow. You must know that."

But young Dhonal was in no mood to be reasoned with. Also, having stirred his men to action, he found that he could only control them by giving them further, and more vigorous, activity. O Flaherty raiding and piracy continued until winter locked the ships in harbour and made a muddy wilderness of Connemara. So far, there had been no retaliation. The plundered herds were slaughtered to provide winter food for the three castles between which the family travelled: Ballinahinch, Castle Kirke and Bunowen. Apart from that, there was only one other result of all the raiding: Dhonal was now nicknamed 'Nacugga' – 'of the Battles' – by his admiring followers and, after a time, he grew more proud of this title than of the lost one of tanist.

Dhonal Nacugga he had become, by his own efforts, and would remain.

Without warning, Graunya took note of his presence again. It was not that she had lost interest in her son but that she had grown adult enough to encompass both of them.

The Christmas festivities were in full spate in Castle Kirke, which was situated on Lough Oirbsen and was more spacious than Ballinahinch. It was crowded with guests. Log fires and lanterns cheered every room. In solemn procession, food was carried from the kitchens and eaten to the music of pipe and viol.

Graunya was wearing a gown of O Malley Blue – that intense shade that had a hint of green in its depths – embroidered with silver, and her raven hair was caught up at the back of her head with a jewelled pin. With tireless energy, she joined in every dance which the Feast Master called, and knew that the eyes of all the men present were upon her, but none so intently as those of her husband.

The chain of the dance led up to where Dhonal was standing. She broke away from the pattern, touched his arm and smiled at him. For a moment, he hesitated, then went with her through the curtain that opened on to the deserted solar. It was warm in the small apartment although the fire was low; there was no other light; the candles were all out.

He kissed her with a fierceness he had never felt for her before tonight. Whether she wanted him, or only another son from him, mattered nothing at all now. She was the woman other men desired and he, Dhonal Nacugga, had sole right to her; he would exercise that right.

She did not dispute it with him. She was fifteen years old and knew her own mind.

Chapter 6

THE main stronghold of O Flaherty was Aughnanure – the 'Plain of the Yews' – a century-old fortress on Lough Oirbsen, farther south towards Galway city than Castle Kirke. Nine years previously, Dhonal Crone had moved out to make room for an army of workmen: stone-masons and joiners, layers of copper and tinplate, carvers of wood. Now their task of renovation was complete and the castle worthy of a chieftain again, its forty-foot tower of six stories ready to receive his great household within double curtain walls.

To his grand-nephew, Dhonal Nacugga, he entrusted the smaller castles of Kirke, Ballinahinch and Bunowen; and the Lady Eilish spent much time instructing Graunya – who was expecting her second child – in the running of these three fortresses.

Soon after the Easter festival, Dhonal Crone and his lady were rowed away south-eastward on the long journey to their new home, leaving the younger couple in Castle Kirke.

It was one of those rare, heat-hazed mornings when broken reflections in water mend quickly to give a flawless image – trees, rocks, resting birds, all motionless, all quiet. . . .

Graunya flung her hands above her head. For the first time in her married life she felt entirely free, although she would miss Dhonal Crone and Eilish. Behind her, the island castle was almost deserted: she and Dhonal would re-staff it with young people of their own choosing. Its chests were emptied, its tables stripped; she would fill and cover them with her unused dowry linen and plate. She would make changes in a routine that had become too rigid.

Dhonal, too, surveyed his new domain. No one, now, would question his comings and his goings; there would be no grey-beards to shake heads over his plans. He would defy everybody, even the new tanist, Thighe the Furious.

He turned to Graunya and saw his thoughts mirrored in her eyes. They clasped hands in the spontaneous, childish gesture that belonged to the early days of their marriage and, laughing, ran into the silent empty hall.

"Where's Bran?" Graunya asked, looking around: the dog was seldom far from her heels. Then, through the open door, she saw him, still standing at the water's edge, his head held side-ways as though watching or listening.

"Bran!" she called, "Bran —" And he came slowly, with reluctant obedience, walking tensely, ears pricked. "What ails you, big dog?"

Something seemed to be troubling him but she attributed this to the departure of the chief and his household. She patted him absently and went to find the few serving women who remained, and the nurse who cared for young Owen.

Dhonal called after her.

"I'll have to be away a night or two: the food stocks are low."

"Yes. We need both meat and fish. . . ."

When she looked out a short time later, she saw his boat far down the lake and others racing from the mainland to join it. She smiled. Dhonal had a way of attracting company and, now that he was supreme lord here, he would have an even larger escort of young men than formerly, all calling him 'Nacugga' and coming back to dine with him! Such adulation was life-blood to Dhonal and she knew that she had to become part of the entourage, or lose him.

She decided to organize her new household quickly so as to be ready to join the next hunting party herself.

As she turned away from the window, she saw Bran again, standing rigid among the rushes, his long nose pointing towards the wooded shore. Normally, he clamoured to be taken in the boat with Dhonal. . . .

The serving women came, with much laughter and chatter, to begin unpacking the dusty chests that were carved with the Seahorse emblem. His nurse brought young Owen for a kiss from Graunya before his morning sleep. The kitchen steward appeared to discuss the main meal with her; and a single boat, with only one man in it, nosed its way to the castle steps. Graunya went out to meet the oarsman and recognized him as a member of the physician family O Lee. He was young and well-built; grey eyes very clear in a bronzed face.

"My father said I was to come today," he said starkly. "I am called Magnus."

"Welcome to Castle Kirke." She led him indoors and up to his father's old apartment, remarking as they climbed the stairs together, "You wasted no time in coming. Were you not tempted to hunt and fish with the others first?"

"I was tempted," he replied solemnly. "Then I thought it unwise for the castle to be left unmanned."

"Oh? Why?" She stood back to let him pass into the tiny room.

He shrugged.

"Any fortress is liable to be attacked, even with a full household. How many male retainers are left, for instance?"

She regarded him with a cool hostility; this was none of his business. Still, it would be uncivil not to answer his question; he was young, awkward and direct, serious to the point of pomposity; such youths were easily hurt.

"Oh, a couple of gallowglasses somewhere," she said lightly. "Five men and three scullions in the kitchens. The stables have half a dozen youths under two men. And" – mischievously – "there's an old fellow in the herb garden, watching bees!"

Magnus O Lee grunted and began to examine the jars and surgical instruments which his father had left for him. Then he unpacked a hessian bag he had brought, by tumbling its contents out on to the straw palliasse: some clothing, much worn; a pair of cowhide shoes; a wooden comb. . . . Finally, a small lidded basin, the only item which he treated with any care.

Graunya began helping him to put his clothing away in a cupboard. She picked up the basin and removed its lid; there was a greenish-white substance inside. He took it quickly out of her hands.

"New medicine?" she asked idly. "What is it made from?"

"If I were to tell you that," he replied, almost sullenly, "you would have no faith in it. The ingredients are simple but the process of preparation is complicated."

"What does it do?"

"Prevents wounds from festering."

"It smells," she said, "like the mould on stale bread. . . ."

His curt, unsmiling manner irritated her. After all, the physician was not an important member of the household until old age and many cures brought their own respect; even then, he was not allowed to attend a woman in childbirth. Rumour had it that old O Lee once crawled through a hole in the wall to deliver a mother; his own daughter, the midwife, could not extricate the child and sent him a frantic message – with a bundle of women's clothing for disguise in case he were discovered! But now old O Lee was a kind of patriarch who attended the chieftain only. . . . Which reminded her —

"Your father left a packet in my keeping," she told Magnus, "to be given to you on your arrival."

"A-A book?" He seemed suddenly excited.

"I believe so." She went and fetched it. He received it from her with reverence; untied the linen tapes; opened the many folds of the covering. Inside, lay a tooled leather rectangle, folded double, into which was bound a number of manuscript pages on vellum. The faded writing was in Irish and Latin and one page bore the date: one thousand, four hundred and thirty-four.

"It's . . . it's the Book of O Brasil!" she whispered.

"Yes. The greatest treasure of my family. . . ." He was like a man who had seen a vision; indeed, if legend was to be believed, this book had supernatural origins, some of the medical information in it having been given, by sea-spirits, to the first O Lee physician. . . .

"Let me look!" She leaned over his shoulder, her hands touching his arms. But the pages were incomprehensible to her – ruled and divided like a complex astrological table. Then she saw that lists of various diseases, with their treatments, were

74

arranged in parallel columns, headed: Prognostics, Region, Season, Age, Constitution, Causa, Signum. . . . It was nothing very wonderful after all. But Magnus O Lee was looking at it and handling it as though it were the Word of God.

She left him in the small, crowded apartment and spent the remainder of the day in furious activity. At twilight she went down to the lake shore to rest: water always calmed and restored her. She believed that, once removed to a dry, inland place, she would begin to die. . . . The lake was breathtakingly beautiful in the muted afterlight, with little blurs of mist beginning to form upon its moon-coloured surface. Her spirit expected tranquillity from it, and yet all she felt was tension, wariness, a prickling of eyes. . . .

In the next instant, Bran leapt from the rushes with a high, strangled yelp and plunged into the water. Black boats, crowded with men, glided from the mainland cover. And Graunya began to race like a deer for the fortress. She flung her full weight on the massive door, slamming it from the inside and dropping the bolts while, without ceasing, she screamed at the full pitch of her lungs. . . . She knew that the entire household would be in, or near, the main hall, awaiting the evening meal. She began to tear down weapons from the walls, flinging them upon the floor and yelling instructions; then, armed with a clumsy longbow, she raced for the upper apartments and got the leading boat in sight through a loophole; the light was poor and growing worse but she hit the craft just below the waterline with a long, slicing shaft, and heard the hide rip. . . .

Her retainers were in position now at every aperture facing the mainland, and feet were pounding upward towards the battlements. Without breaking the rhythm of her defence, she shouted orders to her women:

"Open oil-barrels and roll them down the steps. Light every torch you can find; throw them into the boats as they approach after firing the oil."

Under firm direction, the women were calm. They moved quickly. . . . Graunya called for a stable boy.

"Go out by the back way and let all the animals loose. Protect yourself first, then light bales of straw."

Some of the boats had reached the island and dark shapes of

men were swarming upward towards the fortress. She heard one of them cursing as he blundered into a barrel; then lighted torches began to rain from the women's hands and great pools and rivers of oil burst into flames, the inferno spreading to the lake shore and on to the water itself. Following boats began to retreat in panic but already the fortress door was under the axes of those who had landed safely.

She left the loophole and ran towards the ground floor, shouting for everyone to join her there. A pall of smoke thickened the inner darkness, but the fire outside glowed orange through the windows and reflected itself on the opposite walls. The pounding and splintering of the door was a deafening noise, through which sounded the scrape of scaling ladders. There was no help for it now but to let the invaders enter, and then grapple with them inside. From an upstairs apartment came the wailing of her son. . . .

She formed her people into some kind of order and tried to make sure that each woman had a short knife and each man a sword or spear, but the confusion was very great.

Above her head, a rope squeaked on beams.

"They're within!" she thought, balancing a dart in the palm of her hand. The fireglow picked out a man's figure, crawling on all fours, but he was moving outward along the oak planks towards the glowing window, a knife gripped in his teeth, the rope coiled around his waist. As he climbed through the aperture and out of sight, she recognized Magnus O Lee. An instant later, a ladder crashed outside.

Now the pounding of hooves reverberated through the building and a high wild whinnying filled the air, muting the crash of an axe cleaving the door. The axe was shaken from side to side, widening the gap until a whole plank fell inward and a hand groped for the locks. . . .

Graunya lifted a two-edged blade above her head and brought it down, sickeningly, on the man's forearm. She expected his pain to shriek through her own body; instead, she heard herself muttering into the warm blood which spurted up in her face, "There is one hand which will never violate my infant son!"

The great gap in the door was widening under other hatchets, forming a jagged frame for the fiery picture outside. Black forms of men and maddened horses jostled one another. The invaders drew back for the final charge. This time, they would enter. . . .

She ordered her people to stand in two lines and hold their weapons ready. A queer kind of elation filled her as she waited. Then she saw O Lee outside, fighting to divert the charge. And, in the same moment, her steward leapt through the door, brandishing a cleaver. The horseboys followed, then the little scullions. And, in the midst of it all, she saw Bran pounce on a man and bring him down.

After a long scuffle, the field began to clear. O Lee was using his rope to tie up captives, the steward and some boys were piling others into the few undamaged boats and pushing them away from the shore. The stable lads were quieting the horses and bringing them in.

It was over. A full moon was rising beyond the southern stretch of the lake and, clear against its light, a handful of fleeing craft could be seen.

O Lee came to her, panting and begrimed, dragging his prisoners.

"Who are they?" she demanded.

"Joyces. . . ."

She began to understand: Dhonal had raided the neighbouring Joyce Country last autumn, and driven some of its cattle to his own territories. This reprisal was carefully planned against the time when the chieftain would leave for Aughnanure.

"We deserve their enmity," was all she could manage to say, for this senseless preying of native upon native choked her with anger. Her country was weakening itself internally at a time when outside pressure was growing heavier every day. "Send them in one of our boats to the mainland," she ordered, "and have them turned loose there."

He beckoned to two of the stable men and repeated her instructions. The tall Joyces looked back at her as they were led away. Then O Lee knelt among the wounded, unconcerned about the loss of his prisoners, and she went to help him. Their eyes met briefly in the moonlight.

"How did you tie that rope so quickly to the rafters?" she asked.

"Quickly?" He cut the bloody tunic from a man's shoulder. "It took me a full hour earlier in the day."

"Then you knew what was to happen?"

"I surmised," he said wearily, "when I saw every man in the district rowing away this morning. I tried to warn you —"

Swiftly, she accepted the fact that this youth had more foresight than her husband. She swallowed the faint animosity which she still felt towards him.

"If ever I form an army," she said jokingly, "you will be one of my captains!"

"I will serve proudly," he replied, and went on working. . . .

Like a forest fire in the wind, news of the Joyce raid spread from one peasant hut to the next, and from fortress to fortress: O Flaherty's wife had defended her castle! Rhymsters went to work, setting the exploit to music and, like the O Malley bard years previously, they became attracted by the nickname, 'Graunuaile'. It fitted a verse rhythm which depended on vowel sounds. . . .

When Graunya's second son was born in the autumn, people travelled leagues to attend the christening, mainly for the purpose of meeting his mother; some were curious, others sceptical of the wild stories in circulation about her. Now, it was said, she intended to reopen the Abbey of Cong!

Only two things were certain: she had defeated the Joyces and within a month of that, had reorganized a small section of the O Flaherty fleet for trade. Many interpretations were put upon this latter move but the one nearest the truth was that she had given her husband nominal command of this fleet in order to keep him occupied. Certainly, there had been no raiding since the previous Easter, Dhonal Nacugga having been in France and Spain with his ships, and the mud-hut dwellers of Connemara were deeply grateful for his absence. It was they who paid most dearly for a lord's ambitions: his men and horses were quartered upon their villages when he was away from home, or their dwellings and crops were burned by his enemies. This year, their corn stood high in the steep little fields.

As her own mobility decreased with her pregnancy, Graunya

had gathered a band of active men inside the fortress to guard it day and night while Dhonal was away. She did not affront their pride by commanding them; she appealed, instead, to their reason.

"A prosperous countryside is to our advantage. See that the people are left in peace and no new enemies made for them." It was a revolutionary idea to consider the welfare of peasants but perhaps there was some sense in it. . . . Their crops and cattle would be fuel for other wars.

But Graunya would have no idlers in her company.

"Every strong man should be able to support himself, his family, horses and dogs, either by hunting, farming or trade." The men of the guard either accepted this, or were dismissed.

Now Graunya sat, eyes closed, feeding her new infant, and the youngest O Lee nurse – Peg – was with her. From the lake shore and the water below, a great tumult was proceeding – people shouting, oars splashing – but it was quiet in the women's apartment except for the sucking of the child.

Graunya asked Peg O Lee, "Are they nearly ready?"

"Yes, I think so. The O Colgans are unwinding the standard and the MacKilkellys are falling in behind. Richard O Duane is ordering everybody about! Oh, there's Dhonal Crone now and the Lady Eilish —"

"Are there many other women?" – sharply.

"Y-e-es, I can count six – seven – *nine* whose names are unknown to me."

"Damn them all!" Graunya said. She was in no condition for their scrutiny, still hollow-eyed as she was from the child's birth only three days previously. "Why must they all flock for this infant? Not a soul outside the household came when Owen was born."

"You are the great lady now," Peg said tactfully, "and better known. Besides, it's no small undertaking to break the King's seal on Cong!"

Graunya's mouth curved into a smile in which wickedness and pride were blended.

"My son is an O Flaherty," she said, "and has a perfect right to his baptism in the Royal Abbey." She was not afraid of the consequences, only sorry that she had not attempted it for young Owen as well. She had been too timid then, had accepted the order of dissolution too easily. But now she had armed strength behind her, and confidence for the act of defiance. This was her son's birthright, to be baptized in the place where Roderick, King of Connacht, spent his last heart-broken years. She intended to uphold it.

While the sounds from outside became more urgent, Peg O Lee helped her to dress. As she fastened the cloak-pin at the shoulder for her, their faces were close together. Graunya said, in the soft purring tone which she used for dangerous statements,

"They might not cheer so loud if they knew that your brother had delivered my infant. . . ."

The nurse dropped the heavy gold pin and stooped to retrieve it. From her knees she cried, "I have implored you not to speak of that. . . ."

"What do you suppose they would do?"

"They would burn his eyes out. Oh, why did you force me to bring him to you?"

"Because I wanted him to have experience. He can follow me where you cannot. Now cease worrying and pin my mantle: he is safe with me."

The Royal Abbey of Cong was splendid even in desolation. Briars and nettles which choked the ambulatory of the cloister led the eye upward to the magnificent floral carvings of the doorways. Inside was the library, stripped of all its treasured manuscripts and records. Beyond the Chapter, the *Diaconium Bematis* was empty of sacred vessels. The worn passage leading from cloister to silent refectory had lichens growing between its flags and, on the west wall, six empty windows looked out on what had once been the dining-hall of the Connacht Kings.

But it was only the Church which concerned the travellers from Castle Kirke. They had brought two locksmiths with them to open the west door; it creaked inward on its hinges to reveal the sixty-foot height within. Double that distance away shone the three lights of the east window over the high altar.

Graunya went into the sacristy with the old hermit-priest from Ballinahinch lake for the ceremony of purification. All the others remained by the font at the west door, Lady Eilish holding the infant who was to be called Murrough, and Dhonal proudly marshalling his young men in the earnest hope that the entire party would be challenged, so that he could fight. . . .

The sacristy was dark and had a strange warm smell like that of human occupation; the priest lit a taper and began to pray quickly over Graunya's bowed head; he would be glad to leave this eerie place where the spirits of the departed hovered thick and the presence of the Escheator-General still made itself felt. If English soldiers came again. . . .

He noticed that Graunya was staring past him. She got up suddenly from her knees and blew out the taper.

"Come away," she said. "Let us leave here at once."

Huddled in a round-headed doorway behind the priest, she had glimpsed a group of Augustinian monks, their habits hanging in shreds from their emaciated bodies, their eyes blank with dismay at this intrusion. After three years of wandering and cave-dwelling, they had returned to the only home they knew, climbed in by the dormitory windows and tried to resume their shattered lives, hunting and fishing by night, hiding by day.

Graunya had realized from the beginning that, if she allowed the baptism of her son to be performed in the proscribed Abbey, it would not remain a secret. Crown officials would hear of it. Some action would be attempted against her. She cared nothing for that; but the presence of the pathetic monks was a different matter. If the Abbey were re-examined, they would be discovered, and hanging would be the least of their punishments.

Dragging the protesting priest by the wrist, she ran down the nave of the church and grabbed the infant out of Eilish's astonished grasp.

"I have changed my mind," she said loudly. "I want to return home and have my son baptized there. Where are the locksmiths? See that everything is put back as though it had never been disturbed."

She pushed the bewildered party out before her and drew the west door shut. Everyone began to grumble and complain. They were furiously angry with her for bringing them on this

81

long wildgoose chase; and Dhonal, in particular, chose to argue the entire matter with her.

She said something to him in a low, vibrant undertone and he went away, scowling. Then she heard a woman's voice jeer:

"Lost her courage! How much now for O Malley fearlessness?" A cackle of laughter followed and another woman said:

"Did you know who *really* foiled the Joyce raid? It was Magnus O Lee, her physician. *She* merely sat in a corner and wept!"

Their jibes were like sticks breaking across her back. The men were shambling off towards the boats. She might never recover the ground she was fast losing: if once she gained a reputation for cowardice and lack of purpose, the guard she had gathered and trained would drift away from her. Yet she dared not tell anyone in this motley gathering the truth.

She walked up to the group of women who had spoken.

"Sometimes," she said quietly, "it takes more courage to retreat under the gaze of one's friends than to advance in the teeth of one's enemy."

Catherine, the sixth Queen, was in her private apartment when she heard the news which she had always dreaded: Henry had turned against her suddenly in one of his rages because she had argued religion with him. He had set his name to her indictment.

The result of this course of events was too familiar to be regarded merely as a cruel joke. Indictment led to imprisonment, and imprisonment to execution. The Queen's motherly little figure crumpled. She began to weep with a low moaning sound and, afterwards, became hysterical.

Henry heard her screams and asked, with genuine puzzlement, what was the matter? He had forgotten the signed accusation, forgotten the mild argument from which his senile fury had blazed up. Constant pain was blurring his memory.

His attendants told him what had happened and he made a slight gesture with his fat, bejewelled hands, signifying that it was a small matter to which only a woman would attach importance. He, himself, would go to the Queen and explain that it was all a mistake. The articles against her would be withdrawn.

It was a great effort for him to move. Both his legs were grossly swollen under the awesome weight of his body. He hobbled to Catherine's apartments.

She sprang up and retreated from him, her eyes wild with terror.

"Kate, my Kate —" he said, astonished. "What has become of you?"

He sat down heavily, regarding her with the hurt childish expression which used to touch her heart in the early days; now she recognized it as a sign of wanton destruction, like that of an infant hammering his toys and wondering why they break so easily.

"Your Grace, you have accused me —"

"Nonsense, nonsense! It was Gardiner and Wriothesley."

He shifted the blame, made excuses, exerted all his charm of manner.

After a long time, he succeeded in calming her, then invited her to visit him that evening. As soon as she entered his apartments, he began to talk of religion again, hoping to trap her.

"A woman's place," Catherine said humbly, "is on the footstool, not in the chair of argument. I bow before Your Majesty's wisdom in all things."

She had saved herself this time. From now on, it must be unblinking vigilance over every word spoken or written if she were to survive. Henry could not be relied upon for any constant opinion: in July, he burned a woman at the stake for speaking against the Mass; in August, he asked the King of France to assist him in abolishing that same sacrifice. Keeping in step with him was like jumping from one squelching hummock to another in an endless bog.

Dhonal knew that his position in the fleet was a false one. This autumn, Graunya had come on board herself and sailed with the herring cargo to Spain and, although she deferred to him in all matters, Dhonal was well aware that the real authority rested with her. When he issued orders to the men, there was a slight hesitation – a cocking of the eyebrow in her direction – before he was obeyed.

If he could have ignored his wife, he would have done so but the truth was that she was a far better admiral than he, and he often needed her advice. Her apprenticeship had begun in the cradle, and she had learned her trade from Owen O Malley and Dhonal Crone O Flaherty, two of the best captains in Connacht, while he, Dhonal, had lived inland until his fifteenth year. Had he not been her husband, he might have stepped down to serve under her at sea but, as her lord, and father of her children, such subservience was unthinkable. He had to maintain his position as head of the fleet.

Now, leaning on a coiled halyard, he asked himself gloomily, 'Why does she have to come at all? Why can she not stay at home like every other woman?' – but he knew the answer well enough: other women were ordered by their husbands to remain behind, and obedience was ingrained in their natures. But Graunya had never been trained to obey anyone except a superior whom she had acknowledged of her own free will. She had never acknowledged Dhonal, even while growing big with his sons. . . .

Well, he had had enough of this bedevilment. He would go secretly to Dhonal Crone and ask him to withdraw from Mannin Bay the small fleet which he had left for the use of the lesser fortresses. Dhonal Crone had lost two galleys and a curragh recently; even Graunya would not be able to argue against these gaps in his own fleet being filled from Mannin. And, without ships, she would *have* to stay at home. . . .

In the Tower of London, the old Duke of Norfolk was awaiting execution. Midnight struck. He was to die at dawn, the twenty-eighth day of January, fifteen forty-seven.

A single taper cast gigantic shadows on the walls where other prisoners had scratched their names during the long waiting.

The guard clanked along the passage, rattling keys.

"Here, this one," he bawled, and flung Norfolk's door open to admit a hooded priest.

"Let us pray," the priest said, kneeling beside the prisoner. "*In nomine Patris, et Filii et* . . . be of good heart. There is hope."

"How?" Old Norfolk did not care much now. His son, his one treasure, had gone before him to Tower Hill ten days previously.

"... *et Spiritus Sancti* ... the King is dying."

"*Amen*. He has been dying many times before now."

"He will not last until morning; they have sent for Cranmer. You know what that means?"

Norfolk shrugged. He had served Henry all his long life. He had renounced the Pope for him. And Henry had rewarded him by beheading his son. What was freedom to him now?

"The King will live," Norfolk said wearily, "long enough to be sure that I am dead."

At Whitehall, Henry lay propped up in the mighty bed, his tongue thick in his mouth, his arms incapable of movement. A slow chill was creeping up from his feet, damping the fires that had raged for months in his cauterized legs. He could no longer speak but his last words to his family hung in the death-smelling air.

"Kate, my Kate, it is God's Will that we should part. I order all these gentlemen to honour thee, and treat thee as if I were living still. ..."

"Mary, my daughter, I pray thee be a mother to thy brother. For, look you, he is little yet, this Edward."

He did not ask to see his other daughter, Elizabeth.

It was nearly one o'clock in the freezing January morning when Archbishop Cranmer arrived, breathless, from Croydon. Never again would he be asked to twist the Sacrament of Matrimony to suit Henry's peculiar needs. ...

"Do you die in the Faith of Christ?" he whispered to the sightless King. And swore, for ever after, that Henry pressed his hand and would be saved.

Chapter 7

THE fortress of Aughnanure rose grim and formidable out of the rock wilderness of Iar-Connacht. A narrow arm of water separated it from the mainland and it was said that salmon swum under the foundations, to spawn in a black pool there. Constant gurgling and lapping noises penetrated cellars and dungeons.

Dhonal Crone had caused many alterations to be made at Aughnanure, and one of these he had had to do himself, because the workmen would not touch it; this was the sealing of the Flagstone of Treachery. Dhonal Crone wanted it wedged and mortared, so that never again could an O Flaherty host release it with his foot under cover of the mighty dining-table. It was a huge slab of native green marble, four feet wide by nearly six feet long, and an iron bar – set into the floor on either side – ran through the middle of it. The chair of an unwanted guest could be placed over this stone and, in response to certain pressures, it would revolve, casting man and chair into the black waters below.

Once, the conquering Norman de Burgo had sent his son to collect rent from an O Flaherty chieftain, who drowned the boy beneath the Flagstone of Treachery, then hauled his body upward again and had the head hacked off, to be sent in a sack to de Burgo with the message,

'*Here is O Flaherty's rent!*'

There was a darkness about the Castle of Aughnanure which no amount of costly decoration could lighten. It stared broodingly towards the city of Galway, cursing every invader of its ancient territories. And the citizens feared it more than the sweating sickness, never knowing when an army might emerge once again from within its grim walls, to threaten and loot and burn. In order to protect themselves, they were fortifying their West Gate, and a stone-mason was even now working on an inscribed slab to be hoisted into position above it,

'*From the ferocious O Flahertys, good Lord deliver us.*'

This was the heartfelt prayer of Galway city, re-echoed every Sunday inside St Nicholas's.

Dhonal Nacugga had nearly reached Aughnanure through the February twilight, when the malignity of the place seeped out and enveloped him, transforming his simple mission – to have the chief remove his ships from Mannin Bay – into a sinister act of treachery against his wife. He was taking away her playthings because he resented their importance to her, and his own inability to manage them. Her command of the little fleet diminished him, as surely as her popularity with the crew had robbed him of the tanist title. She would always overshadow him now. . . .

Always? No: there was another way. He could put her from him, reduce her wifely status. Now that the influence of the Church was weakened, many lords were divorcing their wives: Clanrickarde had three, all living. . . .

In spite of himself, he shivered, before calling out to the sentries.

The lofty dining-hall, with its floral carvings and coloured glass windows, was warm, gay and crowded. There was a background of music to the conversation. The wines were French, the fruits Mediterranean.

Dhonal Crone O Flaherty presided over all, with his ollavs, his poets and his Feast Master grouped behind him. His chief guest was Walter Bourke, tanist to the MacWilliam, and Walter's red-headed stepmother, Finola; with their escort they were on their way from a trading visit to Galway, and were breaking the long journey to Carrigahowley. . . .

Dhonal Nacugga found himself placed beside Finola. It was sixteen years since they had met and he did not recognize her at first. His childish memory of her was as a haughty, cruel and overbearing woman who had once lashed out at him with a horsewhip. Now she was saying, in a soft indolent voice, "Dhonal! What a man you have become!" – and there was admiration in her strange green-blue eyes, and a veiled interest which excited him. He forgot that he had been reared to regard her as a stepsister although there was no blood relationship between them (his father had married her widowed mother, who died long before Dhonal was born of another woman).

He passed her his newly-filled goblet and, afterwards, drank from it himself. Her perfume rose to his nostrils. The curve of her breasts filled his vision. To him, this woman was a flame-coloured rose, fully opened, heavy with her own awareness; and Graunya, by comparison, a dark slender bud, withdrawn within a prickly palisade of spiked leaves.

When the meal was over and the hall loud with music and dancing, Dhonal went out, alone, and sat on the stairs. He felt sick and dizzy from too much wine. A cold oblong moon shone through a high window and, beyond, the winter sky was silver grey, pinpricked with stars.

He saw Finola coming silently towards him. Her golden sandals mounted to the step where he sat and paused there beside him. He put his arm around her knees and she did not move except to stroke his head and press it against her thigh. She was all softness and perfume and rich, fur-trimmed fabrics shimmering in the moonlight. He stood up and he was taller than she was. The child's image of a towering woman holding a horsewhip over him, faded. Now that he was a man, Finola was little and unresisting. The hood of her mantle slipped back, uncovering the red-gold hair; and the moon shone full in those eyes that had a strange inward focus.

He gathered all her robes in the sweep of his arms and climbed slowly with her to the upper apartments, seeing nothing except her face against his shoulder. The noises of the hall receded into utter silence and he dreamed that he was climbing upward to the sky, like the Enchanted Lover, leaving all earthly contacts and responsibilities behind.

"This is the hour for which I was born male," he said. And

those were the only words spoken between them until the oblong moon began to shift her light from the stairs.

"You must go now," Finola said softly.

The prospect of leaving her appalled him.

"How can I go anywhere that you are not?" There was nothing else in his life except this woman's embrace. No price was too high. . . .

"There will be another time," she said.

"When?"

"When a certain thing is done."

"Tell me of it. I will do it."

"Are you sure, Dhonal?"

"I swear on my mother's soul, if you will only come to me again."

"I will come. . . ." She leaned over him and kissed him. And he clung to her while she continued, in a whisper, "Dhonal – my love – I want you to kill Walter Bourke for me. . . ."

"*Kill* —"

She put her fingers across his lips.

"You are strong and clever, Dhonal. Arrange an accident. No one will know. Only by Walter's death can my son, Richard, become the MacWilliam tanist, and heir to all the Bourke territories. But – oh, Dhonal! – I want you for yourself alone, not merely for this."

Her teeth were sharp against his naked shoulder, her breasts heavy on his chest. 'Arrange an accident . . . you are strong and clever.' It would be an easy thing for him to do. Walter Bourke was nothing to him, either dead or alive. And he had to have Finola; he had to take her again.

"Walter the Tall will die before the moon is full," he said.

He got up, dressed himself and went down to the hall. The torches were all extinguished but there was a glow from the braziers, and men were sleeping in circles around them, their bare feet reaching out to the warmth, their heads and arms and upper bodies covered by frieze mantles. Except for a concerted snore that arose from their ranks, they might have been corpses laid out for mass burial. The chained wolfhounds were wakeful; their eyes glowed amber.

Dhonal could see a chink of light under the heather curtains of the solar. He went in and found the chieftain sitting alone beside a dying fire. A red paris candle guttered at his elbow.

"Where have you been?" the older man asked without turning around.

Dhonal walked over to the fire. He saw the chief looking up at him from under lowered brows, saw the curious flaring motion of the nostrils which used to remind him of a wild horse when he was a boy.

"I . . . ah . . ."

"Don't trouble to lie to me. You have been with Finola. You reek of her perfume."

"Yes, I have." There was exultation and defiance in his voice.

Dhonal Crone shrugged, "You have not been the first and you will not be the last! But take heed of one thing: that woman is unlucky for a man —"

"I can manage my own life."

"Can you?" The sea-going eyes searched his face. "Then why have you come here, unescorted, in the middle of winter? You were a worried man, young Dhonal, when you arrived – until the red-headed woman gave you a side-long look and put adultery into your head instead. This castle is accursed: I feel it corroding my own spirit. . . ."

"Finola is the first real woman I have ever known."

"Your wife has two children by you."

"Sons have made no difference to Graunya's body, and even less to her mind! She is a man-woman, whose only ambition is to dominate." Suddenly, the thought of his marriage filled him with bitterness. One hour with Finola had given him more reassurance of his manhood than four years with Graunya had done.

"You had better speak whatever request you came to make," the chieftain said, "then I may know what is wrong with you."

"First, I want you to remove all your ships from Mannin Bay."

Dhonal Crone's hard hands went limp between his knees.

"Yes," he said then. "Yes, I see. Perhaps it is the only way. But a great sadness to me. . . . Graunya has the feel of the sea and the gift of weather prophecy – you knew that? No? It will hit her hard to watch the ships being taken away."

He looked to his grand-nephew for some flicker of sympathy for Graunya, but there was none. Strange, that a marriage so well planned – that had gone so well in the early days – should settle into two such opposite camps, because the woman demanded equality with her husband. Dhonal Crone felt that he should have foreseen this earlier. . . . He had relied too much on the younger man's bodily strength, not anticipating a contest of wills.

"And the second reason you came?" he prompted.

"I want to be rid of her altogether as wife. I want to be free."

The chieftain said nothing for a long time. Then —

"Graunya must also be consulted," he said. "I will come to Ballinahinch as soon as may be."

The next morning was brightly cold, and the chieftain arranged a hunt to entertain his guests.

"We'll ride towards Moycullen," he said, "and spend the night with our kinsman, Fitz-Rory, at the Castle of Inveran."

Finola was pleased with this arrangement. Fitz-Rory was her only natural brother and she wanted to see him. They had been very close once. She had little faith in Dhonal's promise of the previous night to rid her of Walter Bourke and, if he broke his word, she could put the matter to Fitz-Rory. Instead of her body, she would have to offer gold but it would be less trouble that way: young lovers were too demanding, and this morning she felt old and tired.

Fastening her fur hood close, she kept out of Dhonal's sight.

There was great commotion in the courtyard while riders mounted and handlers restrained their leashed hounds. Then Dhonal Crone called for the gates to be opened and the hunt poured out over the rocky countryside.

Ahead of him, Nacugga could see Walter Bourke riding tall and spare on his unsaddled mount. All morning, he maintained the distance between them, not wishing to hold any conversation with this man whom he must kill. He did not want to know Walter as a human being lest some remark about wife or family, some friendly smile or gesture, tempt him to mercy. He would stalk him as though he were an animal whose death was regrettable but necessary – one that had to be killed quickly, in a secret place, without witnesses to his fall; if it were not done today, the night would be wasted. That was all he thought about, as red deer fled before the hunt – the night, and Finola. . . .

At midday, he looked about him but could not see her nor any of her attendants. A purplish fog was closing in from the north-east. He rode up beside Dhonal Crone and inquired,

"Where are the women?" – and the chief looked at him sidelong.

"I have sent them on ahead to Inveran. Finola complained of feeling ill."

"Ill?" Dhonal could not control the anxiety in his voice. Then he relaxed: it would be an excuse on her part not to be near her stepson when the accident occurred; Finola was clever, and she trusted him to carry out his promise. "I suppose she'll be well later," he said awkwardly, and made to ride away again, but the chief called to him sharply:

"Come back. I'm shouting in the hunt."

"What for?"

"Can you not see the fog?"

"It's a long way off —" Dhonal was dismayed by this change of plan. He had counted on another hour at least. If the men were to ride close together to Inveran now, he would have no chance with Walter. . . .

"Travelling fast," Dhonal Crone snapped, "swallowing the sun." He began to call in the beaters and the dogs.

Before they reached Miny, an eerie darkness had enveloped them. Looking like a phantom host in the swirling mist, they groped their way forward to the Castle of Inveran. After a while, the red glow of torches from the walls guided them. They hallooed and shouted for the gates to be opened. They surged between the fog-shrouded lookout towers, men and dogs and horses all crammed together, struggling to get in.

Suddenly, Nacugga knew that this was the moment he had awaited all day. His horse was flank to flank with Walter Bourke's. There was nothing between them except the floating particles of fog, nothing around them but confusion, one hooded figure looking exactly like another. Had it not been for Walter's height, Dhonal would not have recognized him.

He dared not use a sharp weapon in case the wound were discovered later. He drew his club from under his mantle, leaned sideways and struck the tall man a controlled blow on the base of the skull.

For several seconds, Walter remained upright. By the time he slumped forward, Dhonal had passed him by. The body began to slip. When it hit the ground, other horses pounded over it and no one paid any attention until the sentries came to close the gate against the swirling darkness, and found the Mac-William tanist battered to death.

They carried him into the lighted hall which had been prepared for a feast. Fitz-Roy, the host – red-haired, with a cast in one eye – came and called for O Canavan, his physician, who knelt beside the body, examined it short-sightedly and pronounced:

"This man has died of hoof blows to his head and chest. I would say that he had fainted first, perhaps from hunger and fatigue. An accident. . . ."

Fitz-Rory said quietly,

"I will break the news to my sister. She went to her apartment an hour ago."

Fuming with impatience, Nacugga sat through the gloomy meal which was served late and cold. Finola did not come down and it was almost midnight before he dared go to her, after the long prayers had been intoned around the body, its bruises hidden under a linen sheet, the candles haloed from the cold damp air. No corner of the castle was free from the terrible music of the keening-women's wailing.

A procession of sympathizers filed past the stepmother's bedside, where she lay, restless and flushed, her hands plucking at the heavy covers. Dhonal was the last to enter the apartment. Finola stared at him dully. He bent and kissed her on the mouth, his arms tightening around her, but there was no vibrant response as on the previous night; she merely sighed and turned her head away from him as soon as he released her lips.

"Finola – I did as you wished —"

"Yes."

"Is that all you have to say to me?"

"It was well done, Dhonal. But the hour is late —"

"What is the matter with you?" he demanded fiercely, shaking her. "You said . . ."

"I say now that I am tired. Leave me alone."

"Leave you – alone?" A fist clenched in his stomach. "Have you forgotten why I did it, what you promised? Finola, you will keep your part of the bargain. . . ."

"Tomorrow."

"Tonight." His grip was hurting her arms. Her whole body ached in all its joints. She felt him fumbling with the coverlets, then with the neck-cord of her gown.

"Go away," she said, so quietly that he hardly heard above the rasping of his own breath. "Go away. I am ill —"

"What makes you so with me?"

She wanted to laugh at the conceit of it but her lips were stiff with sudden cold.

"A chill is no respecter of persons. That damned tavern in Galway – the waters were forced back up the sluices whenever rain fell! The floors were awash and stinking all the time we were there."

"You stayed in the city overnight?" Slowly, he drew his hands away from her.

"We stayed for a week. I have influential friends who can obtain permission for me, even if I *am* a proscribed O Flaherty!"

He sat up and looked at her narrowly. She seemed to have aged ten years since their last meeting. A faint revulsion for her came over him when he saw how her lips were dry and wrinkled like those of an old woman. What if she had caught something in the city? Four years ago, an outbreak of sweating sickness there had choked the gutters with dead. There was always an epidemic of some kind, lurking or raging, inside walled towns; the regular inhabitants seemed to be armed against these things; it was the occasional visitor who caught them. The native Irish had a horror of close-packed communities and the pestilences which they bred, and this inborn fear was beginning to grip Nacugga. He stood up.

"I – I apologize for having troubled you. I will go now."

She nodded heavily, trying to moisten dry lips with a tongue that was bright scarlet; her teeth were chattering with cold.

"Tomorrow," she whispered, "I will be better and . . . will pay . . . my debt to you."

Debt: the word struck him like the lash of a bull-whip. . . .

He ran from the apartment, down the stairs and out through the kitchens, to wash his hands and face in a freezing trough. He felt contaminated and defiled in body and spirit and, for the first time, the full guilt of Walter's murder struck him as the keening-women's wail rose high and clear on the frosty air. It had been so quick, so spontaneous an action at the last, that it had not seemed like murder until now. . . .

He wanted to leave Inveran without a moment's delay but knew that he dared not: he would be expected to make the long journey to Carrigahowley with Walter's body. All he hoped was, that Finola would not be of the funeral party, for he could not bear to look at her again.

At dawn, the corpse was slung in a canvas hammock between two pack-horses. A fine drizzle of rain was falling as the cortège lined up behind it, led by Nacugga sitting his horse between Fitz-Rory and Dhonal Crone: Walter's body would never be out of his sight.

They waited for Finola but she did not come. After a while, one of her serving women appeared to say that her mistress was too ill to move.

The funeral procession set off without her.

While the body of Walter Bourke was being borne through dismal mountain passes on its last journey homeward, sixteen strong men were struggling, at Windsor, with the huge coffin of Henry the Eighth. Over the open grave, the white staves of the household officers were snapped, as symbols of a reign ended, and the titles of the child-King, Edward, were proclaimed. Now the assembled clergy had not only a new King, but a new Supreme Head of their Church, aged nine and a half years old.

On the day before his Coronation, Edward made his royal progress from the Tower to the Palace of Westminster, attired in a gown of cloth of silver embroidered in gold, his small waist encircled by a belt of silver filigree set with rubies, diamonds and true lovers' knots of pearls. His doublet and buskins were of white velvet, his cap so thickly set with diamonds that it made a halo for his pale gold hair, dazzling in the February sunshine. Under a canopy carried by six noblemen, he rode a milk-white horse that was caparisoned in crimson satin sewn with gold damask and pearls; but, when it was discovered that the tall noblemen hid the child-King completely from the people's view, it was arranged that Edward should ride a few feet in advance. So it was that the glittering white and gold figure stood out alone against the armoured horsemen in their surcoats of blue and purple, scarlet and emerald.

A peal of cannon sounded from the arsenal of the Tower as he crossed the City frontier at Mark Lane. And the delirious crowds yelled, "God save the King!"

At Cheapside, the Mayor and aldermen were waiting to present him with a purse containing a thousand crowns. He leaned down to take it; it was large and heavy – too heavy for him to hold. With difficulty, he passed it to the Captain of the Guard, who grabbed it just in time before it fell.

That purse was the first tribute to Edward as King. And it had proved too much for his strength. The Crown would be heavier. . . .

The royal procession moved on into Fleet Street and Temple Bar.

That night, Edward slept in the great bed where, holding Cranmer's hand, his father had died. Very early in the morning, they awoke him for his Coronation.

Carrigahowley Castle was like a place of the dead. No sooner had the MacWilliam buried his son, Walter, than a messenger – arrived from Inveran – told him to prepare a second grave for his wife, Finola. No details about her last illness were known. No one of the funeral party had noticed anything amiss with her before they left Inveran, except Dhonal Nacugga, and he was locked in a dazed silence. Through the bitter cold of a late February day, he sat on a rock by the grey sea, staring at some spectre invisible to everyone else. He felt nothing, heard nothing; his withdrawal from reality was complete until Dhonal Crone went out to talk to him privately.

"My son," the chieftain said, leaning on the wind, "I, alone, understand your feelings. I accept, now, that you loved Finola."

"*Loved* her?" The younger man turned sightless eyes upon him. "Have you gone mad? She was a whore."

"Then why are you mourning her like this?" the chieftain asked gropingly.

A curlew called thinly out of the grey distance as his grand-nephew replied, "I am mourning myself, my body and my soul. Send one of the men down here with a horse, and bid farewell to David Bourke for me. I am going home to Ballina-hinch."

Dhonal Crone gave him a long thoughtful look; there was a word in the Irish language which described the expression in Nacugga's eyes, but it had no single equivalent in any other tongue. It signified a mixture of terror and despair, stirred by a kind of madness.

"I am coming with you," Dhonal Crone said, laying a sympathetic hand on the other's arm. Nacugga started as though the hand were red hot, and shook it off.

"Come if you like," he replied roughly, "and take your damned ships away with you when you leave. Were it not for them and my unnatural wife, I had never set foot in Iar-Connacht."

The evening meal was ready at Ballinahinch Castle when they arrived but Nacugga refused to eat. He went into the solar and slumped on a bench. Graunya excused herself to Dhonal Crone, left her own food untouched and followed him. She was aware of some great change in her husband but could not decide if it were physical or not. Dhonal Crone had told her, hurriedly, about the MacWilliam's double bereavement, yet she could not connect this news with Dhonal's strangeness.

He was disinclined to talk to her, and pushed her away when she tried to approach him. Then he leaned back against the wall, eyes closed.

She went out quietly and called Magnus O Lee.

"I think my husband is sick. . . ."

When O Lee entered the solar, he stood still for a moment,

looking keenly at the man who was either asleep or unconscious, stretched out on the bench. Then the physician went to him and put his hand on the right side of his abdomen, pressing and moving it while bending down to listen. He straightened up sharply.

"What is it?" Graunya whispered. And he spoke to her tersely over his shoulder:

"Do exactly as I say and ask no questions. Your children and the entire household are in grave peril unless we move with all speed. Gather food and water supplies, oil, linen and blankets; have them transported to the mainland and, from thence, to one of the ships in Mannin Bay. I am taking your husband out to sea. No one must come with us."

"Except me," she said with finality.

O Lee swung around irritably, his mouth open to argue; but something in her appearance stopped him – a kind of mature dignity that added inches to her height, making her the mistress, not to be gainsaid.

"Then I must warn you: it will be many weeks before we can have any contact with people again. We must live as lepers, you and your husband – and me, on one lonely ship."

She nodded slowly.

"I will order the provisions," she said. Then: "What is Dhonal's sickness?"

"An enteric fever: a devil out of the flood-waters of cities. . . ."

Chapter 8

THE ship, *Moytura*, was eerily quiet without her crew. Stark-masted, she lay off Errislannon Point in a dripping dawn mist, her empty dinghy moored alongside.

Below deck, a lamp burned over Dhonal Nacugga's straw pallet, heightening the rose-coloured tint of the eruptions on his skin and the cracked scarlet surface of his tongue. He was growing daily thinner and weaker; sometimes, he mumbled in delirium; more often, he was deathly quiet, only his eyes alive to the subdued activity around him, as Graunya and O Lee changed his linen or scrubbed the bare boards about his pallet. They maintained a rigid routine of work and rest, so that their only contact with one another was in the brief moments of handing over the vigil, as now.

"How has he been?" O Lee asked, closing the hatch behind him.

"Restless this last hour." Graunya straightened the blankets over her husband; then, in order to turn his pillow, she slipped her arm under his shoulders and supported his head against her side. Feebly, his hand groped at her.

"Finola . . ." he said.

She tried to lay him down but he clung to her with sudden, feverish strength.

"Finola, oh my love – I will do anything —" The cracked lips were sucking at her clothing, the skeletal hands tightening their grip.

O Lee moved quickly, brutally, to release her, and pushed her away, then held a cup of goat's milk to Dhonal's lips.

"Drink," he said harshly but, behind him, Graunya's strangled voice cried,

"Do you think you can silence him for ever? Do you think you can bind his hands so that they do not speak the truth to me?" And he put the cup down, defeated.

"No. For how long have you been aware of it?"

"For two days. And you?"

"Longer than that."

"I see. He took the fever from her hands. And we risk our lives to save him —" Her face was contorted with passion.

O Lee sprang up and shook her by the shoulders.

"You cannot be jealous of a dead woman," he shouted.

"She is not dead. She lives in his brain. And I am a prisoner here because of her — cut off from my home and children, watching my husband die. Oh, God curse her soul! May everything she leaves behind her be as defiled as we are now. May the son of her body never know a day's happiness." She began to cry chokingly like a furious child, and O Lee's hands dropped from her shoulders.

"You are tired," he said. "Go to bed" – and made to turn away.

He knew that she was near breaking point: the loneliness, the worry for Dhonal's life, the terror of her own infection had been undermining her stability from the beginning, but she had propped her courage with an unshakeable belief in her husband's love for her. Now the prop was broken, the whole edifice tumbling down. O Lee looked at her with compassion; this was not the young girl of the Joyce raid nor the shrewd merchant-woman bargaining her wares. This was an eighteen-year-old wife, caught between a husband who had betrayed her and a physician who had imposed an impossible discipline upon her – to work and watch and sleep, day in, day out, on a phantom ship, without gaiety or normal human contact. And he knew now that he had made these rules for his own protection, not hers. Since that very first day in Castle Kirke, he had wanted her.

He took her very gently into his arms.

"There is always love somewhere," he said. "Remember that, Graunya." He smoothed the dark, curling hair back from her forehead with a hand suddenly unsteady, for there was no tenseness or resistance in her, only gratitude.

Over her bowed head, he looked towards the sick man and saw the fevered eyes fixed upon them both, bright with acute awareness. The cracked lips moved soundlessly for a moment before the words came, harsh and loud.

"For such . . . a lust . . . I murdered the MacWilliam tanist. . . ."

O Lee could not save Graunya from the knowledge of her husband's crime. All her life she would have to live with it, watching for its seeds in her children, feeling the growth of violence and ruthlessness within herself because of it – for her part of the guilt, and because Dhonal's love was gone from her and hers from him.

That night, the ship moved uneasily in a heavy swell and, before daylight, she was pitching and rolling. The wind came fitfully in sudden gusts of tremendous force. The storms of the March equinox were early this year.

In Galway harbour a barque broke her mooring and was driven out to sea, then carried northwards between the islands. From the deck of the *Moytura*, Graunya's unsleeping eyes watched the barque's crazed progress like a huntress watches her prey. She would take that vessel for compensation of the emptiness within herself. It would be hers indisputably, a solid, predictable thing to do her bidding, if she could survive the stretch of heaving, snarling water that lay between.

She climbed down to the dinghy and, leaning on the oars, forced it away from the fever ship. She drew a perverse pleasure from the danger and the discomfort. . . .

On an evening in early April, Dhonal Nacugga was carried by litter into his castle of Ballinahinch. He could not walk unaided nor eat solid food. The youths who had once hunted and raided so energetically under his leadership now looked at him askance, barely recognizing this yellow-skinned, hollow-eyed wreck of a man.

It was Graunya who claimed their attention. She had altered in a startling manner: her face, grown thinner, had a sharp definition which made the blue-black eyes unnaturally large. She had cut her hair up to the lobes of her ears so that it was shorter than was that of most of the men present; and, for the first time inside the castle, she was wearing the kind of clothing which she had only worn hitherto at sea: a straight leather jerkin laced over a rough wool shirt; worsted braes and high boots. Her hips were as flat as a boy's and, when she walked, she put her heel down firmly.

Here was a woman who had no further interest in pleasing men, only in dominating them.

Uneasily, they watched her and she stared back at them levelly, measuring herself against each one of them individually and finding none of them superior to her.

They whispered among themselves, casting sidelong glances at Magnus O Lee: he had been with her; he must know what had happened. Perhaps he was her lover. . . .

Graunya was too occupied to consider idle gossip. The seven weeks of her absence had coincided with the busiest time of year, that of lambing and sheep-shearing and, now that the wool was ready for market, she was determined that it should not be sold in Galway nor to any travelling merchant when she could double its price by shipping it to Spain. But Dhonal Crone had taken his fleet out of Mannin Bay, without explanation or apology, leaving her only the *Moytura* and the barque which she, herself, had salvaged. She had no means of acquiring other ships because the citizens of Galway were forbidden, by law, to sell any craft whatever to the native Irish, and the boat-builders of Clifden and Cong had timber for small craft only.

She turned the problem over in her mind, concentrating on the positive issues, rejecting any idea of abandoning the wool voyage: the Connemara territory could not support itself without trade; its rents were low and difficult to collect, and Dhonal would not be strong enough even for hunting until the end of the summer, if then. There was only one solution: to join her father in his voyage south. Owen O Malley always sold his own spring shearing abroad.

She wished that she could take further council on this decision which was bound to be unpopular, but there was no one to whom she could speak except O Lee, and he was locked in his apartment, engaged in some all-absorbing labour which excluded her.

Calling to her hound, Bran, she went with him into the hall. The masterless men were sitting about in tight little groups, talking or gambling, their evening meal cleared away. They looked slovenly and degenerate. When they turned towards her, there was hostility in their eyes and she wished that she had worn a gown and mantle to come among them.

"I am taking the wool to Spain," she said in the sudden watchful silence. "I want a small crew —"

An old man gave a cackle of laughter.

"For what?" he demanded. "Curraghs?" – and the others hid their mouths behind their hands.

"For the *Moytura*," she said sharply, "thirty men. And ten for the new barque."

"What protects us if we are attacked?" another asked, shuffling his feet in the straw.

She drew her breath in slowly, trying to quieten the pounding of her heart.

"The O Malley fleet," she said, and waited for the uproar. . . .

It came at her in a wave of antagonism, all the age-old enmity of one tribe for another – that same instinctive force which had rejected Dhonal as tanist – fierce, jealous, bitter and illogical. To the Irish, Ireland was not a country but a myriad separate territories of shifting allegiances. The Oath of Supremacy to the English King was easier for them to take than an oath of confederation among themselves. The idea of any kind of union was abhorrent to them.

Graunya stood with her slim legs apart and her hands behind her back. When the shouting had died down, she asked quietly, "Can anyone think of a better idea? Can any one of you here bring me ships and galleys, or obtain Spanish prices for our wool in Galway city?" Then she began to walk among them, looking into their faces. One man shook his hair forward across his eyes, the sign of withdrawal from enemy questioning; her first impulse was to lash out at his insolence but, instead, she brushed the *glibb* away with her own hand.

"I am your friend, O Kilkelly," she said, "who gives you wine instead of buttermilk and water. Your prosperity is linked with mine. Now, will you sail with me?" It needed only one man to turn the tide of opinion. If a single monument of pride and obstinacy toppled, the rest would follow, for the men were easily swayed, volatile and often unreliable. Consciously, she willed this one to agree, her eyes boring into his, her breath on his cheek. She pressed her feet against the floor as though she could draw additional strength from it, and stretched her body upward from the base of the spine.

Without warning, the man bent one knee.

"Take your pick of all my kin," he mumbled, not knowing what had happened to him except that some unknown energy out of her proximity had overwhelmed him.

She was never to understand this kind of victory. It was a power like the laying-on of hands for healing – the power of the consecrated, the chosen of the gods, and it awed her, compelling her to reverence it and use it sparingly. . . .

Before the end of the month, she was sailing under the Seahorse emblem with thirty-eight men and two captains. Her father, in the *Santa Cruz*, saluted her vessels as he swung past to take command of the entire fleet; and Cormac, from the deck of the *Naove*, cupped his hands and shouted, "Graunuaile!" – laughing and waving his cap.

It was good to be among O Malley ships again. Even if her own crew were O Flaherty dependants, at least they were volunteers; she had forced no man to sail with her and they had known from the beginning that they would carry the White Seahorse at their masthead instead of the Golden Lizard. All the tensions of the past slipped away from her like water under the bows and she felt free, full of confidence. She would take her cargo down the dangerous north-west coast of Portugal, where it would bring the best price, and then return to La Coruña to buy a long, fast galley. Little by little, she intended to build a fleet of modern vessels that would hold their own with any wealthy merchants' in the realm.

She was eighteen years of age and considered marriage and childbearing distractions belonging to the past. She would never sleep in Dhonal's bed again, and soon it would be time for her sons to be sent out for fostering to some distant castle, leaving Ballinahinch desolate. Even to herself, she would not admit how great a wrench this parting was going to be, for she loved the boys fiercely, particularly Owen, the eldest, a quiet, solemn little boy who called out all her protective instincts. Murrough was different – rowdy, independent and unaffectionate – he seemed equipped from birth with the means of defending himself and obtaining his own way. Owen missed Graunya when she was absent – Murrough did not, therefore she intended to exert her influence on the O Flaherty chieftain for Owen to be fostered in Aughnanure, where most of the household knew him. Murrough would be quite happy among total strangers.

Dispassionately, she made her plans, shrugging off – as signs of weakness which had to be eliminated – any stirrings of her own feelings. All tenderness had died within her in the moment of struggling out of O Lee's arms, after her husband's fatal utterance:

'For such a lust I murdered the MacWilliam tanist.'

All human contact was tainted for her by the crime bred from Finola O Flaherty. Love and desire and lust ran together to form a putrefying whole from which she retreated, outraged in every sense. Francis Derham and Katheryn Howard: Finola O Flaherty and Dhonal Nacugga – love and death, love and death. . . . No arguments of O Lee could reach her, no pleadings of pure friendship – for the gentleness of his arms had betrayed him.

Out of her withdrawal, she had chosen a man's world, and her creative powers were directed towards that alone, denying every instinct of her womanhood. Only in the half-light of wakefulness into sleep did her body admit a need of physical love, and weep over the wastage of its complex perfection. Dhonal's punishment was hers also; she had taken it upon herself both to inflict and to suffer, with the hard righteousness of the young, the intolerance of the untempted.

Brehon law would have ignored Dhonal's adultery, and asked

only family compensation of him for Walter's murder; but his wife was implacable. . . .

By a masterpiece of timing between wind and current, she ran the *Moytura* and the barque from La Coruña to Oporto, then south to Mondego, drove a hard bargain for the wool, and afterwards rejoined her father at Ferrol, where he helped her to choose the new galley. She derived as much pleasure from this purchase as would another woman from choosing silks and laces, and insisted on taking a place at the oars when the craft was tried. Its performance delighted her; fast and manœuvrable, the danger of its shallow draught was offset by a high prow and curving gunwales.

As they returned to the harbour, a tall galleass was casting off. On her deck stood a group of dark-clad men and, looking up, Graunya recognized one face. She said to her father, "Surely that is Don Pedro de Ricalde?" And O Malley replied, "Aye," gruffly, glancing away.

"Do you suppose he's off to the New World – Hispaniola, Mexico, Peru?"

"Maybe."

"I wonder," she persisted, leaning forward on the trailing oars, "what became of his mission in Ireland. . . ." The passage of the galleass rocked the smaller craft and, for an instant, the tight-skinned face of de Ricalde was directly above her, and she remembered the MacWilliam's words:

'Missionaries on the decks – racks and thumbscrews in the holds.'

"It failed," O Malley said briefly. "We have enough foreigners on our lands."

It was his way of telling her that he had decided to take the Oath to young Edward the Sixth, a more ardent reformer than Henry had ever been. . . .

Edward had two main ambitions in life: to be a good King and to convert his sister, Mary, to Protestantism, but the one was proving as difficult as the other. He was surrounded by zealous advisers, all pulling him in different directions, and the most importunate of these was his uncle, Thomas Seymour, the newly created Lord High Admiral.

At the age of thirty-eight, Seymour – still unmarried – was one of the most handsome men in the realm. His ambition was as boundless as his manner was imprudent: he was vain, loud-mouthed and jealous, obstinate and rash, but he still had great charm for women. Even on dry land, he had a consuming piratical fire and his stock of oaths was inexhaustible.

Seymour owed his high position to the fact that he was the young King's uncle, and brother to the Protector, Somerset, but this latter relationship brought out only the worst in his character: he, Thomas, believed that the guardianship of Edward the King should have been given to him and not to his brother, who was now the first noble in the land because of this trust.

Seymour intended to even the score by marrying one or other of the royal ladies. Mary was too religious to tolerate him, and the Council – headed by Somerset – firmly opposed any mention of a match between him and the fourteen-year-old Princess Elizabeth; so he would have Catherine, the Queen Dowager, who had loved him long before Henry had taken her.

They were married secretly, within three months of the old King's death, while Elizabeth was still living with her step-mother.

The effect of Thomas's presence upon the household was immediate: boisterous and unconventional, it became his habit to enter Elizabeth's chamber first thing every morning, flinging the door open and roaring, "Good morrow, good morrow! How does my lady?" – and bursting into raucous song.

If Elizabeth were up and dressed, he would slap her heartily on the back, or take her on his knee to make her giggle. If she were still in bed, he would pull the curtains apart with a great clatter of brass rings and, pretending to be a grizzly bear, come clawing and growling at her while she burrowed deeper and deeper between the sheets, shrieking, waiting for him to tickle her! It was all more fun than she had ever had in her life.

When her governess remonstrated with the Admiral about the constructions which could be put upon his behaviour, he raised his eyes to heaven and bellowed, "God's precious blood!"

Still, after that, Catherine began to accompany him on his

hilarious morning visits, so as to silence the evil tongues which found more than an innocent romp in them. It was remembered that Seymour had wanted to marry Elizabeth rather than the Queen Dowager. Well, perhaps he would take both of them in the end. . . .

When news of his secret marriage reached the King, Protector and Council, they knew that the pirate-Admiral had made fools of them all because he was still asking their permission! They resolved to watch him more closely in future, and this surveillance would extend to the Princess Elizabeth, who was reported to be in love with her stepmother's new husband, blushing whenever his name was mentioned.

The murmur of gossip concerning the situation swelled to uproar until, finally, the Queen Dowager – now expecting Seymour's child – sent Elizabeth away. But it was too late: the Princess's name was unbreakably linked with that of the Lord High Admiral. Then, in September, after seventeen months of marriage, Catherine died in childbed. . . .

The watching Council tensed itself, waiting for Seymour to make his fatal move. A strict record of his activities had been kept, from which it was obvious that he intended to seize power: he had a large army near the borders of Denbighshire around the provisioned Castle of Holt; he had money in Bristol, enough to finance a rebellion; he had a friendly agreement with several pirates – he, the Admiral, whose business it was to protect shipping – and now, secretly as he thought, he was making inquiries about the dowry lands of the Princess Elizabeth, as a preliminary to marrying her.

Seymour's audacity was founded on the young King's love for him – a love founded, in turn, on gratitude for large gifts of money. Whatever went wrong, Edward would save his handsome, generous uncle, who wanted only to rid him of a tiresome Protector while dusting himself with a little of the power and the glory. . . .

On the night of January sixteenth, fifteen forty-nine, the Admiral let himself into the Privy Garden which led to the King's bedchamber. He had to see his nephew alone in order to clear up some recent misunderstandings, and this was his only means of doing so.

In his belt, he carried a loaded pistol, more from force of habit than evil intent.

Gently, he turned the handle of the outer door. At once, the silence was shattered by the furious barking of a small dog, Edward's pet. The dog leapt out of its basket and sprang at the intruder, who grabbed his pistol from his belt and, cursing, shot the animal. It whimpered once, writhed and then lay still. As Seymour stared down at it, the inner door burst open, and Edward the King stood there in his nightshirt. He looked from the smoking pistol to the empty basket, from his uncle to the dead pet dog and, suddenly, his eleven-year-old face was entirely Tudor, the eyes cold and slanting, the mouth compressed.

Elizabeth was at Hatfield when Thomas Seymour was arrested and taken to the Tower. Within a few days, two of the Princess's most intimate servants were forced to join him there; these were questioned about the relationship between her and the Admiral and, after an agonizing week, they confessed that there had been an intrigue.

Meanwhile, at Hatfield, Sir Robert Tyrwhitt was interrogating the clever, cautious daughter of Henry the Eighth. He knew by her quick breathing that she was apprehensive but he could not break her simple story, nor her subsequent obstinate silence. In baffled despair, he wrote to Protector Somerset: 'Nothing is gotten of her but by the greatest policy.'

The Protector himself tried to make Elizabeth talk, and sent spies into her household, but she merely folded her beautiful hands and refused to be moved; whatever it was that had passed between her and the Admiral was locked behind her tight little bosom for ever.

"You know what people are saying?" Tyrwhitt persisted now, leaning menacingly towards her. "That you are with child by Thomas Seymour. . . ."

She smiled without showing her teeth, and then caressed her own tiny waist.

"Let me come to the Court and show myself there as I am —"

"No. No. That is impossible." Any contact between her and the King, her brother, had been strictly forbidden by Somerset.

"Very well. I say nothing." And her mouth closed like a trap.

She was very frightened and entirely friendless; surrounded by spies; badgered by letters from the Protector; crushed by the fate that was fast overtaking the man she loved. But, through it all, she remained defiant, an enigma that baffled wily statesmen and trained interrogators, none of whom could trap her into an admission of a definite plot to seize power with the doomed Admiral. She concentrated on saving herself in a nightmare game of one small mouse with a roomful of stalking cats.

Elizabeth knew that there was no hope now for Seymour; of the thirty-three articles brought against him, thirty remained unanswered; and the King would not lift a finger to save the man who had killed his pet dog.

On the twentieth of March, England executed her Lord High Admiral. He died bravely, unrepentantly, and the people murmured against the Protector who had signed his death warrant – Somerset, his own brother. But Elizabeth never broke her silence, nor betrayed by the flicker of a pale-lashed eye whether or not Tom Seymour had been her lover.

From that time on, she was a force to be reckoned with and feared; learned, astute and self-contained, she acquired a watching patience while, deep in her soul, the spot warmed by Seymour froze rock-hard.

Two women, as yet unaware of each other's existence, now shared a unique conviction: that the physical love of man would have no more dominion over them. Elizabeth Tudor and Graunya O Malley pursued their private ambitions with ruthless singlemindedness.

Chapter 9

PIRATES were flourishing increasingly in the Atlantic, harrying the trade routes; so, to combat these dangers, Owen O Malley and Dhonal Crone O Flaherty combined their fleets. Under this sensible arrangement, they extended their voyages to North and West Africa, and set about arming any ship big enough to carry cannon.

Graunya, however, was more interested in newer and faster craft than in mounted guns, which she regarded as dangerous, cumbersome and inaccurate. She now commanded over ninety men, picked and trained by herself, and was quite content to rely upon their hand weapons as long as she could sail under the general protection of the armed ships. Her own contribution to the safety of the fleet lay in a pair of new twenty-oar galleys that could carry up to seventy fighting men between them if the need arose.

The *Moytura* and the barque, *Maeve*, both unarmed, sailed deep within the fleet, carrying timber, fish, hides or wool abroad according to the season, and returning laden with foreign merchandise.

By the autumn of the half-century, Graunya was wealthy enough to place an order for a carrack, to be built to her own design, in a Spanish shipyard. It would be ready in the springtime, during her twenty-first birthmonth, and would fly the White Seahorse exclusively, because O Flaherty ships were now forbidden the harbour of Galway, and she still had need to trade there occasionally (although Limerick and the north offered friendlier markets).

No native O Flaherty was allowed to enter Galway city under any pretext whatever, and the clan's ancient right of burial in St Nicholas's had been revoked, owing to the turbulence of funeral parties.

In his seaboard Castle of Bunowen, a fuming lord awaited his wife's return. The messenger who had just ridden in from Mannin Bay – to say that the ships were being unloaded there – had innocently mentioned the order for the new carrack, and Dhonal was black-browed with rage.

"Another forty men," he gritted, pacing up and down the solar. "That's what it will take to crew this new one. . . ."

He had lost nearly a hundred men to Graunya already. Now she would demand another two score, taking only the fittest from among the volunteers who would surge forward. What plague was on these men to want to serve under a woman? Gold: that was it – gold. Her trading voyages never lost; she was too astute, too weather-wise. And she paid her crew at the first foreign port so that they could go mad in the markets there, buying trinkets and scent for their womenfolk at home. . . . He considered that she pandered to their lowest tastes, gambling and singing and drinking with them on the voyage, her language broadening with every season.

But he dared not send her away from him now; she was too popular, too widely known. And, if she went, she was quite capable of taking the men and the ships with her. No; Connemara needed her trade, blast her!

Rage against the world now sustained Nacugga. Simmering or erupting, it had made of him a more fearless hunter, a more reckless raider than he had ever been, and its pulsating energy drew men to him to help clear his forests, drain his land and swell his herds until he held the richest territory in Connacht. If anyone had a mind to connect his sickness of two and a half years back with the death of Finola O Flaherty, and the accident to Walter Bourke, they kept quiet about it – in Connemara, at any rate. Farther afield there were still guarded murmurings, although it was the name of

Fitz-Rory, rather than of Nacugga, that was put forward as the killer. . . .

A great uproar in the hall brought him to his feet: Graunya and her crew were home. He heard the stampede as his own men rushed to welcome them, then the chatter of the serving women and boys, and the baying of the hounds led by the frenzied voice of Bran. . . .

The entire castle leapt to life as soon as Graunya set foot in it. With deliberate strides, her husband went down to meet her. The doorway was crammed with jostling men and women, all moving slowly backwards into the torchlit hall and, for a moment, he could not see her, only guess at her position by the way in which the crowd radiated out from some central attraction. Then he heard her voice:

"Dhonal – Dhonal!" And she was coming towards him, laughingly dodging the leaping hound, her arms filled with the prodigality of gifts which she always brought – a pile so high that she could scarcely see over the top of it.

They went up to the solar together and he glimpsed her face clearly for the first time since her arrival.

"For the love of God," he shouted, starting back, "what has happened to you?" There was a gash above the bridge of her nose, and both her eyes were blackened and swollen.

She lowered the gifts carefully on to a bench, shrugged, and replied over her shoulder, "We were attacked off the Kerry coast. No losses —"

"But your *face*, woman!"

"The blackness will go, a slight scar remain: O Lee put some of his magic ointment on it! Here, try these hawking gloves I brought for you."

He was appalled at the spoiling of her beauty, enraged by her unconcern. She was still his wife and had no right to blemish herself in this manner. He grabbed the hawking gloves from her, flung them upon the floor, then took both her wrists in a fierce grip.

"How did it happen?" he demanded.

"Let me go," she said evenly. "I never answer questions under pressure."

"I'll hold you until you tell me, by God!"

"That you will not do. . . ."

She moved so quickly that he lost track of the sequence. A hooking kick buckled his knees and then his crossed arms were forced up behind his back until it seemed that the joints must snap. She released him after a moment and stood with her feet apart, glowering at him, her eyes sparking.

"Where did you learn that devil's grip?" he moaned, rubbing his shoulders.

"From a Turk in North Africa."

"Then why did you not use it on the man who blackened your eyes?"

Suddenly, the corners of her mouth twitched.

"Because he was one of ours," she said. "I stood too close behind him when he swung his hatchet, and the blunt edge caught me. It will never be an honourable scar, merely a reminder of bad judgement."

She closed her eyes, remembering the pain and the blindness and how the scalding tears had run down her cheeks under O Lee's hands. Recalling his gentleness, her expression softened; and her husband, watching her, felt a great surge of relief that she had not been killed. Much as she annoyed him, he still loved her in a way curiously painful to himself.

Without warning, he caught her tightly against him and stroked the back of her neck where the medallion chain was fastened. . . .

The caress surprised her as much by its warm comfort as by her own immediate response to it. She was lonely for her sons – both of whom had now been sent out for fostering – and she needed more children to fill their places. Dhonal was inseparable from that need. The revulsion which she still experienced in his presence was a spiritual rather than a physical one, and she could control it by a blocking of the mind.

Throughout the winter, they hunted wolf and deer together, and threw their hawks up into the crisp air, as though the companionship of six years earlier had never been interrupted. They sat side by side at the dais table – Graunya wearing Spanish gowns and jewellery and little velvet slippers; the scar on her forehead covered by cosmetic paste – making lively conversation with the throngs of guests and upper members of the great double household, so infrequently assembled that its strength was often underestimated: sea-captain and hunt-leader, portriff and bailiff, paymaster, cargo-master, brehon and maritime judge. . . . The fame of these mighty gatherings soon spread far and wide, attracting more and still more distant visitors until, in February, even the Norman Clanrickarde himself came, drank too much and pronounced loudly:

"This household is more powerful than that of Thighe the Furious. I say that the lord of Connemara should be the O Flaherty tanist!"

Thus, Clanrickarde put into words, and gave sanction to, an idea which many people already held privately: that, if Dhonal and Graunya were prepared to resume their early vital partnership, then, between them, they could rule a large slice of Connacht. 'Fortune favours the strong' was the O Flaherty motto, based on the old truth that any petty chief who showed unusual strength was favoured in new land divisions. More land meant more tenants – fighting men – cattle – the Irish form of wealth rather than gold. . . .

And there was one other sign that Nacugga's influence was widening: lately, a priest of the Society of Jesus had settled in his household – Irish born, Spanish trained, as was usually the case now since the original failure of the Counter-Reformation. The 'Jesuits', as their enemies sneeringly called them, did not waste their educated company on weak lords. If they sat at a chieftain's elbow, one could be certain that that elbow was worth guiding.

The significance of the omens was not lost on Thighe the Furious; sacred though he was as tanist, he decided to protect himself against possible challenge, and increased his personal army in Moycullen. Neither was it lost on Dhonal Crone, the Chief-of-All, who wanted no split within his own huge clan; nor on the nervous citizens of Galway, to whom all O Flahertys were devil-begotten. There was a tenseness around the territories of Dhonal Nacugga. . . .

As soon as the March gales had blown themselves to a whimper, Graunya prepared to set off for Spain to take possession of the new carrack.

After much argument, Dhonal had allowed her to choose

thirty-five extra men from his lands, and these she distributed among her father's ships for the outward voyage. But her lord had made one jealous condition: that she leave Magnus O Lee behind at Bunowen when she sailed. O Lee's reputation as a healer was increasing, and the men had great faith in his ability; a wound which he had dressed never turned septic.

Graunya was loath to sail without O Lee. Sickness on board ship was a serious matter when it arose. But she was in no position to argue with her husband, so she answered with an eye to soothing him, "Dhonal, I cannot see that you are in any danger if you behave prudently."

"Prudently?" he shouted. "What has any man ever achieved by acting thus?" His following was based on a reckless bravado which had become a part of his character, and he had to maintain it.

"A long life," Graunya said crisply, and went to tell O Lee that he would not be sailing with her in the morning.

He received the unqualified news without comment, but tumbled the contents of his hessian bag out on to his mattress with a deep sigh – though whether of anger, disappointment or apprehension she could not judge, for he never confided in her now or invited questions about either himself or his work. Since that one caress on the fever ship, they were more remote from each other than strangers – for strangers have a chance of meeting, but these two always forestalled chance by avoiding each other. . . .

While it was still dark, Graunya and Dhonal set off together for Mannin Bay at the head of a considerable army. The crew and supply wagons had travelled overnight, and the ships were ready to join O Malley's fleet, due at daybreak. Farther south, they would rendezvous with O Flaherty, as always.

It was a sad, wet morning, fretted by dying gales, and the grey beach was strewn with purple wrack. A curragh was waiting to take Graunya out to the *Moytura*, whose lamps burned mistily above distorted reflections. Dhonal's men crowded about him, clashing their weapons, impatient to be off on other business, and he shouted at them, half jokingly, "Save your strength! We'll march on Galway yet. . . ." as Graunya reached up to kiss him good-bye. With her arms still resting on his shoulders, she stared uneasily into his face. The men were shouting and stamping and, through the uproar, she felt the tension of Dhonal's body as he prepared to speed away from her.

"Leave Galway city alone," she said earnestly. "Do not challenge Thighe the Furious —"

He wiped her kiss away contemptuously.

"Whoever gives me that advice," he said loudly, "is a Judas to my ambitions. But what do you care? You weaken my guard, leave my household unattended, and welcome clan *Maulya* into my waters." Then he strode away from her, followed by those men who had been standing close enough to hear his words. They all began to mutter among themselves, looking back at her menacingly over their shoulders.

She stepped into the curragh and, feeling suddenly cold, wrapped her cloak tightly about her. From one point of view, she knew Dhonal to be right; his words lashed at her own unnatural way of life, and the thongs of accusation did not uncurl, either then or later. She had never been an ideal wife for him — or for any man. Her rare moments of passion and submission were interspersed with long periods of complete withdrawal. . . .

The dampness had flattened rings of blue-black hair against her forehead, and her skin glistened in the first faint light of dawn.

"Get out to the *Moytura* quickly," she snapped at the man hunched over the oars.

She was impatient to be free of the sight of land, and angry that Dhonal's mood had turned ugly in the moment of parting, after they had lived together for almost five months with scarcely a quarrel. Ever since his illness, he had been unpredictable. . . .

As the curragh heaved itself over the shore breakers, a fist clenched in her stomach and, gripping the gunwale, she stared at the oarsman in consternation.

"My God," she said, "I'm going to be sick!"

His bellow of laughter was the friendliest sound she had heard that morning, even though it came to her through waves of nausea. . . .

"Graunuaile – seasick! Oh, that's good —" Then he ceased laughing, shipped his oars and scrambled towards her, to hold a wet rag against her forehead. He was an old man, father of many.

"There, there," he said, "you're among your own people now, Graunuaile!" – giving her the name by which she was always known at sea; and, after a moment, asked softly, "Does the Lord Dhonal know about his child?"

She leaned against him as though his chest were the solid door of home, and shook her head. No, she had not told her husband of her pregnancy in case he made it an excuse to prevent her sailing.

The old man patted her arm and went back to the oars.

"We'll return long before it's born," he said comfortably, "and the deck of the new carrack will be under our feet."

The fleet was away for three months so that it was near the end of June when the Aran Islands were sighted again to starboard. Because Dhonal Crone could no longer moor his ships in or near Galway harbour, he had to make for Kilkieran Bay; therefore, he altered course and signalled his farewell to O Malley, who continued to sail due north, with Graunya's new carrack – the *Regina Caoli* – on his landward side.

The evening sky was heavy with raincloud and a thick mist hid the coast of Connemara, but Graunya was determined to see the Skerdmore rocks if she could. This remote and uninhabited cluster held an unbreakable fascination for her, stemming from a childhood game that she and Cormac used to play from the deck of the old *Santa Cruz*. Depending on light and position of view, the Skerd group took on different aspects: sometimes, it was a walled city, with towers and belfries within, lying misty blue and dreaming under a summer sky; other times, it was the gate of hell, belching orange smoke and, if you looked unblinkingly until your narrowed eyes ached, you could see frenzied figures dashing madly hither and yon, trying to escape. Then, again, it was a line-astern of ragged ships; or a dense forest with red deer leaping over the treetops. . . .

There was no end to the pageant of Skerdmore and Graunya continued to play the child's game with undiminished enjoyment on every trading voyage. Were it not for the rain this evening, it might have been the best view of all so far, because the *Regina* had the highest fo'c'sle of any ship she had known. It was like standing on a swaying tower amid creamy clouds of canvas with the wind making harp music in the rigging. She would never take this ship for granted, never ignore one detail of her sturdy perfection from the steering gear that was an engineer's pride to the Seahorse figurehead, so vibrantly expressed that the very wood seemed to snort and ripple.

Between the carved ears, she sighted Skerdmore. Then the ship plunged and the rocks swung upward on the smudged horizon, appearing to hang there for an unnatural time, sinister and menacing, before beginning their apparent descent upon the Seahorse.

"A battery of guns," Graunya said aloud, "mounted over spiked gates."

This aspect had never shown itself before. She half-closed her eyes. Outside the walls which supported the inhospitable gates, corpses hung from gibbets, and black birds circled overhead. . . .

She blinked: the illusion vanished. An undistinguished huddle of dripping rocks slipped by the starboard bow to be swallowed up in the rain-mist of the desolate coast.

Off Slyne Head, she began to gather her ships for the run into Mannin Bay while her father sailed on, alone, towards Inishbofin, where Cormac, his tanist, now had his residence. . . .

The deck of the *Regina* was lively with men as the twin galleys drew ahead to pilot her, and the *Moytura* fell in astern with the little *Maeve* alongside. It was to be a triumphant homecoming. Then the *Regina*'s lookout shouted, and pointed in the direction of Mannin Bay. A curragh was approaching on a zigzag course, oared by one figure, while another waved a red cloth that flared a warning in the grey dusk.

Tensely, Graunya waited, and the men clustering around her became quiet. She was the first to recognize the curragh's occupants as Magnus O Lee and his sister, Peg.

The girl had to be helped on board because she was faint from exhaustion, and O Lee had the appearance of a man who had not slept for weeks.

Graunya signed to her crew to draw back.

"What is it?" she asked urgently.

"You can't go in – to Mannin," O Lee panted. "Your husband has been killed. . . ."

When she neither spoke nor moved, he continued, "Dhonal prepared a march on Galway city. Thighe the Furious heard of his armed advance – went out to meet him . . . thinking his own territory in danger —"

"Thighe killed Dhonal?"

"No. One of his men. The tanist was willing to talk first, but his guard got out of hand. They were inflamed by rumours."

"And now?"

"The castles of Ballinahinch and Bunowen are fortified against you, and men are waiting in the bay to seize these ships. . . ."

She looked at him in stupefaction.

"Fortified against *me*? By whom? What wrong have *I* done?"

"Dhonal's men say that you betrayed their lord. They have joined forces with his brothers, and with Thighe, to claim the castles and the ships from you."

She remembered the scene on the beach, and Dhonal's last angry words, overheard by many.

"I see," was all she said, turning away. He started after her.

"What are you going to do?"

"Call a meeting of my captains and their crews. They must decide whether we fight or not."

He caught at her cloak.

"There can be no question of fighting. . . . You are outnumbered three to one and the enemy is entrenched around the beach and in the castles. All the settlements have been burnt out and the common people fled. I could only save my sister —"

"I will inform my men of the position."

It was almost dark and heavy rain was falling. She crossed the deck.

"Send a light signal to the *Moytura* and the *Maeve*," she ordered. "I want all the leading men of their crews here. Call in the galleys and then extinguish our lanterns."

In the dripping dark, they waited. She spoke once to O Lee. "Did he suffer?"

"No. It was quick."

She nodded and retired into her own thoughts. The position

of a chieftain's widow was not enviable under the best circumstances: in theory, she could claim one-third of his wealth after all his debts were paid, and she could recover her dowry. In practice, she was destitute, because most chieftains died in enormous debt, and Dhonal was unlikely to be an exception; many members of his guard were Scottish mercenaries, claiming high fees, and anyone whom he had ever raided would now demand compensation. The longer she considered the matter, the more futile it seemed to attack: even victory would give her nothing more than two beleaguered fortresses, and years of lawsuits. For her own part, she preferred to keep the ships – which would be accounted as O Flaherty property – and forgo all other claims. Her sons would be given their inheritance when they came of age. But the feelings of the men had to be considered; it was their lord, as well as hers, who had been killed and they had a right to vengeance which she could not deny them.

With a sense of foreboding, she watched the captains and their senior crews gathering, heard their growling and their stamping. They knew that something serious was amiss and their blood was up. Restless after a cramped voyage, they were spoiling for a fight, even among themselves.

She remembered the aspect of the Skerd rocks; the gibbets and the black birds. . . . Was this, then, to be an ending for them all?

Her steward touched her arm.

"Every man is present."

Nearly a hundred of them jammed the *Regina*'s deck in the darkness. The warm rain soaked their woollen clothing, and the heat of their bodies sent out a heavy oiled smell in a mist of vapour.

"I pray you not to interrupt me," she said, "nor make any decision nor tumult until I have finished. Await the orders of your captains."

She was short of breath from the movement of the child within her. Never had she found it more difficult to speak. There was no question of choosing words, of weighing one sentence against another to produce the desired effect – that of reasonableness and caution – and, after a few seconds, she knew that she should have addressed the leaders, privately, at first. It was too late now. Her speech came starkly, each phrase like a whip on bare shoulders, and there was uproar within a moment of its completion.

"We'll fight . . ."

"We know our way in through the darkness —"

"We'll kill – kill – *kill*!"

Knives flashed out of krisses; darts, swords, clubs were brandished; hatchets, axes, every primitive weapon known to these volatile men who yelled and stamped and would not be controlled. . . .

She heard the rattle of the anchor chain being wound in, felt the shudder of the planks under her feet. . . .

"Light me a torch!" she shouted at a mad-eyed youth who tried to rush past her. After some groping and cursing, he transferred the flame from a guttering candle to an iron claw full of waxed fabric.

She held the blazing brand over her head and made for the fo'c'sle. Flakes of light fell around her, giving her a weird unearthly appearance; heads turned, eyes followed this one streak of brilliance in the wet darkness.

"Fire!" Graunya yelled at the full pitch of her lungs.

It was the dreaded word on board a wooden ship. It froze men into an immobility of terror, but she had trained them rigorously for such an emergency and now the lesson took control of their minds and actions: they dropped their weapons and assembled quickly in some kind of order. . . .

Still holding the torch, she advanced to the 'tween-rail and looked down at them; then, deliberately, with one hand, loosened the thong of her cloak. The wet fabric fell in a huddle at her heels. The linen of her white smock began to absorb the rain, to cling to her enlarged breasts and stomach until she seemed huge, naked and awesome under the wavering light which cast a grotesque shadow. Hypnotized, the crowd below watched her. She leaned forward.

"I will slit the throat of any man," she said evenly, "who makes another move without his captain's orders."

She had them under her control now. She could talk to them. . . . Carefully, she outlined the position on the mainland and prophesied the consequences of both victory and defeat.

"If you decide to attack," she continued, "your captains, and not I, must be your leaders. I am too far gone with this child to risk becoming a prisoner of Thighe the Furious; you know well that the unborn of a dead lord belongs to the elected of his father's clan; but Thighe and Dhonal Nacugga were enemies, and I would save my child from his father's murderers."

Raindrops were hissing on the torch, curling it about with smoke, gradually extinguishing it. They saw her figure fade before their eyes, leaving them in darkness as though she, alone, had been the source of light. And, suddenly, inexplicably, she was the mother of them all.

O Flynn of the *Moytura* stepped forward and shouted up to her, "Graunuaile, what do you think we ought to do?"

Oracularly, the disembodied voice replied, "We ought to save our ships for another, and greater, day. Let those men who have wives and families on the mainland depart from us if they wish; we will think no ill of them. But we, who remain, will slip past Mannin in the night and make for Clare Island; we have accepted O Malley's guidance and protection in the past; I think he will not fail us now."

"So it shall be done," said O Flynn. He was the senior captain and not in the habit of consulting anyone once his mind was made up. "To the galleys, those who would leave. To their stations, every other man."

Twenty-seven members of the combined crews chose to return to Connemara. While the *Regina* waited for her galleys to be brought back after landing them, her navigator worked out the new course. Long before dawn, the ghostly ships swung nor'-nor'-west to clear High Island and Inishark.

Chapter 10

Edward the Sixth, King of England, was more weary than he had ever been in all the fifteen years of his life. A recent attack of measles had weakened him, and the daily pressures of his great office were increasing as he approached his majority: there was pressure from the Catholic powers in Europe for the Princess Mary to be allowed her private Mass; pressure from Bishop Ridley for the relief of London's poor – hungry and diseased in their filthy alleys; pressure from the ruthless Duke of Northumberland, who had climbed to full power as 'the king behind the King' over the headless body of Protector Somerset.

England was in religious chaos. There were still more Catholics than Protestants, and the Catholics were militant. If anything should happen to King Edward before he married and fathered an heir, then who would save the infant Reformed Church from half-Spanish Mary Tudor, who must succeed him?

On a night in February of the year fifteen hundred and fifty-three, the Princess Mary sat by her royal brother's bedside and knew that he could not live to see another summer. He had an abscess on the lung which caused him to spit blood, and his right shoulder was noticeably higher than his left.

Weeks went by. He rallied a little, failed again. But, as long as a spark of life remained in him, Northumberland would not let him rest, for the Duke's power depended upon that of the King.

The royal physicians were ordered to administer stimulants

instead of sedatives: Edward was allowed no merciful unconsciousness from his bouts of coughing and his bedsores.

Northumberland's only hope was to cheat Mary out of the Crown (and Elizabeth also, in case she should marry a foreign Catholic) but, to gain his ends, he needed a little more time before Edward died, and time was purchased at a hideous price. . . .

A woman who swore that she could cure the King with potions was engaged, and the helpless boy was given into her hands. The potions contained arsenic, which, at first, stimulated the invalid to brilliant mental awareness. In this state, he nominated his Protestant cousin, the Lady Jane Grey, as his successor to the throne – eliminating, on religious grounds, the claims of his half-sisters, Mary and Elizabeth; Jane was safely married to Northumberland's son – and Edward still had enough strength left to bully his ministers into signing the device.

Now the arsenic exacted toll for the brief rally it had permitted: the King's thin arms and legs swelled, his fair skin darkened and his nails and hair began to fall off, his fingers and toes became gangrenous. The entire body fell into hideous, living decay while the mind remained fully conscious.

"Lord God," the boy-King had prayed while he could still speak, "deliver me out of this wretched life and take me among Thy chosen; yet, not my will but Thine be done. . . ."

Seldom had so young and good and sincere a King been asked to die so painfully.

In the late afternoon of July the sixth – while thunder grumbled in the distance – the King's friend, Henry Sidney, took the pathetic body into his arms and cradled it there against his chest until life went out of it.

Northumberland had to act quickly. His ruse to kidnap Mary and Elizabeth failed but, within the week, he had his daughter-in-law, the Lady Jane, crowned Queen of England.

She reigned for nine stormy treacherous days; then the gates of the Tower clanged shut behind her and the entire Dudley family, as Catholic Mary rode into London at the head of her victorious army.

Elizabeth, with a train of a thousand horse, went out to meet her half-sister, and greeted her as Queen.

They were a striking contrast, these two daughters of Henry the Eighth. Mary was thirty-seven, a small thin woman with greying reddish hair and light eyes. Few people remembered that she had once been attractive – that her brother had had to reprimand her for gambling and dancing and dressing too lavishly! Now, worry and persecution had lined her face, and ill-health stolen the bloom of youth away. Her mouth was thin, tight and downward drooping at the corners.

But Elizabeth, at twenty years of age, was full of youth and anticipation. She carried her slender body with a kind of majesty, and her head of red-gold hair with conscious pride. Her eyes were narrower than Mary's, more alert and suspicious; it was impossible not to notice the sharpness of their glance although she kept their upper lids half dropped under thin, arched brows. She was fully aware that the people were looking at her rather than at Mary – the dowdy little Queen whose magnificent courage had astonished everyone but inspired no one – and Elizabeth smiled at the cheering crowds, drawing them to her pure English self, away from half-Spanish Mary.

She held the tasselled rein high to display her beautiful hands.

A Venetian at Queen Mary's Court was writing a letter.

'Genuine Catholics,' he penned, 'are very few here, and there are none under the age of thirty-five.'

It was an astute observation, although more true of the towns and cities than of the country districts. Mary had inherited an island where the Reformation was nearly twenty years old and, although people were willing to hear Mass for the sake of outward show (as even Elizabeth did) nothing would induce them to welcome back the authority of the Pope. Neither could any force break the hold of the new owners on Church lands.

The clergy themselves were in great confusion, for many of them had married during the two preceding reigns. Now celibacy was the order of the day!

In Ireland, hopes soared at news of the Catholic coronation. Masses were sung in the long-empty monasteries by priests who had dreamed of this homecoming during many bitter years. But their joy was short-lived. Irish nobles were no more willing to give up Church lands than were their English counterparts; greed spoke the same language in both countries.

O Malley, however, welcomed back the Austin friars to Murrisk and called his entire clan together for a great *Te Deum* there in the early spring. Cormac came from Inishbofin with his wife and children and a great host of followers; the newly-married Donald and his men marched from Cahirnamart; Melachlin, the chieftain's brother, from Roonah, and all the associated families of the Umalls assembled, to form a mighty congregation that stretched from the sea to the foot of Patrick's mountain.

Graunya's fleet occupied a good stretch of the bay. She had four large ships now, two barques and half a dozen galleys. Many members of the original Connemara crews were still with her but she had drawn on her father's territories for the remainder, making a complement of about two hundred men and choosing McNallys, McInerneys and O Dowds as her best material. The ollavs of the tribe had allowed her to hold Clare Island as her own territory, on condition that she had the mouth of the bay patrolled during all seasons for the greater protection of the Umalls; and her brother, Cormac the tanist, gave her a roadstead for her larger craft between Inishbofin and the mainland, on the private understanding that she judged his weather for him!

Owen and the Lady Margaret having removed permanently to the Castle of Belclare, Graunya set about building a fortress on her island, beside the old summer residence. And there she lived all the year round – except when away on voyages – in grim seclusion.

She was twenty-five years old, in the full flower of her womanhood, a legend – from Scotland to the west coast of Africa – of vibrant beauty and extraordinary strength of character. Her Seahorse pennant was as well known in Portugal as in Connemara, and only her own family called her Graunya now: she was Graunuaile to everyone else. . . .

The candles were lit on the friary altar, the robed priests waiting, as she entered this place of disquieting memories for the first High Mass there since her wedding. In deference to the occasion, she wore woman's clothing, and a black lace veil covered her cropped curls.

Heads turned as she walked to her bench nearest the altar, but she looked neither left nor right as she genuflected before the tabernacle, crossed herself, and moved into her place.

A small voice whimpered at her elbow and, turning quickly, she saw that her little daughter, Moira, had followed her into the church although she had been left outside in Peg O Lee's care. Graunya bent down and gathered her in her arms, her expression softening as she caressed the yellow silk hair and downy skin of Dhonal Nacugga's child.

From near the west door, a man was watching the mother and daughter intently. All through the *Kyrie* and the *Gloria* he watched, and craned his neck when the congregation stood up for the Holy Gospel. He had a long Norman face with dark hair and beard, both unkempt; his eyes were startlingly green-blue; he was about thirty years of age or more, and his body had the sparc toughness of one accustomed to arms and armour. Even now, in the House of God, he was wearing a vest of mail, and his helmet rested on the floor beside him.

Not without cause was he known as 'Richard in Iron', son of David Bourke of Carrigahowley. Finola O Flaherty had been his mother. . . .

As the last notes of the *Deo Gratias* died away, Graunya left her bench and hurried out of the friary church, carrying the child against her shoulder.

"Take care of her," she said to Peg O Lee, kissing the little one on the back of the neck as she handed her into the nurse's arms, "and let her not wander again. I will be away with the *Regina* for a week or so."

Graunya's latest commission was a strange one; she had been approached by the Earl of Ormonde – 'Black Tom' to his friends, of whom she was one – to anchor in a deserted cove of the Bristol Channel, there to pick up passengers who would pay well for secret transport to Germany, France or Ireland. . . .

Her merchant's mind approved the venture, her restless spirit welcomed any deviation from routine; but she was careful not to mention the plan to anyone except her most trusted navigator and captain because, deep in her soul, she knew that she would be censored by many of her own people for carrying terrified English Protestants out of range of Queen Mary's heresy trials. Still, knowing that these people were being burned and butchered at the rate of four hundred a day, and having no personal quarrel with any of them, Graunya was disinclined to be talked out of a good business deal on purely religious grounds; Black Tom Ormonde himself was a Protestant, and one of the finest men she had ever met. And her own Celtic God was a gentle God, so that Queen Mary's inquisitional fanaticism in His name sickened her. . . .

She was stepping into her skiff on the shingly beach of Murrisk when Richard-in-Iron Bourke came striding after her, having elbowed his way through the crowd.

"Graunuaile —"

"Yes?" She did not recognize him. He had had no beard at their last meeting, thirteen years previously.

"If ever you need reinforcements, I have a healthy band of Clandonnel Scots. . . ."

This direct statement out of the blue puzzled her momentarily. Then she replied, "My followers are sailors, not landsmen, and we undertake no raiding. All our ships are fully crewed."

"The offer is for the future," he said, pulling at his beard and staring at her with his bold, blue-green eyes. "You understand? The future: I to lead by land, you by sea."

Slowly, she recognized the words as a proposal of marriage. There had been so many these last few years that no new formula surprised her, but this one was certainly unique – a kind of grand military and maritime alliance!

"I thank you, but must refuse," she said, keeping her face straight. That was always her answer. A widow she was and a widow she would remain. Marriage did not suit her temperament, she had said once, knowing full well that the real truth was simpler: the man was not born who could dominate her. Magnus O Lee remained her friend, and saved himself from destruction by never aspiring to be either lover or husband to her. . . .

She pushed the skiff away from the shore and had rowed

several yards before Richard Bourke shouted after her, while tearing off his vest of mail, "At least, hear me further —" plunged into the clear water and began to swim.

"What do you want?" she asked as he came alongside, spluttering.

"To prove myself to you."

"I can see that you are a man," she laughed, "and you must be wealthy to employ Scots. Now, go back before you drown."

"Would you care?"

"No."

"What would make you care for me?"

"Nothing. I have all the men and all the wealth I need."

"But no title. I could give you that. Some day, I will be the MacWilliam Bourke. . . ."

She shipped her oars carefully and he put a confident hand on the gunwale. Above the dripping beard, she recognized the green-blue eyes as exact copies of Finola's except that they had no inward slant. Then her brows came down thunderously, puckering the scar, and her long chin jutted. She looked vicious and formidable, utterly unlike the woman in the church cuddling her child. The next thing Richard in Iron knew was that an oar had smashed down on his fingers, and the skiff was shooting away under a stroke that knocked him backwards.

Graunuaile might remain unwedded if she wished, but Mary Tudor could not do so. It was vital that the Queen should marry and give birth to an heir if the Catholic succession were to continue; and her ministers urged her to choose an English subject as consort.

But Mary listened only to her cousin, the Emperor Charles the Fifth; and the Emperor's fatal advice was, that she should marry his son, Philip, who was then a widower. The match would bring England within the orbit of Spain, and preclude any alliance with France.

In vain, Parliament protested. Unheard, the English people murmured. Mary was determined to marry the alien and unsmiling Philip of Spain.

By proceeding with the arrangements, she drove the entire

country into the arms of her half-sister, Elizabeth, and stirred rebellion to a searing flame which almost consumed her throne: Wyatt's rising nearly succeeded, although its failure was complete in the end. . . . A long line of bodies dangled in chains on the banks of the Medway. The city of London became a place of horror and desolation where traitors' heads and quarters spoke a warning from the gates, and twenty gallows stood to recall a day of awful butchery on which the Lady Jane Grey, too, perished.

The Queen had one further precaution to take before her bridegroom set foot in England. On Palm Sunday morning, in a downpour of rain, a barge nosed its way to the Traitors' Gate of the Tower and the Princess Elizabeth was taken ashore from it. She began to climb the green lichened steps, then sat down suddenly in the wet and the slime.

"Oh, Lord," she cried to the watching warders, "I never thought to have come in here as prisoner. Bear me witness that I am no traitor. . . ."

She was unacknowledged heiress to the Throne, and death was very near to her.

In July, Mary and Philip were married, and the huge Spanish retinue of the bridegroom did nothing to gain the friendship of the English people. There were brawls and quarrels everywhere between these two races that had nothing in common. A rumour that the Archbishopric of Canterbury was to be given to a Spanish friar brought a howling, fist-shaking mob out into the London streets.

Philip of Spain – now uncrowned King of England – was careful, affable and in a hurry to leave. Mary was too old and staid to stir his blood. Worse, she was passionately in love with him and never let him out of her sight. His only thought was to escape from her and her gloomy country: hers, to bear him a child.

When Cardinal Pole gave solemn absolution to the nation, Mary knelt in ecstasy and announced herself pregnant. By January, she was wearing her old-fashioned girdle undone and her body was swelling visibly. By February, she had lashed her Parliament into a fanatical campaign against heretics and, with fire and faggot, began to empty her prisons so that the heir might be born into a cleansed, all-Catholic country.

'Bloody Mary,' her people christened her, whispering behind their hands. And the great exodus began of those lucky enough to find ships willing to carry them away from the country.

Graunya made no trading voyages that spring. Instead, with the *Regina Caoli*, she helped ferry human cargoes and, by the smell of their sweat, learned the terrors of religious persecution. Nor was she the only Catholic to side with the Protestants: in London, the French and Venetian ambassadors spoke with admiration of the martyrs' courage, and roundly condemned the Queen in letters to their masters.

The signs of Mary's pregnancy increased; but April passed, and then May, without a child being born. By August, the entire business had become a farce, and Philip – embarrassed – quit England for Flanders, leaving his consort to a nun-like round of religious duties in a monastery at Greenwich. The phenomenon of false pregnancy had withdrawn its signs from Mary, and it was said she wept until her cheeks were grooved.

On the sixth of November, fifteen hundred and fifty-eight, she recognized Elizabeth as her successor. Eleven days later, she died.

In January, Elizabeth was crowned Queen of England. She made no immediate religious changes but the signs were there for all to read, that this was the true daughter of Henry the Eighth, though long branded as illegitimate. For the Christmas Day Mass before her Coronation, she forbade the celebrant to elevate the Host and, when he refused to obey, walked out noisily. And, for the opening of Parliament on January twenty-fifth, when the Abbot and monks of Westminster met her in broad daylight with tapers burning, she shouted dramatically,

"Away with those torches! We can see well enough. . . ."

Everyone was beginning to see very well indeed. Even John Knox regretted his most recent literary work, entitled *First Blast of the Trumpet against the Monstrous Regiment of Women*.

'God hath revealed to some, in this our age, that it is more than a monster in nature for a woman to reign and bear empire above men. . . .'

Women, he further declared, were painted forth by nature to be weak, frail, impatient, feeble and foolish; they were the port and gate of the Devil; their covetousness was insatiable. For a woman to rule men was the subversion of good order and justice, and men were less than beasts to permit such an inversion of God's order. . . .

To which outburst, Calvin cautiously and diplomatically replied,

'There are occasionally women so endowed, that the singular good qualities which shine forth in them make it evident that they were raised up by Divine Authority.'

Elizabeth read this exchange, and smiled. . . . She intended to prove that a woman could rule successfully.

On remote Clare Island, another woman was already proving the same thing. There, the title of a ship was being transferred to its owner – *Regina*: Queen. . . . In the Irish language, there was no direct translation, but only a title formed from two words, 'ban-rioghan': She-King.

Thus was Graunuaile acclaimed on the day that her fortress was completed and the Seahorse banner run up above its enduring walls. For Cormac, the O Malley tanist – 'the best captain of a longboat in the Two Umalls' – had been drowned at the mouth of Killary, and his sister was now second-in-command to the chieftain until a new tanist could be elected.

No man of the tribe was in any haste to challenge her authority.

Chapter 11

IN her island fortress Graunya had a private apartment facing
south. It contained a trestle bed, a chest full of books and a petch
for hanging the few feminine garments that she owned. There
was a priedieu under a wooden image of the Virgin and Child,
and a sheepskin rug on the floor beside the kneeler. Two ships'
lanterns hung from the beams. Yellowing maps – fast becoming
obsolete with the discovery of new lands and oceans – covered
the bare walls, along with weapons, fishing gear and an old
spiked collar once worn by her hound, Bran, whom she knew
must be dead long since in the Castle of Ballinahinch. . . .

The window was the only one in the fortress to contain clear
glass – the expense justified, in her opinion, by the magnificence
of the view: sea and sky and a multitude of islands – and, under
the window, an oak table was wedged, along one side of which
a row of notches had been cut with a knife.

The significance of these notches was known only to
Graunya: they were a record of her sons' birthdays – seventeen
for Owen, fifteen for Murrough, the sixteenth almost due.

She was allowed to see the boys once in a while by secret
agreement with Dhonal Crone. He would put them aboard one
of his ships in Kilkieran Bay, so that she could row in from her
anchored fleet for a brief hour with them. It was a sad, furtive
arrangement which galled her soul, but the only alternative was
to do battle with half the O Flaherty tribe – still baying for her
blood after nearly seven years – and thus lose the friendship of
their chieftain, which she valued.

But even Dhonal Crone was cautious in his dealings with her: he knew her power and guessed the strength of her feelings; therefore, under no circumstances would he allow her to take the boys on board one of her own ships in case she made a dash for Clare Island with them. They were his responsibility until they married or came of age, to take over their inheritance. . . .

She drew a knife out of her kriss and went over to the table. She would make the sixteenth cut now for Murrough. It was August. He had been born in September . . . after the Joyce raid . . . before the journey to Royal Cong . . . an eternity ago!

Murrough belonged to the beginnings of violence in her life and his character marched in step: he was wild and intractable.

She smoothed off the notch with her fingers and a vision of Murrough's face rose up before her: the shining, honey-coloured eyes and mass of dark brown hair waving from brow to neck; the broad freckled nose; strong teeth that flashed white with ever-ready smile. Surely he was a son of whom any mother ought to be proud! And she *was* proud, although the boy showed no return of similar feelings for her, the most famous woman in Connacht. Once he had his hands on the gifts she brought him, he treated her like a stranger – until the time came to wheedle for more! There was an unscrupulous quality in Murrough's charm which disturbed her even while she was responding to it. . . .

How different was Owen, her eldest son; gentle and with-drawn, like the forest creatures among whom he had been con-ceived. When the time for parting came, after one of his mother's visits, he would turn his head aside so that she should not see how his eyes were big with tears.

Between Graunya and Owen stretched the spiritual bond of the firstborn. . . .

Their recent meeting – this spring past – was the most private one they had ever enjoyed because Murrough was not present. When she asked where he was, Owen replied, flushing, "He – he had to go to the mountains with his young men."

"You mean he is preparing a raid?"

"No, no!" – quickly. "Our chieftain has forbidden that. But Murrough likes to train with his companions —"

"– Rather than see me?" She was hurt but not surprised;

there had always been a faint antagonism between her and her youngest son; perhaps because he was so like his father. . . . She shut him out of her mind and, with deliberate heartiness, said to Owen, "Let us talk about your forthcoming marriage.Is Catherine beautiful? Do you love her?"

"Yes, and yes again!" he laughed; then, earnestly, "You will be able to attend our wedding?"

There was no reason why she should not do so. Catherine was the daughter of Edmund Bourke of Castle Barry – a kinsman of the MacWilliam – and she and Owen would be married in Bourke territory, where Graunya was always welcome.

"Yes," she replied. "Certainly, Owen. The end of August. . . ." – although, even as she spoke, it occurred to her that she might meet many people during the festivities whom she did not wish to meet – Thighe the Furious, maybe, with some men who had once made up Dhonal's bodyguard; or O Flaherty women with long tongues and longer memories; or Richard Bourke, the most persistent of all her suitors. . . . Near-drowning at Murrisk had not deterred Richard in Iron; nor failure to be elected tanist when his father, David, died; nor two serious clashes of arms (one, with his half-brother, Thomas, that cost him a hundred and fifty men; and another that resulted in a six-month incarceration in the dungeons of Gallen); nor Graunya's repeated refusals to see him or accept gifts from him. He was obstinate as a suitor and indestructible as a warrior – qualities which might have appealed to her had they not been negated by her secret knowledge that his wealth and power was built on dead Walter's bones. . . .

Now she replaced the knife in her kriss and, leaning her palms on the notched table, stared out through the window. It was a dull, airless morning, everything shrouded in thick mist; the weather had been like that for two whole days. When the convent bell rang the Angelus, it had a muffled, funereal tone.

Before Graunya had finished her brief prayer, her ten-year-old daughter burst into the apartment, high-spirited after hours in the schoolroom which she entered at five o'clock each morning.

"Moira, my love," her mother said, relieved at the intrusion, "come, talk to me. Tell me what you did today." The child resembled the Lady Margaret, her grandmother, with whom she lived for nine months of every year, spending only the summer on Clare Island with Graunya. She had fine, butter-coloured hair and delicate skin.

"It's Tuesday," Moira replied, "so we had languages. We read in Spanish about Ignatius of Loyola, how he founded the Society of Jesus. Then we translated a chapter of Cicero *De Senectute*. After that, we prayed in French for Scotland. . . ."

"For Scotland?" Graunya asked blankly.

"Yes. That they shall cease to insult the Holy Mass there and receive their Queen in peace."

"Oh. I see." That prayer would have been inspired by Sister Michel, born in Paris and an ardent supporter of the House of Guise; her brother was master of a fishing vessel which had a licence for these waters. He kept the little nun well informed.

"Do you know about Scotland, my mother?" Moira persisted.

"Only a little. John Knox leads the Congregationalists. And Elizabeth of England would like to see all French Catholic interests there suppressed. She is afraid of Mary, Queen of Scots."

"Why is she afraid?"

"Because Mary Stuart is a Catholic and has a strong claim to the English throne should Elizabeth die childless. . . ."

Graunya glanced through the window again. The mist was thickening and growing strangely dark. If Sister Michel's brother were right, Mary Stuart's ship would be on the high seas by now (Elizabeth having refused her a safe-conduct through England) and might even have arrived in the dour kingdom which she had left as a small child to marry the Dauphin of France.

The thunder of cannon from royal galleys awakened the inhabitants of Leith. They had not expected their Queen on this dark, wet Tuesday morning, but they tumbled out to greet her and to prepare the Palace of Holyrood for her occupation.

Mary Stuart, a royal widow at not quite nineteen years of age, was tall and pale-complexioned with dark-brown eyes and a wealth of chestnut hair. Vivacious, light on her dancing feet, she was a woman no man could resist – no man, that is, except John Knox, who thundered against her from the moment she stepped on to Scottish soil.

"If there be not in her a proud mind," he declared, "a crafty wit and an indurate heart against God, my judgement faileth me!"

Mary's crime was to have Mass said in her own chapel. The Protestant nobles had bristled at the sight, but contented themselves with destroying the altar candles. . . .

"One Mass," Knox screamed, "is more fearful to us than if ten thousand enemies were landed in the realm to suppress our religion. . . ."

Mary took her sewing to the Council chamber and bent over it patiently while her advisers talked.

Her heart was sick for France. . . .

Graunya gave a deal of thought to her son, Owen's, wedding. She wanted Catherine Bourke to like her as a woman, to accept her as a mother-in-law, but was only too well aware that her reputation would probably frighten the young bride; therefore, she paid great – and unaccustomed! – attention to her appearance. She had two gowns shipped from Spain, where she had ordered them specially in the spring; one for travelling, and one for the wedding ceremony and feast.

The loose travelling dress was in fine black graine, with a red and white striped petticoat and a white frill at neck and wrist; she chose a wired, heart-shaped cap of black lace and pearls to keep the dust of the bridle-paths out of her hair (which she had coaxed to shoulder length), and gloves of fine perfumed leather – slashed at the knuckles to make room for her finger jewellery – protected hands lovingly cared for these many weeks, although no amount of creams and lotions could soften palms calloused by rope and oar.

It was the other dress which worried her. Under Spanish sunshine, the fabric had looked demure enough; now it glowed with terrifying opulence – cloth of gold raised with peacock-blue velvet. Worse, the wide hem was stiffened for the new farthingale fashion which even the ladies of the Royal Cities were finding difficult enough to manipulate. . . .

"I dare not wear it!" she cried to Peg O Lee, and began to close the wooden box in which it had travelled from Spain; but her eye lingered on the beauty of its embroidered bands, its little corded waist vee-dipping at the front, its delicately gathered sleeve tops.

"Try it," Peg coaxed, "and wear it to the evening meal today. Once you became accustomed to it . . ."

Peg lifted the hooped skirt over Graunya's head. The tight-fitting bodice began to take shape as the concealed hooks were fastened.

"There!"

"I'm sure one ought to wear corsets with it," Graunya chuckled.

"You have no need of them."

Her waist was very small above the gentle fullness of the skirt. She found that she could walk with ease, and that the hem was not obtrusive. Viewing herself in the only mirror that the fortress owned, she was surprised at how her own strong colouring toned down the richness of the cloth.

"Very well. I *will* wear it."

"This evening?"

"Yes. Watch their faces" – and the two women went off into peals of laughter.

The hungry, bearded men, sitting with their backs against the walls, were indeed worth watching. Many of them had never seen Graunuaile in a skirt of any kind, and only a few remembered the last great days at Ballinahinch. Now they looked, open-mouthed, at their She-King advancing into the grim, armour-bristling hall; and a kind of glory touched their eyes.

Graunya had expected to be amused by their reaction. Instead, she felt her throat tightening. They were so simple, these rough courageous men of hers, and she had denied them pleasure which it had been in her power to give. Their pride in her had been a sexless thing: now it was charged with the emotion men feel for a beautiful woman. She could have asked them for a crown in that moment and been given it.

She said grace and sat down among her captains. As the meal

began, her white-robed harper sang an old song, unbidden, which she had not heard for many a year.

'*Oh, Clan Maulya of the sea-sent treasure. . . .*'

A fierce affection for her tribe possessed her. She was King and Queen, both – her father, broken-spirited since Cormac's death, was delegating more and more of his own power to her – and she would never split that office by remarrying unless the needs of the clan could be better served by her doing so. It was a dedication. . . .

Next morning, she set out for Castle Barry, taking twenty armed men with her, and Peg O Lee to help her dress. They rowed in a single galley to Cahirnamart, where Graunya's younger brother, Donald, held the old fortress near the river mouth.

Donald's children flocked to greet the visitors and Graunya found herself gazing speculatively at the boys, wondering if they would grow up to be warriors and sea-rovers, or if – like their easy-going father – they would prefer river-fishing and playing the pipes! They were all healthy, sturdy lads, and she encouraged them to a game in the moored galley.

The remainder of her own journey would be made on horse-back, her men walking alongside and Peg O Lee riding with the pack-mules. . . .

Graunya never liked travelling inland. As soon as the smell of the sea grew faint, she became restive and despondent; but, today, the paths leading to Castle Barry were so crowded – there was so much to watch and listen to – that she became absorbed in the journey and only looked back once: that was from the height of Sheehaun, to stare down at Clew Bay with its herd of hump-backed islands, and the great cone of Croagh Patrick rising on the south shore above Murrisk.

"How distant Cliara seems from here," she remarked to Peg, pointing to the horizon, which appeared to stretch southward from Achill Head in a misted, silvery line; above this, balanced in cloud, was the pale blue summit of Knockmore which sheltered the island fortress.

A beggar came pestering them for alms and, farther on, pedlars and jugglers and mummers with painted faces were pressing determinedly towards Castle Barry for the wedding, and all of them wanted Graunya and her escort as first customers. She chose an elderly news-monger from the throng, and questioned him mercilessly as he loped along beside her mount. Where had he come from?

"Out of the north, lady; O Donnell territory in Ulster."

"Why so far afield?"

"Because of the fighting there this two years; our crops and villages burnt; brother against brother. . . ."

It was the old, old story, a dispute about the chieftain's tanist. Con Bacagh O Neill, dying of senility, desired that his bastard son, Matthew of Dungannon, should succeed him. But Shane, another son born in wedlock, took up arms, murdered Matthew and chased the old man into the Dublin Pale.

Shane – 'a haughty, courageous, drunken man' was the news-monger's involved description of him, 'and as full of wiles as a fighting salmon' – was very strong now, and was hiring huge bands of Scottish mercenaries. He had even stolen the wife of Calvagh O Donnell, his neighbouring chieftain!

"And what is the O Donnell doing about *that*?" Graunya asked. To her, it was all a fairy story, invented to pass the time. What went on in the Province of Ulster was of no more personal concern to her – or to anyone else in Connacht – than if it were happening in the Kingdom of Muscovy.

"Not much he can do." Her informant was breathing hard and she slowed her horse. "Shane O Neill has him chained in a dungeon while he makes a mistress of his wife!"

She glanced sideways at the ageing man; his face was grimly set, his fists clenched. Suddenly, she realized that he was speaking of the present time, and of a situation which concerned him personally.

"So the O Donnell's territory is without its chief?" she asked softly.

"It has a new one by strong hand," he gritted. "Shane O Neill's. I will not live under the rule of a usurper!"

"Why, then, do you not help fight him?"

"Too old, too broken in wind. I must wait for the Queen's Lieutenant to clear him out —"

"*What?*" She reined her horse sharply.

"The – the Queen's Lieutenant, my Lord of Sussex; he has marched on Ulster with an army!"

"Blood of God," Graunya shouted, "you all deserve what you get! You squabble like children among yourselves until the enemy moves in. . . ." It had happened with the Normans; it would happen again now – to Ulster; then Munster in the south; finally, to Connacht. . . .

She flung a coin on the ground and urged her horse to a canter; men and mules lengthened their stride to keep pace with her, nearly knocking the bewildered news-monger down as they passed.

The eve-of-the-wedding feast began at sundown. Graunya, in her dress of blue and gold, occupied one of the six honoured places at the dais table; these belonged to the prospective bride and 'groom, with the parents of each. But Graunya, being a widow, was partnered by the new MacWilliam, Richard the Third, successor to David of Carrigahowley. He was an old man who had been tanist for thirty years; very gallant and gay and twinkling; astute as a fox behind a mask of apparent imbecility.

"And why do you not marry Richard in Iron, eh?" he demanded now, spearing a flake of boiled salmon with his hunting knife. "Not his fault that he failed to be elected as my successor, you understand."

"I have decided not to remarry," Graunya said patiently. "Whether Richard in Iron were tanist or not would make no difference." She was looking down the length of the lighted hall, picking out the odd familiar face from among the crowds at the tables, from which a deafening babble of conversation arose. She was relieved to note that there was no sign of Richard in Iron. . . .

"He has the Castle of Carrigahowley now," the MacWilliam continued, "*and* Gweeshedan. Oh, yes; his father, God rest him, left a goodly inheritance to all the boys—"

"But Richard got dead Walter's share, even if he lost the succession?"

"Eh? Oh, yes, yes. Quite rightly too. One of his half-brothers is sand-blind and the other limps: a man needs all his faculties to defend his lands."

She knew that: and Finola had known it also. . . .

"But when the leader is a woman," the MacWilliam continued, laying a roguish hand over hers, "she needs all the strength she can muster."

"I am not the O Malley chieftain," she said. "My father is wise and competent, and will elect a new tanist in due course."

"But your younger brother – Donald the Piper?"

"He —" The scar on her forehead began to tighten.

"Look!" The MacWilliam drew a horseshoe, open end facing west, with the point of his knife on the white linen cloth. "Here is Clew Bay. And here" – he stabbed the knife between the open ends of the shoe – " is Clare Island, held by you. To your north, in Achill, lies the territory of your maternal uncle, Red Thighe O Malley; to your south, Inishbofin, defended by your dead brother's growing sons. Now, move in along the south shore of the bay: Roonah" – another stab of the knife – "held by Melachlin O Malley, your father's brother. Around Murrisk, armed O Malley settlements. East of there, the Castle of Belclare, from which a track runs south, to Moher Lake behind Croagh Patrick, where your family has a strong *crannog* as a last line of retreat. . . . A magnificent chain of defence, you say, reinforced by three fleets of ships! But what happens after we pass Belclare? To east and north, your clan is undefended except by your irresponsible brother in Cahirnamart. You have no friend between that crumbling fortress and" – the knife circled to Achill again – "the lands of your uncle, Red Thighe."

"So?"

"So you need allies *here*" – the point of the blade pricked the north-eastern extremity of Clew Bay – "in Carrigahowley; and *here*" – it moved north-west – "in Corraun. I need hardly remind you that Richard in Iron holds Carrigahowley!"

"And that I ought to marry him for the sake of his fortress?" She was laughing heartily. "What about Corraun in this dynastic plan?"

"I was coming to that." The MacWilliam was in deadly earnest now. "The Corraun peninsula has just passed to a kinsman of mine, another Richard —"

"*Deamhain a' Chorraun?*" The nickname had stuck in her mind because it amused her: 'The Devil of the Reaping Hook'.

"Yes, I have heard of him. Not a man with whom it would be wise to quarrel, by all accounts."

"That is so. But you have never met him?"

"No."

"There he is down below us, at the head of the second trestle."

The Lord of Corraun, as though he could have heard the words over the clamour of conversation and music, looked up just as Graunya's eyes singled him out. For a long moment, they stared at each other without aggression or self-consciousness – the measuring stare of two alert people – then the MacWilliam whispered in Graunya's ear:

"Well? How about the Devil's Hook for your daughter?"

"My *daughter*?" She was startled. No one had ever broached the subject of a husband for Moira before.

"Certainly. An excellent match. We will discuss it further very soon. With him to the north of you as son-in-law, and a fine harbour for your ships in Carrigahowley —"

"That will do," she said with finality. "No doubt my daughter will marry in due course. But I will not. Why should it interest you in any case?"

"Because Bourke territory lies between the Umalls of O Malley and the rest of the country. It is to Bourke advantage that O Malley should be strong when the testing time comes. I think it is not far off."

"What form will it take?" She was thinking of Ulster. . . .

The MacWilliam shrugged.

"Who can know the mind," he asked, "of that valiant liar, Queen Elizabeth?"

Chapter 12

QUEEN ELIZABETH seldom attended a full meeting of her Council; instead, she favoured small private sessions, calling together only those men whose experience was relevant to the matter under discussion. With her principal secretary, the harassed Sir William Cecil, at her elbow, she was now giving her attention to the affairs of Ireland – a weak spot in her realm since recent troubles with France and Spain, either of whom might invade England through the western isle.

The Earl of Sussex, her viceroy in Ireland these past six years, was one of those present.

"What else could I do?" he excused himself. "I had less than nine hundred men! The rebel, Shane O Neill, can call up four to five thousand, and has cattle on the hoof to feed them."

He was asking to be relieved of his office, and the Queen was considering Sir Henry Sidney in place of him.

Sidney was a slender man with a dark, pointed beard after the 'Prince of Spain' fashion. Fastidious in dress, he tried to avoid the extravagances that were turning his fellow-country-men into the strangest-looking beings on earth – their enormous breeches stuffed with rags and bran; their necks stretched above linen frills stiffened with that new-fangled substance called starch! Sidney did not want to return to Ireland, where he had already spent one term: he found the climate too damp, and the nobility of the Pale out of touch with European culture. He wanted to remain in his Penshurst castle with the Lady Mary, his wife, and their young son, Philip. . . .

"You will leave in January," the Queen rapped, "and take a strong line against the traitor, Shane O Neill. He has made himself sovereign of Ulster by murder, rape and double-dealing. We can no longer tolerate such a state of affairs!" – and she cast a withering glance at the retiring Sussex.

"That is true, Your Grace," Sidney murmured.

"See to it then. . . . By the by, how fares Hugh of Dungannon, the Irish page in your household? What age is he now?"

"Almost sixteen, Your Grace, and unrecognizable as anything but a true English subject."

"He shows no Irish sympathies?"

"None whatever."

"Then it might be safe for him to travel with you next year. He must take up his title as soon as his murdering uncle is disposed of."

Sir Henry Sidney had a great affection for young Hugh O Neill, a page in his household these last seven years. He had snatched the youth from the wilds of Ulster, lest his fate become that of his father, the Baron of Dungannon, whom Shane O Neill had murdered. A pathetic little rascal horseboy the nine-year-old orphan had been when Sidney swung him on to his own saddle – his clothing ragged, his few possessions bundled into a sack, his foster parents too frightened of the Lord Chief Justice even to kiss their charge farewell. . . . But the white-lashed eyes shed no tears either then or later. There was a silence and a withdrawal about the lad which even his subsequent mastery of the English language did not break entirely. Sometimes, it worried Sir Henry; he found himself glancing covertly at his red-headed page, wondering how deep the process of anglicization had really gone – or was it merely a veneer that would crack and peel as soon as Hugh was brought back to Ireland? He was Baron of Dungannon now – Shane O Neill having murdered his eldest brother, Brian, also – and, some day, he would be Earl of Tyrone, if he remained faithful and obedient to the Queen.

For her part, Elizabeth was confident that this experiment of educating Irish nobles' children in England must be a success. She had high hopes that Hugh O Neill would subdue troublesome Ulster for her. With Sidney and Leicester as his patrons, the castles of Penshurst and Ludlow his background, rich men's houses in the city of London his wider experience, how could he be other than loyal?

She put the matter out of her mind and, turning to Thomas Butler, Earl of Ormonde, smiled. Rumour had it that Black Tom was her lover – that he had ousted Robert Dudley, Earl of Leicester, in her affections; and certainly there was some strange bond between Queen and Anglo-Irish subject. They were of the same age and related through the Queen's mother, Anne Boleyn; but their affection was more than cousinly. It had a deep, mysterious side, spiritual and telepathic, upon which no finger could be put as upon the passionate and scandalous alliance with Leicester. . . .

"What is your opinion, my lord," Elizabeth asked Black Tom now, "concerning the suggestion for the other Irish provinces – that a President be set up over Munster and Connacht?"

"I consider the idea a worthy one, Your Grace. A stern but tactful President, with a full Council acting under him, answerable to your Viceroy, should solve many problems."

"Good. In the case of your own southern province of Munster, then, we have decided that Sir John Perrot would serve us admirably."

Ormonde was pleased with the choice, Sidney delighted: John Perrot had enlivened the latter's boyhood days at the Court of Edward the Sixth, when his wit and humour had made even a dying King laugh. Red-headed Perrot was outrageous, impecunious, unconventional and widely popular; he never denied the story that he was a bastard son of Henry the Eighth. . . .

"And Connacht?" Ormonde prompted. "Inaccessible territory, but Galway is a fine port town."

Elizabeth busied herself with some papers. Then, as though she had forgotten the question – or never heard it – she talked to Cecil for a while.

"Your Grace," asked Sir Henry Sidney in a voice which demanded reply, "who is to be President of Connacht while I am in office?"

Elizabeth looked at him sharply. Her eyes were very pale,

and the faint pock marks on her fine white skin showed more clearly than usual. Sidney was too direct and masterful for her liking; she would cut his title down from Lord Lieutenant – which she had intended to bestow upon him – to Lord Deputy. And he would have to manage with the same number of troops as Sussex had done; she would spend no more. . . .

"We have appointed Sir Edward Fitton," she said in a voice like snapping sticks, and bent again over her papers.

For the first time since they had entered the apartment, Sidney and Ormonde looked at one another. They were not friends, these two, although there were many points of resemblance in their characters: leadership, diplomacy, a high intelligence. . . . But now they were united by a common consternation: Fitton was the last man either of them would have chosen to rule the Province of Connacht; ruthless and sadistic, he might be the stick that would stir a wasps' nest.

Elizabeth was watching them from under lowered lids. She waited until they opened their mouths to speak, perhaps to argue with her or query her royal decision; then she silenced them by rising to her feet, her gown huge in the sleeve and skirt, wasp-thin in the waist.

"The first thing to be done in Connacht," she said, in her harsh unfeminine voice, "is to break up the troublous clan system. This cannot be accomplished by affability – not in the case of these barbarous tribes which menace our city, in any event. For years, the Mayor and burghers of Galway have complained about the threats and depredations of the O Flahertys. Their chieftain, Dhonal Crone, is an old man, too feeble, apparently, to keep his people in order: therefore, our instructions to Sir Edward will be, to replace him by one who will be obedient to our wishes."

"It will go hard —" Ormonde began, but stopped himself. He understood the sacredness of the tribe in that country where he, himself, was an 'old stranger', a *shangoll*. But how could the old – grown more Irish than the Irish themselves – explain to the brash, new, insensitive invader? Or how could an ambitious man, sitting at the feet of an awesome mistress like Elizabeth Tudor, say to her, 'In Connacht, there is another woman whom they call "queen". . . . Treat her gently and she might become your good subject. Bully her, and you will push her into rebellion, backed by ships and men as loyal as your own; for this woman is beautiful, and of centuries-old lineage.'

Ormonde had known Graunuaile for nearly ten years. He had watched her fleet grow, from the time she had first carried a cargo of wine for him from the Levant. He had gone down to the harbour to sample it; had stayed to dine and gamble with her and some of her men. When she lost, she paid promptly; when she won, she did not crow; she was like no other woman he had ever known in all the years of his Court upbringing. When the others left, he tarried with her in the lamplit cabin, talking of Italian books, which she read with some difficulty but seemed to know well. . . .

He remembered her clear profile and her quick brown hands and the rustling scarlet silk of her petticoat which he would have liked to see crumpled on the boards. But she had said, with full awareness:

"No" – a little wistfully, he thought – "no. I do not allow my own men to touch me." And she had backed away from him, feeling for the door clasp.

"Do you not want any man?" His breath was harsh between his teeth.

"Did I say that?"

"You said that none might touch you."

"You forget who I am" – she drew herself upright until she seemed tall – "how extraordinary is my life; that I stand for ever accused of having sent my husband to his death. For me, one unguarded moment could be my last on earth. And to take another man might be to lose two hundred, for I hold them all in a kind of hopeful love-bondage. If you care anything for me, be on your way."

He did care. There were other women with whom to lay and then forget. This one was to remain in his mind. . . .

The Queen was speaking again. "We shall proceed with the plantation in Leinster which my royal sister failed to complete. And the carrying of wool to foreign ports by native Irish vessels must cease; it is interfering with our own trade. The merchants are complaining."

Ormonde knew that Graunya carried at least one wool cargo

abroad every year, some of it raw, the rest made up into rough mantles whose weaving employed a hundred poor women of Umall. These cabin dwellers had never known anything but grinding poverty before Graunuaile came to care for them; would she allow their livelihood to be snatched from them now, because fat and greedy merchants were petitioning the Queen? He thought not. He knew her well enough, and decided that she would take to illegal running with the same enthusiasm which she had displayed in ferrying his Protestant friends out of Bloody Mary's reach. The challenge of prohibition would be strong wine to her Viking blood.

For his own part, Ormonde wished her luck. If John Hawkins could do it with stolen slaves between West Africa and the Spanish Main, then this Irishwoman could carry the fleeces of her own flocks to whatever markets she chose. . . .

A messenger entered the Council chamber with a billet for My Lord Secretary. He fingered his long, smooth beard as he read it, then whispered in the Queen's ear. Without moving, her body seemed to grow tense and brittle. Her hand clenched over the leather notecase that had her personal device of the Crowned Falcon embossed upon it.

She relaxed with conscious effort and said, "The Queen of Scotland has given birth to a son."

Nobody made any comment. They knew what it meant to her, this confirmation of Mary Stuart's womanhood beside her own barrenness. It made no difference that Mary's consort was the vicious, effeminate Henry Darnley whose bed the Scottish Queen had not graced for many a month: this same yellow-haired Darnley who, in the spring, had murdered David Riccio with fifty-six knife wounds because he believed the Italian musician to be his Queen's lover.

Nothing mattered except Mary Stuart's arrogant claim to the English throne, should Elizabeth die childless: and now there was an heir to bolster that claim.

Elizabeth gathered her regal skirts about her, and withdrew from the meeting.

Ormonde was right about Graunuaile's reaction to the embargo on the wool trade. Within a week of the new order being issued throughout Connacht, she had assembled her captains and navigators around the notched table.

"We need a new course for Spain," she said. "Instead of hugging the Connemara coast, we must keep far out to sea, not bearing south-east until France lies on our port."

"That will be dangerous," O Flynn pointed out, and the O Dowd captains murmured agreement. "Apart from storms and the greater length of the voyage, we will be in pirate waters."

She straightened up and looked him full in the eyes, her own crinkling with amusement.

"Then we shall be in good company, my friend, being smugglers ourselves. . . ."

She knew that, for her, the days of courtesy at sea were over. To be caught while carrying prohibited goods was either to hang or drown unless one could fight one's way out. She had no cannon except the little guns of her father's *Naove* – nothing except the pikes and longbows of her crew, and a few muskets among the officers. A Frobisher or a Hawkins would demolish her entire fleet inside an hour – if he could catch it! Speed was her ally; that, and her almost sinister accord with the elements, which her own men reverenced as God-given. These things were ordnance enough for her until she could carry her first prohibited wool cargo abroad, and spend her profits on powder, shot and new guns.

Meanwhile, her hands were full of another project. She had been given a new site to defend, north of Clare Island, on the wild and mountainous Island of Achill: her mother's brother, Red Thighe, having died of old age, his territories there had been newly divided according to Brehon Law. The elders of the tribe had decided that no one was more capable of defending her rights than Graunuaile, therefore they allotted her that portion of land nearest to her existing domain – from Achillbeg to the awesome cliffs of Minaun that were fretted into caves and pillars by the shark-infested ocean.

At Kildavnet, backed by the tremendous hills, she began to raise her second fortress, an extension to Red Thighe's ancient castle. Her ships could be brought up the Sound to moor, safe and hidden, at its steps.

The view was magnificent. She felt like an eagle on her own battlements. North-westward, the mountains marched to Achill Head, where Croaghaun ended in a colossal cliff, sheer and overhanging, nearly two thousand feet high. South, lay her garrisoned fortress of Clare Island; south of that, Inishbofin, held by Cormac's sons; and, in between, her own son, Owen's, Inishturk.

From the south and west, then, this fortress of Kildavnet was impregnable. But eastward, across the narrow arm of the Sound, lay the Corraun peninsula; Bourke territory; land of the Devil's Hook. And the Celt in her blood distrusted the Norman in his, although these elements had pulsed together for more than two centuries. If it came to open warfare with the English, whose side would the Norman *shangoll* take? Elizabeth trusted them as her faithful subjects – made friends with some of them, like the Earl of Ormonde. But the Irish thought of them as natives, who spoke and ate and dressed as they did themselves. The final choice rested with the *shangoll*, and Graunya had no intention of being caught on the wrong side of that choice: she had to secure the Devil's Hook before it was made. . . .

On this clear September morning, when the air was thin and the heather deepening to purple, she invited Magnus O Lee to climb to the top of the new fortress tower with her. She liked to sound his opinion on any fresh undertaking without actually asking his advice; that would be pandering to masculine pride! Now she faced the low eastern sun, and heard the Seahorse banner fluttering above her head as she pointed north-eastward towards the lovely old Castle of Doona.

"If we had some of our men in there," she said softly to O Lee, "our approaches would be more secure." There was a little purring sound at the back of her throat.

He glanced at her sharply to see the magnificent dark-blue eyes unblinking as those of a hovering bird, and the mouth firmly outlined beneath the uncompromising straightness of her nose. He said,

"The Devil's Hook has men enough of his own to garrison Doona."

"I know that. Fine men with curved knives in their krisses! But he has no ships."

"You would give him some?" He was joking. . . .

"If he were my son-in-law."

He drew a deep breath so as not to answer her with the rage which he felt. After a moment, he managed to ask, "Can you ply no better trade than to barter your daughter for stones?"

"She could be worse mated. And mind your tongue, O Lee." The old spiked stakes of their antagonism were beginning to show once more; these two, who had shared so much, could never find an easy friendship together.

"I have minded my tongue for a length of years; let me unleash it now. You have made Clare Island your chariot with a leading rein to north and south of Clew Bay. You have exploited your advantage, even over your own father —"

"My father is, and always will be, Chief-of-All!"

"Why, then, did you prevail upon him to move out of the Castle of Belclare?"

"Because my fool brother, Donald the Piper, could not maintain Cahirnamart alone. It is better that the chieftain should hold that fortress."

"Although the river damp cripples his ageing muscles?"

"The O Malley is a strong man," she said obstinately, "and Cahirnamart needs him. He knew that himself or he would not have agreed to move after my mother's death. . . ." How easy it had been to persuade him, then, when the new-dug earth was piled above the Lady Margaret's coffin; how gladly had he left Belclare, that was full of memories, to the keeping of his brother, Melachlin, from Roonah.

"You always manage to justify your actions," O Lee growled. "Nothing is important now except to push your line of defences north, to close the ring of the bay as effectively as the mountains do."

"It is a good strategy. Why do you quarrel with me over it?"

"Because flesh and blood means nothing to you in the pursuit of your own ambitions. The next sacrifice is to be little fair-haired Moira to a murdering barbarian like Richard Corraun Bourke. . . ."

To his surprise, she began to laugh heartily.

"You have never met the Devil's Hook, have you, Magnus?

153

A most civilized man, I assure you, gay and dashing and brave!"

"Why do you not take him yourself?" An unreasonable jealousy stabbed at him.

"Because I am thirty-six years old, he twenty-five! Anyway, I have no wish to marry —"

"Neither has Moira. She wants to take the veil."

"A lunatic ambition in these times! I am saving her from the Queen's men."

He saw that there was nothing further to be gained by arguing with her. Whether she realized it or not, she had a fatal habit of imposing her own will upon others – always for the best reasons, from her point of view, but not necessarily from theirs.

'She is growing harder every day,' he thought as he descended the newly-cut steps and heard the workmen hammering and chiselling all around him. 'Now I see land-hunger in her eyes. This is only the beginning. . . .' And his heart sank with dismay, for he recognized that she was building a kingdom, as so many petty Irish leaders had tried to do before her, to the misery of their people and their own ultimate destruction by other petty leaders. He saw how she was closing all gaps against land invasion. Ever since news had reached her that Sir Henry Sidney was burning and preying in Ulster, in his pursuit of Shane O Neill, defence had become an obsession with Graunuaile, to the neglect of trade.

She had shouted at her father's ollavs in the meeting house, "Neither the Lord Deputy, nor any other Englishman, shall enter Umall except across my dead body!" Immediately after that, they had given her Kildavnet: fanatics were needed at the outposts!

Now, she wanted Doona. Later, it would be Carrigahowley, Richard in Iron's fortress. . . .

O Lee had no quarrel with Graunya's general policy. She was a clever, a dedicated and a courageous woman, as well fitted to rule as any man. She could lead, and she could command obedience, respect, sometimes awe. But there was a hard core of ruthlessness in her when dealing with people which disturbed him because it had no higher aim than mere tribal passion: a fierce determination to protect what was O Malley's as though the Two Umalls were a separate country from Bourke lands and O Conor's and O Flaherty's.

The physician felt in a groping twilight way – because his trade was healing and not raiding – that there must be a more spiritual concept somewhere, a wider interpretation of unity, as protection against the invader.

But he had not found it. All his life, he had been a seeker, critical and aloof from the rooting herd; and he had chosen to stand behind Graunuaile because he sensed that she was of the stuff of legend. Now, for the first time, he began to doubt his instinct concerning her – began to search the heavens for a new ideal. . . .

The Scottish settlers in Ulster finished Sir Henry Sidney's work for him: they murdered Shane O Neill in revenge for old injuries. . . . Sidney led his soldiers back to Dublin and stuck the rebel's head on a spike over the gates; even in death, pride and self-indulgence remained stamped on the wolfish countenance of this leader who had sought only his own power.

Down among the crowd of Sidney's men stood the young Baron of Dungannon, Hugh O Neill, staring with white-lashed eyes at his uncle's severed head. And an echo of Shane's mocking words came back to him from the swirling river.

'I care not to be an Earl unless I be greater and higher than such an English title. My ancestors were Kings of Ulster: and Ulster is mine, and *shall* be mine!'

Hugh of Dungannon considered the words too noble for the murderer who had spoken them. All evening, while he gamed and dined in Dublin Castle, he could not get them out of his mind.

'My ancestors were Kings of Ulster. . . .' That was true of himself also, even though his father had not been born in wedlock; but illegitimacy meant little in an Irish tribe where the firstborn did not necessarily inherit. If the chieftain liked his bastards, they grew up with his other sons.

'Ulster is mine —' No; only Dungannon, a very small part of that vast province. Farther north, there was a new chieftain called Turlough O Neill whom the people preferred to this English-reared and half-forgotten son of murdered Matthew.

'— and *shall* be mine!' That was in the lap of the gods, or of Queen Elizabeth. If young Hugh behaved himself, he might be given the Earldom which his uncle, Shane, had so despised. Hugh's mind was trained to think along English lines: to prefer an investiture at the Queen's hand to an inauguration at the Sacred Stone of Tullahoge with all its attendant ritual of white rod and golden sandal and the tribesmen standing shoulder to shoulder as bodyguard for the O Neill.

Now Sir Henry Sidney had time to deal with Connacht, that quiet and obscure western province which had already waited three years for its President to take up office.

Sidney could delay the arrival of Sir Edward Fitton no longer. Together, the pair rode into Galway attended by an impressive retinue.

"Do not rush things here," the Lord Deputy advised Fitton. "It is a slow country – very old, proud, suspicious. If you would coax it to your hand, make no sudden violent movement."

Fitton's was a rigid mind moulded during the reign of Edward the Sixth, when idol-wrecking was a hobby. He was in a frenzy to begin his work. No sooner had the gates clanged shut behind the Lord Deputy than he ordered his men into the Church of St Nicholas, there to destroy every ornament and image which might still carry a breath of Popery from Queen Mary's reign.

From St Nicholas's, they rode outside the walls and ranged through the wilderness of Iar-Connacht, tearing down shrines, burning any building which even looked like a church or oratory. They were too ignorant of conditions to feel any fear. . . .

In his saddlebag, the new President carried a document signed by his Queen, and written in careful Latin so that even the Irish might be able to read and understand its content.

'*Non est sufficiens nec idoneus ad officium illud exercendum* . . .'

This was the patent dismissing Dhonal Crone from office as Chief of All the O Flahertys, and setting up in his stead – against all tribal custom – a member of the non-ruling branch of the family, Murrough *na Thuaigh*, 'of the Battleaxes'. . . .

Fitton returned to Galway in an even greater hurry than he had left it. Out of rocks, bushes – and castles which he had not known existed – the entire O Flaherty clan had arisen with a bloodcurdling yell. The thunder of their united onslaught shook Galway city while the new President panted inside the walls.

A large part of quiet, obscure Connacht was in furious rebellion. . . .

Chapter 13

THE dungeons beneath Shoemakers' Tower in Galway city were full of priests and Connacht rebels, crammed twenty or thirty to a dark, rat-infested cell by order of the Lord President. He had broken the power of the O Flahertys by making them quarrel among themselves, some siding with the old chief, Dhonal Crone, others with the new one appointed by Elizabeth: it was always easy to divert the Irish by creating internal strife founded on feuds and jealousies. . . .

There was only one captive who was confined alone, and this was not in deference to her womanhood but in recognition of the amount of trouble she could cause: during the twenty-four hours since Graunuaile had been brought in, she had shouted and cursed for the first twelve, then lapsed into a silence so ominous that her jailer had ventured inside the grilled door, only to have his neck almost broken in the grip of small hard hands which knew where to press.

A companion rescued him and, together, they decided to put her in irons as soon as they had refreshed themselves with a mug of beer.

Meanwhile she sat, cocooned in her frieze cloak, crosslegged on the earth floor, her blue-black eyes as expressionless as those of a tethered animal which, through sheer exhaustion, has ceased to kick. Confinement was a discipline entirely horrible to her. Thinking about the locked smallness of this space, and the foulness of the air, she began to have difficulty in breathing. It was a distress which she had never been able to overcome, this terror of being forcibly restrained from free movement in the open air.

"Oh, God," she prayed – although prayer was an infrequent exercise to her – "send me freedom at any price!"

It came with miraculous speed: the grating of a key – the door flung open – a voice shouting,

"You! Come on out and no capers."

The English words were unintelligible to her but she recognized a direct command and immediately resented it. She stood up slowly, rearranged her mantle and then refused to move farther. The two exasperated jailers had to carry her out.

"Blood of Christ," one said, "there's no pleasing some people!"

"What do we do with her?" asked the other, who still had her in his arms and was surprised at how so light and small a woman could have caused such uproar earlier.

"She's *their* responsibility now" – jerking a thumb at six blue-clad members of the 'Young Men' militia – "let us be rid of her. Put her down before she claws your eyes."

The half-dozen guards were clattering up and down the rush-lit passage while their captain signed a paper for the jailer.

"What did you say her name was?" the captain asked.

"Graunya O Malley –"

She folded her arms and laughed out loud.

"*Graunuaile*," she shouted, so that all the occupants of the other cells might hear.

"Be quiet, woman, or I'll have you gagged." The captain signed to the six guards to close in around her, and one tied her hands behind her back with a biting cord. Panic hammered again in her throat at this new restriction.

'They're taking me to the gallows,' she thought, 'out near the Hospice of the Templars —'

"March!"

Automatically, she fell into step as though this were some pleasant land journey with her own men. She put her heels down firmly. The captain looked sidelong at her.

"You march like a man," he said in Irish.

"I am a leader of men," she replied without turning her head. The dungeons on either side were full of O Flahertys and their lieges, watching her through the open grilles. She would give them her straight back as an abiding memory.

The guards hustled her to the top of a long flight of steps. If they turned north now, it was the road to the gallows. . . .

They turned south-west, towards the city streets. The moon was rising.

"Where are we going?" she demanded of the captain. He was young and darkly handsome in his pale-blue pourpoint. She had heard the jailer call him Captain Martin.

"To the President's house."

"For a trial?"

Martin laughed pleasantly.

"Mere Irish are not accorded trials unless the Lord Deputy be present. You attacked a Galway merchant ship: you know the penalty."

"I did *not* attack her. I defended my carrack from being rammed by her."

"Your defence, madam, was a good deal too spirited. You chased her with blazing guns and every kind of weapon for seven miles, cutting yourself off from your own fleet in the process!"

She stared at the rhythmic heels of the man in front and said nothing. It had been a bad business, an unpardonable error on her part. She should have let the merchantman go. But the *Regina* was rearing like a wild horse, and all the men were shouting, drowning the cautious warning of her innermost mind. She felt intoxicated. Nothing had mattered except the chase – the splendid, glorious sea-chase with the wind screaming and the tall *Regina* slicing the crisp water —

Then three armed pinnaces had come skimming the Galway Roads, cutting her off from the following guns of the *Maeve* and the *Moytura*. The quarry turned and showed her teeth: she had been a decoy. Two more ships began to move in from the Aran Islands. The *Regina* was surrounded. Her supporting galleys could not reach her. Rather than wait for them, or the barque, or the old *Moytura* to advance to their certain deaths, she had lowered the Seahorse pennant and run up a white flag.

It was then that the men had taken matters into their own

hands and she had not been able to control them. Instead of submitting, they fought —

Seven MacNallys were dead and three Conroys; the *Regina* impounded, badly damaged; the rest of the crew – most of them wounded – prisoners on board. Graunya was the only one to be taken ashore. . . .

Now she and her guards were marching through a district of prosperous houses, but the dark streets were empty except for soldiers on patrol. Since Fitton had come, Galway was a changed town, grim and close-walled, every Irish contact forbidden and even foreign ones scrutinized suspiciously. Some of the old inhabitants had crept away, preferring the dangerous freedom outside to the guarded tension within. There was a rumour that Galway's trade was beginning to suffer; that the merchants were not quite so proud nor the warehouses quite so full. . . .

Inside Sir Edward Fitton's brightly lit residence, there was music and dancing and the rattle of dice.

The Lord President sat picking his yellow teeth. He was a black-haired, round-headed man, his unwieldy body covered in a suit of dark-red velvet 'drawn out' in grey silk and lavishly gold-braided. His starched ruff gaped open at the front of his thin neck. Although an unattractive man physically, a dozen girls and women hung about him, laughing, trying to flirt with him. These were wives and daughters of the Fourteen Families of Galway whose menfolk were Lynch mayors and Bodkin burghers, all guests tonight of their Lord President, their accents betraying long contact with the Irish whom they despised.

Watching them archly was a little Mistress Jane Smyth, who had made the precarious sea-voyage from the Pale with her father, Chief Apothecary of Dublin Castle. Jane did not know that her parent was nicknamed 'Bottle Smyth' and that his reputation was for successful poisoning rather than curing. . . .

"Now, Mistress Jane," the Lord President said to her, "how can we entertain you, eh?"

She tapped a cork-soled shoe impatiently.

"I am still waiting, my Lord," she replied, "to see your prize prisoner. I shall not believe that you have caught her until then."

Fitton put his toothpick in his waistcoat pocket and walked over to the window.

"She should be here any minute," he said.

The moon was up, making a grey mist of lawn and trees, with the sea barely breathing beyond the cannon-bristling walls. Now that the first panic was over, Fitton felt safe in Galway. Those rebels not already under lock and key, he would mow down with muskets; he would burn every blade of grass in Connacht to starve them; he would blockade the coast with Government ships. . . . Or – a much cheaper way, which would thereby commend itself to Her Majesty – he would incite them still further to cut each other's throats by creating more new chieftains, re-dividing lands, setting brother against brother. The execution of Graunuaile would provide a good starting-point: her clan was already in some confusion because it had no tanist, and its chieftain was ailing; remove this woman from command of the ships and there would be chaos —

Jane Smyth's little pointed face was looking up at Fitton.

"Are you going to hang Graunuaile?" she inquired, bright-eyed.

"Certainly, my dear. She is a smuggler and a pirate."

"I have never seen a *woman* hanged. . . ."

"You will, tomorrow morning." He could hear gates clanging at the rear of the house, then feet marching over the cobbles of the kitchen yard. "Here she is now. . . ."

The President's guests crowded around – mayor and merchant, burgher and bailiff with their swarms of womenfolk; a few new English clerks, uncomfortable in their pease-cod doublets – to stare at the wild woman of whom they had heard so much, and none of that good.

"Well, well, not very big, is she? I had expected a giantess!"

"Don't go too near; she seems as though she might bite. . . ."

"What extraordinary clothing – those tight breeches – and her jacket looks like Spanish leather, upon my word!"

"Perhaps you might have it if you get near enough to the scaffold —"

Graunya was still squinting against the sudden light. She

heard the tittering of the women above loud masculine guffaws but her ears were strained for another sound, a repetition of one she had heard outside: the call of a curlew. Here was one sea-bird that would never venture inside a city garden; she knew that, but her captors did not. . . .

The Lord President beckoned to the Irish-speaking Captain Martin.

"Tell her we wish to be entertained," he said. "Loose her hands and let her dance for us."

Amused, they all watched while the message was translated to her. She said something low and fierce, then looked around intently at the crowding faces, her eye raking the Lord President's, committing it to memory and, after that, the pointed countenance of little Mistress Smyth.

From directly under the window, the curlew called again. She knew what she must do. . . .

"Tell them," she said to William Martin, "that I will dance the male part in a Galician *jota*, if the smallest woman present will partner me. And I require the curtains to be opened; it is too hot in here."

Mistress Smyth was delighted at being singled out for attention; to have danced with a woman sea-rover who was hanged next morning would be a considerable social asset.

Servants hurried to draw back the heavy brocades on their jangling brass rings. Musicians struck up an urgent throbbing tune with a fast drumbeat. . . .

Graunya looped her mantle around her right wrist, lifted her head high and swung her arms above it to represent the 'bull's horns' of the dance. Her body – backward leaning from the waist – was taut and slender, the hips flat. She snapped her fingers at Mistress Smyth —

"*Jota–a–a!*"

– And manœuvred her nearer the small-paned window, trying to judge her weight by eye alone.

Together, they spun into the gay mountain rhythm of northern Spain, faster and more violent with every beat. The onlookers stamped and shouted. There was a blur of flying petticoats, and a frieze mantle whirling like a gigantic bat. Without warning, the mantle enveloped Mistress Smyth from head to foot and Graunya's arms locked around her small body, spun, and threw her. . . .

Glass shattered. The prisoner dived through the neat hole in the mullioned window.

When the guards reached the lawn by a more orthodox route, all they found was Mistress Jane Smyth having hysterics inside a frieze mantle.

A coil of rope with a grappling iron at one end was thrust into Graunya's arms as she lay, gasping, in a tangled hedge.

"Over the wall," urged the voice of her son-in-law, Richard Corraun. "Make for the harbour. A galley is waiting."

Like two black bats, they streaked away, running, climbing, dropping down into nameless alleys, flattening themselves in shadowed places as the sentries marched past. The harbour walls were the highest and smoothest, needing three agonizing throws of the ropes before the hooks caught. . . .

Then the freedom of the sea opened up before them and they were racing westward in a long galley with ten men of Corraun at the oars.

"How did you know where to wait for me?" Graunya demanded of her son-in-law.

Richard Corraun, alias the Devil's Hook, put his own cloak around her, grinned whitely in the moonlight and replied, "Madam, my lady mother was a witch; she left me her second sight!"

Graunya made a playful swipe at his head, although she was half inclined to believe – and not for the first time – that there was something supernatural about him. Indeed, in this weird light, his ears looked strangely pointed under his crisp, dark hair and, even for a Norman, he had an uncommonly long nose and chin. Then, remembering that her daughter's time was due, she asked soberly, "Is Moira well?"

"Very well. I saw my new-born son before I left."

"She – she has a son?" The news filled her with an emotion which she had never felt at the births of her other grandchildren: an excited tenderness mixed with a kind of contentment for the future that was almost a belief in her own immortality.

The Devil's Hook was still grinning at her.

"Why do you suppose I rescued you from the hangman? To enliven the christening feast with your new dance, of course! I must have a few windows glazed at Doona so as not to spoil the climax. . . ."

Together, they went into fits of suppressed laughter.

Graunya's relationship with her son-in-law was one of the happiest she had ever formed with any man, but it was impossible to be serious with the Devil's Hook, however grave the issue. In the end, she always went back to Magnus O Lee to talk things over. . . .

"I'll wager my best brood mare," she said now, "that even O Lee has to laugh when we tell him. Will you bet that he only smiles?"

To her surprise – for he was as avid a gambler as she was – Richard Corraun did not bang a fist into a palm and shout, '*Done!*' Instead, he half turned his head and said, so quietly that the beat of the oars almost obscured his words, "O Lee has gone away."

"Indeed? To where? When will he return?"

"I think he will not return, Graunya. He took the Book of O Brasil with him."

She said nothing for a long time, and her body shrank inside the big cloak. All the exuberance of the escape went out of her. O Lee was her most trusted man, dearer to her – in spite of all their arguments and fighting words – than she would ever admit.

But, if he had taken the Book of O Brasil with him, then he was not coming back.

"Oh, Corraun," she cried, holding out her hands to her son-in-law, "*why* did he go? What did I do to him that he should desert me after all these years?" There was a sob in her voice but she would not weep within sight of the oarsmen.

The Devil's Hook sat close to her on the rowing bench.

"Listen," he said urgently, serious for once. "O Lee's services belong to the O Flahertys. I think he has gone back to Iar-Connacht because his own people need him. The rebellion there is only beginning —"

"What do you mean? It is over. Fitton has won."

"If Fitton thinks that, he is a fool. The first attack on Galway city was a wild, unplanned affair which, naturally, failed. Submissions followed it — but submissions, mark you, without hostages! Would you believe a promise, made under duress by one of your own people, without pledges?"

The truth was bitter to her but she had to face it.

"Our own people," she said, "will promise whatever is most convenient at the time, or whatever suits their emotions!" She had never felt more foreign from them; her own word was her bond.

"That applies equally to the English, it seems. Fitton swore to leave unmolested anyone who aided him against the O Flahertys. He got Clanrickarde that way, and Thomond; now he is raiding *their* lands, and throwing down their churches. Graunya, will you not see? The rebellion is spreading south to Thomond, and north to our own doors because Clanrickarde is our kinsman; if even his sons rise, the Mayo Bourkes will aid them."

"Then O Lee should have stayed where he was," she said obstinately, "for, if the Bourkes come out, the O Malleys are in rebellion too, being their lieges."

"If and when that happens, maybe he will return."

"He'll return in his own good time, blast him," she shouted, suddenly furious, "and maybe I'll be dead by then!"

The Saint Nicholas medallion around her neck danced with rage in the moonlight. Death — old age — loneliness. . . . All the things she abhorred. Her children gone their own ways — perhaps she should have remarried!

Her son-in-law read her mind accurately.

"Why do you not take my kinsman, Richard-in-Iron, for your own protection and companionship?" he asked quietly.

She thought for a long moment.

"Because, whenever he comes to my mind, I see not the man but his possessions: the castles of Carrigahowley and Gweeshedan; the great stretch of coast linking your lands with Cahirnamart. I see the greedy inward curve of my own fingers, and the dead face of Walter the Tall."

Alone and on foot, Magnus O Lee travelled southward into

Iar-Connacht, his hessian bag tied to his back with crossed cords. It was autumn but there was no sign of harvest, only of recent burnings: everywhere that he remembered cornfields and villages, he now saw black ugly scars on the face of the countryside, though whether inflicted by the enemy or by the people themselves in some private dispute, he could not judge. There were sheep, seeming no bigger than daisies, high up in the mountains, but no cattle, so he decided that these had been taken out to the islands – a sure sign of uneasy, distrustful times, of raiding and counter-raiding. He knew his way well enough to keep clear of the tracks and saw hardly a living soul. The big red deer, that used to graze with the cattle, had the slopes all to themselves, unharassed by *bodhagh* or churl.

Once, he stumbled on a pile of branches and a woman screamed; stooping to reassure her, he found her suckling twin infants. Her only garment was a tattered cloak.

"Where are your menfolk?" he asked her.

"Dead." She appeared not to care.

"How?"

"A war called Shrule."

A war: a battle. He had heard from a shepherd about some kind of clash near Shrule, between Fitton's troops and some of the Bourke clan, but he had no details of it.

He gave the woman a bird he had killed, knowing that her own days and those of her infants were strictly numbered; winter would kill all three. It was the peasants who suffered, whatever the war. In the old days, the monasteries would have cared for them; now priests and monks were in even worse case than peasants, living in caves and caverns. . . .

He moved on. At the far end of a birch wood was a small burnt-out church, a ragged paper nailed to its door. The paper bore a Latin translation of one of the Queen's memos to her Lord President in Connacht.

'. . . and whereas we understand that divers houses freight with friars remain in some parts of Connacht unsuppressed – compel them to abandon these places – which same houses may be used for the habitation of such Englishmen as we mean shall have estates there. . . .'

O Lee smiled with one side of his mouth.

"I wish such Englishmen joy," he said, "of roofless homes and blackened acres and wood-kerne circling them in the winter nights!"

Late that evening, he reached his destination, the Castle of Aughnanure, and found it double-guarded and unwilling to admit him until he showed the Book of O Brasil. This fortress, housing the lawful chief of the O Flahertys, was too near Galway city to be casual in its defences.

But, within the lighted keep, there was no sign of unease. The tables were spread, the various members of the great household in their accustomed places around their lord, Dhonal Crone. He sat with his back to the tapestry which bore his ancient arms above the motto 'Fortuna Favet Fortibus', while his musicians played on their eight-stringed harps and his ollavs talked and his feast-master directed the bringing in of covered dishes.

"So you have come back," was his sharp greeting to O Lee. "Why?"

"To acknowledge you as my lawful chieftain above the head of the usurper, Murrough of the Battle Axes."

"We do not speak the name of the Queen's O Flaherty."

"I withdraw it." O Lee spat in approved fashion.

"Well, sit down, sit down. Your father's chair has waited for you long enough."

O Lee had a curious sense of continuity as he faced the crowded hall from his dead father's place. The past was reaching out and gripping him; he could not fool himself that he had come back of his own free will: there had been ancestral compulsion. . . . He was one link in a chain of unvarying design stretching back into the mists of the Beginning. How many O Lees had sat in this chair at the chieftain's left elbow? How many more would do so? . . .

None at all, if the Lord President of Connacht had his way. At that moment his troops were less than three miles from the castle, sweating and straining to bring a cannon within range of its walls before daylight. And, guiding them over the difficult approaches, was the Queen's O Flaherty, Murrough of the Battle Axes, and his liegemen. Fitton had promised Aughnanure to this upstart if he would help dislodge the old chieftain.

In the quiet hour before dawn, the cannon pointed a finger of doom at the outer walls.

Graunya lay sleepless inside her new fortress of Kildavnet. She could hear the lap of water down below the steps and, away in the mountains, wolves crying under the big stars of an autumn sky.

Restless, she got up, dressed, and looked out to see that the sentries were in their places. Clew Bay was moon-coloured within its ring of black hills. The ships lay in their own dim reflections beside the empty mooring of the lost *Regina*. That ship, and the men who had died in her and those still held prisoner, léft a bleak space in her heart, made even colder by O Lee's apparent desertion. An unfamiliar kind of fear gripped her; not a physical thing which had climax and ending – that she understood – but a low-toned, monotonous apprehension, feeding on doubt, anger and helplessness which slowly sapped her confidence. . . .

Around the tip of Achillbeg, a curragh came gliding towards the Sound. She felt, rather than heard, the beat of its oars and was waiting for it on the dark steps before even the sentries were aware of its approach.

The oarsman was one of her many spies sent into Iar-Connacht to keep her informed of what occurred there.

"Graunuaile, there is bad news – the Castle of Aughnanure has fallen."

Her impulse was to shake him by the shoulders and tell him that he must be mistaken: Aughnanure was impregnable. Instead, she put her hands behind her back in familiar pose, and asked quietly, "Where is Dhonal Crone?"

"Fled to the mountains with a few attendants."

"Was O Lee with him?" Hope surged briefly.

"I could not find out. Fitton is tearing the territory to pieces and moving north. Many of the household were killed —"

Many killed. . . . Yes, that would be O Lee's way of going; it would never occur to him to save himself if anyone needed his assistance! Suddenly, she felt weak and empty. It was an effort to drag her mind to other matters.

"What news of my sons?"

"Owen O Flaherty took his household out to Inishturk with a great herd of cattle, then returned to fortify Ballinahinch; he is there now, aided by Thighe the Furious. Your other son, Murrough, is in Castle Kirke, in the path of Fitton's advance —"

"— With his wife and children?" Her heart turned over sickeningly.

"No. They are coming to you for protection. I saw them safely out of Killary — the Lady Onora, her five sons and about twelve attendants, men and women."

"So many — coming here?"

"More, besides those few from Castle Kirke."

"I see." She began to pace up and down the jetty. Everything had fallen upon her at once and her mind was in a state of confusion; she did not know how to support those new arrivals for the winter when, owing to the loss of the *Regina*, her biggest ship, foreign trade was at a standstill almost. She had never been so impoverished, either in goods or in men.

After several miles of pacing, she stopped suddenly, nodded her head and seemed to have reached some conclusion. She went into the guardroom, where the men were sleeping on the floor under their mantles, and awoke five of them.

"Take messages at once to Clare Island — Inishbofin — Cahirnamart — and Doona. Tell the households that Aughnanure has fallen and that Black Fitton is marching north. They must prepare to defend themselves."

The fifth man stood irresolute, not having been given a destination.

"You are for Carrigahowley," she told him, when the rest were outside. "Repeat the same message to the Lord Richard-in-Iron Bourke, but tell him further that Graunuaile is on her way to talk to him. That is all."

Not once, during the many years of his attempted courtship of her, had she approached Richard-in-Iron. Now she had to know what he intended to do: whether to join the Queen's forces or throw in his lot with the Irish. In her opinion, all the old Normans were fence-sitters until somebody pushed them off on to one side or the other. The Queen depended on their loyalty to England, the land of their ancestors. The Irish — their adopted people – expected their aid in any dispute with the Queen's Government. But religion was becoming the deciding factor. The Normans were Catholics. . . .

Graunya decided that a man as powerful as Richard-in-Iron needed a correspondingly powerful push to ensure that he fell on her family's side of the fence.

Quite dispassionately, she made up her mind to marry him.

Chapter 14

ACROSS the courtyard of Carrigahowley Castle, two bands of armed men faced each other in the September twilight. Only the vigilance of their mounted captains kept them from each other's throats. Those guarding the keep were Clandonnell Scots, mail-vested, bare-legged, contemptuous in their professional military pride of the long-haired Irish rabble around the outer gates.

Graunuaile's escort continued to eye the mercenaries whose presence in their territory they resented. These Scots came in as paid soldiers of the old Normans – the *shangoll* – married Irish wives and amassed wealth and land. If their wages were not paid promptly, they ravaged the countryside. The Bourkes employed large troops of them in Mayo and Galway, and the Lord Richard in Iron's bodyguard alone numbered nearly five hundred gallowglasses.

It was growing late. All the men were hungry, and bored from standing around these four hours. . . .

"How long more, do you think?" one of the Clandonnells muttered to a companion, who shrugged and replied:

"It could take all night. They say this Graunuaile drives a hard bargain, whether for fish, wool or marriage!"

"You believe the Lord Richard'll take her?"

"Aye. Now that he has been elected tanist, he takes what he wants, poor fellow, and never thinks of the price." The Scot looked around at his armed compatriots and laughed; wages were high among the Clandonnells and Richard-in-Iron always paid. The alternative was desertion and stolen cattle.

The other nodded towards the restless Irish, who were now pacing about like fenced wolves.

"Well, if he imagines we're going to share quarters with that pack —" he began, but was interrupted by the ringing of the Angelus bell from near-by Burrishoole.

For a moment, Scots and Irish prayed together while, within the keep, a Dominican priest arose from the council table to lead the Salutation.

"The Angel of the Lord declared unto Mary . . ."

Graunya stood with her head bowed as the age-old words washed over her. She had won the long day's battle. The marriage terms were entirely in her favour: free access for her men to the castles of Carrigahowley and Gweeshedan; anchorage for her ships alongside Richard-in-Iron's own fleet; the command of that fleet for one trading voyage every year. . . .

A clerk was writing the last words of the contract, watched by Shane MacHubert, the Bourke lawyer.

"Remain only your signature and the Lord Richard's, my lady," MacHubert said.

She sat down slowly, took the quill from him and glanced around the table at her own councillors: seven captains and commanders drawn from Clare Island and Kildavnet; the old poet, O Dugan, representing her father, who was now too crippled to travel far; her uncle Melachlin's brehon and two ollavs from her nephews' households on Inishbofin. She was well represented, well advised and argued for, but not one of these men understood her true position as O Lee would have done. O Lee would have fought against this marriage with every weapon of wisdom and contempt at his command: to him, it would have been a prostitution. Graunya knew that, even while her other councillors were nodding at her and at the dripping quill in her hand.

She looked down the length of the table to where Richard-in-Iron sat waiting, arms folded across broad steel-ringed chest (some people said that he slept in his armour!) and, behind him, she saw the faces of his bastard sons and all their eyes were fixed upon her, blue-green as Finola's had been.

"I require one more clause in the contract," she said.

Richard-in-Iron leapt to his feet and brought his fist down hard on the table. His size and strength were intimidating. . . .

"What is it now?" he roared, continuing to beat clenched fist on wood.

She waited, tight-lipped, for the din to subside, never taking her eyes off his dark, bearded face. She willed him to be quiet, to submit to her.

His tantrum died suddenly. He sat down, muttering, "What more is it you want?"

"For you to put all your other women away."

"*What?*" He was on his feet again, pushing around the crowded table towards her. . . .

"I will not tolerate them," she said with finality. "Your sons are welcome, but not their mothers."

There was a tense silence. Even Graunya's own councillors were shocked by her final demand. It was every lord's right to have women apart from his wife if he wanted them and could afford them.

Richard Bourke was leaning forward on his clenched fists, breathing hard and staring at her with hot eyes. Ever since that day in the church at Murrisk, he had coveted her. Because of her, he had no lawful wife. Now he was over fifty years old, elected tanist at last to the MacWilliam title, wealthy, powerful. . . . His last ambition was to take this woman, who so obsessed him that, beside her, the desirability of all others palled.

"Let them go," he said, shrugging. "I agree." Then, with another burst of defiance, "*But for one year only* . . ."

Graunya smoothed the skirt of her dark travelling dress.

"Then the marriage is also for a twelvemonth," she said; and the Dominican priest cried out sharply:

"This is a perversion of the Sacrament —"

But she rounded on him, shouting, "Not so! We are merely agreeing in advance to what is often done afterwards. Many lords divorce their wives – put them away without reason and take others. Clanrickarde has done it, and Thomond and the O Neills! May not a wife have equal freedom? And, furthermore, a year is long enough for a man and a woman to get a child; is not that the primary purpose of marriage?"

"Yes, but —"

"Very well. The terms of the agreement need not concern any consciences except mine and the Lord Richard's. It may be that we will live the rest of our lives together but, if we do not wish to do so, either of us may dismiss the other after a twelvemonth."

It was the loophole she had sought all day. To be bound for life was too high a price even for ships and castles and wealth; but, given the use of these things until the following autumn, she was confident that the advantage would be hers.

She raised an eyebrow at Richard and he showed white teeth in a bearded smile. The clause had his wholehearted approval. He motioned briskly to the clerk to insert it above his own signature, just made, '*Risteard in Iarainn de Bourca, tanist an MacWilliam. . . .*'

MacHubert handed the document to Graunya, indicating that she should sign underneath Richard Bourke's name, but she ignored this and wrote firmly beside and a little above it, in angular Gaelic script, '*Grainne Ui Maille*'.

The Dominican asked coldly, "When is this ceremony to be performed?" And, shaking sand over the ink, she replied, "When all the terms of contract have been carried out: my men quartered here and in Gweeshedan; my Seahorse pennant flying above the Lord Richard's fleet for the autumn trading voyage. . . ."

The smile died from Richard's lips.

"You are going to sea *before* our marriage?"

"If I delay any longer," she said reasonably, "it will be too late in the year to avoid storms and heavy seas."

"But surely you could wait until the spring?"

"I could. But will Black Fitton hold back his advance to accommodate us? Do we not need powder and lead and more new weapons? Have you all forgotten the situation not twenty miles south of here?"

Sheepishly, they dragged themselves back to reality, and agreed that she should take command of the entire fleet from the following morning.

Inside Dublin Castle, a frowning Sir Henry Sidney was

reading his western dispatches, delayed for weeks by muddy winter roads. He was appalled at the picture that was emerging from each successive dispatch.

"This man Fitton," he burst out at last, "has done more damage in Connacht than an army of infidels! Listen to this"– he spun around to face the Archbishop of Dublin, a leading member of the Council, who was hovering at his elbow – "listen to the wailing of our Lord President!"

He read aloud:

"The province is now entirely out of our control. Everywhere the barbarous clans have arisen against us so that we leave Galway city at peril to our lives. We cannot trust them nor depend upon them, so tangled are their loyalties through intermarriage and fosterage. They fly into a frenzy when we throw down their churches, and yet they are the most irreligious people on earth – robbers, murderers, adulterers. I beg of you, my Lord Deputy, to send reinforcements and food to Her Majesty's troops here for they are starving, the last supply ship having been robbed by a sea-clan named O Malley, led by a truly ferocious woman."

On that final word, the Lord Deputy choked, and handed the papers over to the Archbishop.

Archbishop Adam Loftus was a big smooth man who changed his religion to suit each successive reign: for the time being, he was a Protestant.

"Hmmm," he grunted after careful reading. "Well, it seems obvious that President Fitton must be removed from office when women begin to frighten him!"

Sidney regained his self-control by stroking his dark pointed beard with fine hands.

"Yes," he said then. "Removed, but not replaced."

"You cannot leave the province ungoverned —"

"By no means. But neither can I create another President. Thanks to Fitton's incompetence, the title of that office is now without honour."

He beckoned to his secretary.

"I wish you to draw up a draft of a letter to Her Majesty the Queen, explaining these matters in detail, and recommending that a Military Governor be appointed to Connacht in place of President Fitton. Be very tactful – Her Grace will not be pushed! – but suggest the name of Sir Nicholas Malby as possible Governor. . . ."

The secretary bowed and retired.

"Malby?" Loftus probed.

"Yes, a good military man. Hard and straight as a Toledo blade. Not the type to allow women to snatch his rations!"

The Archbishop laughed; then asked, "But what will Her Majesty do with Fitton, if she agrees to dismiss him?"

"What does she do with all her good servants? Gives them a few thousand acres of Irish land and calls the result a plantation! The theory is that, in a generation or two, the Irish forget that the land ever belonged to them."

"But they *don't* forget," Loftus said with a strange sidelong glance, and Sidney brought the tips of his fine fingers together carefully.

"Would *you*?" he asked, looking at the Archbishop. "If the Gilberts, Grenvilles, Courtenays and Carews drove you out, would you forget? Land is like blood, my friend; a bond; a passion. Its defence can become a religion. And this is what I fear, both in Connacht and in Munster."

Sidney was a man of sensitivity and foresight, who carried out – with great efficiency – orders with which he did not always agree. This was his second term of office as Lord Deputy in Ireland, and he had grown in wisdom with the years. He knew with utter certainty that further trouble was about to arise out of his recent Parliament in Dublin, when land titles had been interfered with and Protestantism forced upon an unwilling people, both Irish and Anglo-Irish. The news from Connacht infuriated but did not surprise him; he had never expected the wild and backward chieftains there to understand the 'Surrender and Re-grant' principle of lands and titles, or to pay Crown rents without a murmur; but he had hoped for a tactful President to educate them in English law, and lead them gently into the Queen's fold.

"God damn Fitton," he said softly. "It will take years to uproot the weeds which he has sown."

He would visit Galway himself as soon as he could but,

meanwhile, there was trouble enough both in Ulster and in Munster. The north was still seething over the slaughter of women, children and wounded on Rathlin Island the previous summer, by Essex and his young commander, Francis Drake. And the turbulent south – in arms these seven years – was still being urged into confederacy against the Queen by the followers of exiled James Fitzmaurice Fitzgerald. . . .

Although Sidney had complete confidence in Sir John Perrot, the Munster President, the situation in that territory worried him unceasingly. He knew that there were Catholic priests somewhere at the back of the general unrest, and that Catholicism in Ireland was reviving after years of laxity. If it became a nationwide symbol to the people. . . .

It was February before the Lord Deputy reached Galway and made his ceremonial entry into the city with the Sword of State carried before him.

He found sad changes along the familiar streets – houses deserted, empty stores crumbling into ruins. The once-proud Mercantile Republic had withstood three years of intermittent siege. The inhabitants – forbidden all Irish contact by Sidney himself on his last visit – had been thrown back upon their own resources, and were ragged and starving. Their only supply line, the sea, was now as dangerous as the menacing country outside their walls.

Sidney wasted no time. He ordered Fitton to retire to his own residence, there to begin packing his belongings. Then he sent commissioners into every part of Connacht, inviting the leaders to come to him under safe-conduct. While he waited for them, he doled out justice in the law court. The dungeons of Shoemaker's Tower were emptied – some by the hanging rope, some by chaining to the oar in galleys, a few by freedom.

At night, he dined with Fitton, not because he liked his company but because he wanted to know more about the tangled circumstances of the Connacht rebellion.

Fitton said sullenly, "My Lord, you are wasting your time waiting for the leaders to come in. They skulk in their mountains and fastnesses, and among the out-islands. They will not come in of their own accord, you mark my words."

"They'll come if they're fairly treated." There was an edge to the Deputy's voice. "It is to their own advantage to make peace, being as much weakened by war as anyone else. They're not fools. . . ."

The Lord Deputy was prepared to wait and his patience was rewarded. Slowly, the Irish began to come in: first, the heads of the minor clans, MacPhilbin, O Kelly, O Madden, Costello, Prendergast. . . . He treated them with courtesy and strict fairness; explained to them (with some difficulty, for their only common language was Latin) the new system under which their territories were to be administered.

"Gentlemen, if you will surrender all your lands and titles to Her Majesty, the Queen, these will be re-granted to you at once for a nominal rent, less than that which you now pay to your own liege-lords. In return for your money and cattle – and for a small yearly hosting of men and horses – you will receive Crown protection against the incursions of your neighbours. No longer will you be in thrall to your own chieftains – for even the greatest among you is a mere *urragh* to one greater: O Flaherty to O Conor, O Conor to O Donnell and so on – and no longer will you have to support Scots for the same protection which England will give you. Surrender to the Queen: she will re-grant and pardon."

The tribes were weary of being raided; holding their lands precariously by election; of living by eternal vigilance. The Lord Deputy's proposals appealed to their strong family instincts; land to be passed from father to eldest son, that land and its cattle to be inviolable, and impartial assize courts to settle all disputes. Yes, these were the answers to their ancient problems. . . .

They surrendered. They urged their kinsfolk to come in. Daily, ex-President Fitton watched the list of submissions grow. The Lord Deputy had accomplished, in a few weeks, what he had failed to do in as many years. He could not resist an occasional thrust at Sidney.

"Has Richard-in-Iron Bourke come in yet?"

"No. Not yet."

"He won't come. He is the strongest man in Connacht; keeps hundreds of Clandonnells. He will defy you. . . ."

179

"I think he is merely being cautious. I have sent the Dean of Christ Church to reassure him."

"And to pardon his wife, the pirate Graunuaile?"

"Among other things, yes."

"My Lord, you are nourishing vipers," Fitton sighed with the air of a man unjustly dismissed.

Sidney waited in a state of increasing tension. If Richard in Iron refused to come to him, then all his plans for Connacht must collapse. He wanted to shire the province – to divide it into four manageable parts – but, as the Lord Richard owned most of Mayo, one way and another, his surrender of land was vital to the scheme. The Lord Deputy was in no position to use force against this wealthy, arrogant chieftain whose wife was reputed to be a fierce sea-rover, intractable as the Atlantic itself. Only this winter past, she had terrorized Galway, blocking its food supplies with a pack of snarling galleys. He heard, too, that she had fortified the harbour of Inishbofin as a roadstead for her larger ships, so as to be within striking distance of the city. . . .

Obviously, she was not the type of woman to surrender easily. Doubtless, she was at the back of her husband's refusal to come in.

He turned the problem over and over in his mind. Then, quite suddenly, the solution came to him in the recollection of something which Fitton had said.

'Keeps hundreds of Clandonnells. . . .'

That was it! Richard Bourke's strength lay in his Scottish mercenaries. Take them from him and he was merely another landowner, as anxious for protection as the next man.

It was nearly three o'clock in the cold spring morning but Sir Henry got up, dressed, and called for the senior members of his staff.

"I want some fit, intelligent men to ride into Mayo. They are to make secret contact with the heads of the Clandonnell families there: the MacSheehys, MacDowells, MacCabes, MacRorys, MacDonalds and MacSweenys, asking them to come to me without delay. When they arrive, I will invite them to hold their livings or *bonaghts* from the Queen instead of from Richard Bourke. I will raise the amount of that *bonaght* until

Her Majesty secures their services, whatever the cost. After that, the Lord Richard is powerless to resist or rebel."

It was a masterly plot. And it succeeded. In the end, it was his Scots who forced Richard in Iron's hand, by their desertion of him for better terms. He became, overnight, a leader without an army, his lands wide open to whatever neighbour chose to raid him.

The Crown had made itself his only refuge.

Graunya was pacing about the painted room that had once been Finola's: now its rugs and draperies were put away, its windows unshuttered to the sea winds, but still she often awoke in the night to a sense of suffocation. . . .

"Richard, I am going to Galway with you," she said.

"No. I'll go alone. We cannot trust their pardon of you —"

"And I cannot trust your good sense not to be trapped into some fool promise!"

In many ways, her husband was a child. When the Clandonnells deserted him, he had put his head in her lap and wept with shuddering sobs, bewildered and broken-hearted. Since then, all the swagger had gone out of him, giving place to a kind of dignified humility which did not commend itself to Graunya as a virtue. She would not accept defeat as her husband did, but poured her own men into Carrigahowley and Gweeshedan, filling the gaps thus left in the Kildavnet and Clare Island garrisons with escaped rebels from Iar-Connacht. She railed and stormed at Richard until she was hoarse but the only result was that he became more patient and childlike than ever; he even discarded the armour which had given him his nickname and, at nights, slept with his arm under her neck and his hand on her breast. Utterly changed from the confident, lustful man she had married, Graunya was at a total loss to know what to do with him. It was against her instincts to abandon anyone who depended upon her: she decided to protect her husband until he recovered from whatever fairy-calm it was that had robbed him of all purpose and aggression.

His voice came to her now from the curtained bed.

"I cannot allow you to ride to Galway with me —"

"We are not riding. We are going by sea."

"Why?"

"Because, that way, we can put up a braver front. Our ships look better than our army!"

"I do not see that it is important," he sighed. "Come to bed, Graunya." The more troubled and apprehensive he became, the more he needed her in his arms; he had no other women now, nor felt the need for them. . . .

"No. Be quiet. Listen!"

The sentries were admitting a rider into the courtyard. The porter's keys rattled. Voices sounded within the keep.

The Lord Richard got up, wrapped a cloak about him and hurriedly followed Graunya out of the apartment. Torchlight blazed up the well of the stairs. Soldiers and retainers were gathering noisily.

The messenger ascended to the first landing, knelt before Richard Bourke and said in a loud, clear voice,

"Hail, the MacWilliam!"

So the great title was his at last. . . . The new MacWilliam crossed himself for the soul of the old one, just departed.

Graunya came to him and kissed him on the cheek and on the lips. She looked exultant.

"We need not go to Galway," she said urgently. "The desertion of the Clandonnells means nothing now – as the MacWilliam, you have an army of twenty loyal tribes instead!"

More and more people were pushing their way into the keep, cheering and demanding wine. It seemed that Richard did not hear her for the noise. He said, like one in a dream, "I must put on my armour and go down to them."

"Tell them that we will not be sailing tomorrow —"

He followed her back into the sleeping apartment and, swiftly, she began to dress him in long red tunic with embroidered belt, and gold sandals – his feasting regalia. She was kneeling on the floor, tying the thongs of the sandals for him with her quick brown fingers, when he put his hand on the back of her neck and began to caress her shoulders under the loose gown.

"Graunya," he said gently, "I must have my armour and my travelling clothes. The Dean of Christ Church has my word that

I will set off for Galway tomorrow. Would you wish a broken promise to be the first act of the MacWilliam?"

For a moment, she stared up at him, ready to argue. Then, in some curious way, the image of her father, as chieftain, was superimposed upon her husband, giving his body a kind of sanctity.

She kissed his hands.

"Be wise," she said. "Be careful when dealing with the English Deputy."

Chapter 15

THE interior of St Nicholas's church was as bare as a winter's tree. Not a fresco, not a niched image remained of all the richness that had once adorned it. The lovely stained-glass windows were gone for ever, replaced by the cold clarity of frosted lights, in this last remaining place of worship inside Galway city.

To Graunya – and to every Catholic now assembled here – these changes symbolized the Reformation. The warm, colourful old religion which had suited the Irish temperament was being ruthlessly suppressed.

She watched impassively as her husband knelt before Sir Henry Sidney, and the great Sword of State touched him.

"Arise, Sir Richard Bourke."

Richard stood up, his English-cut mantle of crimson velvet proclaiming his new allegiance. By sacred oath, he had sworn homage and fealty to the Queen; had received the Seneschalship of his own territories under an English sheriff and – as grand climax – the Order of Knighthood.

Graunya was entirely unmoved by the ceremony. To her, Richard's new titles were empty and meaningless, a mockery of his dignity as the MacWilliam. She felt no gratitude to Sir Henry Sidney for this mark of the special friendship that had sprung up between him and her husband.

On her Uncle Melachlin's arm, she left the church (Melachlin had submitted in the name of the O Malley), her veil of lace-edged cobweb lawn floating from its high wired collar to her sandalled heels, muting the intense crimson of her gown.

Outside, in the sunny churchyard, the congregation stood in noisy groups, so intent on gossip and the examination of each other's finery that they failed to notice the last act of the drama: the Earl of Clanrickarde's rebel sons, Ulick and John, being taken away in chains although they had bowed their knees with the rest.

"It seems," Graunya muttered to her uncle, "that there is one law for the still-powerful, another for the vanquished. . . ."

Sir Henry Sidney and the MacWilliam came out of the church together, crossing the cobbles to where Graunya and Melachlin O Malley stood. The Deputy bowed, greeting her in Latin, "I trust you enjoyed the ceremony, my Lady Bourke."

As he straightened up, he met her eyes and there was animosity in them.

"Do not call me that," she said, very low. "I am Graunuaile, wife of the MacWilliam: these are the only titles I recognize."

Sidney shrugged, preparing to walk away.

"As you wish, madam!" But Richard turned to him quickly, craving his pardon for her. . . .

Suddenly, she was sick of the entire farce – the kneeling, the fawning, the childish reverence with which her husband regarded Sidney's friendship. But she had learned to control her temper and her tongue: now she must be devious and cunning also to obtain the only favour which she wanted for herself.

"My Lord Deputy," she said, "one moment, I beg of you."

"Yes?" Sidney was disarmed by the beauty of a smile which had all the sudden radiance of the Queen's.

"I wish to make you an offer. You have imposed a yearly rent of two hundred and fifty marks sterling upon my husband for his lands —"

"I have."

"— and, furthermore, you have ordered him to find two hundred men for Her Majesty's service. I offer you this number out of my own ships' crews, as well as a pair of powerful galleys, for the pursuit of the Queen's enemies upon the sea."

For a moment, he was completely puzzled. This woman had shown him nothing but hostility during the five days of her visit to Galway; now she was offering to take her husband's services upon herself, and to give more than was asked. Sidney was well aware that, by comparison with her, the MacWilliam was a mere babe in arms, malleable, trusting, full of gratitude for trifles. . . .

She read his mind accurately, and smiled at him more radiantly than before.

"You have taken our Clandonnells from us," she said, masking the anger she felt. "We have few foot and horsemen left but, as a seafaring tribe, we have plenty of sailors. I am asking you to accept these instead."

"And the galleys?"

"Merely for good measure."

He did not trust her. Her appearance too much belied what he knew her to be. This small-boned, agelessly beautiful woman was a ruthless leader of sea-rovers, taking prey even of English supply ships. What wide interpretation might she not put upon the term 'Queen's enemies'?

"Which ships did you plan to attack?" he asked carefully.

"Those that are a common menace to us both: infidel corsairs. The Umalls have lost both men and animals to them in raids this winter past."

It was quite true that Clew Bay's newest enemies were Turks. Since autumn, they had been coming up from some hideout off the Munster coast, swooping on the mainland or islands of Connacht and making off with brood mares, cattle and sheep. They were vicious fighters, ruthless killers, and the Clare Island and Kildavnet garrisons had lost ten men apiece to their curved knives.

"Surely your people defended themselves?" Sidney asked.

"They did, most valiantly. But we are denied the right of pursuit beyond our own coastlines." Bitterly, she remembered the loss of the *Regina* in prohibited Galway Bay.

"You want the freedom of all western Irish waters?"

"My Lord, I do." More than anything in the world, she wanted this, the loosing of the leash that held her. . . .

He fingered his pointed beard. There would be some advantage in granting her request: she would help clear this wildest of coasts, and her commission would prevent her from attacking any English vessel.

"Very well," he said. "I will have the necessary letters

drawn up for you. But you understand that any act of smuggling, or piracy against Her Majesty's ships, or land raiding from the sea will render these letters void immediately? And I will not have this city of Galway molested in any way."

"I have never molested it," she replied truthfully. The robbing of the supply ship was an act against Fitton, not against Galway. . . .

"Then let me have proof that your activities are directed only against Turks and their like: send me either prisoners or their heads!"

He bowed formally and again prepared to walk away but Richard-in-Iron caught at his sleeve.

"Let me accompany you —"

"Sir Richard, I have much business before leaving Galway in the morning."

" – I mean, let me ride with you to Athlone."

"For what purpose?"

"In gratitude for the tokens you have given me!" – and the MacWilliam drew a silk cloth out of his belt which, opened, uncovered a little pile of trinkets. "See, here is the locket containing your son's miniature; and here the ring you wore one night the Queen danced with you; and here —"

"*Richard!*" Graunya's voice cut across his words like a whip. She began to speak rapidly in Irish so that Sidney could not understand. "You will cease this boy's game. . . . We have done what we came to do. Now let the Queen's Deputy ride on alone."

"No. I respect and admire him: he is my true friend. I will ride to the borders of Connacht with him."

"If you do that, you can continue on into the Pale!"

"But, Graunya, I will return in a few days —"

"To Carrigahowley?"

"Where else? It is my home."

"Where else indeed. . . . Think on that."

"What are you saying?"

"That I am sickened by your lapdog attitude to this man. Give it up at once or, by God Himself, I'll fortify Carrigahowley against you!"

"You could not do that —"

187

"No? For every man of yours inside there now, I have ten. Make no mistake, Richard; if I want to keep you out, I can do it."

"But *why*? Why have you suddenly turned against me?"

"I have not turned against you. I want you to come home with me: your own people are waiting to inaugurate you as the MacWilliam, and this is the only title that matters. Show me that you respect it more than the Order of Knighthood."

Sidney could see that Sir Richard was suffering a lashing from his wife's tongue but he had no idea what the passionate argument was about. All he knew was that he was extremely sorry for the big man, so, laying a hand on his shoulder, he drew him away, saying kindly, "Sir Richard, I will be honoured to have your company as far as Athlone. You can bring the Sheriff FitzAlexander back with you from there."

Then, turning to Graunya, he said curtly, "Madam, my clerk will deliver the promised letters to your ship before sundown." Pity she was such a firebrand: she was very beautiful. . . .

The Lord Deputy turned on his heel and strode smartly away. After a moment's hesitation, the MacWilliam followed him.

Graunya stood looking after them both. She was breathing quickly and her colour was high. Melachlin O Malley touched her arm cautiously.

"Graunya, you wouldn't lock the Bourke out of his own fortress? That would make him seem a fool before the assembled tribes."

"He *is* a fool," she said harshly. "I have done with him. . . ." And Melachlin shook his head, wishing that her father were there to convince her of her wickedness: Owen of the Black Oak was the only one she had ever heeded but now Owen was like a mighty tree, felled by sickness that robbed him, even, of speech.

The Castle of Carrigahowley was grey under an evening mist that blotted out the hills and blurred the sea. Its gates were grimly shut. A stranger might have thought it uninhabited until, looking more closely, he saw hooded sentries pacing the high ramparts, and archers in position at every vantage point.

Along the desolate track from Glenhesk, Sir Richard Bourke rode homeward with the English sheriff by his side, their respective escorts strung out in single file before and behind.

"We are almost there," Sir Richard said heartily, and signed to his bugler to sound the horn; its notes seemed to lose themselves in the mist, and then come echoing back from the unseen heights of Nephin Beg. A cold trickle of moisture ran down the neck of Sheriff Edmund FitzAlexander. . . .

Graunya was standing on the walk of the East Tower when she heard the horn. Her uncovered hair was black and shiny as sealskin from the increasing downpour, and rainwater was trickling over her face but she appeared not to notice. Her gaze was fixed unblinkingly on the track far below.

At the first sign of movement upon it, she called, "Arms – ready!" down the well of the stone stairs, and felt the men respond to her own tension.

She moved forward, leaning her palms on the rough wet stone. Horsemen were approaching the castle, looking up, puzzled, at the inhospitable walls. Then her husband rode past them, shouting for the gates to be opened.

Total silence greeted him. He retreated and began to circle the East Tower. . . . She felt a certain sympathy with his bewilderment, and her resolution slipped a notch.

"MacWilliam!" she shouted, leaning out.

"Graunya. . . . Open the gates."

"For what?" She was almost laughing.

"For us to enter, of course. We have a visitor —"

"Who is he?"

"Sheriff Edmund FitzAlexander."

At once, she froze into rigidity. The spark of tenderness which her husband's arrival had begun to fan, died within her.

"Neither of you shall enter here, nor any man of yours. Go!"

There was a hasty conference down below in the dripping gloom, then FitzAlexander rode stiffly forward.

"Madam, in the name of the Queen and her Lord Deputy—"

She balanced a knife in the palm of her hand. He saw the gleam of the blade – felt Sir Richard rush past him in case she threw it, to put his armoured body between her and the sheriff. . . .

"Graunya, in God's Name, let us have an end to nonsense. I demand admittance, as lord of this castle and as your husband." He stood up threateningly in his new English stirrups and, drawing his sword, held it lancelike above his head. His men interpreted this as a signal to attack and rushed forward, howling, to batter the gates ineffectually with their clubs while, from a safer distance, the sheriff's escort fired their muskets.

It was all the excuse the garrison needed. They flung themselves into the defence of Carrigahowley as though Black Fitton and his artillery were outside instead of its lawful owner. The rights or wrongs of the matter did not concern them. While the light lasted, they fought on. . . .

The rain ceased and a thin moon showed. The sounds of battle died into a sea-lapped silence. Graunya came out again on to the walk of the East Tower.

"MacWilliam!" she called.

There was a stir in the darkness down below.

"I am here" – grimly.

"Do you admit now that I can keep you out?"

A long silence; then —

"Yes." He was wet and hungry. "What more do you want?"

"For you to send the sheriff away to Gweeshedan."

A longer pause.

Suddenly the voice of Richard in Iron roared out with all the force of a patient man exasperated beyond endurance:

"I'll see you in hell, Graunuaile, before I break my promise to Sir Henry Sidney. Where I go, the sheriff goes, and bedamned to you! Anyway, it is a term of contract."

So he had recovered. . . . She was glad. She had no compunction now in fighting him to the last ditch, and the word 'contract' put a new weapon into her hand.

She leaned farther out, as though playing at being a stone gargoyle.

"MacWilliam," she yelled, "*I – dismiss – you!*" And that was the end of their eighteen-month-old marriage.

Sir Richard and the sheriff trailed off to Gweeshedan, leaving Graunya in possession of Carrigahowley until some means could be found to dislodge her. It was a castle which a small garrison could hold for a long time against a large attacking force. . . .

But she had no ambition to remain cooped up within stone walls. Leaving as many men as she could spare to guard the fortress, she marched out at the head of the remainder, and was gratified to find Richard Bourke's big flagship, the *MacDara*, still riding at anchor below Lough Feeagh. After only a brief struggle with her conscience, Graunya commandeered the ship and made for the out-islands. All her other large vessels lay in the harbour of Inishbofin, and her galleys were drawn up on Clare Island strand.

She wanted to collect the entire fleet and call a meeting of her captains to decide what methods ought to be adopted against the marauding Turks. It was now the month of April, the beginning of long, bright days, and twilights that would glimmer on for hours, in greens and silvers and purples. . . . She was confident of being able to clear her home waters of corsairs before the onset of another winter.

The familiar outline of Clare Island showed against an early morning sky. Its eastern face was already beginning to brighten as the *MacDara* drew nearer. Then the lookout shouted briefly and Graunya went to the fo'c'sle.

She could just make out the dark mass of the fortress, the paler blur of limewashed huts huddled behind the old summer residence. But something was wrong: there were no sea-birds anywhere. . . .

A pall of smoke hung between the summit of Knockmore and the Strand.

Even before the *MacDara* dropped anchor, her crew could see that the roofless dwellings were still smouldering within. Instead of a row of galleys on the beach, the corpses of their own kinsmen were being floated by the incoming tide – corpses stripped and mutilated in the manner which only infidels employed.

Graunya went ashore in the first pinnace. She recognized the dead faces of men who had served with her for more than twenty years and, all at once, the full tragedy engulfed her, pulling her down to suffocating depths of despair.

She sat among the dead, touching them and keening over

them like a woman who had lost her reason. The men coming in from the *MacDara* stood apart from her, awed by such grief and by the devastation of the island, until one of their O Dowd commanders shouted at them to search the fortress for wounded and dig graves for the others; then he, himself, went to Graunya.

"Come, this weeping won't mend matters," he said gruffly. "I'll take you to your nephews on Inishbofin."

She looked at him, wild-eyed.

"It was my fault. All this. A judgement upon me for what I did to the MacWilliam —"

"No. It would have happened in any case. All that is important now is revenge."

"Revenge!" She seized on the word and it bore her to the surface of sanity. "I pledge myself to that. I have no other purpose in life. . . ."

She stood up resolutely, but a sick dizziness came over her so that she stumbled against O Dowd.

Steadying her, he said, "It is the sight of all this —"

But she looked at him in a queer startled way and replied, "No. No, I think not . . ." and began to walk towards the fortress, past the smoking ruin of the old summer residence where she had spent so many childhood days. Her mouth twisted into a bitter smile.

"You have had the last word, Richard Bourke," she said aloud, although she was alone. "When I need all my strength to avenge my dead, you burden me with your child."

She was forty-six years old gone springtime but, by some alchemy of moist air and frugal living, the bloom of youth was still on her skin and she had the body of a young girl. The lime waters of Connacht had preserved her teeth and the rich depth of colour in her hair, but it was her own intensity that gave her the incandescense which attracted men to her, and held them through the years. As long as she had purpose, this quality would remain, and now it glowed blindingly after momentary eclipse.

She strode on up to the fortress, where a few wounded men had survived, and began to question them mercilessly concerning the invaders: how many ships had they? – from which direction had they come and to which departed? – what were

their weapons, their clothing, the rigging of their vessels? . . .
By the time she had finished, she had a clear mental image of
her quarry – bigger and more formidable than she had previously imagined, but no longer unknown.

She gave her orders to the crew of the *MacDara*.

"You have a ship and two pinnaces; go to every corner of the
Umalls and demand galleys, men, weapons, provisions, in my
name. Bring me my vessels from Inishbofin and command my
nephews there to attend me. Bring my son, Owen O Flaherty,
from Inishturk with all his liegemen. Find Murrough O Flaherty
and his sons, wherever they may be scattered in Connemara or
Iar-Connacht. Get the Devil's Hook from Corraun and
Melachlin O Malley from Belclare. Tell my brother, Donald
the Piper, that I require his curraghs but not his company. And
withdraw the entire garrison from Carrigahowley – I need the
men here when the fleet is ready. . . ."

The response to these summonses was a measure of her
authority: every man came with his vessels, big or small, and
the sea-army grew from day to day.

Graunya worked without ceasing to make order out of what
might have been chaos: she distributed weapons and provisions, gave the protection of smaller craft to larger ones,
juggled with her crews until she obtained the balance she required. . . .

There were great numbers of rough young men, untrained for
anything except fishing and farming, and these had to be disciplined and taught the use of arms. To give them confidence, she
posted them around the island as sentries, making her instructions as lucidly brief as she could.

"Anything that tries to land on this territory without my permission is an enemy: attack it: kill it."

They understood. With a mighty fervour of enthusiasm, they
awaited the sailing, swimming or wading ashore of any unfamiliar being whatsoever.

"Enemy from the sea: attack: *kill!*" became their slogan.
From daily repetition, it burned into their slow peasant minds.
They were never to forget those words, taught to them by
Graunuaile herself. . . . And, one day, she was to lament their
teaching with a wail that would stay in their uncomprehending

hearts until the day they died. But she could not foresee that now. Her only concern was the weather and the western horizon.

On the morning of May Day, the fleet was ready to sail under the pennant of the White Seahorse.

Graunya had hoped for a quick scent of her prey but the summer wore on and no Turk was flushed. She used the fleet like a giant comb to rake the Atlantic from Donegal to Kerry. She sent the long fast galleys into every cove and harbour, and ransacked the islands, but no corsair was found.

"They must be in the Narrow Seas," she muttered, "or disguised as merchantmen in some city port."

With Sidney's letters in a leather bag around her neck, she took the *MacDara* east of Aran and into Galway Bay, where she scrutinized every vessel. Fitton was gone and the new Governor, Sir Nicholas Malby, not yet arrived so that the Galwegians merely watched her progress apprehensively and took no action, but they wrote down a long list of complaints against her, to be presented to Sir Nicholas as soon as he was installed. . . .

By the end of August, she was big with MacWilliam's child. Her son-in-law, the Devil's Hook, begged her to give up the chase, or appoint another admiral.

"No!" She rounded on him. "Only I can co-ordinate all these vessels. If I withdraw, there will be fighting and argument, for every man is a leader in his own heart. . . . The corsairs will return with the early darkness. We have only to wait a while longer —"

"But how much time have you left, Graunya?"

"It makes no matter: I have carried a child at sea before now. Still" – tapping the St Nicholas medallion against the leather bag – "it might be as well if you returned home to Doona and brought Peg O Lee to me."

Peg was nurse to Moira's son, Richard Oge, in Doona Castle. Four days later, she was on board the *MacDara*, which Graunya still insisted on commanding. The flagship was lying off the wild Donegal coast, straining at her anchor before a steadily increasing south-easterly wind. The galleys and smaller craft began to run for shelter. It was growing dark under a tattered belt of raincloud.

Peg O Lee had no interest in the elements. Her only concern was to deliver her mistress's child safely and, after one glance at Graunya's tense face, she hastily began to unpack her belongings.

By midnight, the *MacDara*'s main cabin was dense with lantern fumes, and its boards awash from the huge quantities of water which the ship was taking over her bows. She pitched and rolled; rose up like a frightened horse, held her unnatural position for a breathless time before plunging into what seemed like the ocean bed. . . .

To Peg O Lee, it was all a hideous nightmare. The violence of the storm hurled her carefully prepared bowls and basins to a shattered chaos and deafened her ears to every sound except its own trumpeting. With the weight of her body, she had to wedge Graunya into a corner of the cabin and, crouched there, her own muscles racked, a half-delirious idea possessed her mind: that the storm and Graunya's labour were somehow riding together, galloping with increasing tempo towards their climax, the one as uncontrollable as the other.

"Oh, God, if only my brother were here!" the midwife wept, crawling about in the water that slopped and swirled around her and her charge. But there had been no word of Magnus O Lee for nearly seven years except a vague report that he was in Spain with the rebel Fitzmaurice.

Suddenly, the *MacDara*'s timbers ceased to strain. She appeared to have sailed into some sheltered place, or else the wind was dropping. For the first time in many hours, Peg could hear the voices of the men. She could even stand upright to reach the cloths stowed away above the hatch in readiness for the birth.

It was time now. She dropped to her knees again, listening to Graunya's breathing and, after a little while, to the cry of the male child delivered into her hands.

"You have a son. May God be thanked!"

"I do thank Him." Graunya held out her arms for the infant and spent a long while looking at him by the light of the swinging lantern. "I think I'll call him by an old family name," she said then. "*Thibboge* . . . unless his father has other ideas."

"Y-you're going back to Sir Richard —?"

"Yes. If my child were a girl, I would not do so: but a boy needs his father. You agree, little Toby?" – and she kissed the mottled skin of the newborn's forehead while Peg stood smiling, ankle deep in salt water. . . .

It was three hours until dawn and Graunya slept, oblivious of the discomfort of wet straw and sodden blankets, having often suffered these things before. She awakened to a grey light from the open hatch and a sound of bare feet thudding urgently over the deck. The *MacDara* shuddered from some violent impact. Grappling irons rasped. There was a shouting, and a clashing of weapons. . . .

"*Turks?*" She tried to get up.

Dimly, she could see old O Flynn bending over her, his face dripping blood, and he was shouting, "They're here. They're taking us. We're boarded!" while Peg O Lee pounded him with her fists, screaming:

"Leave her alone – leave her alone! Can you do nothing without a woman?" – and then the shouting from above increased, and the *MacDara*'s bows ground against those of the enemy ship.

Graunya thought quite lucidly, 'They'll kill my child. I have to defend him.'

She got up, dragging a sodden blanket around her. She had no plan, no single clear idea except that the infant for whom she had laboured all night must be saved. It was an animal instinct, blind to all conception of personal safety. The fearless ferocity of wild motherhood had possessed her.

Snatching a rusty short-sword from the cabin wall, she concealed it under the blanket and staggered out, barefoot.

The Turks were in full possession of the *MacDara*, and the foam-flecked sea empty of all hope of aid. The *MacDara*'s crew, seeing that their fleet was utterly scattered and they, themselves, without a leader, were laying down their arms and huddling under the poop-deck while the Turks rampaged and looted. Their dark-skinned commander was barking out orders when, suddenly, he seemed to choke and stood like one bewitched, staring at the strangest figure he had ever beheld. In the dawnlight, it rose out of the depths of the ship and came slowly towards him, holding him with a pair of intense eyes that gleamed through tangled hair.

His men felt the withdrawal of their commander's attention and turned to stare. Like cattle drawn by some unfamiliar object, they moved inward, forming a close circle around the woman in the blanket. It was many months since they had seen a woman. . . .

The *MacDara*'s crew sprang from their huddle and began to engage the Turks while Graunuaile laid about her, left and right, with the short-sword. She lashed her men to greater efforts, not with encouragement but with abuse:

"Cowards: oafs: serfs: may you be devil-cursed who cannot do one day's work without me! . . ."

They fought like madmen, trying to match her frenzy.

In the end, it was she who took the corsairs' flagship.

Seven other ships of the marauders' fleet, trying to reform without their leader, ran into the line of Seahorse vessels sailing to rejoin the *MacDara* after the storm. They, also, were taken, and one hundred and fifty Turks killed.

Chapter 16

FOR four years, the rebel James Fitzmaurice Fitzgerald had hung around the ports of northern Spain, begging ships, men, arms, supplies, for Ireland, but to no avail: Philip the Second would not sanction an expedition.

Then, suddenly, in the early summer of fifteen seventy-nine, circumstances altered: Francis Drake, in the *Golden Hind*, looted the treasure of the *Nuestra Señora* in Spanish waters. This loss of four hundred thousand pesos to an English pirate decided Philip; he would use Ireland as the spearhead of an attack against England. . . .

In a house overlooking the harbour of La Coruña, Fitzmaurice fell to his knees when he heard the news, and recited the prayer that was the motto of his family.

"*In omni tribulatione . . . spes nostra, Jesu et Maria.*"

"Amen," said Doctor Nicholas Sanders, who was kneeling by his side.

They formed a strange alliance, the Anglo-Irish nobleman and the Continental-trained English Jesuit. Fitzmaurice, warm and spontaneous by nature, had held his ragged band of exiles together by the sheer inspiration of his own faith. He had firmly grasped the idea of a Holy War against the Reformation, and was to light an enduring flame from it. . . .

Doctor Sanders, theologian, logician, and composer of a virulent tract against Queen Elizabeth, was a man more suited to the book-lined quiet of great Church libraries than to the rough comradeship of a rebel army. Austere and humourless, he knew himself unbeloved by the rank and file, and incapable of loving them. But he was a soldier of Ignatius Loyola and his orders were clear: to maintain the Counter-Reformation in Ireland at whatever cost it might demand, even to fighting against his own fellow-Englishmen.

The dark, long-limbed Fitzmaurice walked over to the window and stood looking down on the ships in the harbour. He waved to a man crossing the open space in front of the house and then said, over his shoulder, to Doctor Sanders, "O Lee is coming."

Firm footsteps sounded on the stairs; the door opened and Magnus O Lee came into the room, embraced Fitzmaurice, bowed stiffly to Doctor Sanders.

After the news had been told to him, he asked tersely, "When do we sail?"

"June," Fitzmaurice replied. There was an undertone of intense excitement in his voice. "We are to have two ships with a full fighting crew of Spaniards as well as our own men. Doctor Sanders is to be created Papal Nuncio, and the Pope has agreed to bless our banner. This will be carried by the missionaries —"

"*Missionaries?*"

"Of course. All our passenger space must go to them. They are reinforcements for the Irish friars, now very hard pressed indeed with the new troubles in Connacht."

The Jesuit's voice came coldly from the shadowed part of the room.

"You think, O Lee, that we should not carry missionaries?"

"I think it would be better, first, to win back Munster from the Queen's forces."

"How? Can the Irish fight successfully without an ideal?"

Magnus O Lee hooked his thumbs in his belt and brought the fingers slowly inward to form clenched fists.

"No." He thought of the split in the mighty O Flaherty tribe – Dhonal Crone against Murrough of the Battle Axes – and how his own loyalty to the real chieftain had sustained him through a bitter winter in the mountains. Then, without warning, the idealism had vanished: a great cause became a sordid squabble as the rival leaders outdid one another in acts of treachery and cruelty. Hardship and old age had made of Dhonal Crone a bitter, flinty man, concerned only with the title and perquisites of chieftainship, not with its responsibilities, its neutrality within the tribe. He laid siege to a small castle in Iar-Connacht whose aged O Flaherty lord refused to fight on one side or the other, and put the lord's family to the sword, crying, "Now let a cowardly line die out entirely!"

When Dhonal Crone led his followers within the castle, Magnus O Lee remained obstinately outside. . . .

He had made his way southward into Munster, where James Fitzmaurice was fighting a losing battle against President Sir John Perrot. Exile was the only alternative to execution for the beaten leader. O Lee had gone with him to Spain.

"Magnus," Fitzmaurice said now, turning away from the window, "you know that we must have other ships to meet us off the Irish coast? I hear that the O Malleys of Umall have a great fleet, one of the strongest in the country since adding Turkish craft to their own. You have lived with this tribe; can they be persuaded to support us?"

The role of persuader did not appeal to the physician. He knew that Graunya had married Richard-in-Iron Bourke, and that the entire Bourke clan from both Mayo and Galway was up in arms against the new Military Governor of the province, Sir Nicholas Malby. There were regular troops in Connacht now for the first time – Malby's Horse and the Berwick Bands – making a fiercer resistance necessary from a people already weakened by years of warfare.

He replied soberly, "I think it very unlikely that the O Malleys will sail their fleet to Munster when it is needed for the defence of their own coastline." He hated to damp Fitzmaurice's enthusiasm but knew Graunya well enough to realize that she would take care of her own territories first; any place outside the Umalls was a foreign country as far as she was concerned and, on the seas, she *was* the O Malley tribe.

Thinking about her, he smiled, and an old emotion stirred in him. He wanted to see her again, to talk to her, to touch her. . . . She was the only woman who had ever meant anything to him. But now she was another man's wife, just as she had been in the beginning. . . .

Fitzmaurice was looking keenly at him.

"I think you will go to Connacht, nevertheless," he said, the heavy lines of his thin face relaxing. "You will try to persuade Graunuaile?"

O Lee had not realized that Fitzmaurice knew her name, or what she meant to him.

"I will try," he said. "When do you wish me to leave?"

"As soon as we can arrange a passage for you. You will be given all details of our proposed landing —"

The voice of Doctor Sanders cut in harshly, "Is that wise? He might be captured; tortured to make him talk. . . ."

"The risk is less with this than with any other man," Fitzmaurice said gently. "He knows both Iar-Connacht and Umall. I believe that he would die rather than betray us."

No man ever disappointed James Fitzmaurice once he had made this act of faith in him.

O Lee knew that he must persuade Graunya to sail to Munster, not merely for Fitzmaurice's sake, but for her own. It was vital that she should meet this man who, alone, could show her how insignificant was the existing tribe beside the mighty nation that could be, under one leader.

One leader! There was the stumbling block of all Irish efforts against their enemies. The fiercely individualistic tribes, split by centuries of internal strife, would not accept central government by their own, or any other, people.

It was this tragedy of their nature which James Fitzmaurice Fitzgerald set out to reverse.

Graunya was on Clare Island, supervising the cleaning of her ships, when she saw the curragh coming out from Roonah. Without moving from her perch on the scaffolds, she watched it; the summer morning was calm, faintly hazed, and there was no swell between island and mainland so that she had the craft in sight all the time. . . .

She wiped the tar from her hands on the seat of her leather breeches, signed to the shore sentries not to challenge the oarsman, then went down alone to the beach.

'Strange,' she thought, 'how little a man alters – the way he holds his shoulders, tilts his head. . . .' Magnus O Lee might have been rowing up Lough Oirbsen on that summer morning before the Joyce raid, for all the change that she could find in him.

He shipped one oar, trailed the other, and turned sideways to slide the curragh in by the jetty. For an instant, their eyes locked and she felt as though he had touched her.

He waded ashore, dragging the curragh. When its prow was clear of the water, he left it there as if he had forgotten it, and came towards her. They stood face to face, not speaking. Neither saw the other as they were then, but only as the remembered image of youth. For one blinding moment, there was pure love between them, generous, uncritical, joyful in reunion.

Then Magnus said, "Graunya, I have been sent with a message for you —" and, at once, the splendour died within her.

"Sent?" She bit her tongue on the words that should have followed: '*so you would not have come otherwise . . .*' Unspoken, he still sensed them but made no excuse; merely stood there with his hands by his sides, watching her shell close against him as it had always done.

"– from James Fitzmaurice."

She recovered quickly, became brisk and impersonal.

"You had better come up to the fortress. Is it a matter for me alone or for the other tribe leaders?"

"You may have need of their advice but your vote will still be the deciding one." He looked at the impressive array of ships, some afloat, some hauled up on the beach for scraping and cleaning; many of these vessels he had never seen before. "Fitzmaurice wants your support for an armed landing, financed by Spain and the Pope."

"Indeed? When?"

"Early July, all being well."

"What are his terms?"

"There are no terms, Graunya. Fitzmaurice's enemies are mine and yours also. You come as a volunteer or not at all."

She turned her back on him and began to stride ahead.

"Have you any idea what Connacht is like under Malby?" she shouted. "Do you know that we have reaped no crops for three years? – that our rents are doubled from what we agreed with Sidney? – that the entire clan depends on the fleet for food and arms? This province is a wilderness; my husband and I and other leaders hunted animals without rights or seasons. We have nothing to give. Go away!"

He caught her by the arm and spun her around.

"Listen to me; I have little time. Fitzmaurice is fighting for a country, not a province. If he fails, you fail ultimately. Can you not grasp the immensity of what is at stake? – land, religion, the future of an entire race!"

She looked at him dispassionately. The image of youth crumbled; he seemed worn and haggard, as though he had put the last ounce of his strength into the appeal. She noted, for the first time, the white streak at the front of his hair, and how his grey eyes had lightened to a more pronounced clarity. Strange eyes always; now, when the sun caught them, they had a quality of the crusader's zeal. It was impossible to ignore them.

"Why did you leave me?" she asked fiercely. "Was I so small, so despicable, that you had to find another leader?"

His hands, still grasping her arms, took a gentler hold like the prelude to an embrace.

"Graunya, you are a mighty woman to your own clan. There has never been anyone like you before, nor ever will be again. But the days of the clan are numbered. I am asking you to preserve a faith and mother a nation."

It was a moment that would not come twice between her and O Lee – between her and destiny. She must grasp it at once or refuse for all time.

"And if we fail utterly?" she asked.

"We fail together. I will never leave you again."

He felt the hardness go out of her under his hands.

"Magnus – promise – that you will come home when it is over?"

"I promise." All at once, home to him meant wherever she was.

She took the St Nicholas medallion from around her neck and slipped the chain over his head. That was to be his abiding memory of her – standing on tiptoe, her arms extended, giving him the one trinket which she had cherished all her life; her talisman of safety.

. . .

203

In June of that year, James Fitzmaurice sailed out of the port of Ferrol and, a month later, landed at Dingle in Kerry. The friars, led by Doctor Nicholas Sanders, stepped ashore under their Papal blessed banner, and dispersed throughout the country. These men had been trained at Douai and Rome, in the 'Seminary of Martyrs', where the contemplation of a traitor's death was part of their spiritual exercise; they lived imaginatively through the horrors of arrest, trial and execution until they reached the point of self-oblivion. No plans were made for their re-embarkation; they were to preach the new militant Catholicism of the Counter-Reformation until they were taken. . . .

Fitzmaurice moved to Smerwick harbour with his Spanish and Irish soldiers. He sent an impassioned appeal to his cousin, Gerald, Earl of Desmond, to join him, but only Desmond's brothers had come when, five days after the landing, Graunya arrived off Smerwick with a fleet of galleys.

O Lee took her at once to Fitzmaurice and left them together in the new fort which the Spaniards were hastily constructing. Amid an uproar of shouting and hammering, the two leaders took stock of one another and went into conference.

"We must make contact with the O Neill in Ulster," Fitzmaurice told her urgently, trying to mask his agitation over the non-appearance of Desmond, on whom he had counted. "He has promised us a Scottish army if we can provide transport for the men. Are you willing to undertake this?"

"Certainly. My galleys are very fast." She never lost an opportunity to praise her own men to strangers; if the words returned home, their moral effect was greater than if they had been spoken direct.

Fitzmaurice smiled, "They'll need to be fast, to get by Malby in Connacht!"

She did not answer his smile. She had a premonition of disaster.

"I think Malby is on his way south," she said, worried.

"If he is, then the English are short of troops. You bring the Scots to us here and we will outnumber Elizabeth's forces."

It was impossible not to respond to Fitzmaurice's optimism, but she knew Malby better than he did; she had met the

Military Governor in person when he first came to Galway, having journeyed there with her husband to appeal against the savage increase in their rents. The appeal went unanswered: Malby was a man of iron. He had been harassing Bourke lands ever since, as determined to collect the moneys as Richard in Iron was determined not to pay.

If Sir Henry Sidney were still in office, Richard would have gone to him for redress. But Sidney had been recalled after complaints against him by Archbishop Adam Loftus and the Dublin Council. . . .

Graunya did not underestimate the dangers of transporting Scots to Smerwick. There was no love lost between them and her own men, with whom they would be packed knee to knee in the narrow galleys. Also, there were English patrol boats off the Ulster coast, and others would certainly be sent west and south to reinforce the troops already marching on Fitzmaurice. She no longer had a safe-conduct for her fleet – Sidney's letters being now void – so that any adverse change in the weather could drive her into an enemy port.

Fitzmaurice was watching her closely, seeing her examine each difficulty from the impersonal viewpoint of the born leader.

"You will do as I ask?"

"I have said so." Uneasiness sharpened her voice.

He stood up and held out his hand to her.

"O Lee was right: you are a very brave woman, Graunuaile."

She looked up at him searchingly. Her heart was cold with a nameless fear but, because this man asked, she would proceed with her mission. For her, it was a strange compulsion, the desire to submit to another's authority. O Lee had told her that Fitzmaurice had a kind of magic but, whether she accepted him as a leader in his own right or as an extension of O Lee's idealism, she was never to know.

A freak storm drove her galleys into the mouth of Shannon, grounding them in Desmond territory. All but two were broken up; these were captured by the Earl's bailiffs, and their crews sent prisoner to Limerick as common raiders. But Graunya was taken to Desmond himself. . . .

.   .   .

205

James Fitzmaurice, desperate for aid against the advancing English troops, set off by land for Ulster.

To change their weary mounts, his men commandeered some horses from the plough in Iar-Connacht. An outraged peasantry rose against them, murdering their leader for this crime against the sacredness of food-producing land in a starving province.

Over the dead body of James Fitzmaurice, the great Desmond banner sagged, supported by two thorn bushes.

'*In omni tribulatione . . .*'

It seemed that all was over.

Desmond's castle of Askeaton was a remote island fortress nearly four hundred years old. Lichened grey stone without, black marble within, it looked towards the mudflats of the Shannon with arrow-slit windows, grimly resentful of having been stripped of its treasures nine years back, when the crippled Earl first went prisoner to London. Now it was an echoing shell, housing the returned hunchback who hobbled about on two gnarled sticks: Gerald, fifteenth Earl of Desmond, in whom the glory of a romantic line had dwindled to a feeble spark.

The Great Hall of Askeaton was ninety feet long, quite empty except for a carved chair at the dais end with a lighted torch bracketed to the wall above it. In the chair, a figure sat wrapped from neck to ankle in a red cloak, even his hands hidden in its folds.

Until she stood before the Earl of Desmond, Graunya was confident that, when he heard her explanation, he would let her go. But as soon as she came face to face with him, she recognized him as the kind of enemy she feared most – weak and craven, a man who would throw his nearest kin to the dogs to save himself.

". . . But how *can* I release you?" he asked petulantly. "The English officials in Limerick are holding your men; it is only a matter of hours before they talk —"

"My men will not talk."

"I envy you your confidence in human nature! Mine, alas, has been shattered."

"Let me go now. Say I escaped —"

"Admit to another failure? No; my stock is low enough. I was restored to the home of my ancestors on the strict understanding that I became a Queen's man. As such, it is my duty to hand you over."

Her contempt for him showed in her face.

"It was your duty to help Fitzmaurice. . . ."

His hands moved under the cloak.

"You forget that I helped him once and paid most dearly for it: six years as a beggar in the backstreets of London, but without a beggar's freedom – watched, followed, my every word reported. . . ." His face twisted. "Let that be my gift to my country; six years of humiliation. No more. We are beaten. Let us submit."

For a moment, pity overcame her revulsion. She dropped to her knees beside him, her bound hands clasped.

"A broken spirit can mend," she said earnesly. "You are the head of a great house; one word from you and all Munster would rise behind you. You have a debt to your noble forebears."

"Dead men are not the creditors I fear!" His hands moved again and the mantle fell open, revealing the outline of misshapen legs and chest. Involuntarily she drew back and he gave a shout of laughter. "You like your men big and strong, eh, Graunuaile? Like Black Tom Ormonde, my enemy and your lover?"

"*No* —" She sat back on her heels, appalled at the contortions of his face as it leant towards her. His hands, small as a child's, shot out from the mantle's folds and gripped her wrists.

"You have been Ormonde's woman. I hate him. I hate you because you love only the strong, the perfect bodies which you wish to reproduce in your children. It is a woman's instinct."

"I can revere a man's mind!"

"Then why do you look at me with loathing? I am not a coward. But no one has a right to ask help of me, who has to be lifted on to my horse, carried to my bed . . ."

"I—I had not understood that. Forgive me."

His shouting died to a self-pitying mumble.

"The Queen desired Ormonde, despised me; therefore he was lifted up, given honour and position. I was left in the streets for English urchins to jeer at – I, Desmond, born of kings, the flame of my manhood stifled in this miserable, useless carcass!"

She groped for some word of consolation but only the impersonal phrases of the Church came to her mind.

"Can you not accept it as the inscrutable Will of God?"

He laughed derisively.

"You may have heard it said that I am a lukewarm Catholic. . . . God forsook me at my birth. He has no Will in my regard except to torment."

His eyes looked inward on blackness. Then he groped behind the carved chair for his sticks.

"See," he jeered at himself, "the Earl of Desmond creeps out on all fours unless there be a servant to take him on his back!"

He was terminating the interview and nothing had been decided. The prospect of not knowing her fate unnerved her.

"What are you going to do with me?" she demanded.

He sighed.

"I am sending to inform the Governor of Limerick jail that you are here, in case your men have not broken and told him already. You will be closely confined until his guards come for you; I would not trust you to mine for the journey."

At the mere thought of imprisonment, she began to suffocate, and panic edged her tongue.

"Desmond, you snivelling wretch," she shouted at him. "Four hundred years of chivalry were blighted at your making —"

He gave her an odd look; then, with immense effort, stood up alone, sweat starting on his forehead under the lank black hair.

"Take this woman away," he called to the bailiffs waiting in the corridor. And her last sight of the Earl of Desmond was of a man in a flowing red mantle, the deformities of his body hidden by the heavy folds. Just for an instant, his face reminded her of James Fitzmaurice, his cousin.

The interior of Limerick jail was a vast cavern packed with humanity, thick with their stench and their noise. It was impossible to believe that any kind of order could prevail here and yet, when the horrified senses grew accustomed to the place, a pattern was evident; there was a definite stream of comings and goings – new prisoners being brought in, who were immediately besieged for news of the outside world; others, taken away for trial, given pathetic messages, to be delivered if they escaped the gallows.

The death-rate was high from disease, untended wounds and starvation. To alleviate this latter, the prisoners were allowed to crowd under a grating that opened on to an alleyway, so that passers-by could throw down scraps of food. But, as the days darkened into autumn, the streets of Limerick city emptied, and those who had to walk them hurried by, their mantles blown about their legs, their wind-buffeted ears deaf to the pleas from the prison.

Graunya had found eleven of her own men and, under her leadership, they clung close together, sharing what little came their way. She devised means of keeping their minds and bodies active. She fought to maintain the human spirit in them, in this place not fit for animals.

But, in the ninth week of their imprisonment, the belated news of Fitzmaurice's death trickled down through the grating, and the heart seemed to go out of her. She withdrew into apathy.

Now it was the men's turn to coax and enliven, to tell stories, to invent gambling games with sticks and pebbles. But she could not respond to their efforts, nor rid her mind of the conviction that O Lee must have died with Fitzmaurice.

In November, she was accorded a brief hearing before a magistrate.

". . . Woman, what is your trade?"

"Lawful maintenance by land and sea."

The magistrate instructed his clerk to write, opposite her name,

'Raiding and piracy.'

It was a death sentence. She knew it and did not care. She was foul with the dirt of the prison, where, in any case, she would die before the winter was out.

"Do you wish to appeal?"

It was a mere formality but she hesitated; the memory of her three-year-old son, Toby, being fostered by Moira and the Devil's Hook, tugged briefly. Then she realized that she should have considered him before setting out on her last adventure.

"No."

The magistrate nodded his approval. She closed her eyes, waiting for the sentence; an unnatural calm had attended her lately, bound up with an extreme weariness and depression that drugged the senses. She was in her forty-ninth year, the rhythm of her womanhood beginning to falter.

The rustle of papers caught her attention.

". . . You are to be transferred," the magistrate was saying, "to the keeping of my Lord Justice Drury. . . ."

Drury, the substitute Lord Deputy since Sidney's recall. . . . She could make no sense of the matter. Why —?

Then a stray piece of information fitted. Black Tom Ormonde had returned recently from a three-year stay at Court. He was now the Queen's General in Munster. As such, he would be close to the Lord Justice and, without becoming involved himself (for he was cautious of his position) could have instigated this move on her behalf.

She was not entirely grateful to Black Tom. In her estimation, the most he had achieved for her was a postponement of execution; the least, an exchange of Limerick jail for a private dungeon under Drury's residence where her case could conveniently be forgotten.

In this latter surmise, she was correct. Sir William Drury was in poor health and had retired to his mansion at Waterford. She only saw him once, on the night of her arrival there, when she was too wretched from cold and hunger to know or care much about anything.

She had a dazed impression of trying to reason – in cumbersome Latin – with a sick man whose irritability mounted with her every word; of being dismissed from his presence – taken down a very long flight of stone steps, the lower ones green from trickling water – pushed into a cell – the door bolted on blackness and silence. . . .

When he was alone, Sir William Drury dipped his quill and wrote a letter which would have to await the appointment of a new Lord Deputy.

'. . . I send you one Grania O Maile, a woman who has impudently overstepped the bounds of womanhood, and been a great spoiler; chief commander and director of thieves and murderers at sea, to ruin this province. . . .'

There: that was good enough for a hanging at least.

Sir William Drury was weary unto death of the rebel Irish. He had spent the summer on board ship, trying to prevent the Fitzmaurice landing of which his spies had warned him and, afterwards, failing miserably to take the Spanish garrison at Smerwick. His Queen kept him short of troops and money. He had not enough ships to carry provisions. Now he was reduced to executing pedlars and blind beggars in an attempt at quieting the country, because the Dublin Council had decided that those (probably friars in disguise) were the real seed-spreaders of rebellion.

But he had promised Black Tom Ormonde that Graunuaile would be kept 'safe and quiet' until the new viceroy arrived. There was a rumour that Ormonde himself might be appointed. . . .

Drury leaned back in his chair. Rumours were usually wrong. In his opinion, the new Deputy would be Lord Arthur Grey de Wilton.

He stood up wearily, tidied his papers and prepared to retire for the night. There was an urgent knocking on his door. A mud-spattered messenger stood before him, bearing dispatches from Limerick city, marked '*Most Urgent*'.

He read them once – twice – his incredulity increasing. Then he groaned and said aloud,

"It cannot be true. . . ."

Gerald, fifteenth Earl of Desmond, had come out in rebellion against the Queen.

Chapter 17

To Graunya, the greatest torment of her new captivity was its total isolation. Month after month, the only human beings she saw were her two jailers, neither of whom could speak any tongue except English, a language she had always failed to understand.

Concerning the state of the country, she remained in complete ignorance. From the mouth of Shannon to Youghal, the rebel-hero Desmond was blazing a meteoric trail whose sparks flew wide, some landing even in the Pale itself; she heard no single word about these things. To her, Desmond remained a coward and an informer. In snow-covered Connacht, Richard-in-Iron Bourke was fighting for his title and his life against the terrible vengeance of Malby; again, she knew nothing of it.

Cut off, apparently forgotten, she began to die a little. . . .

But, in England, there was another captive who knew exactly what was happening, not only in her native Scotland, but in France and Spain and Italy as well: Mary Stuart, though a prisoner, still dined under a canopy of state and received foreign envoys; still plotted and intrigued for the restoration of her crown renounced twelve years previously at Loch Leven; still cursed the fatal day she had fled across the border into Elizabeth's country, exchanging the wrath of her own Lords for the devious proceedings of the English Queen.

Captivity had not been kind to Mary's health or appearance: at thirty-eight, she was becoming round-shouldered; the angle of her jaw was blurred; her movements had slowed because of rheumatism and a persistent pain in her side. Some days she could hardly walk, much less mount her horse for the chase that she loved (for she was a fine horsewoman).

Age was overtaking her body but maturity eluded her mind; she was still the rash, ruthless, passionate woman who had arranged her consort's murder so that the stormy Earl of Bothwell – who had already seduced her – could call himself her husband. . . .

Now, with her pretty lapdogs on her knee, her embroidery frame cast aside to make room for them, she looked like a discontented child awaiting a chance to indulge in further mischief, as though there had not already been enough. . . .

Under pretext of playing with the dogs, she examined every corner of the vaulted room. Her custodian, the Earl of Shrewsbury, was easy with her, but Elizabeth's spies were everywhere.

Satisfied that the apartment was empty, Mary went to her desk and began to write. She always wrote fast, seldom pausing to think. . . . Her letter was to one of the foreign envoys.

' . . . And in the event of reliable means of communication between us failing, let us agree to use alum on thin white cloth or paper, which has been soaked in water twenty-four hours beforehand; when wetted again, the writing will appear white and clear enough to read.'

This was a new trick she had learned recently but old ones were not to be discarded: pushing letters into the high heels of slippers; writing between the lines of every fourth ·page of books; chalking messages inside bales of cloth. . . . It was all part of a game that amused and excited Mary, relieved her boredom. She had no sense of her own danger.

'As a sovereign prince,' she had argued for twelve years, 'I am answerable to God alone, and subject to no law. I am Queen of Scotland, and heir to the English throne.'

Many men still loved her as a desirable woman. Thousands more, including the Pope, still depended on her as the focus of Catholic hopes. When the great invasion came, she would be freed, given the crowns of both Scotland and England.

But, for this to be accomplished, the childless Elizabeth must first be assassinated. . . .

England's red-headed Queen was notoriously lax in her

personal safety precautions. She travelled by open barge and carriage, approachable, vulnerable, archly confident of her people's affection for her. She walked through the crowded Exchange with only a pair of flirtatious ladies in attendance. To kill the excommunicate Elizabeth would be a comparatively simple matter, and there were many Catholic volunteers for the assignment – Spaniards, Italians, even Englishmen.

Mary Stuart believed that the days of her own captivity were drawing to a close – that, soon, she would be with her young son, King James, in Scotland, sharing his crown and his life. So utterly absorbed was she in the great adventure, the dream of power, the lies and schemes and intrigues, that she failed to notice how the edge of the axe was turning towards her.

Graunya had lost all count of time. She knew that one summer must have come and gone since her removal to Waterford because now it was deathly cold again, as when she first arrived here.

Sometimes, she imagined she could hear the sea pounding on some distant beach, and it was a January sea: she knew its voice. But, then, her mind was wandering a good deal. She imagined impossible things – that she was driving a galley through a winter's gale; that she was nursing her son, 'Toby of the Ships' as the men called him, *Thibbode na Long*, in memory of how the day of his birth had brought captured Turkish vessels to swell the O Malley fleet; or that she was sitting around the notched table with her captains, planning new voyages. . . .

"Dreams of an old woman," she said aloud impatiently. "I have been buried alive."

She talked to herself whenever she had the energy; sang, cursed, prayed – anything to convince herself that she was still human. But it was a losing battle: loneliness was the one thing she had never learned to combat because all her life had been spent surrounded by people, her own people, whose consciousness flowed towards her even when they were silent.

Her failure to communicate with her jailers was not entirely a failure of language, but of race.

She heard one of them approaching now, his step faster than usual. The heavy door creaked open.

"Come!" he said, his lantern searching her out among the straw in her dark corner.

She squinted painfully at the light as she stood up. Her joints were stiff and swollen, so that she walked as though in chains although she had never been fettered here.

"Out. Along there. I don't think you can run away."

In the passageway, he fastened her cloak for her with sudden fumbling sympathy. She stood like a child, her chin lifted obediently, only the enormous eyes moving, questioning, 'Where am I going? Is it to execution?'

"You're going to my wife," he said paternally, wishing that he could make her understand. "She'll wash you; give you some clothes. Can't send you to the new Lord Deputy looking like a river-rat."

At the head of his troops, Lord Arthur Grey de Wilton was riding grimly towards the unquiet province of Munster. After six months in office, failure stared him in the face – failure to capture Desmond or to prevent the spread of rebellion.

Behind him, in the Wicklow mountains, lay the sinister valley of Glenmalure, a place that would haunt him to the day of his death. Into its marshy ravine he had ordered his men to advance – against the advice of older captains – and had then watched them being sucked down until, helpless, they were hacked to pieces by the wild O Byrnes. Now these jubilant clansmen were burning and raiding to within twenty-five miles of the Pale. The Catholic Viscount Baltinglas had joined them, bringing Plunkets, Dillons, Aylmers, Brabazons and Nugents with him. Kildare was wavering in his allegiance. Even Black Tom Ormonde was strangely restless.

It was all crippled Desmond's fault – Desmond and his cursed Papal banner that was stained with Fitzmaurice's life-blood. Once religion came into things, there was no knowing where anyone stood: old enemies united; Queen's men deserted the Royal standard. This must be the most baffling country in the entire world, and Glenmalure was its symbol – a green and smiling valley that, still smiling, swallowed the brave red and blue jackets of the Deputy's troops.

Lord Arthur Grey huddled into his fur collar. Even the hail-stones here had sharp edges.

"God, what a wilderness!" he gritted to the frail young man who rode by his side. "Look on the chart, Spenser, and find me the name of that river over there."

With numb fingers, the viceroy's secretary smoothed out the map, shielding it under his mantle from the wind.

"The Barrow, my Lord. There is an old bridge about two miles on, at a place called Leighlin."

Spenser's teeth were chattering but he made a great effort to hide his misery from the Lord Deputy. If Grey thought him unfit for this climate, he might send him back to London! A poet had to earn a living somehow in a materialistic age when even a success like that of his *Shephearde's Calendar* – published two years previously – brought little enough money. But the fame it had earned him was responsible for his present position as secretary to Lord Grey; the Earl of Leicester had recommended him for it. . . . He was pathetically grateful. He would never complain about the terrible conditions under which the Queen's army in Ireland was forced to live : underfed, underpaid, many men without shoes, many more dead or dying of 'Irish ague' – that mysterious disease which could decimate an army within six months of its landing. It was said that the Irish themselves never suffered from it : they were inured to the everlasting dampness of this wretched island where it rained on nine days out of ten. . . .

Edmund Spenser could never be at ease in Ireland although the beauty of the desolate countryside cried out to his poet's heart. But it seemed to him that there was an insidious poison in the very air which attacked the mind as well as the body, and he feared for his own fragile genius : there was a poem he wanted to complete – *must* complete, or it would tear him to pieces from within. Its title was *The Faerie Queene*. . . . But for how long could inspiration survive here, where even a man like Grey, his hero, crumbled morally – became a sadistic monster?

He thought about the siege of Smerwick the previous autumn, and felt sick in his stomach at the cold brutality of it – Spaniards and Italians coming out, confident of Grey's promised mercy, trailing their sad rolled ensigns from Fitzmaurice's earthen fort; the troops turned loose upon them, and upon their women-folk; the ensuing butchery and slaughter. . . . Then, stripped bodies laid out upon the beach, even death accorded no reverence. Some of the women had been with child.

Grey turned sharply in his saddle, beckoned to the commander of the following company. An intensely handsome young man rode up, his groomed beard and moustaches defying the weather to ruffle them. He had dark curling hair and insolent eyes.

"Raleigh," Grey said, "there is some kind of gathering on the other side of that bridge: have it investigated."

Captain Walter Raleigh detached four musketeers from his company and gave his orders in a marked Devonian accent. Spenser, watching, envied him; he had assurance, physical beauty, a hard shell of callousness to protect him from the things that so troubled the other; Raleigh would go far, especially if the Queen's eyes ever rested upon him. . . .

The musketeers rode cautiously forward, squinting against the blinding hail. They returned bearing a letter for the Lord Deputy.

'. . . I send you one Grania O Maile . . . chief commander and director of murderers at sea. . . .'

"Bring her here."

The entire company was halted now. Men were craning their necks to see what was going on. Grey read Drury's letter again and frowned.

"The name is familiar," he said to Spenser. "Grania O Maile – I think I came across it in some dispatches of Sir Henry Sidney's in Dublin Castle. 'A most famous feminine sea-captain,' he called her. . . ."

Flanked by mounted guards, the prisoner rode across the hump-backed bridge. Her frieze mantle was pearled with hail. The hood had fallen back and she could not replace it because her hands were bound to the horse's rein; the fingers had numbed to a corpselike pallor. She was only half conscious, her entire being withdrawn, diminished, giving out no spark. She seemed small as a child inside the voluminous dress which the jailer's wife had given her.

The Deputy rode forward.

"You are a sea-captain? – a leader of armed thieves and murderers?"

She stared at him uncomprehendingly out of eyes that seemed
too big for her face.

"Answer me, woman," he shouted. "Are you a pirate?"

Suddenly, the question appeared absurd. Some of the men
began to laugh. A terrible fear gripped the Lord Deputy: he
was being made a fool of! It was all some ghastly posthumous
joke on the part of the late Justice Drury. This pathetic little
bundle of skin and bone was the wrong prisoner.

"Are you," he asked, enunciating carefully, "Gran-i-a O
Mail-e?"

She recognized the English version of her name and nodded,
just as a great gust of wind, howling along the surface of the
river, struck her in the back. She bent forward like a reed,
having neither strength nor weight to withstand its force. Grey
could not decide whether she had acknowledged her name or
not. The whole business was time-consuming – perhaps some
trick to delay him in his pursuit of Desmond. Lord Justice
Drury was dead and could not be taxed with the matter.

"Oh, take her on to Dublin," he said impatiently to the
Waterford party. "I'll deal with her when I return there."

Her guards closed in, pushing her mount forward; as she
passed by Edmund Spenser, she looked up briefly, feeling his
eyes on her face.

The poet had a moment of intensified vision. Every detail
of her appearance stamped itself simultaneously upon his mind
– the blue-whiteness of her skin under its scalloped veil of
wet, dark hair; the shadowed hollows of cheek and jawline that
had an air of unearthly fragility; the extraordinary eyes, fixed
on some inward distance that was longer than time itself.

He, and he alone of all the grinning escort, felt the thread of
strangeness brush him with this woman's passing. And he
shivered.

It was the month of March before Grey returned to Dublin
with a sizeable band of prisoners, many of whom were friars
or Jesuits. His policy in Munster was beginning to bear fruit:
pardon for any rebel who came in, bringing a captive kinsman

or priest. By this means, the Lord Deputy had laid hands on one of Desmond's brothers, and executed him according to the fearful Traitors' Code. Likewise a Clanrickarde Bourke, pressed to death between oak beams in Limerick; and two ordained followers of Doctor Nicholas Sanders, dragged to the gallows after having their arms and legs broken over the anvil at a forge.

Grey was confident that the net was closing around Desmond. The rebel leader was being pushed back into hungry, mountainous Kerry, whose coast was now blockaded by English ships so that neither food nor reinforcements could reach him. It could only be a matter of time before he and Sanders, his inspiration, were taken.

Meanwhile, the urgent problem was to find space for the new prisoners. Executions must not be rushed through before valuable information was extracted by rack and burning boot. . . .

Grey sat down to study the dungeon plan of Dublin Castle against a separate list of offences and names of old occupants.

"Good Christ," he said abruptly to Spenser, "this O Malley woman has been at the Government's charge for eighteen months, in Limerick, in Waterford, and now here. And do you know what for? *Raiding Desmond's lands* . . . the very thing we are trying to encourage."

Spenser adjusted the narrow sleeve bands around his thin wrists and replied carefully,

"Obviously an official blunder, my Lord."

"And one which must be rectified! I want to look into the entire matter. Have her brought up at once for questioning."

"She does not speak English —"

"No, but Sidney's report mentions that her husband was proficient in Latin. Perhaps she is also."

"Yes, my Lord."

"Hurry, then. I'll see her in the lower guardroom . . ."

So, once more, Graunya quit her place of confinement to face an inquiry. But, this time, she sensed a subtle difference in the atmosphere. Whether it was little Spenser's obvious concern for her, or some undercurrent of pleasure in the Lord Deputy's manner, she could not decide: but she smelled freedom and prayed God to guide her tongue.

"Grania O Maile, you were sent to Limerick jail by the Earl

of Desmond," the Lord Deputy said to her in Latin. "What was his complaint against you?"

She was tempted to preface her reply by a hot denial of Desmond's charges, but Spenser – standing behind the Deputy's chair – coughed sharply and she looked at him. His face was tense with warning. If ever an unspoken message flashed between two people, Spenser's eyes said, 'Tell the bare truth.'

"Desmond's complaint was, that I had raided his territories with my galleys."

"This was true?"

"My men and I were taken on the south bank of the Shannon, where the Earl's estates are." She was feeling her way. . . .

"You live by raiding and piracy?"

"No. By trade, I am a sea-captain, not a pirate."

Grey looked keenly at her, then smiled encouragement.

"But you would not hesitate to pick up an illicit cargo if provisions at home were scarce? The Earl has a wealth of sheep and cattle. . . ."

Puzzled, she sought Spenser's face again. He nodded, quite definitely.

"I might do that," she said, gropingly.

"To Desmond only? Because you dislike him?"

Without thought, her answer flashed out.

"*I despise him!*" – and Grey nodded, satisfied.

"That is well," he said. "Desmond is an arch traitor. You did Her Majesty, the Queen, a service when you tried to raid him. As the Queen's Deputy, I apologize for your long and unjust confinement."

She was entirely bewildered at the turn of events but kept her face closed and inscrutable.

"I am free?"

"Quite. One of our patrol ships – the *Swiftsure*, under Captain Richard Bingham – is leaving Dublin Bay tomorrow; sailing north around the Ulster coast, then southward to Connacht and Munster. It will take you home."

Involuntarily, she glanced down at the tattered dress that hung loose upon her, and Grey smiled with the air of a man who knew women.

"Spenser," he said, "take my Lady Bourke to the Castle

bath-house, and have some gowns and mantles delivered there for her approval at my charge."

The bath-house was white with steam, and loud with the chatter of officials' wives, some of them eating and drinking from trays and vessels brought to them where they lay – like Roman matrons – on the massage slabs. This was the gossip centre of Castle life, but its language was English so that Graunya gained no information from her three-hour stay there. What she did gain was more to her liking at the time : a body that gleamed with scented oils ; hair washed and brushed, coiled high with silver pins ; nails shaped and polished ; and a gown cut for the new French farthingale, whose padded hips disguised her extreme thinness.

She considered it unfitting to board a ship, as passenger, without baggage, so ordered three more gowns to the Deputy's charge, cosmetics, slippers, gloves, mantles, a riding hat and a wired cap ; all these to be packed in baskets and delivered at once aboard the *Swiftsure*, lying on the north bank of Dublin Bay.

Her pleasure in the purchases was not entirely feminine ; there was an enormous satisfaction in making them that was partly defiance of officialdom, and partly exuberance in the first flush of being free. She felt like a young girl, light and gay and beautiful, and was astonished – on looking into a mirror – to see a mature woman, dignified and imperious.

"Graunuaile!" She tried to pin her identity with the familiar title but, immediately, an attendant arrived, bearing the food she had ordered.

He bowed and said in English, "My Lady Bourke."

Captain Richard Bingham, commander of the *Swiftsure*, was fifty-four years old, and settled in the conviction that the world had a grudge against him. Born a younger son, he had spent his life in the Queen's army and navy, and was always posted to the most troublous and plague-ridden parts of her realm.

Yet distinction evaded Richard Bingham. He had known the bitterness of unemployment – of having to beg his old commander to find him another position. He had been inside the Tower for six years, after being involved in one of the many plots to put Mary Stuart on Elizabeth's throne. He had been turned down by Francis Drake as second-in-command of the expedition to help Don Antonio of Portugal. . . .

The result of all this was, that Bingham was a bitter man, resentful of the success and authority of others. Whatever he did – however well he did it – turned out badly. His superiors bawled at him for actions of enterprise and initiative which would have earned another man a title.

The latest example of this unfairness had happened at the siege of Smerwick the previous autumn. . . .

Old Admiral Wynter was in command of the fleet, and Bingham was Vice-Admiral aboard the *Swiftsure*. By good seamanship, the *Swiftsure* reached the Kerry coast ahead of the flagship, where it was learned that Italian troops, sent by the Pope, were reinforcing the Spanish garrison. Without waiting for his Admiral, Bingham sailed to intercept the Italians and, by his prompt action, did more to accomplish the fall of Smerwick than anyone else.

But Wynter flew into a towering rage with him and berated him before his own men. . . .

Now, here he was on coast-patrol again, no farther up the official ladder than ten years ago. And, crowning insult, he was being made to carry an Irish passenger! Her luggage littered his deck. He was to make a detour into Clew Bay to deliver her to the Castle of Carrigahowley: Deputy's orders. And who was she? One of the Connacht Bourkes who so plagued his friend, Sir Nicholas Malby.

Bingham had no use for women. He was unmarried. A girl had laughed at him once for being undersized. . . .

Graunya knew nothing whatever about Captain Richard Bingham when she stepped aboard the *Swiftsure* at four o'clock of a March morning, and felt the swell of the brimming tide under the timbers. She was excited, elated and restless. She wanted to examine the ship.

"Madam, you will go below!"

No one had ever ordered her to do that. With an effort, she submitted to the captain's authority; heard the swish of the hawsers being cast off, the groan of the capstan's turn. She listened, smiling, to the familiar orders, the strange tongue in which they were being given making no difference to her comprehension. Mentally, she set and adjusted the spread of canvas; took her bearings for the northward course. . . .

They were under way now. She could go on deck.

Bingham met her, glowered at her, indicated that she was in his way. Her black eyebrows came down, puckering the scar: he was being unreasonable! A lively exchange, in several languages, followed, the upshot being that Bingham posted a guard around poop-deck and fo'c'sle, leaving her only a small open space amidships.

The next time he saw her, she was sitting on one of her baskets, dicing and playing cards with a couple of his officers. He called the men to extra duties but had to release others; these immediately gravitated towards the lively passenger in the French farthingale.

By nightfall, he could hear her laughing and singing with the fo'c'sle ratings. . . .

Her presence irritated and distracted him. He felt that he was no longer the master of his own ship. His men were giving him only the surface of their attention but, if he ordered them not to associate with her, he might have a mutiny on his hands.

"Blast her! Oh, blast her to hell," he said. She was an enemy. . . .

The *Swiftsure* was approaching dangerous waters, the narrow North Channel between Antrim and the Mull of Kintyre. It was reported that Thurlogh O Neill was having thousands of Scottish mercenaries ferried across here, using O Malley and O Flaherty galleys for their transport, but no patrol vessel had been able to catch him doing it.

However occupied she was with other matters, Graunya's ear was always close to a ship's heartbeat. Now, through the men's singing and the rattle of dice, she heard its imperceptibly altered rhythm, and her head lifted inquiringly. Seconds later, the cry, "*All hands!*" sent the men scrambling to their posts.

For an instant, she sat motionless, then ducked under the awning and raced to the port rail.

In rain-scudded moonlight, the North Channel was grey and fast-running, the Antrim hills dangerously close. Across the bows of the *Swiftsure*, a flotilla of seven black galleys was streaking for shore, using the V formation of wild-goose flight – a formation which Graunuaile herself had taught the O Malley fleet!

Bingham was trying to cut the crowded galleys off from landing.

"*Fire!*"

A volley of chain-shot broke the nearest arm of the V; then the *Swiftsure* ploughed into the jagged gap, her other light guns blazing. Only the leading galley could possibly make the shore now. . . .

With a helpless sense of nightmare, Graunya watched men struggling in the water, the weight of their armour dragging them down until nothing remained but floating wreckage and a few lightly-clad oarsmen, who began to swim, but were picked off with musket fire. These latter were O Malleys and O Flahertys; the men in armour, Scots.

She saw the leading galley straining for the shore but making heavy progress as though it were damaged. Bingham ordered his single pinnace to be lowered for its pursuit. Given a little time, the galley's crew could still escape.

There was a stone waterjar within Graunya's reach. With great effort, she lifted it, balanced it on the rail just as the pinnace was swung out and hanging directly below, its keel not yet in the water.

The heavy jar dropped like a thunderbolt.

There was a moment of awful silence after the crash; men staring down at the shattered ribs and spine of the little craft before turning horrified eyes upon Graunya. Then Bingham's fury broke like an untethered bull's and his hand seared across her face.

"You she-devil out of hell! I'll kill you for this. . . ."

For a panting moment, he considered the method of execution, then realized that he would have to account for her to the Lord Deputy. No, he would not put himself in the wrong. . . .

"You do not wish to remain on my ship, do you?" he breathed at her. "The men will tear you to pieces for what you have done!"

They showed no signs of it but – "For your own safety, I am going to send you ashore in a coracle; a woman of your sea-going experience should have no difficulty in handling it. Your baggage is confiscated as payment for the craft you have smashed."

Bingham had seen people drown from coracles in calmer waters than these. With immense satisfaction, he watched her climb over the ship's side, her movements hampered by her padded skirts.

Chapter 18

THE round, basket-like coracle spun in the *Swiftsure*'s wake, and Graunya made no attempt to control it with the single paddle. Balance was all-important: she sat cross-legged, very quiet, until the patrol ship disappeared into a haze of moonlight, leaving her alone in the North Channel; then she studied the coastline. A long stretch of it had slipped by from the place where the leading galley had struggled ashore. She must find that place, make contact with her men before they scattered. . . .

In the dark hour before dawn, she stepped out of the coracle on to a beach where dim figures were huddled around a broken galley, and she whistled like a curlew before calling their names, "O Malley – O Flaherty – O Dowd. . . ."

One of Cormac's sons from Inishbofin was the first to recognize her. He came running over the dark shingle, his arms outstretched in incredulous welcome.

"Graunuaile – we thought you were dead: now you walk out of the sea!"

Laughing, she hugged him to her.

The other men came crowding around, talking, touching her, asking where she had been these eighteen months. To her, the sound of their voices was like water in a desert; she closed her eyes and let it trickle over her, not troubling to follow what was said. With a dozen hands guiding and supporting her, she walked up the beach towards the galley.

"Can it be repaired?" she asked, running her fingers over it in the darkness.

One of the young O Dowds answered. "No, not without tools and materials. She's badly holed above the waterline; with twelve of us in her, there'd be no chance."

Twelve: so that was all that remained. . . .

"Where are the Scots you carried?"

"Gone to Thurlogh O Neill. They are sending us back an Antrim man as guide for the overland journey."

She felt the harsh shingle through her fine leather slippers. Allowing for detours, the distance home would be about two hundred miles. . . .

For hour after hour, as the party trudged south-westwards, Graunya listened hungrily to familiar accents telling a strange new story: how the Earl of Desmond had risen in arms for his faith and his fatherland: how the Anglo-Irish nobles of the Pale were supporting him; how O Rourke of Connacht was going to be the link joining Munster with the northern forces of Thurlogh O Neill.

"The whole country is rising," they told her. "We cannot lose!"

But she had aged mentally in prison and her enthusiasm could not leap as high as theirs; they were all young men; their fathers had served under her. She had seen one English ship destroy seven galleys; had watched the disciplined troops of the Lord Deputy at Leighlin; had known a man like Fitzmaurice trampled into the ground by his own people.

She made no comment until the extravagant excitement had died down, then asked quietly, "What of Connacht?" – and the sudden fumbling silence told her the truth: Connacht was dying in Malby's grip.

Little by little, she pieced the story together. The previous year, Sir Richard-in-Iron Bourke had fled before the Military Governor's fury to the out-islands, where a hundred of his men perished in the freak snows of that winter. Afterwards, he had submitted. Now the lovely friary of Burrishoole, near Carriga-howley, was an English garrison.

Malby had taken great prey of sheep and cattle out of the Umalls, and burned Cahirnamart to the ground.

"My father?" she gasped. "Is he safe?"

Yes; Owen O Malley of the Black Oak had been carried on a hurdle to Belclare (his paralysis was too far advanced for him to sit a horse) and he was still chieftain in name, but no longer had jurisdiction even over the fishing rights of Clew Bay: Malby had claimed these for the Queen. The O Malley now paid to fish his own waters. And he had been forbidden to elect a new tanist. . . .

"The fleet?" Graunya asked, desperate for better news. "What is its strength today?" She was questioning old O Flynn's grandson, Shawn.

"The barque, *Maeve*," Shawn said, "and all the bigger vessels are safely moored at Carrigahowley —"

She stopped dead in her tracks.

"At Carrigahowley? Why are they not at Inishbofin and Clare Island?"

"Because the outer coast is swarming with armed English patrol ships."

"I see. Go on. How many galleys have we left?"

This was the question the men had dreaded; they knew how she loved her long, fast galleys. Jerking his thumb backward towards the Antrim beach, one of the O Flahertys mumbled,

"You have seen the corpse of the last one."

Suddenly, she was weary in her very bones, as though she had walked to the funerals of every member of her family.

"Why did you have to take the galleys north?" she asked tonelessly. "What are Thurlogh O Neill's Scots to you?"

Her nephew plucked at her sleeve and, when she looked at him, he was so like his dead father, Cormac, that she blinked: Cormac thirty years ago. . . .

"Graunuaile," he said, "the transport of Scots is our last means of livelihood. Every item of Irish produce is lately forbidden export except to England, and we have refused to send our goods there. O Neill pays us; we carry his mercenaries."

"And now?"

"Now it is over. We will have to scratch a living from the soil and try to protect our remaining herds."

Try to protect . . . but the whole basis of the agreement with Sir Henry Sidney had been that, in return for their native rights, the Irish would be entitled to Crown protection; their 'regranted' lands were surrendered in the first place on the understanding that no troops would be quartered upon them – that rent and service would be sufficient. Instead, the chieftains were being double-robbed. So the old chantings of the bards had not been far wrong:

> *With one of English race no friendship make;*
> *His promises are empty and will ruin thee. . . .*

The bards were gone – proscribed, hunted and killed as 'the most dangerous sparks in this gunpowder isle' – but the bitter truth of their verses was becoming more apparent every day although it was too late now to heed their warnings. England was strong, and united under a clever Queen who was determined to pursue her conquest to the end. Ireland had no central leadership; her sporadic rebellions were unco-ordinated; she cried out for a King to lead her – but never a King out of her own body. Spaniard, Austrian, Italian, she would accept; Irishman, never!

Graunya walked on silently behind the Antrim guide, trying to adjust her mind to the new conditions she would have to accept in Connacht – sheriffs, garrisons, mobile troops throughout the territory; her fleet confined within Clew Bay. . . . She recoiled from the entire picture. It was an exchange of one kind of imprisonment for a worse kind.

This wooded Ulster through which she and her men were travelling was a brooding alien land, full of strange names – O Neill, O Connell, Maguire, O Hagan, O Cahan – and she felt disquieted by them, although there were no English troops.

The first sight of the vast inland water of Lough Neagh soothed her tension for a while but, as the lake receded into the distance until it was a sky-mirror within a black frame of evening-shadowed land, a greater apprehension gripped her: mountains were rearing up, barring the way to the west! There was some force here that would engulf her. She felt its approach and her own unwillingness to resist it.

That night, a man with hand on sword rode into the circle of firelight and surveyed the group of travellers for a moment in close-lipped silence.

"Who are you?" he asked then, authoritatively.

Graunya stood up and walked towards him, slowly smoothing the folds of her skirt. She could see his escort closing in behind him : he must be the lord of these territories. . . .

She said carefully, not wishing to antagonize him, "We are harmless wayfarers making our road home to Connacht. If we have trespassed on your lands, we beg forgiveness."

She looked at him earnestly : the firelight gave him a golden quality, hair and skin and light-lashed eyes. He had a strong neck and shoulders ; fine hands —

"What tribe?" he demanded, motioning to his escort to spread out and surround her men.

"O Malley of Umall." She was standing by his horse's head and the animal nuzzled her neck, its breath warm. The rider leant forward, his voice suddenly vibrant with interest.

"You are the woman they call Graunuaile?"

She smiled, "I am."

He dismounted swiftly. He was not a tall man but he gave an impression of enormous power, leashed and suppressed.

"Hugh O Neill, Baron of Dungannon!" He bowed in the English manner which his upbringing in the Sidney household had taught him. "I offer you the hospitality of my roof rather than of my forest. . . ." He spoke Irish with a curious accent which thinned the more guttural sounds of the language.

She was absorbed in unblinking contemplation of him and did not answer at once. This man's presence entirely satisfied her, as though heroically-dead Cuchuallain were born again, and his beloved Emar standing in her own place. . . .

It was a fantasy which could not survive the light of day, and Graunya – always a realist – knew that. She was twenty years older than Hugh of Dungannon, the elegant, Penshurst-educated, Queen's Baron; and he liked his women young. He had divorced two wives; lived with a succession of mistresses, the latest one being Una, daughter of his greatest enemy, Thurlogh O Neill. . . .

Of all this, Graunya was aware from hearsay, and she tried to keep it at the forefront of her mind as the Baron lifted her on to his pack-saddle.

"You're as light as bog-cotton," he said, his grip lingering ;

then he swung himself up before her and, groping for her hands, drew them around his waist.

O Neill's escort, with her own men walking beside them, led the way through the forest towards Dungannon. The moon was coming up behind the trees – the same moon that had illuminated Bingham's hatred for her aboard the *Swiftsure* now silvered her embrace of a man who called to her in the first instant with a rapture that was spontaneous love.

She laid her forehead against the pleated back of his mantle and smelt the faint fragrance of woodsmoke that came out of the cloth with the warmth of his skin. She felt the jog of the horse's gait beating upward along his spine. Her hands moved gently over the narrowness of his waist, denying that they wanted to caress. And, all at once, she was enveloped by a greater sadness than she ever knew her soul could contain. . . . She, whose understanding of love was limited to what Francis Derham had told her of it, now loved – too late – with a lucid madness. And she had to be her own keeper.

Hugh O Neill of Dungannon was always aware of women: his demanding restlessness led him from one to the other, seeking a satisfaction which he never found. His manhood responded to a young girl's beauty and gave her his children, but his heart remained coldly observant, noting each little stupidity, each failure to match the flight of his own spirit. He was too worldly-wise ever to be disappointed in a woman, for he expected nothing in the first place except a brief excitement – anticipated, calculated to the last heartbeat – although this foreknowledge in no way diminished the vigour of his pursuit.

Yet, sometimes, he dreamed of real conquest: an unattainable woman attained – for a while, Una O Neill had been that to him, the prize snatched from enemy territory, wild, drunken Thurlogh's daughter. . . . But the snatching had been more satisfying that the mating.

Power was O Neill's real passion. Nothing except annihilating defeat could ever shake his confidence in his destiny. Step by patient step, he was building the ascent to a high throne – secretly arming his peasants, extending his landed sway, angling for the Queen's title of Earl of Tyrone – but, for the present, power was here and now, in the gift of the She-King of Connacht. Graunuaile was a legend of unassailable virtue – or lack of inclination, which was much the same thing – and it was Hugh O Neill's single-minded intention to become her lover. Her fame excited him, he himself being still obscure. Stories of her power stirred his envy; he wanted power.

Then, with amusement, he remembered how her escape from Fitton's residence had provided dining-hall entertainment up and down the country for months, and her marriage to Richard-in-Iron Bourke, speculation.

Here was a woman who would not bore him.

He took her hands in one of his and they lay, with a quiet watchfulness, in his grasp. It was a sign language which he understood perfectly. The old excitement, to which a woman's implied assent always gave rise, began to mount in him. He looked at her over his shoulder: she was staring inscrutably at the moon.

"What are you thinking about?" he asked, slowing his mount.

"About you." She had never learnt evasion or subtlety.

"As a woman thinks of a man, either with calculation or with passion?"

She hesitated, searching for the harshest form of denial.

"No; as a mother thinks of a son – how handsome he is, how powerful are his shoulders, how great his gift of command. I have sons older than you are."

He watched the last man of his escort disappear through the trees, then himself dismounted and stood looking up at her.

"Was that intended to shock me into due reverence for age?" He was mocking her but she shook her head seriously,

"Only as a reminder to myself," she said.

"I could make you forget —"

"Doubtless. For one night. Moonlight can be very kind. But the rhythm of my life swings in years, not hours."

"I would ask you again in the morning."

"In the morning, I would be gone."

He walked a few paces away, shoulders hunched. He had a strangely leonine appearance in the moonlight. Then, turning on one booted heel, he demanded abruptly,

"In what way will you think of me if we never meet again?"

"As the one man I could have loved without reservation – had he been born sooner, or I later."

He stood beside her again, and asked, gently now, "What is it you would love in me?"

She bent down to touch his reddish-yellow hair. It was short and curled crisply. She ran her fingers through it with a sense of physical pleasure; and a single rib, shining like coiled golden wire, looped itself around her thumb.

"I cannot say. I do not know you. But there is a power in you that I have never felt in any man, only in the sea – and the sea can carry or drown. You would drown me, O Neill, because I would be humble with you. And humility is no part of my nature."

"Argument is no part of love."

"Once, I would not have argued. Now I ask you not to touch me." She wound the rib of hair around a button of her gown. "Let us ride on to Dungannon. . . ."

Sir Nicholas Malby, Military Governor of Connacht, was studying a large map. It was marked with squares and crosses that spread, like a rash, from O Conor lands in Sligo southward to Thomond, infecting the Bourke territories in between. The squares represented garrisons; the crosses, native castles whose lords had submitted.

Malby was well pleased with the state of Connacht. Under his mailed fist, everything was quiet – so quiet, indeed, that he had been able to visit Munster and the Pale recently. Only one thing now worried him: the garrison commander at Burrishoole had reported that near-by Carrigahowley Castle was in a state of defence, and had armed ships strung out along its coastline and five miles up-river towards Lough Feeagh. There could be only one reason for this: the MacWilliam's imperious wife, Graunuaile, did not subscribe to her husband's submission.

On the table in front of him, Malby had a list of complaints against this woman, drawn up several years previously by the citizens of Galway: she was a smuggler of prohibited goods; a sympathizer with rebels; a constant threat to the trade and peaceful living of the city.

Now she was a silent menace to the Burrishoole garrison. . . .
Malby looked up from the papers.

"Captain Martin," he said, "I believe that this Graunuaile was once a prisoner of yours, in the days of Sir Edward Fitton's presidency?"

"Yes, sir." Martin could hardly control a painful wince; the same prisoner's dramatic escape had cost him several months' reduction in pay, among other embarrassments.

"Then you would know how to deal with her again?"

Martin would, given the chance.

"Very well. The citizens here are demanding action against her, since news of her return reached them. Also, she has refused to give or sell supplies to our garrison at Burrishoole. You will lead a company – armed and paid for by the Burghers of Galway! – to attack Carrigahowley: I want the castle laid open and the O Malley ships taken or destroyed."

"What about the woman, sir?"

"Ummm. The citizens want her arrested but I would prefer not to risk a riot. She is only as strong as her possessions: strip her of these, then give her into her husband's keeping. He values his title, which he holds by my investment, so will see that she remains peaceable once he has control of her."

"But where *is* Sir Richard in Iron?" the captain asked.

Malby looked at him witheringly.

"Inside Carrigahowley, of course, you fool. His wife is holding him prisoner. . . ."

Martin went to make his arrangements for the campaign. His company strength of mixed arms was thirty horse, forty-five foot and twenty Irish kerne, these latter to care for the animals and baggage. The kerne had to be watched day and night, for they were thieves and deserters by nature, but it was impossible to dispense with their services in an army that was always understrength.

By the time Captain Martin's company was ready to leave Galway – proudly inspected by the Burghers, and blessed by the custodians of St Nicholas's – it had one kerne less, and Graunuaile had a spy speeding homeward. . . .

Sir Richard Bourke was lying on his bed in the apartment that had once been his mother's. The long fight against Malby, and then against some of his own kin who chose to dispute the Mac-William title with him, had left its mark: he looked old and worn; he had a thigh wound which did not heal, and the fingers of his left hand were useless from a knife gash across the wrist.

Graunya was sitting beside him, stroking his thick grey hair.

" . . . I think the attack will come from the north-east," she was saying calmly. "The tower guns are ready and I have moved extra men out to the ships."

"There is still time," her husband groaned, "to come to some agreement."

"No. This is unprovoked aggression that is planned. You heard what our spy had to report."

"You should have left the castle open in the first place, Graunya, and disbanded the fleet."

"We have argued long enough about that. I came in here to live in peace and to care for you in your illness. Now I will defend my right to do these things. Malby will not blame you: he thinks you are being held against your will."

His uninjured hand patted her knee.

"How long can we hold out?" he asked.

She smiled, remembering the last siege, when he, himself, had been outside the walls.

"Indefinitely."

She walked over to the window and he watched her with an old man's longing; these days, only her body was close to him; her spirit had gone away somewhere – with another man, maybe. He didn't know. . . .

"It's raining," she said. He heard the satisfaction in her voice, then the certainty, "It will go on raining. . . ."

These were the conditions she needed, the seeping summer moisture that wraught havoc with uncovered troops.

Martin's siege of Carrigahowley lasted for three weeks under a sky that drizzled and poured by turns. In the heat of the July days, suffocating vapours arose out of the sodden earth, rusting the men's armour, crippling their joints, seeping with dampness into the powder kegs.

The horses stood around miserably, cropping between stones, switching flies off their steaming flanks. Flies plagued the tents. Men began to fall sick.

And, all the time, the vigilance of the castle never relaxed for an instant. It seemed to have a thousand eyes, and its supply of powder and shot was inexhaustible, reinforced by a line of armed ships that spat fire.

In vain, Martin looked for aid, either by land or by sea. None came. Apart from the backing of the Burrishoole garrison, the eerie marsh and mountain countryside was as empty of help as was the flat expanse of Clew Bay.

Then, on the twenty-second day of the siege, a solitary horseman arrived with new orders from the Military Governor, who, himself, was on the march, but not towards Carrigahowley.

"Proceed east at once. O Rourke of Breffni is in rebellion."

For the first time in his life, Martin was glad that the hydra had sprung another head.

But the weather which helped to defeat the Burghers' Company also worked against the rebel Earl of Desmond in the Kerry woods: it robbed him of his staunchest ally, the Jesuit Doctor Nicholas Sanders. Exhausted, emaciated, burnt by his own inner fire, the Papal Legate died under the dripping trees. And, in his death, Desmond saw his own end.

The Earl had refused the Queen's pardon; defied three armies; dodged his own traitorous fellows like a hunted wolf. Misery gave the man greatness; he was possessed by an idea that transformed him from a snivelling, broken-spirited wretch into the classical image of a crusader. When even his own followers began to desert him – awed by the devastation of Munster and the terrible deathroll under Black Tom Ormonde's sword – he would neither submit nor fly.

In the winter woods of Glenageenty below the flank of Slieve Logher, he crouched in a freezing cabin with only three companions left to him out of a force of two thousand. It was early on a Tuesday morning, the feast of St Martin.

Six soldiers from the keep of Castlemaine rushed in upon him, led by a petty Irish chieftain whose cattle Desmond had stolen. One of the soldiers, an O Kelly, cut off the Earl's arm;

then – when it was found that he could not walk – tried to carry him. But the rebel was bleeding to death.

"I am the Earl of Desmond —" he cried, before they killed him.

So ended the war of the Geraldines, Ormonde against Desmond, Queen's men against rebels. But when Atlantic gales blew in over the Kerry coast, Desmond's gallowglasses still howled in the wind, and peasants swore that his ghost, on a silver steed, rose out of the midnight waters of Lough Gur.

Rebels' estates were carved into handsome prizes for Englishmen: forty thousand acres around Youghal for Sir Walter Raleigh; fifteen thousand acres for Sir Edward Fitton, ex-President of Connacht; three thousand and twenty-eight acres in Cork for Edmund Spenser, the poet. . . . Interrupting his work on *The Faerie Queene*, Spenser wrote the epitaph of Munster.

> Out of every corner of the woods and glens they came creeping forth upon their hands, for their legs could not bear them; they looked like anatomies of death, they spake like ghosts crying out of their graves; they did eat of the dead carrions; the very carcasses they spared not to scrape out of their graves. And if they found a plot of watercresses or shamrocks, there they flocked as to a feast at the time, yet not able long to continue. In short space, there was almost none left, and a most populous and plentiful country was made suddenly void of man and beast; yet in all that war, there perished not so many by the sword as by the extremity of famine which they themselves had wraught.

These conditions flooded upward into Connacht, where the O Rourke rebellion still smouldered. . . .

There was only one way in which to fight famine and suppression, and Graunuaile grasped it: she took to the high seas. Morality no longer concerned her. She demanded toll of any vessel strong enough to put up some resistance; if it were weak, she took everything. Under the White Seahorse, she harried shipping in the English Channel. She swooped on the harbours of coastal towns in Scotland and in France. Dutch, Spanish, Portuguese prey became all the one to her in an orgy of piracy.

She smuggled guns for Hugh O Neill of Dungannon and, after every meeting with this man, went raiding again with renewed vigour. Some said that she was trying to die, but could not; others, that she had gone mad or was in league with the devil.

To herself, the explanation was simple: her people were starving and she could feed and clothe them by robbing the seas. That she exulted in the danger was incidental. But there was another, and far stronger, driving force within her: in Ulster, a new King was moving towards the Coronation Stone of Tullahoge where the royal O Neills had been inaugurated for six hundred years. He needed the weapons which she brought to him – strange tokens of a stranger love. . . .

Hugh O Neill, Baron of Dungannon, was soon to be created Earl of Tyrone by an unsuspecting Queen Elizabeth, who was watching Spain instead of Ireland.

Spain . . . where the keels of the Armada ships were already being laid down.

Chapter 19

WHEN she learned that there was a Government price of five hundred pounds for her head, dead or alive, Graunya's sole comment was, "Anything less would be insult!"

Still, a certain caution entered her activities as a result. When her ships were not at sea, she hid them in desolate bays of the Ulster coast where they were provisioned by the Baron of Dungannon, in return for Spanish arms.

There was a precious quality about each moment that she spent with Hugh O Neill, a sense of heightened perception that gave her a reckless courage in his service.

Then, in the spring, her husband died, and she returned to Connacht to attend to her interests there. Her feeling of loss and desolation surprised her: she had never loved Sir Richard-in-Iron Bourke but, when the piercing wail of the keening women rose to the Easter stars, she wept for him.

The brehons of the clan forgathered in the dark council room of Carrigahowley Castle – secretly, for they were proscribed by English law – and arranged the new land division according to their ancient custom of *gavelkind*: all titular territories to be returned to the tribe, all else to be divided among the heirs after one-third had been given to the widow for her lifetime.

But, on this final point, the council was noisily divided. Shane MacHubert, the aged Bourke adviser, tottered to his feet.

"I say that Sir Richard leaves no widow," he proclaimed, "for that Graunuaile did send him shamefully from her, and bore him no other son afterwards."

The Devil's Hook spoke up passionately for his mother-in-law's rights – 'Has she not fed us in famine? – defended us by land and sea?' – and many sided with him, splitting the council.

For a while, sitting there straight-backed and dangerous, she let them argue; then, without a word, walked out into the sea-sparkling sunshine and, for a long time, stood looking at the bay and at the distant prospect of Clare Island, Hy-Brazil like against a silver sky.

'What does anything matter,' she thought, 'as long as my son, Toby, inherits Carrigahowley and Gweeshedan? Some day, he might even be the MacWilliam and have all the tribal lands restored to him!'

She smiled a maternal smile that had a little of the tigress in it: 'Toby of the Ships' was her dearest child. Somehow, Owen and Murrough O Flaherty were more like brothers to her than sons – mature men now, both of them – but Toby was only seven years old and she felt closer to him than to any of her kin. One day, he would come to live here in his father's ancestral fortress and she had a pathetic desire to be near him, or near his children, to enjoy their youth and give them the comfort of her maturity. She had always been so occupied with other things. . . . Her present kind of life must end sooner or later. When O Neill was King — Yes, that would be the end for her. Then, peace, normality, the dignity of an old woman!

She went back into the gloom of the council chamber.

"I have but one request to make," she said. "That I be allowed to build a little tower above the mooring; there to end my days out of the swing of the sea."

MacHubert conferred with the robed brehons. Heads were nodded, relief expressed that she had made no further demands.

"The tower will be built for you," MacHubert said then.

"I thank you all. So grateful am I that I will not ask for the return of my dowry."

"Y-your dowry?"

"The garrison of this castle. I shall leave the men for its defence."

The Devil's Hook hid his mouth behind his hand but laughter welled up into his eyes. There was no law to force a woman to take back her dowry if she did not want it; by leaving hers, Graunya was keeping control of Carrigahowley until her son grew up!

The advisers and brehons began to disperse, some of them muttering darkly. Graunya walked over to her son-in-law.

"I am leaving at once," she announced, ignoring his grin.

"Will you not come to Doona with me? Moira and Toby and our own son are expecting you —"

"No. My presence is nothing but a danger. Head-money is like a catching disease; it moves with the victim and only those already infected are allowed to share the loneliness."

He watched her go, a small, thin woman, misleadingly fragile in a soft grey gown, her neatly coiled hair defying the years in its depth of colour. . . .

She returned to Ulster, to the thickening plot with Hugh O Neill, upon whose rise to power she had staked her life, and the lives of the three hundred men who made up her trained sea-army. She had a reserve of eighty men on Clare Island but would only call on them in extreme necessity, because – although ferocious defenders of the fortress there – they were mere churls and *bodhachs*, unfit for the discipline of a scratch fleet moving at peril. . . .

'Enemy from the sea – attack – *kill!*' was still their training motto, its repetition a daily ritual amid the clash of uncouth axes. No one might land on Clare Island with safety except under the sign of the White Seahorse.

In the spring of the following year, Graunya made a trading voyage to Norway for the purchase of six new galleys. While she was gone, Sir Nicholas Malby died in Connacht. Iron-fisted though he had been, he had fought according to certain rough rules of his own, and the Irish respected his memory: their late Military Governor had employed neither treachery nor cunning against them.

Now, with a certain amount of hope, they looked for his successor.

In Dublin, a new Lord Deputy had taken up the Sword of State: red-headed Sir John Perrot, reputed bastard son of Henry the Eighth. Perrot had been President of Munster for nearly fourteen years and a kind of sympathy had grown in his mind for the dispossessed, unruly Irish – a sympathy which he dared not show except in his increasingly frequent bouts of drunkenness or rage when he would flare out at the Dublin Council with blistering oaths. . . .

Malby's death left a gap in the administration. A letter from Westminster gave Perrot instructions for filling it.

' . . . to journey into the Province of Connacht without delay and there install, in the name of Her Most Gracious Majesty, the new Military Governor —'

Perrot squinted at the document with pale-lashed Tudor eyes.

"Faintly remember the fellow," he grunted, rubbing his hearty stomach. "Siege of Smerwick four years back. Ummm. ' – long military and naval service . . . Captain Richard Bingham'."

News of the appointment sped ahead of the Lord Deputy. . . .

Graunya felt the wide arc of her life begin to close into a fatal circle within which friends and foes were to be locked until death separated them. She knew exactly what to expect from Bingham: pettiness that would strengthen into cruelty; the determination of a failure to do all things more thoroughly than his predecessors had done – not for duty, but for the disparagement of their service. Thus did the Binghams of the world go their joyless way, ensuring that everyone within the orbit of their authority paid for past humiliations for which they had not been responsible.

The new Military Governor was installed at Galway in July of the year fifteen hundred and eighty-four, and was knighted in St Nicholas's Church by Lord Deputy Perrot. The city put on its bravest show of splendour for the occasion: mayor and burghers walked in procession; troops marched and rode; cannon thundered from the towers; and all the ships in harbour were decked with bunting.

This was the only honour which Sir Richard Bingham's life of service had been accorded. Far from rejoicing in it, he meditated bitterly on the lost years. If only the office and title had come sooner — Well, now they were his, and he would see that the lackeys jumped!

So began the reign of terror which was to make the administrations of Fitton and Malby seem, in retrospect, like years of pleasant tilting. . . .

When Sir John Perrot came to Galway again, in the following summer, he found a province ripe for mass rebellion against the imprisonments and the hangings and the burnings of villages where native women and children perished. And now Perrot cursed Bingham to hell for ruining the greatest business of the reign: the mighty Composition of Connacht – in preparation these ten years – all drawn up on page after legal page until it was ready for signature by the landowners.

' . . . Acknowledging the manifold benefits they find in possessing of their lands and goods since the peaceable Government of Lord Deputy Sir John Perrot, and the just dealings of Sir Richard Bingham, knight, their chief officer —'

That last phrase was the one that stuck in the throats of the assembled chieftains, many of whom had been ready to sign the Composition for the sake of peace and exemption from taxes. But their hatred of Bingham choked them. If the Composition lied in one thing, it lied in all.

Gathering their shabby escorts and their lean mountain ponies, they rode out of Galway city without a backward glance for the Lord Deputy's magnificence.

One of the few native Irish marks on the mighty document was made by Murrough *na Thuaigh*, 'of the Battle Axes' (who had never succeeded in wooing the tribe away from old Dhonal Crone, the rightful chief). His thunderous name became emasculated to 'Moragh na Doe' in the English form; and he made his cross beside it, for posterity to call him a fool. The ink was hardly dry before Bingham sent eight bands of armed men into Murrough's territory, to plunder and burn and rape 'for taxes due'.

Murrough turned at last and came out in rebellion, joined by Bourkes and O Rourkes and Clanrickardes, O Malleys and Joyces and all their dependent clans. . . .

In some perverse way, Bingham had wanted this rising, if only for the pleasure of suppressing it. With all the energy of a small man who must assert himself, he blazed up through Iar-Connacht into the Joyce Country, killing as he went; then bore eastward to Lough Mask where Thomas Roe Bourke was

243

holding Hag's Castle, 'a round strong fortress with no landing place' as Bingham was to describe it in his official report of its fall. He executed Thomas Roe and his young son.

The Bourkes fortified Castle Barry, were beaten again and watched their eighty-year-old chieftain carried – because he could not walk – to the busy gallows.

'All titles of O and Mac are now abolished,' wrote a jubilant Governor to the Sheriff of Sligo, who was George Bingham, his brother.

Together, these two men were to enforce upon Connacht a régime so harsh, so sinister, so utterly without mercy or morality that the wretched province became conditioned to its terror, as a bear is taught to dance by having its feet burnt. . . .

But, in Dublin, Lord Deputy Perrot was roaring louder and louder against Bingham, referring to him in Council as 'a beggar', 'a bad baggage fellow' and 'a dodkin, the smallest coin of the realm'.

Bingham prepared a list of complaints against Perrot. Perrot retaliated with a longer list. The feud between them became a matter of common gossip which Hugh O Neill was able to retail to Graunya after one of his frequent visits to the Pale.

"They will cancel each other out," he said with grim satisfaction. "Let us be patient."

"But nobody wants to lose Sir John. He is a good man —"

"Is he? For kidnapping the O Donnell's son, Red Hugh, by base trickery and now keeping him locked up in Dublin Castle?"

"I – I sympathize with the boy's misery," she said, startled by O Neill's abruptness; usually, he was most calm and soft-spoken.

"Sympathy is not enough. We must contrive his escape."

"That is impossible!" She was aghast at the idea of O Neill's becoming involved in any act against the Government before he was ready to back it with arms. "Dublin Castle is like a locked beehive. Prisoners' fetters are examined every twenty-four hours. . . ." Instinctively, she rubbed her own wrists where the skin had once been raw.

"Be that as it may," O Neill replied roughly, "I want Red Hugh O Donnell freed." She had never seen him in such a passion of earnestness; even the fact that his favourite daughter, Rose, was betrothed to Red Hugh could not fully account for it.

"But *why*?" she demanded. "I know that he is the O Donnell tanist, and will one day be your neighbouring chieftain, but he is still only a youth. . . ."

"A youth who shows signs of military genius! He has fire, speed, endurance and *instinct* – that unerring sixth-sense of the true Celt. . . . Remember, too, that his mother is the Ineen Dhuv, a Scot of the Isles whose kin were murdered on Rathlin; she has reared her son in purest hatred of all that is English, whereas I have ties of fosterage with the race which my own people will never forgive me."

"Is Red Hugh as bitter as the Ineen Dhuv?"

O Neill laughed, and took her hand in his.

"Bitterness, Graunya, is a dark thing. There is no darkness in him. He is a dancing flame!"

She looked down at their linked hands, symbol of an understanding between them that transcended language, and knew with utter certainty why he wanted the other as his general: because Red Hugh had all those characteristics to appeal to the Irish nature which he, himself, lacked: spontaneity, exuberance, directness – qualities which, allied to O Neill's own cunning statesmanship, could forge a double-edged weapon against the enemy.

She thought for a moment longer, then said decisively, "I will make a plan of the Castle as far as it is known to me, and will write down every detail I remember about the habits of the jailers. But I will not go near the place again; my feet would not carry the weight of my apprehension! You must find someone else to organize the escape."

"Oh, I have," he said softly. "I have. . . ."

For Mary Stuart, though, there was to be no escape. A scaffold, draped in black, dominated the Hall of Fotheringay Castle on the cold, but sunny, morning of February the eighth; it was almost twenty years to the day since the wretched Henry Darnley, King of Scotland, had been murdered by his consort's connivance. Now, two masked executioners waited while Mary

Stuart walked slowly towards them, between the rigid ranks of the Sheriff's company.

She was unappalled by the sight of the block, and unrepentant of all her scheming to have Elizabeth assassinated. Her tears were only for the faithful servants she was leaving behind.

"Ye have cause rather to joy than to mourn," she said to them, "for now shall ye see Mary Stuart's troubles receive their long-expected end." Long-expected, indeed, by everyone except romantic, impetuous Mary – the figurehead of religious hopes to all Catholics, 'the greatest whore in Christendom' to most Protestants.

Pathetically, one of her little lapdogs walked behind her. . . .

The Dean of Peterborough moved forward and renewed his exhortation that she should change her religion.

"Master Dean, trouble me not," she said with dignity. "I am resolved in the Roman Catholic faith; you have nothing to do with me, nor I with you."

Then she stepped on to the platform and the executioners began to disrobe her of her long black cloak, and of the white lace veil that covered her head.

"I was not wont," she smiled at them, woman to the last, "to have my clothes plucked off by such grooms." The little dog crept under the black folds of the mantle as it fell.

Quietly, Mary Stuart laid her neck across the block.

"*In manus tuas, Domine,*" she said, and died with perfect fortitude.

Whimpering, the little dog shook himself free of the mantle and stood, bewildered, in the blood, between his mistress's body and her severed head, which had rolled out of its auburn wig.

When news of the execution reached London, the people went mad for joy. But Elizabeth withdrew herself into silence: she had never wanted the death of this sister-Queen whose son, James, was now heir to the English throne in everything except acknowledgement from the last of the Tudors.

The execution of Mary Stuart had removed one danger from England's shores while another was moving closer: in May of the year fifteen eighty-eight, Philip the Second's mighty fleet

– the most powerful armament ever collected in Europe – sailed out of Lisbon.

There were one hundred and thirty-eight ships in all – galleons of Spain and recently-annexed Portugal; high-turreted galleasses with a spread of sail so enormous that the hundreds of slaves chained to the oars seemed superfluous; classic galleys carrying some of the two-thousand-odd pieces of artillery; heavy transports and provision vessels – every one overcrowded with their combined complement of more than thirty thousand persons: nobles and their servants; soldiers; priests and surgeons. . . . But this was to be an invasion force against England, not a sea-fighting fleet: the cramped conditions were tolerated. . . .

Before even Biscay was reached, the first blow fell. A cook opened a barrel of meat and found it crawling with white worms. . . . Other stores, hastily examined, were in even worse case, the threat of pestilence writhing in the horror of their decomposition.

The Invincible Armada put into La Coruña, where more than a month was lost in cleansing and reprovisioning. Men who had set out gaily from Lisbon were to remember this delay as the leasehold of time running out. . . .

England tensed herself to meet the expected onslaught. Her fleet was ready at Plymouth – smaller ships than those of the Armada and only sixteen thousand men – under Lord Howard of Effingham, Hawkins and Drake.

The great half-moon formation of the Armada, seven miles of Spanish pride from horn to horn, was sighted from the Lizard on the nineteenth of July. English beacons flared their warning along the coast. A grey drizzle of rain was falling, making an early twilight.

The Spaniards struck their sails and drifted for the night. When morning broke, they were on the weather side of Rame Head and, to their incredulous horror, the English fleet was swooping down on them from six miles astern. Other ships of war were beating out of Plymouth with a speed which the lumbering Armada could not match. The high-sea citadels were outclassed from the beginning by the snug, low-lying craft which had been built in the yards of John Hawkins.

A murderous gunfire pursued and overtook the tall ships,

making chaos of their majestic formation. Up and down the Channel the battle raged day and night. Galleon after galleon sank or fled, bewildered by a fiercely-rising wind and a sea in turmoil.

The desperate Spaniards made for the north but were driven to take refuge in the port of Calais. At midnight, appalling furies approached out of the storm-racked blackness – English fireships blazing towards them, spark-spitalled tongues of smoke licking ahead like the devil's pennants, causing panic and flight to the open sea.

Within ten days of sighting England, the battered Armada was forced into a final battle in which four thousand Spaniards perished. A gale was blowing from the south, making it impossible for the huge galleons to retreat through the straits: their admiral commanded them to sail north and try to reach the Atlantic from the shores of Scotland.

"Keep as clear of the coast as possible," ordered this unfortunate commander who 'had no health for the sea', "and take especial care not to fall upon the island of Ireland for fear of the harm that may happen to you on that coast."

In Connacht, Bingham was ready for the remnants of the Armada. He had caused a rumour to be circulated that 'Spanish ships were coming to murder the old and carry the young off into slavery'. For the less gullible, he had a direct order:

"No one shall aid or harbour Spaniards. Whosoever does so shall die according to the Traitors' Code."

His troops and his spies were everywhere throughout the impoverished province, waiting, watching the heaving grey ocean that boiled and thundered among the coastal rocks as though this were December and not August. He was prepared to go to any lengths to prevent Spaniards from landing and joining forces with the rebel Irish.

The out-islands were the greatest danger because, owing to the turbulence of the sea, he could not reach them; but he was well aware that there was someone who could, if she were not there already: Graunuaile.

He conferred hastily with his brother, George.

"We must take a hostage to force her obedience —"

The choice was obvious: her youngest son from the Castle of Doona. His life in return for captured Spaniards. . . .

For eleven days, the Seahorse fleet had been penned into a bay of the Tyrconnell coast by a gale from the north-east. Time and time again, Graunya had tried to round Horn Head, taking the ships out against her every instinct, knowing that the storm had not reached its climax.

Even in the shelter of her cabin, she was buffeted by the gift of weather prophecy that hammered and screamed its warning to her alone. On the nights of August twenty-third and September second, when the freak storms rose to points of frenzy, she was like one possessed by devils. The elements which had always used her as a medium now threatened to destroy her if she defied them.

Across the ragged September horizon, she saw the first galleon being driven south-westward from the Scottish coast: *La Rata Encoronada*, an eight-hundred-and-twenty-ton vessel of the Levant squadron. In its wake staggered the transport, *Duquesa Santa Ana*. Later in the day, the giant Neapolitan galleass, *Girona*, battled against a wind that was beginning to veer southwest. In the wash of these ships, pitiful horses and mules – thrown overboard because of lack of fresh water – struggled and drowned.

Graunya summoned her captains.

"The Spaniards will make no effort to avoid the west coast now," she said, "because their water supplies are finished. I think the first ship that passed us this morning had no rudder, and certainly the second one was holed. Neither of them had a shred of canvas left." She walked about with her hands behind her back. "Their crews must be in a bad state. If they are to land, they will need help. We must be on Clare Island before they reach there."

"But we have been trying for eleven days —"

"I know that." She was more tense than they had ever seen her, as though she were waiting for some familiar nightmare to materialize. "Now we must succeed."

O Flynn's grandson, a junior captain, asked humbly, "Will the wind drop soon, Graunuaile?" And she replied with the dispassionate voice of the oracle:

"No. It will increase in force." She felt the pressure of the storm at the base of her skull.

"How, then —?"

"The galleys. Our best men at the oars. Myself as pilot."

Graunya was never to forget that voyage from Tyrconnell to Mayo in the teeth of a sou'-westerly gale. The sea was running like a mill-race against the galleys; the men leaned their whole bodies on the oars and still made little progress. Several times, the galleys were spun around and forced back over the course they had travelled so painfully.

In any other circumstance of her sea-going life, she would have ordered her vessels to run for shelter but, now, she had to go on. She had to reach Clare Island before any Spaniard landed there: the wild peasants who made up the garrison knew nothing about the Armada. . . .

Off Dooros Point, another huge Spanish ship was being pounded to death, her masts gone, her high poop pitching a hundred yards away as though it were a separate craft, and all the surrounding ocean writhing in the mass of her tangled cordage. There was no sign of human life anywhere near, and the final destruction of this mighty galleon, *La Trinidad Valencera*, was an awesome sight: it reared up and crashed itself upon the rocks in suicidal frenzy with a sound that was more than that of splintering wood.

A day's voyage south to Gweebarra Bay: dead bodies in the water now; great pieces of wreckage rolling round and round; cables and figureheads and casks and – once – about twenty yards of vivid orange silk.

The galleys made no pause to examine anything but struggled on – two more days, two more nights – towards Sligo and Killala, the signs of catastrophe increasing in number, the wind still howling out of the south-west, pluming a ploughed ocean.

Around the point of Benwee Head rushed the full raving fury of the mad Atlantic, to snap oars, lift galley-prows, hold them poised as though by the throats before flinging them down between mountainous waves.

For an instant, Graunya glimpsed *La Rata*, rounding Erris,

dangerously close. The transport, *Santa Ana*, had vanished and there was no sign of the *Girona* either; it was likely that they had been driven back on to the Ulster or Scottish coasts. She prayed that this was so. . . . By the time the galleys themselves had cleared Erris Head, *La Rata* had vanished also. There was just a chance that she had found haven in Blacksod, but there might be other ships —

Graunya dared not risk the narrow passage between Achill and Corraun, so she piloted for the open water west of Inishkea, then bore due south, clearing Achill Head. A south-easterly course from there would bring Clare Island into view, if her oarsmen could bear up that far; two of them had collapsed – one bleeding from the mouth – and there were five broken oars in her own galley alone. She could only see one other craft out of the original six, and that was far astern.

In the trough of each wave, she looked up at a rearing wall of water, poised greenish-grey, curling yellow at the tip but, on the brief summit, there was a sweeping view which she grasped with intensified vision; in a series of elevations, she counted seven huge ships, all in far worse plight than *La Rata* had been. Two were already aground off Clare Island, a queer greenish evening light striking off their brasses and their gildings against the sinister blackness of the island's west face. Little figures could be seen toppling from the sloping decks, scrambling through the gaping ports to thresh and struggle shorewards. Some were already wading out of the sea, dragging themselves up the strand beyond the pull of the shoaling water.

And, waiting for them, was a grim line of armed men, their double-edged axes working in deadly rhythm: swing up behind the head – swing down into the exhausted body of an enemy from the sea. . . . Attack: *kill* – attack: *kill* – until the axe-bearing arms were weary.

Graunuaile stumbled on to her blood-soaked island where dead Spanish faces looked up at her from a tangle of gold chains and jewelled fingers and swords whose owners had been too weak, from hunger and disease, to draw them out of their scabbards. Satin doublets – once white, now as russet as the dead men's silk hose – were slashed to reveal their secret quilting of gold ducats, and the ravaged flesh beneath.

The screams that she had uttered in the first realization of what was happening, died to a long keening wail.

The men of the island garrison came, leaning on the wind, wiping their axes on their sleeves, expressions of dazed ecstasy on their faces.

"Graunuaile," they exulted, "we have saved your island-kingdom!" – while all she could do was moan, "Oh, Christ! Oh, God!" – and search the seas for even one survivor.

But there was none. Only the *Santa Maria de la Rosa* ploughing her doomed passage to the Kerry coast.

In a letter to the Queen, Sir Richard Bingham summed up the fate of Spanish ships that fell upon the coast of Connacht.

> By contrary weather, they were driven upon the several parts of this province, and wrecked as it were by even portions, three ships in every of the four counties bordering upon the sea, in Sligo, Mayo, Galway and Thomond. So that twelve ships perished – that all we know of – on the rocks and sands by the shore side, and some three or four besides to seaboard of the out-isles. Other great wrecks they had, both in Munster and in Ulster, which, being out of my charge, I have not so good notice of. . . .

Bingham executed one thousand, one hundred and fifty-six survivors of the Armada who came ashore in his territories; his brother, George, eight hundred. Western Irish peasants robbed and slaughtered an unknown number, but their chieftains helped nearly five hundred to safety at risk to their own lives and property. In Ulster, two thousand four hundred Spaniards were got safely out of the country; and some remained secretly with Hugh O Neill, who was now Earl of Tyrone.

Before the full toll of the wreckage was known, Owen O Malley of the Black Oak died as he had lived, chief of his nation. But, by order of Sir Richard Bingham, no tanist was allowed to succeed him. Thus, the last elected ruler of Clan O Malley took the old tribal system with him, out of the Two Umalls, for ever.

Chapter 20

W HEN Graunya learned about the kidnapping of her son,
Toby, she lost her sole remaining instinct for self-preserva-
tion: inside the walls of Galway city – where Spanish corpses,
still hanging in chains from the gibbets, swayed in a sad autumn
wind – she submitted to Bingham.

"See now that I have obeyed you," she cried in Latin, flinging a handful of gold ornaments at his feet. "These were worn
by Spaniards whose graves are on Clare Island for you to witness!
Where is my son?"

"In England, madam, being taught a civility which his
mother lacks."

"You will not find it lacking in me from henceforth. I submit.
I grovel. I call you Lord of Connacht. Only restore my son to
his own place."

"The price of ransom is high —"

"I will pay it."

"Very well. These are my terms: all your cattle from Carrigahowley; your brood mares from Kildavnet; your sheep
flocks from the islands —"

"Take them!"

"No, not by seeming force lest my administration be blamed
again" – he had suffered one brief removal from office after
Perrot's complaints against him – "but I will receive them from
your own hand at Castle Barry on Martinmas Day next. Meanwhile, you will admit my bailiffs into all your territories, to

take inventory." No Englishman had ever yet penetrated the remoter parts of the Umalls. . . .

"They will not be molested," she vowed, "nor will I drive any animals away. When will my son come home?"

"As soon as may be practicable afterwards."

"That is your word? He will be restored, safe and well, to the Castle of Doona?"

"In due course, all else being in order."

"All else *will* be in order —"

"You have overlooked one small matter: there is still a price of five hundred pounds on your own head. That amount – which I am forfeiting by not arresting you now – you will bring with you to Castle Barry along with the beeves and mares and muttons."

They regarded each other with mutual loathing; then the Governor signed to his attendants to have her escorted to the quayside.

For a long time after she had gone, he sat staring at the pile of gold ornaments on the floor – his neat-bearded chin cupped in small hard hands – and the gold was reflected yellowly in his eyes. He would accept her possessions – lawfully; and he would take her life – still within the law. He no longer had the hostile interference of Sir John Perrot to watch, for Perrot had given up the Sword of State five months back and had been replaced by Deputy Fitzwilliam, a man old in his suspicions of all things Irish. . . .

Graunya returned by sea to Carrigahowley and ordered the bringing in of all her animals. A mellow autumn sun shone on glossy mares and mud-caked cattle and small rough-fleeced sheep whose meat was lean. She could ill afford this ransom with winter coming on but she had promised to drive no beast away. Still, she decided that a little husbandry was in order: a few dozen beeves slaughtered for salting; a gift of a bull or a mare to friends and kinsfolk; a placid ewe or a furious ram to cave-dwelling shepherds, in advance of a year's wages. . . . It was all well and quickly done before the bailiffs arrived, and still large flocks and herds remained for them to count.

A week before Martinmas, the entire caravan set out for

Castle Barry, the five hundred pounds head-money distributed in small sums among the men of Graunya's escort for safe keeping.

She had to remind herself constantly that the whole painful sacrifice was for Toby's benefit and not for Bingham's, but still she could not compose her mind to what she was doing – giving away almost her entire personal wealth for a verbal promise, and that from a man whom she hated and distrusted. But, if she did not do it, and lost her son as a result, she might as well be dead. For once, she was firmly penned. There was nothing for it but to go on, although she had had a presentiment of treachery from the start. If only O Lee were at hand to advise her. . . . But he was in Wicklow with the rebel O Byrnes, working towards Tyrone's scheme for the release of Red Hugh O Donnell, one attempt having already failed. . . .

November trees were bleak and dripping; tracks turning to muddy streams; a vast desolation which the sight of Castle Barry intensified rather than relieved, as though the spirit of its old hanged chieftain hung above its towers in the tattered sky while the hopes of his heirs guttered in its dungeons.

Sir Richard Bingham, bareheaded but otherwise in full armour under a heavy cloak, rode out to receive the ransom. He had twenty armed men with him, mounted on big English horses that towered over the slender Irish mares.

"All the beeves and horseflesh can go to my own residence at Roscommon," he ordered with a proprietary air, "and the muttons to those garrisons that have need of them." Then, watching his escort collect the last bag of money, he turned abruptly to Graunya, and asked, his voice loud in the dripping silence, "Are you Graunuaile?"

She blinked with astonishment.

"You know that I am —"

"I merely require your confirmation. All your goods are now forfeit. As a rebel and a pirate, I arrest you."

"*But my son —*"

"Traitors have no heirs. You have been behind every act of defiance in this province, and off its shores, for more years than anyone has patience to remember; you were in arms against both my predecessors; you are a notorious rebel through all the coasts of this country and others, and now I believe that you have aided Spaniards." He put his hand on his sword and spoke over his shoulder. "Take this woman to the castle. . . ."

Her men had no chance against plate armour, muskets and chargers. Helplessly, they watched her go, then themselves turned and rode quickly away. She heard their dying hoofbeats in the November twilight and all hope went with them. When Bingham was both judge and jury, one more hanging would make no difference.

In the morning, she was taken on to the green outside the castle walls. The old gallows, worn out with service, had been replaced by a raw new one, the wood and the rope white; she hoped that it had never been used before, that it would not smell of death. . . .

'I ought to be afraid,' she thought wonderingly, 'or at least sorry to leave this life in such fashion!' But she had no feeling whatever. All her sense of outside events had been cut off by a dull fatalism which left her conscious only of anger: anger at her own stupidity; anger against the double-dealing to which she could never become accustomed.

"I will curse Bingham with my last breath," she vowed, speaking aloud in Irish. And, as hands urged her up the wooden steps, she recited a blasphemous litany.

"May the young wife he has just married never bear him a son! May the ghosts of Spaniards and Irishmen sit on the foot of his bed, all night, every night! May he die in darkness among strangers —"

The hangman dropped the noose loosely over her head. She looked down at the Military Governor, willing herself to hold his eye to the end, forcing her curses upon him.

The hangman would not proceed until Bingham nodded – as he had so often nodded in the past —

But now, there was a thunder of hooves approaching, a great shout, a flash of steel. The soldiers wheeled around.

"Sir Richard Bingham?" a voice bellowed. "Let me through."

The rider flung off his helmet and reined his lathered mount.

"Who are you?" Bingham demanded.

"The Lord of Corraun, alias the Devil's Hook, a rebel Bourke!"

"Then you may follow your kinswoman on the rope —"

"Not so hasty! I have hostages for you; my own son and five other boys born of chieftains —"

Graunya shouted, "*No, Corraun, no!*" but he waved a hand airily as though bidding her good-morrow in her own fortress, and continued to address Bingham, " – whose fathers will, of course, be quiet as long as you hold their sons."

"Which chieftains?" Bingham snapped.

"Donald the Piper O Malley; Roebuck French of Gallen; MacWalter the Tall Bourke; MacSweeney the Scot; O Rourke Oge and myself. Enough?"

"For what?"

"For the lady here. As you already have *her* son, I think she will be peaceable from now on. And remember, hanging is less punishment for Graunuaile than restraint!"

Six chieftains' sons for hostages. . . . It was a tempting offer: the Queen was anxious for such youths to be sent to England, remembering what great good had come of educating the Earl of Tyrone at Penshurst – he was holding the north for the Crown!

Bingham looked with regret at the unused rope.

"Where are the youths?" he asked harshly, hoping that he might get them and still keep his prisoner.

"In a secret place. I will only lead you to them if my kinswoman may ride behind me."

"I could hold you here and make you talk —"

"It would do no good. The place is under the ground, in a labyrinth of limestone caves."

"Very well. You will ride under close escort. Take the woman behind you. If you attempt to escape, she will be shot."

So Graunya and the Devil's Hook rode away from Castle Barry on a slender Irish horse with the imported chargers crowding around them, massive haunched. The tracks were muddier than ever from overnight rain, and all the green places were turning to swamp. Corraun plunged into woods and forded streams; guided his mount through bogs that had gravel tracks of which only he knew; waited patiently and obediently for the Governor's cavalry when they were forced to drop a few paces behind.

"How far more?" Bingham raved.

"Just over there. You see the mouth of a cave? That is the entrance."

"Lead on then and bring the boys out."

The hooves of the heavier horses were squelching in a rushy morass. Bingham had no desire to proceed farther, nor to enter the labyrinth without lights. He watched the Devil's Hook and Graunya disappear into the cavern's mouth.

He waited. His escort waited. The silence stretched. Then —

"*Sir!*" shouted an officer, pointing a quavering finger at a distant hilltop. And Bingham knew that he was beaten when the Devil's Hook waved a hand to him before vanishing over the green horizon. . . .

"There were never any hostages, were there?" Graunya panted when her son-in-law drew up for a breather.

He looked at her over his shoulder, and his face was surprisingly solemn.

"You should have more trust in people's affection for you, Graunuaile; *all* the men I named gave their sons."

For the first time since her husband's death, she felt tears prick her eyes but she turned her head obstinately away, and demanded suspiciously,

"How did you reach them in one night?"

He gave a deep sigh for her ingratitude.

"I did not *have* to reach them: we were already gathered together in Cahirnamart. Listen, Graunya: there is a conspiracy to have Bingham removed from office again – this time, permanently. Even some of his own officials are in it, for they are as much sickened by his brutalities as we are. A huge petition is going to the Dublin Council. We need your signature to it as the most famous woman in Connacht."

"That is why you rescued me?"

"Partly," he grinned, "partly!" – and galloped on.

Lord Deputy Fitzwilliam had no more love for Sir Richard Bingham than Perrot had had and, when he perused the list of charges and complaints against him, decided to hold a General Sessions at Galway for the Governor to stand trial there. But the Dublin Council opposed this course, on the grounds that the court would be packed against Bingham. If there were to be a trial, it must be in Dublin. At the end of November, therefore, the accused Governor was escorted out of his province where O Rourke of Breffni was still in active rebellion.

No sooner had he gone than the entire Bourke nation rose again in arms for one final attempt to shake off the English yoke. The O Malleys joined the Bourkes. The clan O Flaherty came out under their once-despised chieftain, Sir Murrough of the Battle Axes (because old Dhonal Crone was dead at last) and, for the only time in its history, there was unity of a kind in Connacht.

Graunuaile led a spectacular raid on the Aran Islands – which were being held for the Crown by Sir Thomas le Strange – and escaped with three galleys full of foodstuffs and a transport loaded with artillery.

This latter she wanted to moor below the Castle of Bunowen, where her second son, Murrough, now lived, so that the weapons might be collected by O Flahertys of Iar-Connacht and Connemara.

But Murrough flatly refused to harbour the transport.

"You mean," his mother asked dangerously – standing astride a bench in a swaying galley – "that you are not with us in this fight?" She had had her own suspicions for a long while that Murrough was playing a double game for his own advantage. His nickname betrayed his English sympathies: *na Maor*, 'the Sheriff'.

He looked down at her from the height of the jetty and, for a moment, he reminded her of his father, Nacugga, by the way in which he stood. . . .

"I am not with you," he said then, and turned away without making any offer of hospitality.

She was too humiliated and angry to consider the rights or wrongs of the matter. If Murrough refused to help his rebel kinsmen in one way, then he must be forced to do it in another.

Withdrawing her galleys and the transport ship northward up the coast, she waited for nightfall, then raided her son's lands with all the vigour of a young tanist taking his first prey.

259

Before dawn broke over the Bens of Beola, three thousand head of cattle were being driven overland towards Umall, and Murrough's prized aviary of hunting-hawks was empty. . . .

Graunya, her matriarchal pride satisfied, continued her journey by sea. She needed reassurance now that her eldest son, Owen O Flaherty, was loyal, although he had never given her cause to doubt him: he had aided and supported her in many of her ventures and – lately – was one of those chieftains who had helped Spaniards, risking his life for their safe return home.

She ran her galleys into the harbour of Inishturk. Owen came striding over the beach to meet her and she kissed him fondly, looking up at him with searching eyes. He seemed haggard and distrait —

"My son, what is the matter?"

"Have you not heard?" He took a pace away from her, his hands still gripping her shoulders from their embrace. "Bingham has been acquitted of all charges. He is on his way back to Connacht. I think there will be terrible retribution for this rebellion. . . ."

It was swift and final. The two Bingham brothers, Richard and George, with their nephews, John and Francis, led their troops to the four corners of the province and laid its spring crops waste with fire. Then they converged on O Rourke of Breffni – having paralysed his allies, the Bourkes – and forced him to retreat northwards from his cannon-levelled fortresses and his blackened lands.

O Rourke fled to Scotland, where he threw himself on the mercy of Catholic King James. But James, needing Elizabeth's goodwill, handed the fugitive over to her officials. The list of his crimes was impressive, one being that he had dragged a wooden effigy of the Queen at his horse's tail.

"Did not this shameful incident occur," thundered the prosecutor, "during the Deputyship of Sir John Perrot? Why was no action taken then?" And eyes turned accusingly on the redheaded son of Henry the Eighth, who had preferred to sympathize with rebels than to make friends with Crown officials.

O Rourke was given over to a traitor's death at Tyburn, which he faced with dignity and courage. Sir John Perrot, confined in the Tower, awaited the Queen's signature to his own execution warrant for treason, but died while Elizabeth hesitated to take the life of her natural brother.

In Connacht, the fight was over and the costs coldly estimated: *to the war against the Bourkes and Scots for the year 1586, £1,476; to the war against all others, 1589 to '90, £3,296.*

All tribes and counties which had risen were to pay these costs, in addition to their normal rents. Graunuaile was ordered to restore what she had taken from the Aran Islands. O Rourke's lands were given over to English settlers, his son and heir turned out to roam like a wood-kerne. . . .

Devastated Connacht paid its debts in cattle, sheep and horses. There would be no harvest to reap this autumn. Many chieftains were living without cover in the mountains, their fortresses taken over by the Governor's troops; and the wolf packs – as though sensing the weakness of the people – hunted even down to the seashores.

The famine conditions which Edmund Spenser had described in Munster had now reached as far northward as Sligo.

Graunya could never trade with Spain again after the Clare Island massacre, so she turned the Seahorse fleet over to deep-sea fishing. Her larger craft could reach the Cod Bank, sixty miles west of Achill Head, and remain there in the otherwise empty Atlantic for weeks at a time. This location had the advantage of being entirely peaceful, free from the interference and humiliating supervision which now bent Connacht's back in slavery, and she returned to it time and again, sailing for home only to land the catch and take on fresh water.

Her men knew that some spark had gone out of her. She would spend hours sitting cross-legged on deck, tightly wrapped in her old frieze mantle, staring unseeingly at the ocean and speaking to no one. They judged that the failure of the last rebellion had broken her as much in spirit as in possessions, because of the brutal killing of her eldest son, Owen: Bingham's nephew had asked Owen to ferry troops across to Inishturk, and feed them there at his own expense. The lord of the island had no choice but to comply. When the men had eaten, John Bingham ordered a massacre. . . .

Every living soul on the island perished – Owen O Flaherty, his wife Catherine, their only son and all their attendants, men and women.

Since that outrage, Graunya had shown little enthusiasm for anything. There was a curiously vacant expression in the dark-blue eyes which had once been so intense. Even when her men persuaded her to gamble with them, she lost and won with equal lack of interest. It was uncanny, especially when moored out here on a flat calm day, the sea an unbroken circle, the sky a domed lid over it, and Graunuaile sitting like a small petrified tree with her straight back against the mainmast. She was sixty years of age and looked older: the bright-foliaged youthfulness which she had kept for so long had been the bubbling of an inner sap; that dried up, nothing but bare branches showed, without hope of another spring.

She talked to herself, silently, in the cavern of her own mind.

'I have no sons remaining. Owen, dead; Murrough, estranged from me; Toby, growing up in England, his childhood lost to me. . . . My lands are all desolate, my castles empty. The only man I ever loved has gone chasing like a fool after an English general's daughter —'

This was the bitterest reality of all: Hugh O Neill, Earl of Tyrone, married to young Mabel Bagenal, twenty-five years his junior! While Connacht was fighting for its life, Tyrone was too busy, with love or lust, to raise a helping finger. Passionately, he had wooed old Bagenal's girl and – when fiercely ordered to leave her alone – snatched her from a house in Dublin and rode away with her, to willing seduction and necessary marriage. . . .

Still, the brain that planned the kidnapping of an enemy general's daughter could also engineer the escape of Red Hugh O Donnell from Dublin Castle.

While it was still dark on Epiphany Morning – the Irish 'Christmas of the Stars' – young O Donnell, with fellow-prisoners Henry and Art O Neill, crept through a privy whose chute opened on to the outer walls.

Tyrone had bribed a jailer to fix a rope from the high chute down into the castle moat. Beyond the frozen water crouched a band of O Hagans, retainers of Tyrone. Some of them went off in one direction with Henry O Neill; the others took Art and Red Hugh westward to the snow-covered Wicklow mountains wherein lay the fatal valley of Glenmalure that had swallowed the Deputy's troops; but the marsh was frozen now, so that the youths' fetters clanged on every stone as they stumbled along.

After a night and a day in the bitter weather, Art O Neill collapsed and had to be carried, before the forty-mile march ended on top of Table Mountain. Here, the O Hagans left him in Red Hugh's arms while they went to find the rebel O Byrnes – not an easy task at any time, for the O Byrnes only came out of their caves these days to raid and burn the Pale!

The O Hagans were gone a long time. Red Hugh's clothing froze into an agonizing bond with that of the unconscious Art O Neill.

At last, he heard them returning and saw the cloud of their icy breaths. They had an elderly man with them as well as several young O Byrnes.

The man bent over Art O Neill, then took him gently out of Red Hugh's arms, saying, "I am sorry – your friend is dead." Then he looked at O Donnell with faded eyes that had a trace of astonishment in them: by all the laws of the Book of O Brasil, this youth ought not to be alive either. Magnus O Lee judged that his stamina must be fantastic. . . .

On his own ageing back, O Lee carried the youth half-way down the mountain to where there was a rebel cave warmed by a fire. There, he examined him carefully and found that he was suffering from severe frostbite of the feet. It was too late to massage them with snow or cold water; gangrene had set in at the tips of the big toes.

Quietly, O Lee put the blade of his hunting knife in the fire and, when the steel was hot, he turned his back on young O Donnell to shield his hands from the boy's sight. Holding the frozen ankles firmly, he amputated the gangrenous toes.

The boy would live, although he would always be lame.

O Lee's three-year mission was almost ended – to restore Red Hugh to Ulster, where his chieftain-father was waiting to hand over the O Donnell title to him, and Tyrone was ready to join him in arms for the most carefully planned rebellion the country had ever known.

Magnus O Lee sighed the sigh of an old man. For himself, he had had enough of patching bodies broken by fighting. All he wanted was to return to his native Connacht, however terrible the conditions there, and keep his long-standing promise to Graunuaile, that he would never leave her service again.

They would not quarrel now. They were both too old. . . . It was a sad, and, at the same time, a comforting thought.

Graunya had imagined that the homecoming of her son, Toby, would be the most joyous event of her life. Instead, when he arrived at last – without warning or explanation from Bingham – several uncomfortable problems arose.

He was fifteen years of age, physically mature, and had been away almost four years; he spoke Irish haltingly, with a strong English accent, and regarded his native province with bewilderment and distaste – the rough, poverty-stricken living conditions of even the greatest lords; the outlandish dress of the people; the primitive food they ate, half-cooked and totally unseasoned. . . .

For their part, the native Irish viewed Toby with suspicion and dislike, even after he had put away his velvets and laces, let his hair grow long and tried to sprout a beard! To them, he was that member of a wild litter that has been handled by aliens and is for ever rejected as a result.

Poor Toby of the Ships! Here he was, Lord of Carrigahowley, son of Graunuaile, foster-child of rebel Corraun and most noble born of the Nether Bourkes, yet people treated him like a leper. Even his own mother was often at a loss for words in his company as she groped to bridge the mental gap between them that was political and religious and cultural.

Without exaggeration or emotion, she told him about the Connacht wars, by way of explaining the wretched conditions of the province; but he interpreted the lesson as an accusation for not having fought in them!

Then, out hunting one fatal day, Toby met the grandson of that O Rourke who had died at Tyburn.

Over the following months, friendship developed between the two boys. Wild schemes for new rebellions were discussed. The young Lord of Carrigahowley was now determined to prove himself wholly Irish by some worthy feat of arms. . . .

Incautiously – for he was not yet conditioned to Bingham's spy system – he put his ideas on paper and sent the letter to Brian O Rourke. It reached Bingham instead. Toby's arrest was automatic.

At the same time, his harmless uncle, Donald-the-Piper O Malley of Cahirnamart, was accused of having been concerned in the murder of some soldiers. He, too, was locked in the Shoe-makers' Tower in Galway.

Now, at last, Graunya shook off her apathy. She had been driven too far and would take decisive action against Bingham, her enemy. But not in the old battering-ram fashion – she had learnt her lesson! – although the scheme, when complete, still bore the hallmark of her directness: gathering her ships, her men, and as many neighbouring chieftains as would accompany her, she sailed for England to petition the Queen. . . .

And, because there was never the least idea of failure in her mind, she not only succeeded, but succeeded brilliantly. Her first audience of Queen Elizabeth was in the Presence Chamber – where many might come and be heard publicly – but, afterwards, she was granted access to the Privy Chamber, to which only chosen petitioners were invited. . . .

During the months of June and July, men of the Seahorse fleet roamed London's thronged streets – where appalling squalor lived side by side with comfort, splendour and even magnificence, all under the ever-present shadow of summer plague – while their admiral spent an increasing amount of time at Court. It seemed that Graunya's presence amused the unconventional ginger-wigged Elizabeth, who admired vitality and courage above all other human qualities; to the Queen, Graunuaile was a female Francis Drake, living proof of her own royal theory that woman was in all ways man's equal! For sup-plying this proof, Graunya was offered the honorary title of Countess, which she refused, on the grounds that —

"I am Graunya Ui Maille of Umall, which title has always been sufficient unto my needs."

Still, she got those things for which she had come, and a few more besides: release – on bonds of good behaviour – for her son, Toby, and her brother, Donald the Piper; confirmation of her first husband's property to her remaining O Flaherty son, Murrough, and his heirs; some maintenance for herself out of the lands of both her husbands. . . .

In a bag hanging from her belt, she carried the most remarkably human letter ever dictated, in the course of business, by Elizabeth Tudor:

> For pity of this aged woman having no title to any livelihood or portion of lands, the Queen desires Sir Richard Bingham so to deal with her that her sons' property shall yield her some maintenance for the rest of her old years. She hath confessed her ill usage of Murrough *na Maor* O Flaherty, who was dutiful to us when his mother preyed him with her galleys. She promises by oath now to be faithful.

Graunya's impression of Queen Elizabeth was summed up by her parting words, in Latin:

"I would, madam, that I had known the pleasure of your gracious presence in my youth; for then should I have learned how to govern."

"Methinks you know it well enough," quipped the Queen. "Sooner you sail with those wild fellows than I!" – and they laughed together, these two women who were, by nature, so much alike.

Chapter 21

THE Seahorse fleet sailed out of the Thames estuary and made its way westward through the Channel, where it was much delayed by fog and, later, by storm; so that, when the Irish coast came in view at last, fresh water was dangerously low aboard.

Graunya decided to risk a mooring off Howth Head on the north horn of Dublin Bay. The old Norman castle of the St Lawrence family there was within the boundaries of the Pale but – secure now in the possession of the Queen's letter – she went ashore in a longboat with six men and approached its gates. It was evening, calm and sunny after the high winds.

An old man peered warily from the guardtower.

"Who is it?"

"Graunuaile, requesting hospitality."

"Aye – aye – we thought so. Saw the ships."

She waited for the gates to be opened but the old man made no move.

"Hurry, fellow!" she shouted impatiently. "The tide waits not even for me." Other faces were now peering through the arrow-slits, and a sergeant clattered out on to the gun platform.

"The gates are closed for the night," he bawled, "and the family St Lawrence seated at their evening meal. They have left orders not to be disturbed."

Motionless, Graunya regarded him for a moment, her eyebrows lowering, puckering the scar. Then —

"The Queen of England opened her gates to me," she cried

ringingly, "and so, also, shall the St Lawrences!" She turned on her heel, snapped her fingers to the men of her escort, and strode away at their head. She was in a black rage that hospitality – the greatest virtue of the old Irish chieftain – should be so ignored in this mad world where all the ancient customs were toppling: she had punished her own son for such incivility, and she would punish Howth Castle, although her ships' guns were of too short a range to reach its walls.

The fleet lay up where it was for the night and, very early next morning, landed a large party to search for water. As they scrambled along a stony beach under the cliffs – led by a scowling Graunya who had not yet made up her mind what action to take against the St Lawrences – a young boy approached them. He was wearing a velvet cloak over his nightshirt, and his bare feet were thrust into felt slippers that were ornamented with gilt buttons.

Graunya had never been able to resist the charm of a small boy. Her expression softened as she went down on one knee before him and held out her hands.

"Who is sleepwalking?" she teased. "And where is he going?"

"To see the ships," the lad replied solemnly. "I am fully awake, I assure you. The porter is my friend and let me out!"

For an instant, as realization of his identity came to her, she held her breath; then, standing up slowly so as not to frighten him, she asked in a casual tone, "You are Master St Lawrence?"

He nodded, wide-eyed.

"Then I invite you on board my flagship. . . ."

Within the hour, the unwatered fleet was far north of Howth while the St Lawrence heir played happily under the Seahorse pennant. . . .

This was the last public act of Graunya's maritime career. She refused all offers of ransom for Geoffrey St Lawrence and demanded only a verbal agreement for his safe return: that the gates of Howth Castle should never again be closed during meals and that an extra place should be laid at the dais table at all times.

Toby of the Ships and Donald the Piper were released from Shoemakers' Tower in Galway. To celebrate her son's return to Carrigahowley, Graunya arranged a marriage for him with Maeve, daughter of O Conor Sligo of the royal house of Connacht; that done she withdrew her own presence and all her belongings from the fortress, and went to live in the little tower of Rossyvera which had been built for her above the mooring.

Her Oath to the Queen precluded her from active participation in any further fighting, should it arise. So – to put temptation behind her – she disbanded the Seahorse fleet. O Malley and O Flaherty nephews became the new owners of barques and galleys, along with sons and grandsons of faithful captains. To Murrough *na Maor* of Bunowen she gave some of the larger ships, and to Toby of Carrigahowley the remainder, these latter to be moored where she could see them from her tower, to complete the satisfying view which it commanded: westward, the Corraun peninsula; south of that, the familiar outline of Clare Island, with Inishturk and Inishbofin beyond; and, across the width of Clew Bay, Murrisk under the cone of Croagh Patrick where lay buried Owen-of-the-Black-Oak O Malley, and the Lady Margaret. . . . Graunya had directed that she, herself, should be buried on Clare Island.

Now that her youngest son was married, and her ships gone the ways of their new owners, she had nothing further to defend or lose. Worse, she had nothing to do and soon became restless. Loneliness tormented her: there were few of her own generation remaining. . . .

And then, one September evening, she looked towards the mouth of the bay and saw a curragh being rowed along a red finger of the setting sun. She went down to the jetty and, when the craft drew alongside, grasped its painter and made it fast to her own belt.

"Welcome home, Magnus," she said softly. "This curragh can only leave again with me in it!"

He gave a deep chuckle of laughter and replied, "I'll do better than that. A longer rope from my curragh shall be tied to the foot of your bed!"

In after years, legend was to swear that Graunuaile kept her entire fleet so tied up; but, then, legend exaggerated many things about her. . . .

For almost a whole month of that golden autumn, she and

Magnus O Lee wandered about together like contented children, filling in the gaps of the times they had spent apart — talking, laughing, feeling the deep roots of old friendship stir with new life.

"Do you not miss the Seahorse fleet?" he asked once, hooking a fruited bramble from the top of a sun-warmed bank.

"Of course. It was my life. But now —"

"Now?"

" — I am not important: an old woman with her rosary hanging from her kriss!"

"What matters then?"

She knew what he wanted her to say: words he had tried to teach her long ago, the truth of which she had only lately learnt.

"Apart from your being home, Magnus, nothing matters except the nation as a whole — neither personal pride nor family nor tribe. The little wars are over; the old ways gone from everything but Faith."

She took the purple fruit out of his hand.

"How peaceful everything is," she said, not knowing that it was the last day of such peace.

Across the Ulster-Connacht border surged the troops of Tyrone under Red Hugh O Donnell. And the Bourke nation marched to join them, with all their lieges.

Hugh O Neill, Earl of Tyrone, was in conference, inside his fortified Castle of Dungannon, with Jesuits, chieftains, and those survivors of the Armada whom he had maintained to train his troops.

"My friends," he said, rising, "the news from Connacht is most excellent. Sligo Castle has fallen to the O Donnell! We hear that Sir Richard Bingham has been driven from its walls and sent into retreat across the Curlieus, with the loss of eight companies. . . ."

The chieftains cheered noisily while the more restrained Spaniards nodded and smiled.

"It was regrettable," Tyrone continued, "that one Ulick Bourke found it necessary to kill Sir Richard's brother George —" He lifted his leonine head and raked the assembled company with a sharp blue eye: no regret whatever showed on any countenance; he chose his next words accordingly. " – instead of killing Sir Richard himself!" There was a roar of approval for this sentiment. Tyrone continued, "But it seems that Her Majesty, the Queen, has now taken his dispatch out of our hands: she has summoned Bingham to appear before a special court at Athlone, to answer charges and complaints."

"That happened before," shouted O Cahan, "and the devil was freed!"

Tyrone tapped an elegant finger on a letter newly arrived.

"Not this time, I think. The Governor of Connacht has disappeared, and he is not at Athlone. My belief is that he has panicked, and taken ship for England. If so, he is a fool: the Queen expects obedience from her officials. He will walk off that ship into one of her dungeons. . . ."

A report of three weeks later confirmed this prophecy: Sir Richard Bingham was confined in the Fleet prison, charged with a long list of offences.

But Tyrone had no further time for the ex-Governor. As supreme commander of the rebel forces, he was directing operations on all fronts: Red Hugh O Donnell, with Bourke aid, was to keep Connacht fully occupied while thrusting eastward to harry English settlers in King's County and Queen's County; bands of wild kerne were to raid Longford, to drive enemy cattle herds northward; trained rebel soldiers must take Monaghan and Enniskillen; the Pale was to have no peace from raids by O Byrnes, O Moores, O Conors and Kavanaghs.

Behind this planned chaos, the leader's brain worked with deadly precision. Every move had been calculated for years in advance. He had been patient – God, how he had been patient! Lies, evasions, declarations of loyalty to allay suspicion; the hiding of men and arms; truces, submissions, humiliations . . . all ended on that September day when he rode to Tullahoge with the priests and the bards and the chieftains, there to be consecrated as The O Neill, Prince of Ulster – the sanctity of six hundred years of kingship invested in his sacred person.

His people would follow him now to the death and, as a king, he would lead and fight and, maybe, die. But, as a man, he would continue to love women.

His third wife, Mabel Bagenal, was dead – her heart broken as much by his infidelities as by the harsh way of life in an Irish rebels' camp – and he had a little Scottish wench of the McDonalds with him presently. Yet he knew that he would have to send his McDonald mistress away soon. His heart was gone from her already – gone to the regal beauty that was Catherine, daughter of the Magennis of Iveagh.

In order to make Catherine his Countess, Tyrone was prepared to risk alienating the Scots. He had six thousand troops in arms and no longer needed new mercenaries.

All that mattered, politically, was to continue his correspondence with Philip of Spain, who had tried twice already to send troops to Ireland and whose ships were now sailing up the west coast once more, recruiting Irish pilots to guide them on future voyages.

Putting both Catherine Magennis and Philip of Spain out of his mind temporarily, Tyrone gave his full attention to the Blackwater fortress, the only English garrison standing inside his borders between Dungannon and Dublin.

"We could take the crumbling fort without difficulty," he pointed out to his council, "but that would relieve the English of a tiresome duty: the provisioning of their three hundred men there. I think a long blockade is best. When the garrison is reduced to eating its horses, supplies will be sent up from Newry under strong escort. We will attack that escort. . . ."

Ten months went by before Marshall Bagenal set out to relieve the Blackwater. He had a force of more than four thousand men guarding the precious food supplies.

With their combined armies, Tyrone and O Donnell were waiting for him at the Yellow Ford. They struck quickly and accurately. Bagenal was killed, his six regiments decimated and the colours of forty companies lost. It was the most disastrous defeat ever suffered by an English army in Ireland.

Alarm spread from Dublin to Westminster. New levies were hurriedly raised in all the English and Welsh counties. Ploughmen, shopkeepers and artisans were bundled into transport ships with beggars, criminals – even lunatics – all of them badly clothed and entirely untrained. Many deserted, many more died of cold, starvation and disease. Such a rabble had the Queen's army in Ireland become that its General hid his troops for shame when he went to attend a conference.

Tyrone was now the man Europe watched. His signature 'O Neill' was beginning to have almost royal significance, with its accompanying seal of the Red Hand of Ulster.

Ulster was Tyrone's. Connacht was O Donnell's. Now for the awful vengeance that was to overtake those English settlers who had accepted Desmond lands in Munster. . . .

Fire and sword became their portion at rebel hands. Those not killed or mutilated in their own homes fled into the walled towns of Cork, Youghal and Waterford, where famine and pestilence had already taken lodging before them. The poet, Edmund Spenser, escaped from his blazing castle of Kilcolman, leaving behind him in the flames the last books of *The Faerie Queene*. The whole elaborate structure of Elizabeth's Munster plantation collapsed in an agony of hunger, plague and death.

Well had the dispossessed Irish learned the lessons of savagery that had been taught them.

Tyrone was master now and he pressed his advantage to the limit. English territories in Ireland had shrunk to a narrow strip between Dublin and Drogheda. The Queen's subjects were refusing to sail to the accursed island that had become a graveyard for military careers. Even when she sent the magnificent Essex – favourite of her declining years – as Lord Lieutenant, his reluctant army melted away in five fatal months with nothing to show except a copy of Tyrone's proposals : that the Roman Catholic faith, under Papal government, should be openly practised throughout the country; that lands should be restored to their lawful owners, and Irishmen elected to State offices. . . . These were victor's terms. They would be implemented when Spanish aid arrived —

But, suddenly, Tyrone covered his face with his hands.

"Oh, God," prayed this cynic – who, according to Essex, cared 'as much for religion as my horse' – "let it come soon, for I am near the end. . . ."

The strain of six years as supreme commander was beginning to show. He was past middle age and his burden of responsibility was enormous. He had enemies even among his own people, and the fiery impetuosity of his loyal followers required eternal vigilance and restraint on his part. Even Red Hugh O Donnell had to be watched: the young fool had no conception of his own limitations, never having failed. . . .

Father Archer, tutor to Tyrone's sons, came to him.

"My Lord, there is bad news —"

"*What?*" The leader's tension showed in the violence of his start.

" – Young Hugh Maguire has been killed."

"Maguire . . . ?" It was impossible. 'The third Hugh' as he was called (next in command to O Neill and O Donnell) bore a charmed life: everyone knew that. . . . But the priest was crossing himself and mumbling his detailed story. It must be the truth —

In that bitter moment, Tyrone felt the tide turning against him.

Later, disasters were to multiply: the loss of Donegal and Assaroe; the refusal of the Scots to supply men and powder; kinsmen beginning to waver – even to go over to the enemy.

Tyrone began to fight a defensive war while the new Lord Deputy Mountjoy marched to the Ulster border with strong, fresh troops, to ring the rebel territory with forts.

"Somewhere, I have failed," Tyrone said, watching old friends desert him. "Could it be that I have tried to give my people a destiny which they never desired – discipline, government, central command? The tribe dies hard. . . ."

For a moment, he visualized the results of utter defeat for himself and Red Hugh O Donnell: death or exile; their vast lands, with those of Hugh Maguire, taken over by the Crown. Planted with English settlers. A new Pale, impregnable inside Mountjoy's ring of forts —

"Oh, God, no!" Tyrone prayed. "Not the proud North; not O Neill's Ulster. . . . Let Spanish aid come soon."

During all these six years of furious fighting by her kinsmen, Graunuaile had made no move out of her little tower of Rossyvera. Impassively, she had watched her old ships, under young new captains, sail northward out of Clew Bay to carry reinforcements and ammunition to Ulster. She had bidden farewell to grandsons and grandnephews who were going proudly to Spain for the piloting of Philip's troops to Ireland. With O Lee by her side, she listened to the reports coming in daily of Tyrone's victories, and her heart exulted for him: she would live to see him crowned King of Ireland! She was seventy years of age, but she would live another twenty if need be.

The Spanish landing was expected to take place anywhere along the west, or north-west, coast. A breathless country waited. . . .

Then, on a midnight in late September, Magnus O Lee came thundering on the door of Graunya's apartment, and she struggled out of brief sleep to understand his words.

"The Spaniards landed six days ago —"

Something in his tone bade her lie quiet for a moment.

"Where?"

"Kinsale."

She groped in the chilly darkness for her frieze cloak, flung it around her thin shoulders and stood up, barefooted.

"Kinsale. . . !" She drew a deep breath, then shouted so suddenly that O Lee started, although he had expected the outburst. "What devil's bastard guided them there? Blood of God, the farthermost southern point of the country! Tyrone will have to fight his way through the forts, then march two hundred miles. . . ."

Raving and cursing, she threw on her clothes, and he waited quietly for the storm to subside.

"What do you want to do, Graunya?"

"I want to go to Clare Island. Now. This instant. Take me there."

In the darkness, her presence was vital and commanding. He went down to the jetty and untied his curragh. Carrying another pair of oars, she joined him and, without a word, embarked and began to row for the island.

The night sky was big with autumn stars, the sea infinite. . . .

It was still dark when they beached the curragh.

"Wait here," she ordered, her voice rasped with exhaustion. "I am going to the summit of Knockmore."

"You need my help," he said firmly.

"I must be alone when I judge the weather —" She remembered that she was speaking her father's words. Eerily, O Lee answered with her own, as though they had hung in the air here for more than half a century.

"I will be quiet."

She shivered, looking up at the dark mass of the mountain. How many O Malley prophets had trodden this path? Every one, from the tribe's beginnings. . . . And she was the last. The gift would die with her, as the legality of the title had died with her father.

The clouds were shifting for dawn as she and O Lee reached the summit. He stood in the hollow of a rock and she went forward alone to the ancient place where O Malley chieftains took their oath to God and to the tribe.

O Lee watched her in the blurred, grey light – her body thin as a thorn tree, her hair shimmering white as its blossom. There was an inhuman quality in her very stillness and, suddenly, he remembered that it was the time of the September equinox, a morning sacred to O Malley weather prophets since the old druidic days.

Somewhere in the western darkness above the cliffs there was a flapping as of great wings and a faint, high-pitched keening sound. . . . The back of O Lee's neck prickled. Then, all at once, he lost sight of Graunya – only for an instant, as though a darker shape had stood between him and her. Some trick of the uncertain light — Then it happened again, and again, as though a circle of wraiths was moving around her where she stood.

He sprang up, scattering stones, and began to crash forward through the heather, shouting, "Graunya – Graunya, come away!"

She turned and looked at him with empty eyes. "Tyrone must not move south," she said tonelessly. "It is to be an autumn of torrential rains, lit only by the green fire of lightning. His troops would have to carry all their equipment upon their backs, for their horses and mules would perish in the mud : and how could men fight after such a march? I must go to him at once and tell him what I have seen."

It appeared not to cross her mind that anyone could doubt her vision.

"I will come with you," O Lee offered.

"No. Toby's wife is near her delivery. She has more need of you than I have."

So, for the last time, a ship and three galleys carrying the pennant of the White Seahorse moved out of Clew Bay under Graunuaile's command. She had reclaimed the vessels from her son Toby's mooring below Lough Feeagh near Carrigahowley, and crewed them with old captains and oarsmen, dragged grumbling from beds and firesides, because all the younger men were gone.

The urgency of her commands awoke them. They sailed, in good order, for the Ulster coast.

But Lord Deputy Mountjoy – although himself nearing Kinsale by now – had not left northern waters unattended. Armed merchantmen, trawlers and barques patrolled every league of shoreline, making a landing almost impossible for an unauthorized craft.

For days, Graunya dodged among the islands of the Rosses, then crept northward for Tory Sound, trying to gain the long deep fiord of Lough Swilly, from whose eastern bank she could reach the rebels. It was a nightmare of danger and delay that called out every last ounce of seamanship she possessed. She began to wish that she had travelled overland; but the ships had called to her for a last adventure and she was glad she had not denied it to them, or to herself and the old men.

Mooring the larger vessel in Sheep Haven, she went ahead with the three galleys only, taking advantage of every narrow inlet for cover. But, at Rinmore Point near the mouth of Swilly, she had to come out into open water, and the guns of the English *Tremontana* stared down at her for an instant before belching fire and iron.

The middle galley took the full blast of the attack and sank instantly. Gallantly, the one astern tried to draw the *Tremontana* off westward, but ran on a reef where it hung like a frenzied beetle, its thirty-eight oarblades unable to reach water before the larger vessel closed in and finished its struggles.

Graunya's galley escaped into Lough Swilly and landed at Inch, in O Donnell territory. An old man was milking goats by the lakeside.

"Where can I find the O Donnell, your chieftain?" Graunya asked.

But the old man shook his head sadly, and mumbled, "Not here – not here, nor any of the young ones; all gone marching south. . . ." And she knew, then, that she was as incapable of averting the ultimate tragedy as when the Armada ships were beaten upon her island. If Red Hugh O Donnell had gone, then Tyrone must follow to support him. The men of Connacht would join Ulster rebels as they passed and, together, the doomed armies would stagger southward – through blinding rain and swollen rivers – until they reached the unknown, open country around Kinsale, where Mountjoy would be waiting for them, entrenched between them and the Spaniards.

As she turned back hopelessly towards the galley, heavy rain-drops of enormous size began to fall, ploughing up the surface of the 'Lake of Sallows' like a hail of lead shot. And she regarded them with a terrible fatalism.

"Let us try to make our way home," she said wearily, "those that are left of us." The weight of her seventy-one years had never lain more heavily upon her. She knew with prophetic certainty that Tyrone was finished, but foreknowledge made it a personal tragedy before it became a national one. . . .

'What has been the purpose of our lives, his and mine?' she asked herself. 'We have fought only to lose everything – men, religion, lands, a way of life, an ancient culture.'

She felt old and near to death. Then she realized that Elizabeth must be old also, staring the same spectre in the face. But Elizabeth was childless, her only heir James of Scotland, Mary Stuart's Catholic son. . . . And, in that realization, lay her answer.

'The purpose of all this has been to gain a little time, to hold out until the tide turns. A little time – and maybe a spark of inspiration for those who will follow.'

Tyrone's defeat would live on as the lament of a nation. And the name of Graunuaile would be linked for ever with his and O Donnell's, Desmond's and Fitzmaurice's, to remind the people how precious was their heritage.

It was reason enough to have lived.

Through thunder, lightning and vicious squalls, the single galley and the vessel that had been left in Sheep Haven made their way back to Clew Bay, and moored at Rossyvera.

Wringing her wet hair as she went, Graunya ran up to the little tower that was her last possession.

"Magnus!" she called, then – with an edge of panic to her voice when he did not answer – *"Magnus. . . !"*

She saw him coming from the direction of Carrigahowley Castle, his grey head bent against the lashing rain, his old shoulders doggedly hunched. And a kind of tenderness for him came over her – a little backwater of the main flood of passion she had known for the O Neill but, nevertheless, a gentle, worthy stream, green-shaded, sun-dappled, even in this of desolation spirit.

"Magnus, my love, where have you been?"

"With Toby's Maeve. She has a son."

He seemed too dazed with weariness to remember that Graunya had come back from a long journey, or to ask her anything about its outcome. She felt no resentment for his lack of interest, only a sudden relief at the birth of an heir for Toby and Maeve.

"Come home, Magnus," she said. "You need rest. We will talk later."

She helped him climb the steps to the tower, then herself went down again to the mooring and shouted to the MacNallys and the Conroys, the O Dowds and the O Flynns, who were awaiting her instructions, "Take me around to Carrigahowley – I have a new grandson who may need these ships one day!"

The men grinned and cheered, their faces shining with the rain that was to help defeat Tyrone and O Donnell. Her own face was wet: she could weep now and no one would notice. . . .

The emblem of the White Seahorse on its ground of O Malley blue shook out its sodden folds as the flagship moved towards the old fortress.

CAVAN COUNTY LIBRARY

Bibliography

1 *A Chorographical Description of West or H-Iar Connacht* (1684) by Roderick O Flaherty, with notes by James Hardiman for the Irish Archaeological Society.
2 *History of the County of Mayo* (1908) by H. T. Knox. Hodges, Figgis, Dublin.
3 *History of Galway* (1820) by J. Hardiman. Connacht Tribune, Galway.
4 *Memoirs of the Binghams* (1915) by R. E. McCalmont. Spottiswoode, London.
5 *The Great O Neill* (1942) by Sean O Faolain, Longmans, London.
6 *The Irish Geneologist*, Vol. 1. Paper read by Commander Antony MacDermott (1940).
7 *The Dictionary of National Biography*, Vol. XLII. O'Malley, Grace (from the *Calendar of State Papers* for Ireland from 1574 to 1596).
8 *The Story of Ireland* by Brian Inglis (1956). Faber, London.
9 *The Stranger in Ireland* (1954) by C. Maxwell (extract from Fynes Morrison's *Itinerary*). Cape, London.
10 *Corrib Country* (1943) and *Connacht and the City of Galway* (1952) by R. Hayward. A. Baker, London.
11 *Blue Guide to Ireland* (1952 edition) by L. R. Muirhead. Ernest Benn, London.
12 *The Reformation in Ireland under Elizabeth* (1930) by M. V. Ronan. Longmans, London.
13 *History of Ireland* (1936) by E. Curtis. Methuen, London.
14 *Elizabeth's Irish Wars* (1950) by Cyril Falls. Methuen, London.
15 *The Islands of Ireland* (3rd edition, 1950) by T. H. Mason. Batsford, London.
16 *The Mountains of Ireland* (1955) by D. D. C. P. Mould. Batsford, London.
17 *Henry the Eighth* (1929) by W. Hackett. Cape, London.
18 *The Last Tudor King* (1958) and *Lady Jane Grey* (1962) by H. Chapman. Cape, London.
19 *Queen Elizabeth the First* (1934) by J. Neale. Cape, London.
20 *Elizabeth and Leicester* (1944) by M. Waldman. Collins, London.
21 *The Shape of Ships* (1956) by William McDowell. Hutchinson, London.
22 *English Costume in the Sixteenth Century* (1933) by Iris Brooke. A. C. Black, London.
23 *Golden Century of Spain* (1937) by R. T. Davies. Macmillan, London.
24 *Dances of Spain* (1950) by Lucile Armstrong. Max Parrish, London.